CATALYST

by

Roberto Rabaiotti

Grosvenor House
Publishing Limited

Roberto Rabaiotti is hereby identified as author of this
work in accordance with Section 77 of the Copyright, Designs
and Patents Act 1988

The book cover picture is copyright to Roberto Rabaiotti
Background image for front cover is copyright to Inmagine Corp LLC

This book is published by
Grosvenor House Publishing Ltd
28-30 High Street, Guildford, Surrey, GU1 3EL.
www.grosvenorhousepublishing.co.uk

A CIP record for this book
is available from the British Library

ISBN 978-1-908596-09-3

1976

Prologue

The three of them stared open mouthed at the occupant of the front passenger seat. The words he had just spoken had reduced them to silence. They could scarcely believe their ears. When they had first met barely twelve months before, it seemed incredible that they would arrive at this moment. As another car passed by, its headlights casting momentary thick shadows across them as the dirty-white beams flashed across the second floor pillars of the multi-storey car park in Cardiff city centre, they instinctively dropped their heads a fraction in their desire to shield themselves from the prying eyes of the driver. They felt on edge and ecstatic at the same time, their delicate conversations with the front seat passenger having finally come to fruition. Only he had been unafraid to hold his head high when this car and all the earlier ones had come by. The decision he had arrived at after weeks of deep contemplation emboldened him and made him feel immensely proud. Having conveyed the decision, a powerful force energised his body and he felt indestructible. He would not duck and dive like the others in the car. He was prepared to put his head above the parapet.

'We'll be forever grateful. The whole Welsh nation will.' Dafydd, who was sitting in the driver's seat, shook his hand, speaking softly and looking him straight in the eye with admiration. The front seat passenger's eyes did not blink in the slightest. Ieuan and Robert behind him each shook his hand in turn and nodded their heads, unable to find the right words to express their feelings. They were in disbelief that anybody could take such a courageous decision, but proud and grateful at the same time. None of them said it, but even the IRA would be stunned by this development, their first steps in gaining credibility with the Irish terrorist group. They needed their help. They were upstarts, a gathering of loose links scattered around Wales, trying desperately to establish a similar movement with the same aim, namely the permanent removal of London governance from their beloved lands.

Their links to the IRA were tenuous, no more than someone who knew someone, but at least it was a channel of communication. Only the IRA had the means to provide weapons and the know-how to plan an effective terrorist campaign and this tiny group of Welsh anarchists craved their support. But the IRA only poured scorn on them. They saw no evidence of their being truly committed or battle-hardened or organised. They were no more than a disparate bunch of idealists playing at being the tough guy without any comprehension of what a terrorist campaign really entailed. They were no better than youthful bully boys, amateurs. The IRA was an army, a true army, they kept ramming down their throats to their embarrassment, with all the disciplines associated with a modern army.

But now, Dafydd knew and Ieuan knew and Robert knew that what the front seat passenger had said would be the game-changer. The IRA would see that they were capable of carrying out an incredible coup, that they had planning and structure and that most importantly of all, they were ruthless. Not only would it galvanise Welsh sympathisers at home and beyond but it would also convince the IRA that it would be in their interests to offer them their support as nationalist fervour enveloped the British Government from a new front. After such a momentous decision, it seemed that the end had finally arrived to the first part of the plan and for a full minute, an eerie silence followed Dafydd's words. It took the front seat passenger to speak first. 'You know what I need.'

The three others in the car lowered their eyes and nodded their heads but doubt strained their faces. He had raised this before and saw once again the confidence drain from their expressions. Not for the first time, he became forthright with them. 'I won't ask again. If I don't get it, we can forget everything, orrite!'

'Don't worry, we'll get it.' Ieuan's words tried to express a degree of certainty. 'We'll let you know as soon as we can.'

'Good.'

'You're sure you won't consider using…'

'No! How many times do I have to tell you? If you mention it once more, I'm outta here, orrite!' Robert looked chastened and turned his gaze away but could not fail to avoid Ieuan's stern look for trying to raise the matter once again. 'Right, I think that's it. You can see my commitment and I won't let this great nation of ours down.' He pulled at the handle and opened the door. 'You've got my number. Lemme know when you've got it. Otherwise, only call me if something is desperate.' His companions all nodded their heads. He got out of the car, shut the door and walked away to the exit. They followed his tread until he disappeared, not uttering a sound.

'Well, it's on. This is it.'

'Unbelievable.'

'Let's hope he won't falter or change his mind.'

'He's really determined. You can see that. It's like he's got no fear at all. Haven't you noticed how much more committed he's become these last few weeks? How many times did he say there's nothing more important in his life and that the cause is beyond question?'

'But still, what he's planning on doing is staggering...beyond words, beyond anything even the IRA would do, just immense.' Ieuan and Robert nodded their heads at the same time in response to Dafydd's words, both of their faces expressing incredulity.

'He's very young. We sure we haven't taken advantage of him and pushed him too far now?'

'So what, Rob! What's up with you? You going all soft or summing? If we wanna play in the big league, this is what it takes. He seemed keen enough to me anyhow. Orrite, all our talk about big links with the IRA and how they're gonna arm an' support us might be a bit of an exaggeration, but who knows? They should be impressed an' it's not gonna do us any harm, will it?'

'Yeah, but all this talk about an undercurrent of Welsh anarchists and youngsters just waiting to be given a lead is a bit over the top. I think that was the convincer for him 'cos he fancies himself as a bit of a leader, someone who people will look up to and respect forever. Young kids all love that type of talk. Makes 'em feel great, like.'

'What's done is done. If we have to be a bit Machiavellian, then so be it. You've gotta toughen up, Rob.'

'But to do what he's gonna do. Fuck me.' Robert shook his head in disbelief. Silence returned and their only movement was a lowering of their faces as another car drove past them.

'Let's not get ahead of ourselves. The whole thing is incredible and a hell of a lot has got to go our way and his way first. But still, I get the feeling if anybody can do it, he can. He's quite exceptional, you know. You sort of feel he always gets what he puts his mind to. But it'll be tough, no doubt.'

'And brave. Brave beyond imagination.' They all nodded their heads in agreement.

'Come on, let's go and 'ave a quick pint in the City Arms and silently toast Joe, our comrade in arms.'

1

'Hey, Joe, can you do us a favour and stop banging on about all this Welsh nationalism rubbish of yours? You haven't stopped going on about it all night. We're trying to have a good time here and you're boring us to death. Look, Sue Jenkins is over there with a couple of her friends. You must've noticed them smiling our way. Come on, let's go over and sit down with them. I'm sure they wouldn't mind.'

'Christ, boys, is that all you're interested in, bloody women all the time? You know there's more to life than that and it's not rubbish, you toss-pot.'

Dave and Pete looked at each other, surprise etched across their faces, both of them startled by the vehemence of Joe's response. For a moment, neither of them said a word and with the air heavy with tension, they both picked up their pint glasses and sipped nervously at their beer, avoiding eye contact. The couple sitting at the table next to them in the Maltsters Arms glanced sideways, their attention attracted by the raised voice.

Despite their unease, David Harris and Peter Williams were not unaccustomed to Joe's fiery and unpredictable moods. The three of them had been close friends since virtually the day they were born. During the summers, their mothers would take them daily to Ynysangharad Park, in the Welsh valley town of

Pontypridd, to play on the swings and slides by the open air swimming pool, while in the winters, they would spend most of their time around each other's homes playing boisterously and noisily, and generally making their mothers wonder whether having children had really been worth the effort. They all attended the same primary and secondary schools and were always in the same class. They were now in their final year at Coed-y-Lan Comprehensive, trying to decide what the next stage in their lives would be.

However, increasingly, Joe's moods and opinions were becoming more extreme. In particular, his condemnation of all things English was so vicious that when a classmate suggested he had some sort of a chip on his shoulder, he punched him so hard in the face, he broke his nose. Such was the incident and the commotion it caused with the boy's parents that the headmaster had considered suspending him, but eventually decided upon the cane and a formal warning that any repeat would result in immediate expulsion.

Typical of Hoppo, as the Dickensian-like figure of the headmaster, Meirion Hopkins, was known to everybody in the school, Joe thought at the time. Soft, weak and incapable of taking any tough action when necessary. Much like the Welsh nation, he concluded.

'Look, Joe,' Pete said eventually and in a sharp tone of voice. 'There's a time and place for everything. It's nine-thirty on a Friday night, we're 'aving a good drink and if we play our cards right, I reckon we could be in with Sue and her friends. You know she's just packed in John Clayton, don't you, so she's definitely available. And don't kid me you don't fancy her 'cos she's the best girl round these parts by far and you know it. What d'you wanna do? We can either go and sit down with them or you can be a pain in the arse for the rest of the evening? It's up to you.'

'I'm sorry, boys,' Joe replied after a moment's pause. 'I was wrong to have had a go at you. Look, I'm not feeling too good and I've got a hard game tomorrow. I 'ope you don't mind if I go home.'

Joe had usually been the last person to suggest going home after a night out. Every possibility was explored to keep the evenings going after the pubs had closed. However, lately, he seemed preoccupied and bored with the routine of same pubs, same drinks, and same conversations. Pete and Dave were now accustomed to his leaving early and, inwardly, both of them felt a little upset that their close friend appeared to be growing tired of their company. Joe's growing nationalism and vitriolic attacks on all things English were departures from his usual happy-go-lucky approach to life where the most contentious conversations revolved around the selection of the Welsh rugby team. Privately, they both hoped that Joe was just going through one of those phases, though of what, they did not know.

Joe slowly rose from his seat, clutching his pint of Carling, which he swiftly finished in two large gulps. As he grabbed his brown leather bomber jacket, which lay beside him on an empty seat, he noticed that Bob, the landlord, was looking his way, a half-smile on his face, giving him the thumbs up. This was his characteristic way of wishing Joe a good game the next day. Joe winked back in acknowledgement, put on his jacket and turned towards the main door.

'See you in the clubhouse after the game?' Pete asked a little unsurely.

'Yeah, I'll be there.'

'Have a good game, but don't bother coming if you lose,' Dave added in a jocular tone, trying to ease the tension a little.

'There's no way those London bastards are gonna beat us and that piece of shit in the centre will wish he'd never come by the time I've finished with him.'

Grinning, Pete and Dave watched as Joe left the pub. Their eyes were not the only ones looking at Joe. From the other side of the room, Susan Jenkins had been observing him all evening. At his departure, she felt a touch deflated but promised herself that at the next opportunity she would make a special effort to get to know him. Immediately, John Clayton had become a distant memory.

* * *

That October evening was the coldest so far that autumn and when Joe opened the pub door, he was met by a rush of freezing air that made his eyes water. After the hottest summer in decades, it seemed scarcely believable that the temperature could drop so much so quickly and plumes of white breath accompanied each of his steps. He rammed his hands deep inside his jacket pockets as he walked purposefully under the yellow glow of the street lights, which were partly masked by the thin veil of drizzle that showered him. But despite the marked difference to the comfortable warmth of the Maltsters Arms, Joe was in such deep thought, his jacket remained unzipped despite his only wearing a thin cotton shirt underneath, and he failed to register the smell of smoke on his clothes that he hated so much.

His usual route home took him past the Old Bridge, Pontypridd's most famous landmark. When it was built in the middle of the eighteenth century, it was for a time the world's longest single-span bridge. The six large holes, three each either side of the bridge's imposing stone structure, gave it a unique appearance that would cause bewilderment to all who saw it. On this particular evening, Joe decided to walk across the wet, glistening tarmac of the road in front of the pub and over to the famous bridge in order to feel as one with an age when Wales appeared to have a great and distinctive identity, which he believed was sadly missing today. He walked up the shallow steps before stopping momentarily at the top. Looking over a wall, he tried to observe the flow of the River Taff beneath him but saw only a wide, black void, the water barely visible or audible. On both banks of the river, the windows of old, low-terraced houses shone brightly like cats' eyes in the night. When he arrived down the other side of the bridge, he cringed at the scattered glass of broken bottles and fish and chip wrappers that had been thrown into the holes by the apathetic youth of the day, examples of whom were at that moment jostling and staggering drunkenly alongside on the adjacent bridge, shouting and swearing.

Where has all the pride and self-respect of this great nation gone? he thought furiously as he continued his walk down Taff Street, the main road that ran through the town centre. Pontypridd was built on the confluence of two great rivers with coal mining traditionally at its heart. The pride of the miners reflected everything that was great about the Welsh nation in Joe's eyes: strength, courage, fitness, determination, camaraderie, responsibility, respectability. But now, on that cold October evening, he saw these characteristics being diluted as mines closed and employment moved towards commerce, shops and offices.

'John Menzies, Boots, Woolworths,' he muttered under his breath, shaking his head as he observed the gaudy corporate colours that seemed incongruous in the murky, misty, grey surrounds. 'You could be anywhere in England. It's a disgrace. And who's closing all the mines and destroying our industry and special way of life? Who's opening all these shops? Why, it's the English, of course. As if they haven't exploited us enough already, they now plan to take us over completely. And who cares around here? Fucking nobody.' He considered throwing a stone through a window but quickly thought the better of it, though he did aim a hard kick at the door of Marks & Spencer, hurting himself more than the solid glass structure.

Joe could never understand why, when compared to the fierce pride of the Irish, Basques and Palestinians, to name but a few, the Welsh seemed content to reflect their nationalism solely in romanticised terms through culture and were unprepared to fight for the country's very existence with meaningful deeds.

'Daubing out English names on road signs is the most you can expect these days. It's pathetic. Where are the people who are prepared to fight and die for their country like in Northern Ireland? Isn't their situation the same as ours? What's going on 'ere?'

The words he spoke to himself and his fury were so intense that he felt the whole town could hear him. On arriving at his home, which was situated halfway up Graigwen Hill, a largely residential area that overlooked the whole town, for some inexplicable reason, he paused before going through the garden gate. It seemed as if a divine force was controlling his actions. He felt, all of a sudden, inwardly calm and clear of mind. He turned slowly around and observed the town's lights below him, seemingly like perforations in the earth's surface with the glowing lava shining through. He recalled the previous night's conversation in the multi-storey car park and the agonising arguments that had whirled around his brain for months on end. He had made the right decision. There was no doubt about it. Things had to change in this great nation of Wales. There was nothing more important than bringing Welsh nationalism to the forefront of world attention and he would be the catalyst for others to follow and fight for true independence.

For the first time that day, he felt at ease. He unlatched the garden gate, strode up the path and round the house, opened the back door and went up to his bedroom. After undressing, he lay on his bed in calm contemplation before falling asleep as content as at any time in his life.

2

On the face of it, the last person anybody would imagine to be passionately nationalistic about Welsh affairs was Giuseppe Chilani. A third-generation boy born to Italian immigrants, who had settled in the Welsh valley towns at the turn of the twentieth century, Joe, or Giuseppe, as his family insisted on calling him, could not point to any exploitation of his forebears by English industrialists for his inner anger. Despite a very Italian upbringing at home and many summers spent in Italy visiting relatives, Joe's affinity was very much with the land of his birth, much to his mother's sadness. Her attempts to make him speak Italian at home always fell on deaf ears.

From his early teens, Joe's good looks, classically dark and brooding, his pleasant manner and sporting prowess made him very popular among his school friends. Without fail, he was always the centre of attention and possessed a charisma that was much envied and admired. He was bright and intelligent as well. His teachers all agreed that a university education was inevitable, possibly even at Oxford or Cambridge, a very rare occurrence during the school's existence.

The subject in which Joe excelled at school was history and his major interest was how society had changed in Wales during the Industrial Revolution of the nineteenth century. The images of children working for next to nothing underground at the coalface, their parents bent permanently at the waist and going blind prematurely through years of cutting coal in seams less than four feet in width, distressed him, and when reading in his room at home, tears often flowed freely. He could barely imagine the slums, the overcrowding and lack of sanitation of the new dwellings and how anybody could survive such conditions. His view was that the English industrialists were arrogant, evil men earning vast profits from their workers' toil with no concept of protection and safety and welfare for those in their employment. Blindly, he would never accept counter arguments that such conditions were no different to numerous other towns in England or that those doing the exploiting were more often than not Welsh themselves.

The English, he concluded, had a history of exploiting the nations they governed and would always look after their own interests first. Joe had been horrified to learn how they had been prepared to allow virtually a whole country's population to die as they had done in Ireland during the potato famine of the mid-nineteenth century, and it was barely believable that Winston Churchill would allow many millions of Indians to starve to death during the Second World War by not providing shipping to transport food to what was the jewel in the crown of all their colonies, and one supposedly under English rule and protection. And this, the same great Churchill, the most revered Englishman who ever lived, adored by millions throughout the country, who, when Home Secretary in 1910, sent in the troops to murder innocent, striking miners in Tonypandy, close to Joe's home in Pontypridd, to quell their desire for better working conditions.

Most of those who suffered under English governance throughout the world eventually rose against them and many colonies gained their independence. Even Ireland was partitioned with the struggle over the north continuing to this very day. But Joe could never understand why the Welsh remained passive, seemingly content to be subjugated by the English, never agitating strongly for their own independence. Such thoughts brought out an intense anger within him that he found difficult to dispel.

Without question, the one teacher who most influenced his thinking at Coed-Y-Lan was Brian Davies, the senior geography teacher. Geogger Davies, as all the pupils knew him, was an active member of Plaid Cymru, the Welsh nationalist political party, and at one time a Plaid member on the town council. Joe had been incredulous when he had lost his seat to a Labour party member, not understanding how anybody who advocated Welsh independence could be ejected in favour of an English party candidate. Geogger Davies recognised Joe's interest in politics from an early age and noticed how the many questions he asked when they were together related to social and economic conditions whilst other pupils of the same age were normally more interested in battles and warfare. On many occasions, Joe remained behind after class to carry on discussions with him and more often than not, these discussions became more political in nature. Geogger Davies knew that he was walking a very fine line personally as teachers were explicitly forbidden to discuss politics with pupils, but such was Joe's interest and brightness and obvious leanings towards an independent Wales, he could not prevent himself from engaging with him. He believed that when Joe left school, he could become a valuable asset to Plaid Cymru, hinting strongly that he should consider joining the political party. Joe felt a real bond with Geogger Davies and promised never to reveal their conversations to anybody else, but he was nothing but scornful of the idea of joining Plaid.

'What worries me, Mr Davies, is that there's absolutely no progress being made if we're to reach our goal of independence. The government will never change anything unless they feel some real pressure and that's gotta come from the people themselves out on the street. If you look throughout history, the English have always capitulated in the end when there was local strife and agitation in their colonies. At the first sign of trouble, they'd try and suppress it with force but eventually, when the pressure on the ground from brave and committed freedom-fighters was too much for them, they'd give in and the colonies would gain their independence. The British Empire on which the sun never set is no more. Why can't we do what other countries have done? The government can see that Welsh people are apathetic and couldn't give a toss. Why should they worry about anything up there in London if there's no pressure on the ground down 'ere in Wales? Politics is no more than a load of hot air. Plaid's MPs can talk for as long as they like in Parliament but they'll never get anywhere.'

'That's a bit unfair, Joe, and not strictly true if you want my opinion and your view on what has happened to the British Empire is very simplistic. You're wrong to believe that about politics. Plaid's MPs are very good. I know them personally and they are very committed. I don't know how much you follow it but they are often raising good, meaningful questions in Parliament which discomfort the government and I think they're making good progress.'

'With respect, sir, does anybody in Wales even know who they are, what they do or what they've achieved? You can count them on the fingers of one hand so it's no wonder you know them all personally. I like to think I know a bit about politics but if one of them passed me in the street, I wouldn't recognise 'im. They're invisible. The Scottish MPs are always on the telly pushing their case, though I don't think they're making much progress either. All the talk and coverage about independence from England revolves around the Irish and Scottish. There's nothing about Wales. Only real pressure in the streets like in Northern Ireland will make those English sit up and listen. You can tell that ordinary people on the ground in Northern Ireland are totally galvanised by what's going on and I bet you that one day, and sooner than you think, Northern Ireland will become part of the Irish Republic.'

'Come off it, Joe, you're not suggesting that violence and terrorism and all the fears and horrors they entail is the way forward, are you? Do you want to live with soldiers in the street and in constant fear of when and where the next bomb will explode? Do you want to worry about whether a loved one has been innocently murdered or maimed by some terrible act of terrorism? That's not the way forward. The ordinary people of Northern Ireland you refer to want peace more than they want independence from England. In fact, the vast majority consider themselves British and want nothing to do with Ireland. They're not galvanised by the IRA, they're disgusted by them. It's only the misguided few who believe in violence.'

'I'm not so sure, sir. Sometimes, sacrifices, real sacrifices, have to be made to achieve what is truly right.

And in such terrible struggles, innocent people will unfortunately get hurt. But whose fault is that? The English, of course, for governing a country that's got nothing to do with them. Look what's happening, sir. It was in the papers the other day that the government's been having some secret discussions with the IRA, despite what they might say in public. Let's face it, they're winning. What they're doing is succeeding.'

'Look, Joe, I want independence as much as you do but you cannot condone terrorist means whatever the cause and whatever the circumstances. Who the hell have you been talking to? What's going on in that head of yours?'

The tone of Geogger Davies's voice was suddenly sterner and he looked directly into Joe's eyes with a stubborn stare. For a brief second, they remained transfixed, neither of them saying a word nor wishing to be the first to break off eye contact. But the master wanted his point to be accepted and understood and it was Joe who finally looked away, a little shyly. However, as he stood up to leave, he looked directly at his master and said quietly with a slight shake of the head, 'You're wrong, sir. I'm sorry but I know you're wrong.'

Not for the first time, Geogger Davies detected real conviction in Joe's voice and beliefs but for the very first time, he was worried and concerned about it.

* * *

If Joe had answered Geogger Davies's final questions directly, he would have shaken his geography teacher to the core. For what was going on inside his head was far too extreme to admit and Joe was indeed being influenced by a clique of militant Welsh nationalists.

They had first met nearly a year before in the clubhouse at Stradey Park, the home of Llanelli Rugby Football Club, the evening after Joe had played superbly well in the under-nineteen level rugby international between Wales and England.

From an early age, it was obvious to all of Joe's family, friends and school teachers that he possessed the strength, speed and co-ordination to become a truly outstanding sportsman. Of even greater necessity, he had the desire and determination, and in Wales, one sport stood out above all others in terms of importance, Rugby Union. At this, Joe was truly gifted and his prowess was admired and revered. Consequently, his popularity among his fellow school friends was total whilst his PE teacher recognised a special talent with the ability one day to play for the senior national side itself.

In his third year at Coed-y-Lan, when only fourteen years of age and barely ten stones in weight, he became a regular member of the school 1st XV, generating explosive power from his five-foot ten-inch frame. This, together with his searing acceleration, would often leave opponents clutching at thin air as he burst past them from his position of centre three-quarters. In defence, a tackle from Joe Chilani would shake up an opponent to such an extent it would make him wonder why he had ever taken up the sport in the first place. Town and county representative honours followed as a matter of course and of particular pride to his school were his four caps for representing Wales at under-fifteen level and six caps at under-nineteen level, three of these as captain. It was the first time for eighteen years that the school had had a Welsh international in their midst and the first time ever as captain.

The defeat of England in Llanelli was the highlight of Joe's rugby career to date. It was his first game as captain and he had led the team with distinction. Not only had he scored two tries, he had laid on two others as Wales won by a huge margin. Several representatives from the foremost rugby clubs in Wales and England were in attendance and they all nodded their heads in approval whenever Joe made a play and what is more, they all agreed that now, at just over six feet in height and fourteen stones in weight, progression to senior honours appeared on the threshold.

In the heaving clubhouse after the game, his fellow centre, who came from the local area, introduced him to a friend of his older brother who had come to watch the game. Dafydd Morgan was accompanied by two friends, Robert Jones and Ieuan Harris, all of whom were in their mid twenties. They were engaging company and fuelled by copious quantities of Felinfoel Best Bitter, Joe spent most of the evening with them, joking and laughing. What intrigued the three friends was Joe's belittling of the English and obvious hatred for them.

'Isn't it brill whenever we play England at rugby. Wharrever the age group, we always stuff 'em. It's the way we show 'em we're stronger than 'em, our way of getting one over them for all the trouble they've brought us.'

'Trouble?'

'You know, all the hardships they've brought upon us Welsh people over the years, for centuries even.'

'Yeah, you can count on the English to cause trouble wherever they are.'

'The thing is, and this pisses me off more than anything, is that people 'ere think all the problems with

England are something that go back in history, but that's rubbish. Can't anybody see that our way of life today is being totally transformed for the worse? If a Martian lands here in fifty, no, make that twenty years time, has a look around a bit and then crosses the Severn Bridge, he won't see any differences at all.'

'This Martian of yours, he's driving then, is he?' Joe, Dafydd and Ieuan all corpsed in laughter at Robert's witticism and spluttered into their beers.

'That's a good one, Rob. Must tell the boys that one back in Ponty,' Joe responded as he wiped away some tears from his eyes.

'You're right, Joe. He'll be drinking Watney's Red Barrel in this very clubhouse next instead of Felinfoel. I agree with you.'

'Come on now, things might be pretty awful at the moment but they can't get as bad as that, surely, can they?' Once again, Joe broke out into a laugh, shaking his head.

'Thing is, being serious for a minute, is anybody gonna do anything about it?' Dafydd's interjection slowed down the merriment for a moment and Joe took the opportunity to sink a good third of his pint. 'More pertinently, are *we* gonna do anything about it?'

Joe's companions took this remark as a signal to take large swigs from their glasses, but each one of them peered over the rims at Joe, curious to see how he would respond. It was a key moment for them; a way of gauging the attitude of their prospective targets, for Joe was a target, like many others they had tried before in their search for those willing to join them in militant action against the English. Only a handful of men and women had bitten so far and none of them as relatively well known as the senior Welsh Schools' rugby captain.

Joe's antennae were acute and he understood perfectly well the meaning behind the question. This was no reference to political activity. The tone of Dafydd's voice and the expectancy in the looks in all their eyes reflected something much more hardline. To his surprise, the question electrified him, seemingly touching a nerve which had been trapped deep inside his body. The flow of current brought it to life. He hesitated before replying, taking the opportunity to take another swig of his beer which the others, now on edge, followed. Amid the chattering groups of rugby lovers in the bar, their little group of four was now an oasis of silence. Dafydd thought Joe needed a little more cajoling, encouraged, at least, that he had not answered in the negative to the implication behind his question. He gambled that a flattering appeal to his leadership qualities would hit home, having observed during the game the relish with which Joe had led his teammates and his lack of fear in inciting them to greater performance as he screamed at them all the historical ills brought down upon them by the English.

'I loved the way the boys followed you on the pitch. You could see they listened to your every word. You were a giant out there. Even Cliffy Ellis in the second-row looked small in comparison an' he's nearly six-foot six. They looked up to you, no doubt about that and considering it was your first time as captain, it was pretty impressive.'

'Yeah, well, thanks for that. Compliments'll get you everywhere,' Joe responded with a smile.

'Particularly when there was that fracas after you shouldered their wing in the solar plexus. How late were you, about five seconds?'

'Come off it, I wasn't that late. Well, p'rhaps four seconds.' The four of them all started to chuckle to themselves. 'Wasn't as if I hit 'im that hard. You'd have thought George Foreman had punched him the way he went down, the English public school prick.'

'The thing is, all the boys ran in to help you when their hooker started 'aving a go at you. You could see they were gonna be by your side. You 'ad their respect, you did. It was superb.'

'Well, thanks.'

'Why d'you hit 'im late 'en?'

'Well, it's obvious, innit? He was English. Isn't that enough?' Joe took another swig of his beer but his smiley face turned serious when, after wiping his mouth, he hesitated before carrying on, looking them all in the eye sternly, 'An English cunt.'

'It's the sort of leadership people need in this country if we're to get rid of them.' Dafydd's voice was lower, more conspiratorial and he glanced left and right to ensure that only his little group could hear.

'You think I can play a part 'en?' Joe's three companions all gave subtle but palpable body movements as their brains understood immediately the significance of Joe's words. He was interested.

'Definitely. Wales needs people exactly like you, a strong and determined leader. They'll follow you to the 'nth degree, no doubt about it.'

Joe swelled with pride. But then Dafydd beckoned his three companions to gather round more closely and he lowered his voice to barely a whisper. His alert eyes darted left and right once more, studying those close by and evaluating whether anybody could hear him or not. 'Joe, let's get serious. I'm not talking kids stuff here. You know what I mean now, don't you?'

'Course I do. I'm not fucking stupid.' Joe's response was almost angry.

'That's good. Look, we can't talk here. I'm gonna be down your way next Tuesday. I know a nice little pub in Church Village, the Hollybush, not very far from Ponty. D'you know it?'

'Yeah, I know it. My auntie doesn't live very far from there.'

'Let's find a nice quiet table around seven o'clock. She won't be there, will she, your auntie?'

'Nah, she's not a pub-goer.'

'Good. We'll have a chat then.'

'Look forward to it.' And the glint in Joe's eye and his energised body language convinced Dafydd, Ieuan and Robert that Joe was on board.

* * *

Joe's meeting with Dafydd in the Hollybush was the first of several over a number of months, culminating in the fateful decision taken in the multi-storey car park in Cardiff city centre. During that time, Dafydd, Ieuan and Robert had initially tiptoed their way around him but found very quickly that not only was this unnecessary, Joe, if anything, was considering even more extreme action than they were. For Joe's part, when he left Stradey Park that evening after the England game, it was as if the very reason for his existence had been unearthed. He was conscious of entering adulthood and he craved such a purpose. All his instincts, bottled up from an early age, that it would probably require a violent struggle to rid Wales of the English, came flowing out. All it needed were the likes of Dafydd to release the cork. He couldn't wait to meet him the following week.

He felt as if he was walking on air, his pride swollen by their complimentary words. This cause would become the most important thing in his life.

During the meetings, Joe had been excited beyond words when he learned that his comrades, and he now saw them as such, were in communication with the IRA and that a violent, nationalist campaign on two fronts would undoubtedly overwhelm the British Government. He also understood that they needed to demonstrate their capabilities by carrying out a 'spectacular', as the IRA liked to refer to such dramatic events. Only then would the IRA see that they were serious and committed, and worthy of all the necessary support. Many plans and ideas were discussed but the most promising revolved around Joe because as the months passed by, his profile was becoming better known in Wales due to his progression in rugby. This was an avenue to exploit.

Joe was also hugely impressed to learn from his comrades that their tentacles reached far and deep in Wales and that a large undercurrent of frustrated anarchists and sympathisers was just waiting to be given a lead. They convinced Joe that there were many already prepared to take up arms which would be supplied by the IRA and that this did not include all those other unknown Welsh men and women who would surely be inspired to join their cause as well. Joe believed an awe-inspiring coup to convince the IRA and energise the hordes of brave Welsh people waiting for such a lead was the only way forward. And his comrades convinced him that he was that special leader, that everybody would follow him. Joe already saw how he was dominating their gatherings, throwing out the most ideas. Yes, he was a leader, there was no doubt about it, and he would lead. But Joe had red lines that he would personally never cross. He was, however, also capable of incredible courage. There would be no turning back from the decision made in Cardiff for nothing would inspire the Welsh people more than an incredible act of courage.

* * *

Joe's all-important rugby profile was gradually extending from schools' rugby to the millions who followed the senior ranks. Since the age of sixteen, Joe had been playing regularly for his town club, one of the most outstanding teams in Wales. Within six months, he was playing for the senior side, rubbing shoulders with the giants of Welsh rugby. After only a handful of games, the question was not whether but when would he be selected for the full Welsh national team? Stunning performances in televised matches against Cardiff and Swansea had raised people's awareness of him considerably in Wales and to the wider rugby fraternity further afield. One incident in the game against Swansea was the talk of all rugby fans for days on end. The great Swansea, Wales and British Lion wing, Gareth Evans, was streaking for the corner to add to his already impressive club record of tries when Joe, starting five yards behind, thundered after him, catching Evans as he was diving for the line. His shuddering challenge jolted Evans into losing the ball and blasted him over the touchline. It took fully two minutes for Evans to regain his feet and he remained glassy-eyed for the rest of the game. In such circumstances, those in the stands and on the touchline would usually berate a player for his lack of speed. On this occasion, such comments were inappropriate for Evans had been in superb form all season, culminating in five tries scored for his country in the home internationals played earlier in the year. All the talk was of Joe's breathtaking tackle.

From the very start of the new season, Joe's form had been so impressive that former international greats turned news reporters, such as Dewi Griffiths, were advocating his selection for the full national side despite his young age. Although he played for Pontypridd every Saturday afternoon, Joe's fitness was such that he continued to represent his school in the mornings, putting the fear of God into his overawed opponents. Although under no pressure to do so, this commitment to his school was appreciated and acknowledged by his teachers and fellow classmates.

The day after Joe's long, contemplative walk home from the Maltsters Arms, Pontypridd were due to play the Harlequins from London. No other side in England typified the rich, upper middle-class origins of English rugby than this club. Even among other English club sides, the air of superiority and arrogance emanating from the Harlequins made them universally despised and no other victory was greeted with greater delight. While the reality was often quite different, the image of the Harlequins was of wealthy City traders turning up in their sports cars, playing a match and then disappearing back into London, dinner suit at the ready, usually with a bottle of champagne in one hand and a dizzy blonde in the other. The difference between the Harlequins and the gritty clubs of the Welsh valley towns was as marked as a pint of beer was to a schooner of sherry.

Although the match was only a friendly fixture, Joe had decided not to play for the school side that morning. He wished to retain all his energy for Joe would be in direct opposition to one of the world's most brilliant centres. His performance would be measured against the very best and it was common knowledge that the match would be attended by two of the selectors for the full national side. For, on this afternoon, Joe would be facing the most glamorous rugby player in the world and captain of England, James Harrison.

'Tell me where you're going again?'

'Pontypridd. It's one of those typical Welsh places with a funny name. Although the word ends in a double 'd', you pronounce it 'preethe' apparently. It's about ten miles from Cardiff. They're a good side, though.'

'Aren't they a bit rough up there in Wales?'

'They're rough wherever I play,' the man chuckled. 'Don't worry, I'm a big boy now and I can look after myself.' The newly-wed Harrisons were contemplating the day ahead over breakfast in their spacious and beautiful Shaker kitchen.

'I'll have three sausages with my bacon if you don't mind. Must keep my strength up. And some real butter on my toast, please. I think I'll pass on the Flora.' They both grinned at the reference to the healthier margarine option they advertised on the television.

'What time will you be back?'

'Probably not till quite late. It takes well over two hours to get there. We'll probably stay an hour or so after the game to keep the natives happy and leave around seven o'clock. The boys have lined up a curry on the way back, somewhere near Bristol. Jerry Harding is going to join us, I heard,' a reference to his fellow England centre who played for the Bath club. 'I haven't seen him in ages. He's been out injured with a pulled groin muscle. It's quite serious, apparently.'

'He's a real dish, is Jerry. I'm sure his pulled groin muscle had nothing to do with playing rugby.' The woman laughed and her husband followed suit.

James Harrison was as content as he had ever been in his life. Recently married to pop star Vicki Adams, who was expecting their first child, his position as captain of England had led to a thriving business and unprecedented popularity amongst the public at large if not necessarily within the rugby fraternity. He could sometimes appear high-brow, particularly in the rugby hot beds of the West Country and North of England, where their particular brand of the game was much divorced from that of the London scene. Nevertheless, and even if somewhat begrudgingly, nobody questioned his brilliance or position as captain of the national side. He worked hard at his game, contrary to the common perception that everything came easily to him. He knew competition for places was fierce. Furthermore, the media was so fickle that every England defeat was greeted by the irrational clamour to change the players, the captain, the coach and the selectors, more often than not, all of them at the same time. He knew that he had to constantly deliver his best and this drove him on to train and prepare for matches with an intensity unmatched by any teammate.

'What time are you leaving?'

'Nine-thirty from the Stoop,' a reference to the club ground of the Harlequins. 'I'd better be off, actually. Now, where's my kit bag?'

'You be careful, honey. Nothing would give the Welsh greater pleasure than to give the England captain a good kicking. I'm sure they'd try and kill you if they could get away with it.'

'Don't worry, I'm used to it.' He shrugged his shoulders.

His calm assurance and inner confidence were once more in evidence, characteristics that had first drawn Vicki to him. Backstage at the Hammersmith Odeon, he had stood out among the fawning froth of hangers-on and she had had no hesitation in accepting an invitation to dinner when he had asked. The media was soon in a frenzy to which he, in particular, was totally indifferent.

'I'll see you tonight. Love you, honey.'

'Love you, too.'

Harrison retrieved his kit bag from the utility room, kissed and embraced his wife and went out the back door to his Mercedes sports car to make the short journey from Richmond Hill, where his Victorian town house stood grandly overlooking the Thames, to the Stoop, only a couple of miles away.

To Joe Chilani, James Harrison stood for everything he despised in the English. Arrogant, domineering and condescending; he believed naively that Harrison had been born with a silver spoon in his mouth. Whilst he could see that he was a very fine rugby player, he never considered him a true team-man. Harrison would seemingly pick and choose the matches in which he played, saving himself for the high-profile games. Because of his rugby fame, Harrison had established his own business, specialising in motivational courses for businessmen. Joe felt that Harrison was selfish and played the game only for what he could make out of it, milking it dry before he packed up and turned his attentions elsewhere.

Joe was blind to the reality. On a recent British Lions tour to South Africa, comprising the best talent from the three home nations and Ireland, it was the Welsh contingent who saw, to their surprise, the true James Harrison. He was hard working, sociable and ever helpful to the more junior members of the squad. As captain, he insisted that the players roomed with teammates from different countries to avoid the danger of cliques forming. Traditionally, the captain was entitled to his own room. Throughout the tour, he relinquished this privilege. In particular, he built up a strong and lasting friendship with the Maesteg and Wales scrum-half, Dafydd Hopkins, who worked at the Port Talbot steel works close to his home. For the greater part of the tour, they roomed together. No two characters could be more different and yet, by the end of the tour, Hopkins's respect for him was total and vice versa.

'You know the real reason he's pals with 'arrison, don't you?' a local from Maesteg Rugby Football Club conjectured. 'He's just trying to get in with his missus so that he can shag Emma, Jo or Tracey from her group, the dirty bastard.'

* * *

While the Harrisons were breakfasting in Richmond, one hundred and fifty miles away in Pontypridd, Joe lay motionless in his bed, fully awake, his head turned to the side, his eyes staring at the reproduction print of Marc Chagall's *I and the Village* on the wall in front of him. He wondered what had attracted him to the picture in the first place and what could possibly have been going through his mind at the time as he struggled to comprehend the subject matter. Must have been one of my more pretentious moments, he concluded. The picture's splash of red, green and white contrasted vividly against the psychedelic patterns of brown, yellow and orange on the wallpaper beneath it. The whole wall looks like a car crash, he mused, or the pool of puke, more like, he had noticed in the doorway of Edwards Sports Shop the previous evening.

His mind soon returned to the commitment he had made, knowing that his intended plan would shock his friends and devastate his family forever. Nevertheless, he was prepared to accept these consequences. He was convinced there were other Welsh people out there who thought the same as him but who required inspiration and leadership so that they, too, could embrace the struggle. A dramatic event would incite them into action. He was sure of it and excited by it. He went over his plan in his head for the hundredth time. It was really beginning to take shape. The softness of his bed and the quiet of the room made for precise thinking and he translated the thoughts softly into words. 'What? Yes. Who? Yes. When? Yes. Where? Yes. How?' There was a hesitation of a few seconds before Joe answered this final question in the affirmative but if there had been somebody else listening to him at that particular moment, they would not have failed to have registered the doubt in his voice. Despite this, the pieces were falling into place but the plan was totally dependent, nonetheless, on another overriding but immensely difficult factor. When that was in place, nothing could stop him.

'*Giuseppe, vieni giù?*'

All of a sudden, his mother's calling disturbed his thinking and the smell of fried eggs, bacon and strong coffee, which he liked so much on match days, began to filter through into his bedroom.

'I'm coming. Give me a minute,' he bellowed.

Joe rose slowly from his bed, took off his pyjamas, put on the shorts and sweatshirt that lay over the back of the armchair and dragged himself across the landing and down the stairs towards the seductive aromas of the kitchen. His younger brother was already seated, his face buried in that week's edition of *Tiger* which had just been delivered. Joe flicked his ear as he passed by.

'Gerroff,' Marco yelled as he glanced up in irritation towards his brother. Joe grinned.

'How many goals has Roy Race scored in the last minute this week 'en?' Joe asked sarcastically.

'Shurrup,' Marco responded without batting an eyelid.

'I dunno how you can read such rubbish.'

'It's not rubbish.'

'How old are you anyway? You should've outgrown comics by now.'

'Look, will you shurrup or not?' Marco's voice was sterner.

'Why, what are you gonna do about it?'

Marco did not respond. But then, as quick as a cheetah trapping its prey, Joe pounced on his brother, placed him in a friendly headlock and ruffled his hair. Marco tried to wriggle free but his brother was too strong for him. Joe was now laughing. A few seconds later, he released him. Marco got up from his chair and faced his brother, his features reddened by the headlock.

'James Harrison is gonna kill you today 'cos he's ten times the player you are. He's gonna make you look stupid.' Joe's face immediately turned as black as night. In a flash, he struck his brother hard across the cheek with an open hand, bringing tears to his eyes. 'You're just a bully, you are,' Marco shouted back as he ran from the kitchen.

Their mother turned from the stove when she heard the commotion. '*Giuseppe, che cos'hai fatto? Perchè piange tuo fratello?*' she asked her elder son, enquiring what he had done and why his brother was crying.

'I didn't do anything. He's just a big baby.'

The boys' mother was used to her two sons squabbling and she knew that it would all blow over as quickly as it had started. She turned her attention back to the stove and flipped the eggs over in the frying pan. Joe sat down at the table and poured himself a cup of coffee. He stared straight ahead, his mood markedly darker, and like on numerous other occasions over the past few months, the picture of the captain of England never left his head.

4

'Right, boys, gather round,' boomed the deep bass voice of Geraint Thomas, captain of Pontypridd Rugby Football Club and massive second-row forward. This charismatic figure stood tall like a lighthouse in the centre of the dressing room, adjusting the thick bands of white bandaging and black tape around his head. He applied some Vaseline across his brows and cheeks, slicking down the two forests of grey-flecked sideburns either side of his scarred face before wiping his hands vigorously on his black and white hooped jersey. Known as Leap because of his impressive jumping ability at the lineout, Thomas was a battle-hardened colossus, now in his fourteenth year of senior rugby and fifth as captain. Although he had never reached the heights of the national team, he nevertheless commanded huge respect throughout the Welsh rugby community. As ever, in his final rallying call to arms before they left the dressing room, he tried to begin with something original. 'Orrite, boys, let's 'ave some quiet,' he commanded. The dressing room hushed as Thomas continued. 'When it comes down to it, rugby is a very simple game,' he said calmly and with feeling, eyeing each and every one of his teammates around him. He brandished a ball in a bucket of a left hand. 'See this thing here, this is a rugby ball, orrite, and all we've got to do is cross their line and touch it down. Easy.'

'Now slow down, Leap, you're going too fast for me. Tell me again what we have to do?' The voice was unmistakably that of Eamon Murphy, Pontypridd's Irish full-back and bona fide comedian. Six years previously, he had left Limerick in the Irish Republic, ostensibly to watch the international match between Ireland and Wales in Cardiff. A long weekend, he had promised his parents and workmates. He never returned. Having got talking to some Welsh supporters that Saturday evening, he eventually awoke on the living room floor of a house in Pontypridd with a headache to end all Hail Marys. The house belonged to Martyn Prosser, the Pontypridd hooker, and the two of them got on famously and became firm friends. Eamon decided to stay on and soon found a job in the local chain works, Brown Lenox, where he had worked ever since.

The rest of the team chuckled aloud. Thomas hesitated and then smiled, accepting how facile his statement had sounded. 'Orrite, come on now, let's concentrate. Let's start thinking about the game.' The expressions in the room immediately turned more serious. 'What we're gonna do today is keep it nice an' tight for the first twenty minutes and then we'll look to move it out wide to you girls in the backs, orrite!' Thomas had been brought up to believe that rugby was a forwards' game and it came naturally to him to disparage the more glamorous backs, though none of the comments were ever taken personally or seriously. 'These Londoners are all fucking soft,' he exaggerated, 'so let's really get stuck in and show 'em what Ponty rugby is all about, fucking 'ard but fair, orrite!' As he expressed this last word, he glanced at Rocky Evans, the team's fiery tight-head prop who always played on the edge of the rules. Evans knew the significance of the glance but it never changed the way he played the game. Indeed, inwardly, Thomas hoped it never would. 'You two in the centre, Joe, Pat, keep close, no gaps. Watch Harrison like a hawk but don't be afraid to 'ave a go yourselves, orrite!'

'Right,' said Pat. Joe did not respond. In fact, he had not heard a word his captain had been saying, so totally absorbed was he in his own concentration, sweat pouring from his brow and dripping on to the rough concrete of the dressing room floor.

'This is a big day for the club,' Thomas carried on. 'It's not often we get to play the 'arlequins and they've got four internationals in their side today so they're showing us respect. If we beat this lot, we'll enjoy our beer a lot more this evening, that's for sure. And remember, a couple of the selectors are 'ere and international places are up for grabs. Right, all of you who wanna piss, gerrit over with. We'll gather in two minutes, usual warm-up and then out we go.'

As the players were about to leave the dressing room, Joe took several deep breaths, his nostrils filling up with the smells of sweat, Deep Heat and wintergreen. They were intoxicating and he felt strong and eager to burst on to the field of play. Through the open door, he caught sight of the Harlequins players making their way up the tunnel towards the pitch, observing live for the first time the famous multi-coloured, quartered jerseys. 'Cunts,' he muttered silently to himself, his eyes never leaving the Englishmen. He heard the distant noise and polite applause as the Harlequins ran on to the field. A few seconds later, it was the turn of Pontypridd. The applause was deafening. Joe had never played in front of so many spectators. Not even the games against Cardiff and Swansea had attracted such a crowd. 'They must be shitting themselves,' Joe shouted over to Pat as he bounced up and down on his toes waiting for the kick-off.

James Harrison was acutely aware of the eager anticipation in the crowd and hoped his teammates would not be unnerved. He himself was calm and in control. After all, he had once played in a Grand Slam decider for England in Paris against the might of France in front of fifty thousand spectators and games did not get any bigger than that.

Rocky Evans was soon in trouble, receiving a tongue-lashing from the referee almost as soon as the game had started for punching Brian Meadows, the excellent Harlequins hooker. The occasion has got to Rocky, thought Thomas. He won't last at this rate. 'Just calm it down, Rock,' urged Thomas, 'we don't want you sent off and you know what this ref is like. He'll 'ave his eyes on you.' Rocky did indeed know this referee. He had sent him off twice previously.

'Sorry, Leap, but I've always wanted to do that to Meadows.'

Brian Meadows was a fearsome character who lived, breathed and ate rugby. As wide as he was tall, with a shaved head, gnarled and scabby ears and narrow slits for eyes that exuded menace, he was considered a hard, uncompromising player as likely to scold his own teammates as much as the opposition players. It was widely believed he could be provoked into indiscretions that could result in penalties against him and possibly even his being sent off. The reality was that his aggression was controlled and disciplined, and he had not played thirty times for England for nothing.

Throughout the first-half, Joe and Harrison rarely came into contact as the game became bogged down at forward. On one occasion, Joe sensed that Harrison was going to break, so he quickened his step to aim a tackle. Harrison, however, moved the ball on as Joe approached him. He held back, his face only inches away from that of the England captain. The latter stared at his opposing centre and saw something that was rare on a rugby field, even at the highest level, a real hatred in an opponent's eyes. It shook him a little.

As the game opened up in the second-half, their confrontations became more frequent, with Harrison invariably on top. On two occasions, Joe attempted to cut inside his opponent only to be hammered to the ground. On the second occasion, the force of the tackle dislodged the ball from his hands and was retrieved by a Harlequin who stole away for a try.

'He's a lot stronger than I thought,' Joe admitted to Pat as they awaited the conversion beneath the posts. In the distance, he could see Harrison receiving the congratulations of his teammates for the tackle that had led to the try. They were all grinning and Joe seethed with fury, desperate to get back into the action.

Midway through the half, Harrison took a pass at pace and attacked a half-gap that appeared between Joe and Pat. Joe accelerated to close him down only to be beaten by a side-step that left him floundering. Never had Joe been beaten without laying a hand on an opponent. It was a humbling and humiliating experience. Whilst on the floor, he heard the crowd gasp as Harrison continued on his sweeping run for a further thirty yards before he was finally brought down by a tackle from Eamon Murphy. The spectators applauded loudly. Although hostile towards English opponents and Harrison, in particular, they appreciated good play from whoever produced it. Joe returned to his position in a rage, wiping away a thick smear of mud from his backside.

The match remained deadlocked at twelve points each as the last few minutes approached. The England captain gathered the ball in loose play and headed off in the only direction open to him, up the right-hand touchline. As he saw the space close down, he slowed his pace and passed the ball inside him to a supporting teammate. Clearly three seconds late and like a grenade with its pin pulled, Joe exploded into Harrison with a stiff-arm tackle so hard and so high it threatened to decapitate him. The force of the swinging arm propelled Harrison across the touchline and he crashed heavily into an advertising hoarding, over which he cartwheeled, head first, before landing at the feet of some standing spectators who needed to take evasive action. Joe immediately went over to the prostrate figure who lay dazed on the ground. 'Make me look stupid, will you? I swear one day I'll kill you, you fucking bastard,' he screamed down at him.

The England captain was seeing too many stars to fully absorb what Joe was yelling at him but one spectator heard every word and was shaken by the sheer intensity of feeling. Her name was Susan Jenkins.

All hell let loose. Three Harlequins forwards ran menacingly towards Joe, like heavyweight boxers leaving their corners at the sound of the bell. As the punches started flailing away, all thirty players became involved in a mighty free-for-all. It took fully two minutes for the fighting to stop. As the teams parted, a certain Rocky Evans lay flat on his back on the sodden turf, the vacant stare in his eyes seemingly contemplating the clouds above, his arms and legs spread-eagled, like a sacrificial offering at a Pagan festival. Brian Meadows never forgot the punches he took or the opportunity for a payback. Although there was still a minute left to play, with the game level-pegging, the referee, sensing real tension and fearing a repeat of the violence, blew his whistle early to end the match. The crowd instantly broke out into loud applause for a fine game. This seemingly reduced the boiling points of the players and handshakes were offered and accepted all round.

'You orrite, James?' Thomas asked, enveloping him with his massive arms.

'Yeah, I'm fine, thanks.'

'Sorry 'bout that tackle. He's been really keyed up all day and he just lost it. He's only seventeen, you know, an' has gotta lotta learn, but he's a good prospect and who knows, he may even play for Wales this year. He wanted to leave his mark, though that's not what he had in mind, I'm sure.'

'Don't worry about it.' James Harrison was used to being singled out for rough treatment. 'He's pretty sharp, I'll give him that. Had my work cut out today.'

Leap Thomas smiled as he left the England captain with a final clasp of the shoulder. As Harrison entered the dressing room, the memory of those eyes so full of hatred played restlessly on his mind.

* * *

The atmosphere in the clubhouse behind the goalposts at the town end of the ground was as ever lively with banter about the game. The Harlequins team and officials departed after about an hour, their coach crammed with cans of beer and cartons of cigarettes as they headed towards the curry house in Bristol, the pub in Swindon and the hangovers in London.

'Well played, Joe.' Dewi Griffiths patted him on the back. Joe almost blushed in acknowledgement as the compliment came from the chief rugby correspondent of *The Times* newspaper and one of Welsh rugby's legendary players. 'You showed some nice touches out there today and your tackling was strong. You held Harrison up pretty well and that's the best he's played all season. Keep that up and we'll see you in the famous red jersey yet.'

'Thank you, Mr Griffiths,' Joe replied politely. 'Let's 'ope so.' Griffiths left Joe and walked over to David Richards, a national selector. Joe hoped that Griffiths would put a good word in for him.

'You eye-tie prat.' Joe was brought back down to earth as he turned his head towards Pete. 'Smacking Harrison like that is gonna stir things up, you watch.' He shook his head in mild rebuke at what Joe had done, though smiling at the same time. Joe just grinned and shrugged his shoulders. 'Dave's keeping a couple of seats for us in the corner.' Acknowledging Dave's waving arm, the two of them crossed the clubhouse and sat down at the small rectangular table where their friend was sitting.

'Wha' you 'aving?' Pete asked, noticing that Dave's glass was almost empty.

'Lager top,' Dave replied before sinking the remains of his glass in one gulp.

'Joe?'

'Pint of Welsh, thanks.'

'One lager top, one bitter,' Pete muttered as he wound his way round the tables and groups of chatting people to the bar as if he were avoiding shoppers on a busy Saturday afternoon in Cardiff. At the bar, he sighed as an impenetrable barrier of thirsty rugby fans was waiting impatiently to be served. Although the three boys were under the legal age for drinking alcohol, neither of them had ever been challenged in the two years of their regularly coming to the club.

'How'd the school get on?' Joe asked Dave.

'Great win; nineteen-six.'

Joe raised his eyebrows. 'Brilliant. Hawthorn are usually quite good.'

'Simon House had a cracking game in the centre. I don't think you'll get your place back next week.' Both of them laughed as they eyed the bar eagerly to see if Pete had been served yet. They were in luck.

'Here you are, boys.' Pete had returned, gripping three pint glasses precariously in his hands.

'Ta, Pete. Tha' was quick.'

'Got lucky. Phil was being served as I arrived so he got 'em in for me.'

Just as Joe was taking his first gulp, he saw out of the corner of his eye the rotund figure of the president of Pontypridd Rugby Football Club, Stan Williams, waddling towards him. His whole demeanour was serious and intimidating, accentuated by the black shoes, black trousers and black pullover he was wearing with the Pontypridd RFC badge on the left breast together with the black and white club tie that he always seemed to wear beneath it. He ignored Pete and Dave and addressed Joe directly. 'Joe, 'ave you got a minute, we'd like to 'ave a word with you in the committee room.' Williams's tone left no doubt that he was expected to respond positively.

'Sure. Hang on a sec, boys.' Joe stood up and followed Williams to a room situated between the ladies and gents toilets in the foyer of the clubhouse.

Pete looked at Dave. 'I smell trouble.'

On entering, Joe almost choked as the smoke swirled around the airless committee room. The walls were stained nicotine-yellow and at the far end of a long mahogany table, Mervyn Hughes and Alan Jones, two committee members, were already seated. Hughes tossed Jones a packet of Capstan Full Strength, from which the latter eagerly pulled a cigarette. The ashtray between them was overflowing, smothering the name of the beer company whose logo embellished it. Sitting down between them at the head of the table but not inviting Joe to take a seat himself, Williams got straight to the point. 'We've been considering that incident with Harrison. I can tell you, the 'arlequins were not very happy about it at all and they've got every right to be 'cos it was totally out of order. You know our club's reputation isn't the best when it comes to dirty play and we're determined to change that. What you did today and because of who you did it to means that the press are gonna 'ave a field day. It'll take us a long time to recover from this.' Williams paused and Joe sensed what was coming next. 'As a result, we've decided to suspend you from the next two games, against Neath on Wednesday and Llanelli on Saturday. We also wanna warn you that this club will not tolerate such behaviour again and that if there's any repetition, your future 'ere will be in doubt.'

Joe was incredulous, unable initially to say a word. Gathering his thoughts, he finally responded. 'I can't believe that. I'm just totally dumbfounded, staggered, I am. What can I say? Not only did the ref not send me off, he didn't even warn me or anything.'

'That's because he 'ad his hands full sorting out the punch-up,' Hughes replied rather smugly. 'We had a word with him afterwards and I can tell you he was really pissed off with you. He admitted he should've sent you off.'

'You know that this and all the publicity that's gonna come about will seriously harm my chances of making the Welsh squad this year as well as giving me the reputation of being a dirty player, which I'm not.'

'Well, you should've thought of that beforehand, shouldn't you? You've only got yourself to blame,' Williams returned, his voice raised as he got up from his chair. 'We'll be advising the press immediately. We wanna be seen to be taking action quickly. That's all, you can go now.'

Joe left the room in a rage, his face twisted in fury, and he paused momentarily in the lobby to calm himself down before making his way back to his friends. He reasoned that what they had done was strictly correct but he couldn't help feeling that their main purpose had been to knock him down a peg or two. While they wanted him to play for Wales one day for the prestige that it would bring to the club, they were too dyed in the wool, old-fashioned, rugby men of a different era to believe that a seventeen-year-old could be ready even if his performances suggested otherwise.

'Narrow-minded pricks,' he muttered under his breath. 'I'll fucking show 'em.' He sat down next to Dave and Pete, who both stared at him expectantly. They could see at once that his mind was elsewhere for Joe did not say a word.

'Well, what 'appened?' Pete asked eventually.

'Read the papers tomorrow,' Joe responded enigmatically. He wasn't in the mood to discuss it with anybody. Sensing this, Dave and Pete kept quiet and swigged their pints. After a moment, Joe awoke from his reverie. 'Same again?'

'Yeah, ta.'

Joe stood up and walked over to the bar. He spotted a gap and nudged his way to the front. As he waited to be served, he felt a tap on his shoulder. He turned round. It was Susan Jenkins, the corners of her mouth stretched in a sunbeam smile. 'You wouldn't mind getting me a coke and two white wine and sodas, would you?' offering him two crisp green notes. 'It'll take me forever to get served.'

At the end of the game, Susan Jenkins had immediately left the ground and gone home. After having her tea, she relaxed a little in front of the television watching her favourite programme, *The Generation Game*, and then changed from her mud-splattered jeans and sweater into an elegant, low-cut, jet-black dress. It successfully showed off her slim figure. At seven o'clock, her best friends, Ann and Helen, arrived at her house to be greeted by her customary 'nice to see you, to see you nice,' pinched from the venerable Bruce Forsyth. Ann had managed to borrow her father's car for the evening and fifteen minutes later, they walked into the Pontypridd RFC clubhouse and into the staring eyes of the now well-lubricated menfolk. Their attentions were gradually moving away from rugby and towards their next great love.

'Of course not,' Joe replied with charm. He took the notes from her hand, not failing to catch sight of the lace trim of her bra down the front of her dress.

Sue and her friends were regulars on Saturday nights, which was also Disco Night at the club. Indeed, when the rugby committee was dishing out the music to Joe, Rockin' Robin Williams, the resident DJ, had started his own particular brand. Rockin' Robin had been the disc jockey at the club for the past five years.

'Hasn't bought a new record in all that time,' Eamon Murphy was often heard to joke.

'Well, 'aven't had a pay rise in all that time either, 'ave I?' Rockin' Robin would retort.

Sue always appeared to be surrounded by male company, or so Joe believed anyway. Consequently, he had never felt comfortable going up to talk to her although he had always found her very attractive. She attended a different school to him, so outside of Saturdays, he rarely saw her. Deep down, he knew the reason he never approached her was the fear of rejection. The drinks finally bought, he handed them and the change over to Sue.

'Thank you. That's really good of you.' Joe noticed that her smile lingered just that little bit longer than normal and nor did he imagine the unnecessary brushing of her fingers against his as he passed her the drinks.

'No problem. P'rhaps we can have a dance later on?' Joe's request was instinctive.

'That'd be nice. I look forward to it.' Her response was warm and accompanied by a wide smile. She finally turned and walked back to her friends. Joe's troubles of earlier in the evening were now a distant memory. Pete's comment the previous day that Sue was no longer seeing John Clayton had not escaped him either.

'Would you like that dance now?' Joe asked two hours later, tapping her on the shoulder. He was more fortified with alcohol.

'I thought you'd never ask,' Sue replied, turning round to look up at him from her chair.

Ann and Helen took sips from their drinks, smiling knowingly to each other. It did not escape Sue that Joe had waited until Rockin' Robin had begun to play some slow records and as the first beguiling notes of Chicago's *If You Leave Me Now* sounded out from the speakers, Joe held Sue's hand and guided her to the dance floor. As they held each other, Joe breathed in the fragrance of Chanel N° 19, not that he knew what it was. For her part, Sue breathed in the lingering stinks of Deep Heat and stale beer. In fact, Joe stumbled once or twice which made Sue think that he had had one or two drinks too many.

'I thought you played really well today.'

'Thanks. I thought I played okay but it wasn't one of my better games.'

'You definitely had the nicest legs out there. I'd get yourself a bigger pair of shorts, though, because I very nearly ran on and jumped on you.'

Joe was taken aback by the comment. A bit forward, he thought, but it pleased and bolstered him, nonetheless. 'Even nicer legs than Mr Wonderful opposite me?'

'Oh, definitely. He's a bit fat, actually. He's a good player, though.'

The record came to an end but they did not leave the dance floor. They waited for the next one to play and never left each other's company for the rest of the evening. When the slow records came back on, Sue did not mind when Joe slipped his hands down her sides and over her behind nor the hint of an erection when they held each other ever more tightly. Joe was embarrassed and moved himself away from her a fraction but he was pleased that she so obviously wanted to be with him.

When the last record came to an end, Rockin' Robin wished everybody a safe journey home and the clubhouse lights came on, momentarily blinding the dancers' eyes. Joe continued to hold Sue gently in the middle of the dance floor and kissed her fully on the lips. At the same time, he ran his hand through her long brown hair and sensitively stroked the back of her neck. Sue felt what seemed like a bolt of electricity pass through her body.

'Walk you home?'

'That'd be nice. I'll just tell my friends and gather my things. See you in a sec.'

'You dirty bastard,' Dave said as Joe collected his kit bag and coat from the lobby. 'Give 'er one for me, will you?'

'You're such a dog,' Joe replied with a smile. He knew that tonight he would act the perfect gentleman, have a nice kiss and arrange to see her again. Sue was not like any other girl he had known. He wanted the relationship to develop seriously and he did not want to ruin it. 'See you Monday, boys.'

The last vision Dave and Pete had of their friend that evening was a little hazy due to the bucketfuls of beer they had consumed. Nevertheless, they registered that Joe was holding Sue's hand as they walked out of the clubhouse into the freezing cold night air.

'Lucky sod.'

That very same evening, many miles away in Balmoral Castle, Prince Charles was restless and finding it difficult to sleep. He had been looking forward to this weekend in the highlands of Scotland for many weeks, away from his official duties and the prying eyes of the media and away also from the rest of his family who rarely ventured to Balmoral at this time of year. It had been discreetly arranged many weeks in advance but instead of the pleasures he had anticipated, his mind was a whirl of activity and when he had gone to bed, he was uneasy and unsettled.

Three days previously, he had been in Wales, at Carnarvon, the castle town in the north of the country which had been the setting for his investiture as Prince of Wales in 1969. What he had hoped to be a day of celebration only succeeded in alerting him to the, at best, apathetic, at worst, downright hostile feelings the Welsh nation had towards him. The turnout in the town had been pathetically low and only women of pensionable age appeared to be in attendance, loyally waving their miniature Welsh flags and Union Jacks. It was significant and disappointing that the principality's national newspaper, the *Western Mail*, had relegated his visit deep into the inside pages, supported by an opinion column that was lukewarm, at best. Similarly, his visit featured low down on BBC Wales television news and he felt humiliated that even the arrival in Cardiff of the pop group, Showaddywaddy, for that evening's sell-out concert at the Capitol Theatre was given greater prominence. You could fill the theatre with ten times the number of people who had turned out to see me. Doesn't anybody care about me anymore? His private thoughts were totally self-indulgent.

In his mind, it was becoming abundantly clear that a recent BBC documentary had adversely affected Welsh public opinion of him. In the company of a distinguished journalist, he had supported the programme in his frankness and openness. He felt that he had come over as a more human and warmer person but now, in the quiet of his bedroom, he was not so sure that the programme had been a success. A small demonstration in Carnarvon had caught his attention and particularly the banner, *Go Home to Scotland*. What did they mean by that? He was puzzled. There was no doubt that he felt a greater affinity towards Scotland. How he loved the summer there, fishing in the beautiful lakes and streams and walking through the heather up and over the hills where the views were unmatched anywhere in Britain. Certainly much of the film had been shot in Scotland, none in Wales, he remembered, and for the most part he had been wearing a kilt. Perhaps it was this that had annoyed them and maybe they had a point. Shouldn't the Prince of Wales be spending more time in his supposed country and be taking a greater interest in its affairs?

My God, I can't do everything, be everywhere and please everybody. He was becoming emotional. I did not ask to be who I am. How my great uncle was right to give up the throne and live in Paris with the woman he loved, away from this constant pressure and glare of publicity.

The thought was delicious. Perhaps he could do the same. What that ghastly gutter press would pay for these thoughts, he reflected.

After a moment, he regained control of his emotions and became calmer as reality and that sense of duty which had been instilled in him since birth returned. I should spend more time in Wales, he conceded, and accept more invitations to visit and speak and engage with the people. As he turned to pour himself a glass of Highland Spring, which he kept by the side of the bed on a silver salver, his partner awoke.

'Is everything okay, Charles? You've been tossing and turning all night.'

'Oh, I'm just a little restless and thirsty, darling. You go back to sleep.'

On finishing his drink, Charles turned towards his partner, pulled the sheets and blankets over himself and held her lovingly in his arms.

'Mmm, that's nice. I love you so much, Charles.'

'And I love you, too, you naughty Mrs Parker Bowles.'

6

The doorbell rang. It was Marco who answered.

'Hello. Is Joe in?'

'Hang on a second.' Having looked suspiciously at the person in front of him, Marco turned his back and shouted in the general direction of the upstairs. 'There's some girl here to see you.' He walked back towards the living room, leaving the poor girl standing alone on the doorstep.

'Charming,' Sue muttered under her breath.

A moment later, Joe came bounding down the stairs, adjusting the collar of his black Pontypridd RFC blazer. He met Sue at the door and gave her a peck on the cheek. Sue crackled with excitement at seeing him again and noticed that the underside of his neck looked quite red and raw. Joe was shaving three times a week by now but being a special occasion, he had ventured a fourth. He knew it had been a mistake when he saw the blotches while looking in the mirror. He had slapped on some Brut 33 aftershave from the bottle given to him as a birthday present by his mother. It was the first time he had used it and it felt as if somebody had taken a blowtorch to his neck.

'Bye, Mum,' he yelled before the door closed behind him with a heavy clunk. 'You look absolutely gorgeous,' he said as they walked to her car.

'Thank you.' Sue's smile could have lit up the darkest of nights. 'You look pretty good yourself.' Joe smiled back, his confidence rising.

The previous Saturday, on the doorstep of Sue's home, Joe had asked whether she would like to go out one evening to the Caesars Arms, a popular country pub close to the village of Efail Isaf, a few miles away from Pontypridd. Sue accepted at once and they made arrangements for the following Saturday. Joe had planned to borrow his father's car but Sue owned her own and was quite happy to drive herself. Joe was very appreciative. He knew it was not always easy to borrow his father's car as he worked late in his restaurant and required it to get home. Having to wait for a taxi on a busy Saturday night after a long, hard day was not very appealing, though his father was always willing to put himself out for his son.

The Caesars Arms was already filling up when they arrived. They made their way over to a small, round, dimpled-copper table in the middle of the pub, close to a supporting pillar. If they had arrived five minutes later, no tables would have been available. Joe went up to the bar and returned with a pint of lager and a white wine and soda. For the first time, Sue noticed a faint graze about an inch and a half long by the side of his left eye.

'Have you been fighting?' she remarked, pointing to his eye. 'You couldn't have got that playing rugby 'cos I read that you're suspended.'

'Now that's where you're wrong,' Joe replied with a cheeky grin. 'I got it playing for the school this morning. Just an accident; caught a knee in a tackle.'

'I like it. Makes you look all tough and masculine like that boxer, John Conteh. He's gorgeous.'

'P'raps I should do the other eye as well then, though there's not much I can do about the colour of my skin?'

Sue smiled and touched the graze lightly with her finger. 'At least they're letting you play.'

'Yeah. They're not as small-minded as those wankers at the club if you pardon my French.' Sue grinned before taking a sip from her glass. 'You go to the Ysgol Gyfun in Rhydyfelin, don't you?' Joe asked in reference to the school that catered purely for Welsh speakers. He knew that she did but it was a way of opening up the conversation.

'That's right. It's a good school. I like it there a lot.'

'It must be marvellous to speak Welsh.'

'I suppose so but I don't really look at it in those terms. We always spoke it at home so it comes naturally to me.'

'I'd give my right arm to speak Welsh. It's a true expression of your nationality, something to be proud of.'

'I'll teach you if you like.'

'Really? That'd be great. I'd love that.' Joe took a quick swig of his drink before carrying on. 'Are you planning to go to uni next year?'

'Definitely. I'd love to go to London and study economics at the LSE. They're the one I have in mind.'

'Why London?' Joe countered, his expression turning a little more serious.

'Well, it's time I broadened my horizons a bit. Deep down, I'm a city girl at heart an' I quite fancy the idea of living in London. There'd be so much to do though whether I could afford it is another matter.'

'You should stay in Wales.'

'Why?' Sue responded inquisitively. The sharp tone of Joe's voice had not escaped her.

'Because Wales can't afford to lose young, talented people like you an' me. If we all leave, Wales will just become an extension of England. There'll be nobody left to preserve the Welsh way of life. Our special identity will be lost. It'd be tragic. It's already 'appening at far too fast a pace. What this country needs are young people fighting for independence, for its own Parliament with real powers. Welsh people with real power to look after this country's interests.'

'I applaud your sentiments but you have to be realistic. The world is becoming a smaller place and the opportunities for young people today are immense. You can't escape global influences. Decisions being taken on the other side of the world, let alone England, are having an effect on the way we live. Look at all the Japanese companies starting up in Wales. Schools will soon be teaching Japanese as well as Welsh, you watch, and I think that's a good thing.'

Joe was taken aback. 'Look, I understand everything you're saying but all I want is for Wales to have its own Parliament so that we can govern ourselves and make our own laws. I'm not saying we should kick out the Japs or anything like that, only the power to do so if we so choose and most importantly of all, to break away from those bastards in England. With Welsh people controlling Welsh affairs, the important and unique features of Welsh life will always be preserved. They're worth fighting for. In fact, I think it's our duty.'

It did not escape Sue's attention that this was the second time that Joe had used the word 'fighting'. She was not exactly sure what he meant by it but so vehemently had he expressed himself that it played on her mind.

'You sound just like some of the boys at school,' Sue said in a resigned tone.

'Say that again, will you?' Joe responded, his ears pricked. He took a sip from his drink, his eyes never leaving Sue.

'I said that you sound just like some of the boys at school,' she repeated bemused.

It's true, Joe thought. There were people in Wales who shared the same views as him, just like his comrades had said. They needed leadership and direction, that's all.

'Tell me about them.'

'There's not that much to tell, really. Just boys who fervently believe in an independent Wales, usually trading crackpot ideas on how to achieve it.'

And this in only one school, Joe mused. There are hundreds of schools in Wales. There must be similar types in those as well. And what about all the people not in school like all those at work or on the dole, of all ages? There must be thousands of them. Suddenly, Joe had a crazy vision of an army of youngsters descending on London, demanding their rights and prepared to fight and die to achieve them. The reality would be much more covert, he knew, but the vision brought a smile to his face, nonetheless. They needed to be galvanised and incited to take action. He would be the catalyst.

From this conversation, Sue saw a side to Joe that she had not seen before. His charm had disappeared and there was an ugly edge to his voice. His eyes were intense. It was not a side to his character that she liked very much but at least he was passionate and bright, so unlike a number of boys she knew. The image of Joe standing over James Harrison flashed across her mind, scowling and threatening, those same intense eyes. That was fine, she thought, but the passion and desire had to be controlled and disciplined. She was not yet convinced Joe possessed those traits.

'Excuse me a minute.' Sue rose to go to the lavatory. It was not that she particularly needed to go but she felt a break from the previous conversation was necessary. Maybe then they could talk about something a bit lighter.

It had done the trick. On her return, Joe was smiling, his demeanour much softer. For the rest of the evening, Sue had not enjoyed herself so much for a long time. Joe's stories of life in a rugby dressing room, of his friendly squabbles with his brother and of his escapades with his friends, all made for entertaining listening. And she often found herself shrieking in laughter at his jokes, usually acquired from Eamon Murphy. When Joe spoke, his eyes sparkled. He was gentle and comfortable to be with. He was also so damned good-looking, Sue reflected. When he looked longingly at her with those large brown eyes of his, with lashes so long she wished they were hers, she could feel herself tremble with excitement. She was frequently tempted to place her hands on his massive shoulders. On more than one occasion, she moved her hands towards him, only to retract at the last minute. She knew that she would find it difficult to resist him. The thought turned her on.

'Last orders!'

'My God, is that the time?'

'Time flies when you're having fun,' Joe clichéd.

As they got up from their chairs to leave, Joe took Sue's short black leather jacket and placed it carefully over her shoulders. In so doing, Sue rested her hand momentarily on his. He smiled. The laughter continued on the journey back to Pontypridd. On arrival outside Joe's home, she switched off the engine.

'Thanks for a lovely evening. I really enjoyed myself.'

'Same here,' Joe responded as he gazed deeply into Sue's eyes. She held the stare with ease.

'We should do it again.' Sue's voice betrayed a degree of uncertainty, hoping that Joe would respond in the affirmative. She need not have worried.

'Definitely!'

There was a momentary pause before Sue carried on. 'Why don't you come round my house next Saturday? I'll cook you something. P'rhaps we can play some music afterwards?'

'Tha' sounds great. You're very kind. I'll bring a bottle or three.'

'Trying to gemme drunk, are you?'

'It crossed my mind.'

They both chuckled out loud.

'Good, about eight o'clock then?'

'Yeah, I'll be there, don't worry.'

Looking into her eyes, Joe cradled Sue's head in his hands and placed his mouth over hers, kissing her longingly. Sue did not resist.

'I'd better go before I do something I regret,' Sue gasped eventually.

'That's probably wise. I'm gonna need a cold shower myself before I go to bed tonight.'

Sue giggled, bringing her hand up to her lips. Joe opened the door of her burgundy Hillman Imp and got out.

'See you next Saturday then.'

'Can't wait.'

7

The following morning, Joe woke up late. Indeed, he was still in bed when his mother returned from church at midday. Nothing saddened Mrs Chilani more than Joe's non-attendance at Mass each week. Although Marco accompanied her regularly, she sensed that even he was becoming restless and beginning to complain as to why he had to go when his brother did not. Her husband, she thought, could set a better example. He only ever went at Christmas and Easter.

During lunch, when all the family was gathered for the one and only time in the week, Joe was noticeably quiet, his mind clearly elsewhere. When his mother enquired as to how his evening had gone, Joe muttered 'fine' but did not expand any further, frustrating her curiosity. After dessert, he grabbed hold of a couple of newspapers which were lying on the sideboard next to the kitchen table and slumped into an armchair in the living room. *LONDON BOMB KILLS FIVE* read the dramatic front page headline in *The Sunday Times*. In smaller print underneath was written, *IRA CLAIMS RESPONSIBILITY*. Tragic, thought Joe, but totally understandable. He then read a number of quotations from eminent politicians deploring the attack. They tried to convey sympathy and a determination to hunt down the perpetrators but Joe believed them to be false words spoken for public consumption.

'That's exactly what I'm gonna do,' Joe said quietly to himself. 'Something unforgettable like that. Only, people have become bored with Irish politics. In my case, the headlines will be earth-shattering as it will be totally unexpected.'

He turned to the sports pages. Pontypridd had lost to Llanelli. He was encouraged to read one line which stated that the team had missed the solid tackling of the suspended Joe Chilani in the centre. He was not best pleased to read in the report of another match, however, that one of his rivals for a place in the Welsh national team had scored three tries, one a solo effort from forty yards. He cursed Stan Williams and his fellow committee members. This was living proof of how his suspension had given his rivals an advantage. It only made him more determined. A couple of pages in, he read an article on Britain's world champion boxer, the featherweight, Ronnie 'Hurricane' Henderson, who was preparing for a fight against a Mexican opponent he had never heard of.

'Fifty thousand pounds he's being paid. It's obscene,' he exclaimed. 'I'd rather see Rocky Evans and Brian Meadows go at it for nothing.' He allowed himself a chuckle.

An hour later, he placed the papers down on the carpet. His father was dozing in the room's other armchair. Joe got up and went upstairs to his bedroom. He shut the door behind him and sat down at the mahogany desk which had been in the family for as long as he could remember. He pulled out a sheet of paper and pen, sat back and pondered. A few seconds later, he wrote the word 'What'. Against it, he wrote a simple sentence. He then wrote 'Who', against which he placed a tick. Next to the word 'When', he scribbled a date.

Against 'Where', he wrote three words. After writing 'How', he thought for a second before scribbling a word though he followed it with a double question mark and a slight shake of the head, his lips pursed. This was a major concern of his. Everything else, however, was in place. Nothing had changed from his initial thoughts and it pleased him that his plans were so well advanced and so clear. Nevertheless, everything was totally dependent on one key factor over which he had only some control. He was desperate to succeed.

'I've gotta do it, I've just gotta do it. I can't let anything get in my way, anything!' So full of determination were the words he spoke quietly to himself and so intense was his desire that he could feel a headache coming on. 'The impact will be enormous, just incredible, it'll be.' These words and the images of the day that appeared clearly in his head shook him to the core. He took a deep breath, taking time to regain his composure, but then reality set in. 'It's a lot easier said than done, but it's not impossible.' At no stage did his resolve weaken.

As the light dimmed outside, he quickly realised that the afternoon had flown by. The small clock on the desk was showing five o'clock. 'Nearly time for *Rugby Special*,' a reference to the BBC's flagship rugby highlights programme. He decided to take a break and, after tearing the piece of paper into tiny fragments, he made his way downstairs, via the rubbish bin in the kitchen, to the living room where his father was now snoring, fast asleep, mouth wide open.

'*Vuoi prendere una tazza di tè?*' his mother asked, appearing from nowhere.

'Tea. That'd be nice. Ta, Mum.'

Mrs Chilani went back into the kitchen. Why does he always reply in English? she thought a little annoyed.

'Oh, no, they're not showing Leicester and Gloucester, are they?' Joe said to himself disappointingly, shaking his head. He had read a report of the match earlier in *The Sunday Times* and by all accounts, it had been a dull, turgid affair. 'No doubt the Beeb has found fifteen minutes to string together to make it look like a classic.'

"*And that's late by Burton on Wheeler, but the referee's allowing the game to continue. That's good advantage played...*" Nigel Starmer-Smith's assured commentary rang out from the television. "*...and Wheeler is not best pleased. I can see him and Burton scuffling just out of shot of the camera...*" A moment later, the camera closed in on the two players. "*You would never believe they are England teammates...,*" the commentary went on, "*...eyeballing each other like that. I have to say that Burton has been well off the pace today and this is the closest he's come to laying a hand on an opponent.*" All of a sudden, the camera caught Burton punching Wheeler flush on the jaw, leaving him writhing on the floor. The referee sent him off without hesitation. "*Disgraceful,*" bellowed Starmer-Smith.

Joe gazed on as the trainer sponged Wheeler's face. It had been the most exciting moment of the match, the incident everybody would be talking about. 'A bit like what I have in mind,' Joe said to himself quietly, 'something on TV that grabs people's attention that they won't forget for a very long time. But in my case,' Joe added chillingly, after a short pause, 'the trainer will be wasting his time.'

After *Rugby Special* had finished, he remained in the armchair and continued to watch the television though he was not really concentrating. Soon, his mind turned to the requirement over which he had only some control but which was essential to the carrying out of his plan.

'It's possible, it's very possible,' he whispered, convincing himself, 'but you're going to have to push yourself harder than you've ever done before.'

This went without saying because only the very best achieved what he needed to achieve for only very special people were selected to play for Wales.

8

'Now where did she say she lived?' Joe pondered this on a dry mild evening as he walked the half-mile from his home through the town centre and up the sharply rising hill to an area of Pontypridd close to the local golf course called The Common. As his vision swept over the wide expanse of green, lit up by the street lights that bordered the undulating turf, he recalled how he used to fly kites there with his father when still at primary school and later model aeroplanes which always seemed to plummet to the ground seconds after their promising take-off. The incline of the hill was very severe and he was pleased with himself that he was neither out of breath nor perspiring greatly when he arrived at the top. He was keen, after all, to make a very good impression. 'Now where is it? Number 2, 4, 6, it must be down by 'ere somewhere.' He craned his neck to see as far ahead as possible. Around the corner, he caught sight of a familiar-looking Hillman Imp right outside number 18, his destination. 'This is it.'

Joe had been in the best of spirits all week for his plan was taking shape and his resolve was strong. Each evening, once home from school, he would dump his satchel, change into shorts and t-shirt and go out for long runs in and around the villages near Pontypridd, pushing himself harder each time. His times had improved each successive day to his huge satisfaction. In order to play for Wales, he had to be fitter than any of his rivals and certainly fitter than he was at the moment. During a weights training session on Thursday evening in the Hawthorn Leisure Centre, his mind began to turn towards dinner with Sue that coming Saturday. I hope her mum an' dad will be out, he wondered nervously. He always felt ill-at-ease in the presence of girlfriends' parents. He pondered this as he sat on a bench by the weights machine, resting for a moment, his arms aching and the palms of his hands bruised and sore.

Now, as he approached Sue's home, these thoughts returned and a few butterflies fluttered inside his stomach. Casting a quick glance at his watch, he rang the doorbell. He was right on time. As he waited, he looked down the front of his blazer and noticed a fine thread of white cotton on the lapel. He brushed it away. Slightly on edge, he ran his fingers around the collar to ensure that it was not upright. He realised that it was the same blazer he had worn the previous Saturday at the Caesars Arms. 'She'll think it's the only one I've got.' Smiling to himself, he nodded his head in acknowledgement that she would be right.

A slim silhouette approached the front door, visible through the frosted glass. He quickly checked to see that his fly was zipped up. The door opened.

'Bang on time.'

'I wouldn't wanna be late for this. It's the only thing I've been thinking about all week,' he lied and with his hand resting on her shoulder, he pecked her on the cheek. Sue blushed and lowered her eyes instinctively for she could feel her spine tingling already.

'Come on in. Excuse the mess.' Sue retreated a step and let go of the door. She tried but failed to sound composed but her apologies were unnecessary for her home was immaculate.

'Thanks.' Joe wiped his shoes in an exaggerated manner on the doormat before crossing the threshold.

'Through here.'

Joe followed Sue along the mirror-bright parquet floor in the hallway and into the living room. The lights there were set more dimly and the room was noticeably warmer. Two brown leather armchairs were positioned either side of a fireplace of brown and white glazed tiles, inside of which flickered a gentle wave of flames from an ornate cast iron grate. Facing the fireplace and with its high back pressed against the wall was a sofa which matched the armchairs. On a low stainless-steel table in one of the corners, and somewhat out of keeping with the seductive atmosphere, a T-Rex LP was playing.

'Great music; I love T-Rex,' Joe stated insincerely once more. He much preferred the harder edge to Slade.

'*Electric Warrior*; one of my all-time favourite LPs. Glad you like it. What would you like to drink? Some wine? Beer? I think there's some gin and vodka in the cupboard as well if you prefer?'

'I'll have a little wine if you don't mind,' and with this, Joe emitted a soft, howling sound, similar to that of a dog or wolf.

Sue smiled. 'Ha ha, the old ones are the best.' Joe returned her smile somewhat sheepishly.

'I've brought some with me.' He passed Sue a bottle which was wrapped in purple tissue paper.

'I was wondering when you were going to hand that over. That's very kind of you, thanks.'

'No problem. It's red so I hope you 'aven't made fish.'

'You're in luck. I've made chilli con carne. I hope that's okay?'

'Sounds great to me and smells even better. Can't wait.' Joe licked his lips. 'The wine's Chianti. I dunno much about wine but my dad goes on about it all the time. I've tried it before and it's really nice. Hope you like it.'

'I'm sure I will. I've got some white wine in the fridge, Liebfraumilch. Fancy a glass of that for starters?'

'Yeah, lovely.'

'Take a seat. I've just got to finish off in the kitchen a minute. I'll get you your wine.'

'I'll come with you. It's always good to see a woman hard at work,' and before Sue could answer, Joe took a few paces back into the hallway, hoping Sue wasn't an ardent feminist for her face turned stony in reaction to his words. He followed closely behind as she led him into the kitchen. She opened the fridge and took out the bottle of Liebfraumilch and poured two glasses. As Joe grabbed a high stool and positioned it beneath him, he caught a glimpse of a multi-coloured trifle in the fridge, with lashings of cream, nuts and cherries on top. It looked delicious.

'Cheers.'

'Cheers.' They clinked their glasses, both of them smiling and gazing into each other's eyes.

'How's your week been then?' Sue asked as she put her glass down and began to slowly stir the chilli, adding some salt at the same time. It bubbled away enticingly.

'Excellent,' Joe exclaimed with confidence. 'I've been training really hard, running and weights mainly. A bit of gym work as well. I can feel myself getting fitter and stronger all the time.' Sue could see how his skin glowed.

'I'm so determined to get into the Welsh squad. I'm desperate to play in the internationals this season.'

'When can you start playing again?'

'Well, actually, I could've played today. My suspension ran out last Saturday but they didn't pick me. I think they were making the point that I can't just walk back into the side. They got thrashed, though, and I heard that Pat in the centre has broken his collarbone, so I'm pretty confident I'll be back next week.'

'So the all-conquering hero returns then?' Sue said playfully.

'I wouldn't say that, but I tell you what, I wouldn't like to be facing me next week. I'm champing at the bit to gerrout there.' Sue noted the determination in his voice. 'I feel fantastic, a million dollars, like.'

'Only a million dollars? Let's hope your opposition hasn't recruited the Six Million Dollar Man then!'

'Very funny,' Joe replied with a smile. 'I tell you, if I'm up against Steve Austin next week, there won't be enough technology to rebuild him afterwards, I can assure you.' Sue laughed and Joe followed suit.

'When's the first international?'

'Mid Jan; Ireland in Cardiff. After that it's Scotland at Murrayfield before the big one; England in Cardiff.' He went quiet for a moment as he pictured himself running out for Wales, his chest heaving in the famous red jersey, the Prince of Wales feathers proud on his left breast.

'What about France?'

'The Froggies? They're later on some time. Can't remember when, exactly.'

Joe seemed less excited at this fixture as if it was unimportant. Sue picked up on this straight away and found it puzzling, especially as the French were likely to be the main competitors to Wales this season.

'What about Italy? Do they have a team? You could play for them if they did.'

'Nah. Italy's a football country. They're crazy for it over there. My dad loves it when they play. All his friends came round the house when they were on the telly during the last World Cup. They didn't half make a racket, shouting at the TV at the smallest of things. My mum kept serving them cake she made specially and my dad must've opened God knows how many bottles of wine. Italy were rubbish, though, so they weren't very pleased when they were knocked out. All they got out of the World Cup was an extra stone in weight and dodgy livers, I tell you.' Sue smiled as she refilled their glasses. 'Lucky they didn't make the final or they would've put on two stones in weight and got proper cirrhosis.' Sue laughed and held Joe's look with her own as she sipped at her drink. Joe took a larger one from his own before continuing. 'My brother loves football as well an' I quite like it myself, too, but rugby's my real love. Italy will never have a proper rugby team, believe me. It's ridiculous to think that the Five Nations championship will become the Six Nations one day, though that's more likely to happen than Margaret Thatcher becoming our next Prime Minister. We'll be in the next century before Britain is ready to have a female PM, take it from me. The Tories must've been off their heads when they chose her.' Joe sniggered and shook his head at such preposterous thoughts.

Sue turned down the gas under the chilli and collected two plates of Parma ham and melon from the fridge. Joe followed her, carrying both of their wine glasses, as they made their way into the dining room, where a table had been set for two. Two candlesticks had been placed in the middle, with the long red candles balancing somewhat precariously on top. The crisp white table linen radiated freshness. The matching set of crockery bore a beautiful blue and white swirling pattern and to Joe's eyes, looked expensive. He was relieved that nobody else was evidently going to join them.

Sue set down one of the plates in front of Joe and the other directly opposite him, where she would be sitting. As she returned to the kitchen to retrieve some matches to light the candles, Joe fiddled with the bottle-opener before successfully pulling out the cork with a loud pop. He was inwardly relieved as he often broke the cork when opening wine at home, much to his father's annoyance, and he did not want to perform a repeat tonight. He filled a different pair of wine glasses with Chianti while Sue lit the candles.

'I've never seen so much wine on the table, red, white. I'll have to go a bit easy.'

'Oh, don't worry about that, let yourself go,' Joe replied with a glint in those large brown eyes of his she so adored. They clinked their glasses once again and with a broad smile, Joe thanked her for the invitation. Neither of them spoke as they both sliced into the lean ham.

'What do you have to do to get picked for the Welsh squad then?' Sue asked in an attempt to start up some conversation.

'Just play well, I assume,' Joe responded matter-of-factly. 'Sounds easy, dunnit, but in fact there are other things you have to take into consideration like buttering up one or two newspaper and TV people and the like. You've got to keep your name in the spotlight. You do that and the selectors will always keep you in mind. It's amazing how influenced they are by the press. I'm not sure they've got a brain cell between 'em.'

'Your name is always in the papers.'

'Glad you notice.' Sue's cheeks reddened, not unnoticed by Joe. 'It's true but not always for the right reasons like this suspension business. But I always try to have a word with the press after the game and I suppose I'm lucky in that I'm only seventeen, still at school and have an Italian name. You could say I stand out a bit. I'm not complaining, though.'

'So you think you have a chance?'

'Yeah, I think so. There's no centre in Wales playing better than me at the moment, that's if those wankers on the committee let me play, of course. Geraint Lewis is pretty much a cert, being captain and all that, but the other position's up for grabs.'

'It would be wonderful if you were selected. I could scrounge some tickets off you.'

'So that's why you invited me to dinner, is it? I knew there was some ulterior motive behind it.' They both laughed. 'I must say, you have a lovely home. Is it just you and your parents? I forgot to ask last time if you had any brothers or sisters.'

Sue's tone softened and her expression saddened a little as she dropped her eyes. 'Actually, I live here by myself. My parents were killed about a year ago in a car accident. I'm an only child.'

Joe was stunned and for a few seconds totally lost for words. 'I'm so sorry. I didn't know.'

'That's okay. I'm getting over it bit by bit, I suppose, though I do have my moments. My grandmother lives down the road and she pops in regularly. In many respects, it's been tougher on her. You never expect to outlive your children.'

'You don't get lonely then?'

'Oh, there's no chance of that. The girls are always round. I wish I had more time to myself sometimes.'

'Who would they be then?'

'Helen and Ann, mainly. Don't know if you know them? Helen Morgan and Ann Jones. They're both in school with me.'

'Vaguely. I've seen 'em around.'

'They're brilliant. A bit mad, but really good friends.'

'You must all speak Welsh to each other then?'

'Yeah, it's our first language.'

'Brilliant, just brilliant. Promise me you'll never let it die. You must keep the language going. Please promise me that.'

'I'm sure we will,' Sue replied, wiping her mouth with her napkin, baffled and somewhat startled at the vigour of Joe's command.

* * *

The conversation flowed easily and the level of laughter grew in direct relation to the quantity of wine consumed. The dinner was devoured eagerly and they clearly enjoyed each other's company very much. When Sue went to make some coffee, Joe stood up from the table and made his way into the living room at Sue's invitation. Once there, he looked through the collection of LPs neatly stacked side by side on a shelf above the record player. He selected David Bowie's *The Rise and Fall of Ziggy Stardust and the Spiders from Mars* and placed it on the turn-table before slumping into one of the armchairs. I'll have to have a double workout tomorrow to burn this meal off, he thought contentedly. He glanced to his right. That day's edition of the *Western Mail* was lying on a small table next to the armchair. As Sue was still in the kitchen, Joe picked it up and began to read the headlines, one of which caught his attention about two thirds of the way down the front page. *PRINCE OF WALES TO STEP UP PUBLIC ENGAGEMENTS.* He read the column underneath. The Prince of Wales was planning to spend more time in the country. The article went on by stating that he wished to have more direct, personal contact with the people, the suggestion being that there would be many more walkabouts arranged and that he would be attending more business and cultural events.

'Hypocritical twat,' Joe muttered under his breath.

'What's that you said?' Sue was standing behind him, holding a tray of coffee and plate of After Eight mint chocolates.

'Oh, nothing; just reading about Prince Charles, that's all. I can't stand the bloke. How can anybody who talks the way he does, with his accent, all la-di-da, claim to be the Prince of Wales? It's just ridiculous. He couldn't give a stuff about Wales. As far as I'm concerned he should live out his life of luxury in Windsor or Sandringham or Buck House or wherever it is he lives, the tosser, and leave Wales to the Welsh.' Joe's voice was raised and his expression serious. Sue could sense that his mood was changing. She was about to change the subject but was too late. 'Who the hell does he think he is, coming to Wales with his false smile just to shake hands with a few grannies? It's so patronising. I bet that when he's out of view of everybody, he can't wait to wash them.' Joe mimicked the Prince of Wales's accent. '"How dare a commoner touch me!" He's such a pompous prick.' Joe was in full unstoppable flow. The Chianti had certainly helped. Sue quietly poured the coffee, her countenance having changed to one of exasperation. 'Just look at him. What does he do? He talks to plants for God's sake. Honestly, people round the world must think he's crazy. And what has he ever done for us? Bugger all. He's better off dead.'

Sue finally managed to get a word in edgeways and replied sharply, 'That's an awful thing to say, you ought to be ashamed of yourself and say sorry.'

All of a sudden, the atmosphere was tense and oppressive. Joe went quiet. Neither of them said a word and they both lowered their gaze, unable to look each other in the eye. After a while, Joe addressed Sue in a much calmer voice and changed the subject. 'You must like David Bowie?'

'God, yeah, definitely. He's superb, my absolute favourite.'

Joe did not respond immediately, seemingly disinterested in Sue's reply. He leaned over and put a lump of sugar into his coffee and took one of the mints. 'Mmm, delicious.'

'I'm glad you like them. You can't go much wrong with After Eights.'

The words spoken were stilted and the tension only eased a fraction. It did not escape Sue's attention that Joe had not apologised. They both quickly fell back into silence. The previous conversation was still on their minds, disturbing the relaxed state they had been in beforehand.

'Another mint?' Sue asked awkwardly after a few more tortuous seconds passed by.

'Sure.'

Joe took one from the plate, discarding the mint chocolate's wrapper on to the tray. Once again, there was a suffocating silence between them. Neither of them could make eye contact with the other. Joe looked at his watch and considered saying his goodbyes. At that moment, Sue excused herself and set off for the bathroom upstairs. She recalled how a similar action at the Caesars Arms had drawn a line under another tense situation and she hoped for the same result this time. As she left the living room, Joe also stood up in order to stretch his legs. His eye caught sight of a line of books on three oak shelves in a corner alcove on the other side of the room. The spines of the books on the upper two shelves were all identical, each having gold leaf wording embossed into a rich black leather. They looked very imposing as only a set of *Encyclopaedia Britannica* can. On the bottom shelf were resting six volumes of Winston Churchill's World War Two memoirs. Although smaller in size than the *Encyclopaedia Britannica*, they looked no less imposing. The books' jackets were buff in colour and each was protected by a transparent plastic cover. Next to these were resting two large books written by the eminent historian, A.J.P. Taylor, one entitled *History of World War One*, the other *History of World War Two*. In complete contrast to the other books on the shelves, the jackets of these two were brightly coloured, one in orange and white, the other in pale-blue and white. The themes of the books made Joe recall the two black and white prints that were hanging in the hallway. One was of a number of German submariners at their stations inside a U-Boat. The other print was of a British Spitfire aeroplane in combat with a German Messerschmitt. Both of the planes seemed at incongruous angles to each other as they fought for domination of the sky. To the right of the shelves, on the adjacent wall, Joe studied a small display of three wartime medals that hung in a square, glass, mahogany case. He was only familiar with one of them, a German Knight's Cross with Oak Leaf Cluster. For a moment, he was transfixed, in awe of such an historical item. Strange things for a young girl to display, he mused. As he continued to stare and ponder, Sue returned. The noise of the door opening startled Joe and he turned to face her. 'I was just admiring your medals. When did you receive these? I never thought you were that old.'

Sue smiled. The ice had been broken. 'Ha, ha, ha.' Sue exaggerated her laughter, enunciating each 'ha' slowly and deliberately and rocking her head to the left and right and then back again in time.

'I would never have thought you were into military history. The books look a bit heavy to me.' Joe nodded his head in their direction.

'Just my normal bedtime reading. What d'you have on your bedside table? No, lemme guess. Autobiographies of rugby players and other sportsmen, I bet?'

'Hey, don't get all sarckie with me.' Joe's reply was playfully stern. He was smiling and he gently grabbed Sue's arms in a mock attempt to rough her up. Laughing, Sue backed away with an extravagant hop. Joe could not bring himself to admit that he was currently halfway through a biography of Barry Sheene.

'Actually, they all belonged to my father. He was passionate about the wars, particularly World War Two. It was a real interest of his. He was always looking out for any memorabilia. There's tons of stuff in the loft; old newspapers, cards, maps, you know, stuff like that.' As Sue spoke, Joe could see genuine sadness in her eyes as she recalled memories of her father. 'Whenever a programme came on the telly about the war, it didn't matter if we were watching something else on the other side, he would always switch over and ignore our protests. We didn't mind, though, because we knew how interested he was.'

'I can see how much you miss him.'

'My mum as well. She was wonderful. A typical Welsh mother really; kind and generous and always with something to say for herself. The house was immaculate and I can see her now shaking her head whenever she came into my room 'cos I'm not the tidiest person in the world. She was never angry, though. My dad could huff and puff a bit but my mum would always bring him back down to earth.' She smiled at the memory. 'She definitely wore the trousers in that marriage.'

'It sounds a lot like my own family. I think Welsh and Italian mothers are very similar. The house is everything to them. My mum can get a bit hot-headed, though. If something upsets her, she goes mad, absolutely bonkers, you know, in that typically Italian way, with lots of shouting and arm waving and the like, and if she's upset at something me or my brother have done, she won't hesitate to smack us about the head. When she's in one of those moods, I tell you, it's better to gerrout of the house. I've never been frightened on the rugby field. I'll tackle eighteen-stone forwards, no problem, but I tell you, I'm shaking like a leaf when my mum goes berserk.'

Sue couldn't stop laughing and in her mind she pictured a woman chasing two boys up and around a house similar to a chase in a Benny Hill comedy. As the laughter subsided, there was a momentary silence before Sue walked over to the record player to lower the volume. Joe was a great fan of David Bowie and he thought the volume low enough already. Sue came back and sat down beside him. He was reclining in one of the corners of the sofa. One of his legs was resting on the middle cushion, with his foot overhanging the front so as not to dirty or scuff the leather. As Sue sat down, Joe, without hesitation, sat up straight and angled his body towards her, placing his right hand firmly on to her arm before looking her directly in the eye. 'I've really enjoyed myself tonight,' Joe said, his voice deliberately low to accentuate the feeling. 'You've put so much time and effort into a wonderful dinner. I'm absolutely stuffed. I feel really spoilt 'cos I dunno what I've done to deserve it.' His eyes never moved from Sue's when he spoke.

'Oh, come off it. Don't exaggerate, it wasn't much,' Sue replied, blushing a little. 'And anyway, I do like a man who eats his food.' She did not try to move her arm away from his hand.

'Wasn't much, you're joking! The meal was fantastic. No, seriously, I'm very lucky. I've had a great evening.'

'Well, I'm the lucky one as well to be in the company of such a handsome person.'

Joe's gaze moved away from Sue and wide-eyed, he surveyed the room as if looking for somebody else. 'Who are you talking about?' There was a mischievous glint in his eye as he turned back to face Sue. His expression was one of feigned bewilderment. 'Oh, you're talking about me. Well, it's nice of you to say.' They both burst out laughing.

Joe leaned back in the sofa but this time he brought Sue with him. She rested her head on his chest, her body wrapped in Joe's arms. He kissed the top of her head.

Neither of them said a word as they enjoyed the warmth of each other's bodies. David Bowie had stopped singing and the turn-table had come to a halt. Joe raised his left arm slightly up her body and his hand rested just below Sue's right breast. She did not offer any resistance. Everything was quiet and still in the room. Joe looked down at Sue and noticed that she was gazing directly ahead, seemingly into space. Her expression was one of deep contemplation.

'Penny for your thoughts?' Joe ventured.

'Just thinking about Mum an' Dad, that's all. That conversation has rekindled a lot of memories. See that table over there, in the right-hand drawer is my father's pride and joy.'

Joe now understood that Sue's gaze was not in fact aimless but that she had been staring at a small walnut table that fitted perfectly below the curtained bay window. What a time to be talking about tables, he thought. The table itself was rectangular and heavily veneered. On top of it sat a crystal vase of brightly assorted flowers, which made for an attractive splash of colour against the beige curtains. The table possessed two drawers, of equal size, which were positioned side by side. Each had a small brass key in their locks, from which hung two olive-green tassels on gold-braided string. Joe had noticed the table earlier for it reminded him of the one in his own living room at home where his mother kept her solid-silver canteen of cutlery. He held Sue a little firmer, hoping that she would turn her attention back to him. Sue, however, began to reminisce. 'Whenever my mum dusted that table, my dad would shout out to be careful, not that she could remotely damage his gun.' Sue broke into a smile as the scene returned to her mind.

For a moment, Joe hesitated, wondering if he had really heard what Sue had just said. 'Excuse me but did you just say "gun"?'

Sue could feel the tension in his body as the word jolted him out of his relaxed state. 'Yeah, it's a World War Two German Luger.' Sue's reply was expressed in such a matter-of-fact manner that she could almost have been talking about a mundane household item.

Joe finally understood what Sue had said. He sat up straight. 'You're joking?'

'No I'm not. My dad had it for years. He got it from someone he knew in Cardiff. Don't ask me who or how. He would've liked to have displayed it but I don't think he ever had a licence so he kept it out of view. He would oil and grease it lovingly until the action worked smoothly. You'd think he was tending to a baby. He fired it once.'

'Wha', it works?' Joe interrupted Sue's flow.

'Oh, yeah. He went up to the woods in Llanwonno one day and fired three bullets into a tree. He was so excited when he told us, though I remember my mum was quite angry with him. I know it's unlikely you'd bump into anybody up there but she still thought it was a foolish thing to do. I think my dad regretted telling me because he came to my room later and swore me to silence.'

Joe was fully alert, registering avidly every word Sue spoke. 'Are there any bullets left?'

'I think so. I remember seeing a box of them with the gun and it would certainly have contained more than three.' Joe was on the point of interrupting her for he was eager to see the Luger, but before he could open his mouth, Sue carried on. As Joe's plan later evolved, it was fortunate that she did so. 'I'll be honest, I haven't opened that drawer since the accident.' Her voice was much lower and there was an inherent sadness. 'It would bring back so many memories as he loved that gun so much and I loved seeing him out the back, in the shed, with it. The pictures and books I can put up with. They're part of the house and have been there for as long as I can remember. In a little while, though, I'll take 'em down and do up the house the way I want to, but not just yet.'

Joe squeezed her arm to show that he felt for her. His mind, though, was racing. He wanted to see the gun but Sue, inadvertently, had given him the seeds of a plan. He needed to think clearly and so refrained from asking her. He needed to gather his thoughts and he could not do that if he remained in the living room with Sue.

'Could you tell me where the bathroom is?'

'Just up the stairs, first door on the right.'

'Excuse me a minute.'

Joe rose sluggishly from the sofa, the meal weighing heavily inside his stomach. He left the living room and walked up the stairs. All the time, his brain was awash with unstructured thoughts and ideas. On the landing, he turned right and saw the bathroom door. On its front was a jokey porcelain tile which featured a small wide-eyed dog with its leg cocked against a tree. He pulled down the brass door handle and went in. Once inside, he pulled on the light cord, locked the door behind him and momentarily took in the bathroom's surrounds. Unsurprisingly, it was very feminine, a hue of pinks and yellows, standing out against the white tiles. A pretty china bowl in the middle of the window sill contained some lavender pot pourri. Joe thought that it had had to be a recent supply for the smell was overwhelming.

Around the bathtub was a vast array of bottles, full of lotions and liquid soaps. Joe walked over to the toilet and sat down on its wooden lid to structure his thoughts. He knew he did not have long and so took a deep breath and concentrated hard, recalling everything he had just learned.

'A gun with ammunition in the right-hand drawer of the walnut table,' he said softly to himself. Almost immediately, he experienced a slight panic attack. 'Is the drawer locked?' As quickly, the shiver of panic subsided. 'The key is still attached. Sue hasn't opened the drawer in a whole year.' He was pleased that he had not asked to see it. 'If I steal it, she'll never know it was missing and even if she does open the drawer, she'll be surprised to see it's not there but she may think her dad had put it away somewhere else, in the shed or attic, perhaps. Anyway, she'd be hard pushed to say that I took it and even if she did, I'd deny it.' Once again, though, an icy panic enveloped him. 'What if she's looking at it now? All this talk may have prompted her to open the drawer. It's unlikely. I'll have to take the risk. The odds are on my side.' The panic subsided. He had been in the bathroom for five minutes but to him it felt much longer. 'I'd better get a move on. How do I steal it? I've got time but I may not have many more opportunities. What if she moves it? It has to be tonight.' He was starting to fret as time pressed on. Indeed, downstairs, Sue had begun to wonder what had happened to him. She walked over to the record player, removed David Bowie from the turn-table and replaced it with the Bruce Springsteen album, *Born to Run*. She kept the volume low. 'I have to steal it tonight. It has to be,' Joe concluded decisively. As he said this, the faces of Dafydd, Ieuan and Robert came to mind and, in particular, the lowering of their eyes and fidgeting of their bodies when he had told them exactly what he needed. It was obvious they would struggle to supply the firearm he demanded despite Ieuan's final confident words in the multi-storey car park. This was an unbelievable opportunity he had to take. It was imperative. 'I'll have to stay the night and take it when she's sleeping.' Once again, he became concerned. 'There are no guarantees she'll let me stay, though the signs are promising.' He had been in similar situations before only to misunderstand a girl's intentions. 'They're just impossible to read, sometimes.' He shook his head in dismay. 'I have to be careful, though. If I'm too pushy, she may get upset and kick me out and bang goes the gun.' He smiled at the unintended pun. He rose from the toilet seat and pressed down on the button flush. Downstairs, Sue heard the faint sound and made herself comfortable on the sofa. Joe bounded down the stairs and almost ran into the living room. He felt slightly embarrassed and tried to make a joke of his delay. 'Sorry I took so long. I mistakenly went into your bedroom and I couldn't resist rummaging through your wardrobe.' Sue gave a half-smile, unsure whether Joe was joking or not. He sensed this and realised how clumsy he had been. 'I'm only kidding.' His face lit up and Sue broke into a broader smile. Joe composed himself and sat down beside her. He took her in his arms and held her gently against him. 'Now where were we? Ah, Bruce Springsteen, excellent. This is a great album. You a bit of a rocker then?'

'Yeah, suppose I am. I think he's brilliant.'

'He's gone a bit quiet, though. Must be well over a year old now, this album, and I've not heard there's another one in the pipeline. Wasn't he meant to be the future of rock 'n' roll?'

'Yeah, that's true. Hopefully he's working on something new.'

'The future of rock 'n' roll? More like a big flash in the pan. Bet we never 'ear of him again.'

Joe slowly moved his left hand and placed it on Sue's hip. After a short pause, he moved it so that it rested on the bare skin of Sue's back which was showing between her trousers and black cotton top, which had ridden up as she positioned herself in Joe's arms. She flinched at the cool touch. Once again, Joe paused, not moving his hand to gauge Sue's reaction. Determining her lack of resistance, he slowly and lightly brushed his fingers back and forth against the small of her back. Sue's face was hidden from Joe. He kissed her on the back of her head, the fine strands of hair momentarily sticking to his lips. She could feel a bulge form in Joe's lap below her. She grinned to herself as she recalled his erection when they had danced in the clubhouse. How embarrassing it must be to be a boy, sometimes. Moving slightly away from her, Joe slowly slid his hand up Sue's back and rested it on the back of her neck, gently massaging it between his forefinger and thumb. Sue closed her eyes for the sensation was wonderful. With a start, Sue unwrapped herself from Joe's arms and turned to sit astride his lap, facing him. She put her arms around his shoulders and placed her mouth over his. They kissed passionately, as if tomorrow was their last day on earth. She held Joe so tightly he wondered whether her breasts would be aching under the pressure for he could feel them pressing firmly into his chest. His right knee was directly under Sue's crotch and she opened her legs a little wider. He started to rock his knee very gently back and forth and the sensation Sue experienced was gorgeous. They stopped kissing and Sue placed her head to the side of his, cheek to cheek. She felt a light scraping from the bristles on his chin. Her eyes were closed and her mouth open. Joe could just make out her low sighs. It turned him on. His penis was now fully erect, jammed inside his jeans and bursting to get out. Sue could feel it beneath her and so looked him straight in the eye. 'Let's go to bed,' she whispered, not waiting for a response and jumping smartly from his lap.

The next few minutes were almost surreal due to Sue's practicality in the circumstances. In the manner of a matron on a hospital ward, she strode over to the record player and switched it off. She then ruffled a few cushions and picked up the empty glasses and bottle from the floor. She strode purposefully into the kitchen, returning without delay, empty-handed. Joe, in the meantime, had risen from the sofa more sheepishly and tucked in his shirt, which had ridden out of his jeans. He made a half-hearted attempt to smooth out some creases. At last, Sue took Joe's hand and led him into the hallway and up the stairs. At the top, she pointed out her bedroom while excusing herself momentarily as she entered the bathroom. Joe continued along the landing and went in. The German World War Two Luger was the last thing on his mind at this precise moment. To tell the truth, he felt apprehensive and shivered with nerves for the only time he had ever spent a whole night with a girl before had turned out to be a disaster and the only time he had actually had intercourse had not been that much better either.

The previous winter, on a school skiing trip, Joe had ended up in bed with a girl from the Cardinal Newman

Roman Catholic School. It was a disaster in that, firstly, her roommate was in the twin bed next to them pretending to be asleep, secondly, she would not put her hands where he wanted her to put them and thirdly, she would not allow him to put his hands where he wanted to put them. She lived up to the doctrine of her religion far too much for Joe's liking. In addition, the fact that she asked him whether he loved her every fifteen minutes was intensely off-putting particularly as he had only met her two hours previously. His desire to invite her friend to join them soon died a death and he craved leaving as soon as possible but could not remember for certain where his hotel was and he did not wish to freeze to death finding out at such a late hour. He eventually pretended to fall asleep and thought about the most mundane things to reduce his ardour. He hoped desperately that tonight's experience would not be the same. At least there wouldn't be a roommate peeping over at them.

That said, staying the whole night was the least of his worries. Of greater concern was the fact that he had only ever had intercourse the one time before. This had been with a girl he had been seeing a year earlier called Charlotte Roberts, who had the reputation of being a bit of a goer and who, unfortunately for her, had a name that rhymed with 'harlot', which Joe's friends were never too shy to remind him of. When he was round her house one evening, by chance her mother had gone out to Bingo, leaving the place all to themselves for a couple of hours. The expectation was too much for him and he came in ten seconds flat, already halfway there before even undressing. He cringed at Charlotte's continual hip movements after he had come, and her soothing words of comfort afterwards made him shudder with embarrassment which remained with him to this day. For months, he worried that her words, "don't worry I'm on the pill", were in fact lies and whenever he saw her, he tried to ascertain whether there was a growing bump in her stomach area. More than nine months had now passed by without the patter of tiny feet so at least that worry was behind him. But now, inside Sue's bedroom, he felt so turned on he was convinced another disaster was highly likely.

The room was pitch-black except for the moonlight from the gap between the two maroon-coloured curtains which lay a white stripe across the floor to the bed. This light and that from the landing helped guide him to a lamp on a small round table next to the bed. He walked over and switched it on. Its shade was made from a red and white check fabric and the rosy light it gave off was very dim. He saw an armchair in one of the corners of the room festooned with soft toys. The bed was a double. The matching linen of the quilt and pillow cases was a bright white in shade with small green, white and yellow daisies sewn into the corners. He began to unbutton his shirt. The armchair was only two paces away and he placed it over its back. He sat down, careful to avoid Snoopy, and took off his shoes and socks. 'Why do my feet always smell so much?' he cursed, wiping them desperately in the pale-blue carpet and sniffing a sock. At that moment, he heard the bathroom door open and Sue appeared in the bedroom. He noticed that she was barefoot. She quietly closed the door behind her. Joe walked over to meet her, placed his hands on her arms and kissed her sensitively on the mouth. He could taste spearmint and hoped that his breath did not smell too badly. It struck him how much shorter Sue now was and she needed to be on the tips of her toes to reach him. Joe took one step back and was about to pull off her top when Sue moved away from him and switched off the bedside lamp. The room fell once more into darkness. He could not see Sue and only felt her presence around him as she quickly stripped off her clothes. Joe stood rooted to the spot. 'Hey, where've you gone?' There was no reply, but a moment later, Sue was once again standing in front of him, placing her hands around his neck and kissing him on the lips. He gave a little jump as she had seemingly appeared from nowhere. He realised that she had changed into a long t-shirt and when he ran his hands down her back to her behind, he noted that she was still wearing her knickers. At least her back was smooth, indicating that she had removed her bra. Joe was slightly taken aback by the fact that she had clearly not wanted him to see her naked and this confused him as to how the rest of the night might pan out. Silently, Sue took a pace back and slipped under the duvet and into the bed. Joe was still wearing his jeans and was now uncertain whether he should join Sue fully naked or not. In his nervousness, he decided on a compromise, jeans off, pants on, but when he pulled his jeans down his pants became so entangled in them he thought it would be the most uncool thing in the world to spend time unravelling them before putting them back on. Accordingly, he stepped out of them, nearly tripping over as he trod and kicked them off and slipped under the duvet next to Sue. His penis was now fully erect having sprung up from the constrictions of his tight jeans like Zebedee in the *Magic Roundabout* and it prodded firmly into Sue as Joe moved to hold her in his arms. This was a girl that Joe most certainly would touch with his bargepole.

As they kissed, Joe placed his knee between her legs and as in the living room, Sue clearly enjoyed his gentle leg movement, but when he tried to slip his hands under the front of her t-shirt, she brought her elbows down sharply to prevent any upwards progression. Joe took the none-too-subtle hint and moved his hands away. Where's this going? he wondered. He next tried placing his finger inside the elastic of her knickers by her hip bone. But when he tried to pull them down with the lightest touch possible in some bizarre belief she may not notice, Sue sharply moved her body away dislodging his finger. They continued to kiss but Joe was at a loss where to place his hands next and the frustrating memory of the girl from Cardinal Newman, whose name he had already forgotten, came to mind. Was there something wrong with him? Was he doing it correctly? His friends boasted about shagging all the time as if it was the easiest thing in the world.

More in hope than expectation, he moved his right hand down between Sue's legs waiting no doubt for a sharp rebuke when, to his surprise, on touching the soft cotton of her knickers, Sue offered no resistance. He thought he had better go gently so as not to push his luck too far and as he rubbed the front of her knickers, he sensed Sue's pleasure straight away. Her hand came down to join his and he was sure she would remove it forcibly. But in fact all Sue did was move his index finger a fraction, inviting him to rub in a particular spot. When she took her hand away, he started the light movement but once more her hand came down to mark the spot more accurately. God, how useless I am at this, he pondered in embarrassment. He decided to rub over a wider area, hoping he would hit the right spot some of the time at least. Sue appeared to enjoy this very much and one or two sighs were even quite loud, but he was now convinced she was just faking it to make him feel good. Before he could think about it any further, however, and much to his pleasant surprise, Sue grabbed his penis and started to run her hand up and down the shaft quite firmly.

'Oooh, not so hard,' he whispered kindly. He was about to add that she was not milking a cow but thought it probably unwise. Sue slackened her grip and continued the movement but then, to Joe's horror, he knew he could not hold himself back any longer and he came, his body shuddering as the sperm shot from his penis. Sue moved away from him smartly when she realised he was coming to avoid the sperm hitting her t-shirt. She was unsure whether she had succeeded or not and looked down worryingly. They had barely been in bed five minutes and it was pretty much all over. Once the overwhelming pleasure of the orgasm had subsided, Joe lay back, turning his face away from Sue and cringed. Useless, absolutely useless, he thought of himself.

'Sorry 'bout that, Sue.'

'Why sorry?' she replied, holding him tightly, her arm across his chest, her head nestling on his shoulder.

'Yuck, it gets everywhere that stuff. Send me the cleaning bill.' Joe grinned and Sue smiled back.

'Don't worry. I've got a load of washing to do anyway.' Sue paused momentarily but then went on, 'No, I'm the one who should say sorry, actually. It's just, you know, our first time together, like, and I dunno, I just felt it right to hold back a bit.' Sue screwed up her eyes out of Joe's vision wondering what his reaction would be. She did not want to lose him and so before he could even open his mouth she added, 'God, I really wanted you tonight and next time you'll enjoy it more, I promise, if you know what I mean. I hope you understand.' Sue braced herself once more for Joe's response, desperately hoping that there would indeed be a next time.

'I understand,' Joe spoke at last, though in truth he did not. 'I really enjoyed it and I'd really like there to be a next time.'

Sue's heart missed a beat in happiness at Joe's reply and she hugged his body even more tightly. It was so warm and hard and muscular and carried the sheen of a colt, just fantastic, she thought, hoping he would think the same about hers.

'That's lovely to know. Make sure you visit the chemist's beforehand. I promise you won't be disappointed.'

'You want me to bring some aspirin in case you get a headache then, do you?' Joe replied mischievously.

'Nooo! You know what I mean.' Sue raised her head and looked him in the eye, a little exasperated. 'You know, bring some johnnies, that's what I mean.'

'Durr, I'm not stupid, you know,' and the two of them burst out laughing.

A few moments later, after a final kiss, Sue leaned across Joe to switch off the bedside lamp. He was soon dozing, Sue's head resting on his chest. Within seconds, they were both fast asleep.

9

Joe's eyes suddenly popped open and with a shudder, he was wide awake. For a moment, he failed to register his surroundings. It was so quiet he could hear his blood rushing like a waterfall in his ears. A faint light was filtering through the curtains. The green luminous dial of the bedside clock put the time at ten minutes to seven. The events of the night before slowly meandered their way through the sleepy fog in his brain.

'The Luger,' he whispered to himself, glancing at Sue from the corner of his eye, hoping she had not heard him. The task in hand came clearly to mind, his sleep now totally shaken from his head. I have to steal the gun, he remembered. A wave of pure panic swept over him as he began to concoct a plan, but fortunately the silence and stillness of this early Sunday morning helped bring some structure to his thoughts. I just need to go downstairs, nice and quiet, take it and the bullets and put them into my blazer pockets. The inside one should be big enough to hold the Luger. At least, he hoped it was. What if she hears me? I'll just pretend I've been to the bathroom.

He looked across at Sue once more. She was sleeping soundly and fortunately for him, in the middle of the night, she had moved over to her side of the bed. Incongruously, thoughts as to what his mother would believe when he arrived home came to mind. She always fretted when he didn't come in from the night before. He wasn't perturbed. He would say he had stayed over at Pete's, like he often said, even if this time she might not believe him, knowing that he had gone round to Sue's for dinner and that she would more than likely probe with further questions.

Joe felt relaxed, calm and in control of his nerves. It shouldn't be too difficult, he concluded. A couple of minutes are all it should take. I just hope the gun's where Sue said it is. Well, no point worrying about it. He looked across at Sue yet again and carefully lifted the part of the duvet that was covering him, trying desperately not to disturb her. He swung his legs slowly from the bed and softly set foot on the carpet. The plush pile felt warm and comforting. He paused. He looked back towards Sue but she had not stirred. He tiptoed over to the door and pulled slowly down on its brass handle. There was a barely audible click but he still screwed up his face and cursed. Thankfully, he was relieved when he saw that Sue had remained motionless.

Unfortunately for Joe, however, and as is so often the case when a partner rouses, Sue had indeed woken up. She had registered in her slumber that Joe had left the bed. She immediately believed he was going to the bathroom so thought nothing of it.

On the landing, Joe walked in slow, careful steps as if the carpet was littered with eggshells. He passed a second bedroom, the bathroom and went down the stairs. So intense was his desire to remain silent that every step felt as if he was crunching gravel beneath his feet and he screwed up his face at the most minimal of sounds. At the bottom of the stairs, in the hallway, he relaxed and reassured himself of the quietness of his movements.

Sue had lived in her house all her life and in so doing, she had developed another sense. She could associate every creak and rustle virtually to the inch from where it came. It soon occurred to her that Joe had gone downstairs. The lack of any sound from the bathroom door handle and hinges convinced her of this. Perhaps he's fetching a glass of water, she considered, or making me a cup of tea. She smiled at the thought but somehow doubted it.

Joe entered the living room. There was enough early morning light to make everything clearly visible. He walked briskly over to the walnut table. He took hold of the tiny brass key, with its olive-green tassel, and tried to turn it to the left. It did not budge. 'Shit.' However, he quickly worked out that the key had not turned because the drawer was not in fact locked. He was more on edge than he had realised and this made him look over his shoulder towards an imaginary sound. Everything remained still. He looked down once more at the drawer and pulled slowly at the ornate brass ring above the key. The drawer was quite heavy but it slid towards him easily and thankfully for him, soundlessly, as if on generously oiled runners. His eyes opened wide and a rush of ecstasy swept over his body for the handgun was there. Although he could not see the Luger directly, its distinctive shape was clearly visible under its yellow felt wrap. Next to it was a small rectangular cardboard box. 'The bullets,' he said under his breath. He picked up the box first and heard its contents rolling around inside. He opened it and saw five small-calibre cartridges. 'More than enough.' He closed the box and placed it on the table. With care, he then took the gun out of the drawer. It was heavier than he imagined, about two pounds in weight, he estimated. He folded back the yellow cloth and stared at the Luger. He allowed himself to touch it delicately as if it were a piece of fine Murano crystal. He thought it looked magnificent, its grey barrel and black butt gleaming as the Luger caught the first rays of morning light. It carried the unmistakable air of quality German manufacturing. After a few seconds, he carefully re-wrapped it and placed it on the table by the vase of flowers. He closed the drawer and turned the key. Somehow, he felt more reassured with the drawer locked. He picked up the Luger and box of bullets and made his way slowly and silently into the dining room.

The faint aromas of chilli and red wine still lingered in the air. His blazer was hanging over the back of a chair. He picked it up by its collar and tried to place the Luger into the inside pocket. 'Bollocks,' he whispered. It did not fit handle first as he had hoped. He strained the pocket to its limit but it still failed to fit. He tried it barrel first. This time it entered easily enough though the gun's handle remained visible over the top of the pocket. It did not fit snugly and there was a danger, he felt, of it falling out. 'It'll have to do. I've got no other choice.' Fortunately, the box fitted easily into the right-hand pocket of the blazer. In both cases, the bulges were noticeable and this worried him. Slowly, so that the Luger would not bang into the chair, he replaced the blazer. He stepped back and stared directly at it. He considered the bulges and reassured himself that his concern was more because he knew what was causing them and that Sue or anybody else would not be overly bothered. Eventually he turned and left the dining room. For the first time, he became conscious of how cold he was feeling, being naked. The timer on the central heating had yet to kick in that morning. He tiptoed back up the stairs and quietly re-entered Sue's bedroom. She was still lying in her original position. A huge sense of relief washed over Joe like a tidal wave when he got back into bed beside her. However, this relief soon turned to worry when Sue immediately spoke to him.

'And how are you feeling this morning, big boy,' she whispered in her best Mae West impression.

'Fine.' Sue had hoped for a rather more emotive response. 'Just been to the bathroom.'

The moment he said it he regretted it. She had not asked where he had been and he hoped that the nervous tone of his voice had not accentuated the lie. He was not convinced. For a few moments, Sue did not say anything. She was sure he had not been to the bathroom. On his return, she had once again failed to register the creaking of the bathroom door as it opened and closed. That extra sense of hers had also convinced her that somebody had come up the stairs and that person clearly had to be Joe. She was puzzled at the obvious lie but the warmth and softness of her bed and the memories of the night before negated her inquisitiveness and she thought no further of it.

Joe, however, was experiencing an anxiety attack and he wondered whether Sue could detect the quickening pace of his beating heart. Although he reasoned that everything had gone pretty much to plan, the fact that she was awake when he returned to the bedroom alarmed him. He had hoped to stay another hour or two, cheekily in the hope that Sue might bring forward her promise of greater sexual activity, but his instinct told him to leave whilst the going was good. Indeed, if he could leave quickly, he could see himself out and there would be no reason for Sue to see the bulges of his blazer pockets. Sue turned towards Joe and snuggled up against his body, resting her arm across his chest.

'I'm gonna have to make a move in a minute,' he whispered coyly, knowing that Sue was unlikely to be best pleased.

'Why so early? Stay a bit longer.' Sue was almost pleading with him, the quiver in her voice highlighting her disappointment.

'I'm sorry, but I do have to go. My mum'll be worried sick. She never relaxes until I come home, particularly if I've been out all night at Pete's or Dave's.'

'Or at another girl's house,' Sue interjected jealously. Joe ignored the remark.

'I usually tell her in advance or ring home if it's a spur of the moment thing. I haven't done either this time.' He lifted Sue's hand and kissed it. Then he moved it aside and got out of bed. He felt ashamed using his mother as an excuse, though there was some truth in what he had said. He unravelled his underpants from his jeans and began to dress himself. 'You don't have to get up. Sleep a bit longer. I'll close the front door after me.'

Sue remained silent and sulked a little. Despite his earlier words of assurance, she feared that he was going to leave and not bother to see her again. However, she perked up when Joe came over to her side of the bed and sat on its edge.

'We'll go out again next week. I've really enjoyed myself tonight, you know, the dinner and everything, like. You're a great girl. What about Friday?'

'I'd love that.' Incongruously and inquisitively, Sue changed the subject. 'Just out of interest, d'you think Pete likes Helen?'

'What you're trying to say is that Helen fancies the pants off him and wouldn't mind going out with him. I wasn't born yesterday.' Sue hid her head under the pillow in embarrassment. Pete will fuck anything, Joe thought with a grin. 'I'm sure he'll be interested. Tell you what, we'll make up a foursome, how's about that?' Joe leaned over and kissed Sue with feeling on the lips.

'That'd be great. Helen would love that.'

'Good. Next Friday then. I'll call you in the week.'

Joe stood up from the bed, looked back at Sue with a smile on his face and left the bedroom. He fairly bounced down the stairs and into the dining room. He carefully removed his blazer from the back of the chair and put it on. The left-hand side was weighed down by the Luger but it felt relatively secure. With his right hand, he lightly tapped the side pocket to ensure that the box was still there. He looked into a wall mirror briefly and pushed back his hair with both of his hands. As he walked out of the dining room and into the hallway, he was startled to see Sue standing directly in front of him. For the first time, he saw that the long t-shirt she was wearing had a picture of a dolphin swimming on its front. Sue was smiling. For some inexplicable reason, Joe stared at the image wondering whether his sperm had caught Flipper on the snout, but the shirt seemed dry enough.

'I just wanted to see you off properly.' Sue raised her arms and placing them around Joe's neck, she kissed him fully and longingly on the mouth. She sensed some tension in his body but he did not hold back. He tried to manoeuvre the left-hand side of his body away from her but without success. Sue could feel the firm bulge pressing against her breast. It was unusual and she had not noticed it before. Bit weird that. Another puzzle to this moody, mysterious but gorgeous boy, she thought. Finally, they parted. Joe searched Sue's face for any clue whether she had detected the bulge or not but she did not register anything untoward.

'I must go. See you Friday.'

Joe slid back the chain and opened the door. He turned momentarily and smiled at Sue before striding down the street. Sue lingered on her doorstep, ignoring the chill wind and uncaring whether the neighbours could see her or not. She was unable to see his face but Joe was positively beaming, his mouth stretched from ear to ear and when he turned a corner and escaped her view, he fairly danced along the pavement as if on air, like Fred Astaire. He thought about the word 'How' which had so concerned him on the piece of paper in his bedroom and the answer 'Gun' which he had scribbled next to it but followed by two question marks. All that worry evaporated as he knew the question marks could now be removed with confidence. He was euphoric. It had been a very satisfactory evening, very satisfactory in all manner of respects indeed.

10

As Joe skipped down the hill, he knew that he needed to find a secure place to hide the Luger. His mood was so positive and his brain so sharp that an answer came to mind without delay. So immersed was he in his own reflections that he barely noticed the chill and fine drizzle of that dank, grey Sunday morning. He was conscious of passing one or two early-risers and wondered what they would make of a well-known figure in the town walking home at such a time, seemingly after a night out on the tiles. He shrugged his shoulders. He was a rugby player, after all, and so his behaviour could hardly be construed as unusual. He was so emboldened he did not hesitate to talk openly and confidently to himself. 'I'll hide the gun in the drawer of my bedside table. I'll lock it, take the key and carry it with me all the time. It's only tiny. Nobody'll know it's gone and even if someone does notice, I'll just say there's some private stuff inside. They'll think I'm referring to porno mags or johnnies, something like that, and Mum an' Dad, I know, won't say anything else. If Marco pushes it, I'll slap him down to size and tell him to butt out of my business.'

He was doubly pleased to know that his bedside table was in fact one of a pair. The locks were identical so he would have a spare key should he lose the first one for any reason. 'I'll hide that one as well. I'll have to do that 'cos if I left it in, it would focus attention on the one missing in the other drawer. I'll hide it in my kit bag.'

Joe always left his kit bag in his bedroom, inside the wardrobe. His boots would be cleaned and his kit lovingly washed and pressed by his mother. They would be left to dry and air in the utility room next to the kitchen. One day, he was surprised to see two pairs of socks, shorts and boots drying there, next to two rugby shirts. Unbeknown to him, Eamon Murphy had slipped them into his bag after training one evening in the hope that Mrs Chilani would turn her loving hands to them, so legendary was Joe's pristine appearance before a match or before training. In returning them to Eamon, who denied all knowledge, Joe feigned a slip in the dressing room as Eamon held out his outstretched hands and dropped them on to the wet, mud-strewn floor in front of him. Joe exaggerated his profuse apology as Eamon carefully tried to extract his belongings by his fingertips from the muck without dirtying them anymore.

Inside the kit bag, Joe kept a very old, grubby and torn plastic bag with the words 'Fine Fare' now barely legible on both of its sides. Within it, he kept an assortment of items; boot studs, stud spanner, scissors, gumshield, Elastoplast, tie-ups for his socks, Vaseline and a tube of Deep Heat. 'I'll stick the key to the inside of my gumshield case with some Elastoplast. Nobody'll find it there.' Being semi-circular in shape, the gumshield fitted snugly into its round case, but there was still room to stick down the tiny key. 'Nobody ever goes into that plastic bag so it'll be safe there.' Nodding his head in approval, Joe was content with the arrangements he had just thought through and confident that the Luger would not be discovered. Finally, ten minutes after leaving Sue at her front door, he arrived in front of his own. It was not yet eight o'clock but he expected his family to be already sitting around the kitchen table, taking breakfast. His mother and brother would leave the house for church at about ten-fifteen. His father would leave even earlier to supervise the cleaning of his restaurant.

Before entering, he steadied himself and attempted to improve his appearance by pushing back his hair and brushing down his blazer with the back of his fingers. It hardly made any difference but he felt all the better for it anyway. He touched the Luger, which remained secure in his inside pocket. He took his house key from a pocket and inserted it in the Yale. The door opened and he walked in, wiping his feet aggressively on the mat inside. At the end of the hallway were three steps which led directly down into the kitchen. As expected, his family was at the table and on hearing the key turn in the lock, they all peered over towards the front door. His father's interest was more a reflex action and he immediately re-immersed himself back into *The Sunday Times*.

'*Dove sei stato?*' His mother's question as to where he had been was said in a tone that reflected both her anger and relief.

'I'll be down in a minute.' Joe failed to give a direct reply, bounded up the stairs two at a time and went into his bedroom. He closed and locked the door behind him and made directly for one of the bedside tables. On opening the top drawer, he saw some old, lime-green exercise books inside. He carefully took the Luger from his inside pocket and placed it on top of them. He removed the box of bullets from his side pocket and placed it next to the handgun. The bullets rattled around freely inside the box, making him think that Sue's father had fired many more than he had let on to his family.

He pulled one of the exercise books from under the gun and box and placed it on top of them. It would be a disaster if somebody managed to open the drawer but at least the exercise book provided another barrier to the lethal contents being discovered, however flimsy, and he felt more reassured. He then closed and locked the drawer and put the key into his wallet which contained a small pouch for coins. He briskly walked round the bed to the other table. He locked the top drawer and removed the key. With just two paces he was in front of his wardrobe. He opened it and pulled out his navy-blue sports bag which had the word 'adidas' and company logo prominent in white on both of its sides. He unzipped the bag and took out the plastic carrier bag, which, with the items jangling inside, he put on to his bed. Quickly, he rummaged through it and found the white gumshield case. He prised it open and removed the reinforced plastic shield. He then picked out the small box which contained Elastoplast and as he could not find the small scissors he usually kept in the bag, he tore off a tiny strip with his teeth. He remembered how Eamon Murphy had borrowed the scissors earlier in the week at training and how typical it was of him not to return them. He placed the key inside the case, pleased that it fitted snugly and placed the Elastoplast over it. Although a little fiddly, he managed to secure it firmly. He replaced the gumshield, snapped shut the case and put it back into the carrier bag. He threw in all the remaining paraphernalia, tucked the bag into the corner of his kit bag, placed some spare kit on top, zipped it up and returned it to the wardrobe. He thought about locking the wardrobe door itself but believed it unnecessary and only likely to lead to greater suspicion if his mother or brother noticed.

With the keys safely hidden, Joe paused for a moment, took a deep breath and sat down on the edge of the bed. He calmly reflected on the events of the previous evening and on his incredible luck in discovering the Luger. With what he had in mind, he was truly staggered to have come across such a weapon and though not usually a believer in fate, he wondered whether some mystical force was helping him in his task. He knew his plan was difficult and even, at times, seemingly impossible but perhaps *he* was the chosen one after all, perhaps it was his destiny and it seemed only to reinforce his resolve. 'If there is something out there guiding me, please give me the strength and ability and luck to carry this through,' he whispered, his neck craning back and his eyes looking upwards. He could not reason out what he was saying but it gave him huge comfort nonetheless.

Almost immediately, his thoughts turned to Sue. He bent down to take off his shoes and removed his blazer, which he tossed on to the back of the armchair. Having done that, he flung himself on to the bed and with his hands cupping the back of his head, he stared at the ceiling. He could hear voices coming from the kitchen and wondered how long it would be before his mother called him down for some breakfast. He recalled the short but exhilarating acts of intimacy in bed with Sue and he craved seeing her fully-naked body next time. But more than that, he acknowledged how at ease he had felt in her company and accepted that he had fallen for her to a far greater extent than any other girl he had known before. He thought about her situation, both parents dead in a terrible accident, and he admired the way she seemed able to move on in life. The thought of his parents dying terrified him. She lived alone and this physical and mental vulnerability endeared her to him and brought out his instincts to protect her. He wanted to hold her and make her aware that he would always be there for her and that she was not alone. As he struggled with his own resolve, it gave him a warm feeling to know that he, too, was not alone, that there was someone from whom he could receive reassurance just by her being there. He knew the times ahead would test him beyond anything he could imagine and that there would be many moments of weakness and doubt. For a brief instance, it crossed his mind whether to confide in Sue. Did she feel the same way as him? Surely she would understand and be proud of him, wouldn't she? He recalled the conversation at the Caesars Arms, however, where she seemed totally underwhelmed by his arguments. This was cause for disappointment but he was so convinced of the need to fight the English for an independent Wales that he could not believe that, in time, not only Sue but the whole of the Welsh nation would be proud of the part he played through the course of action he undertook on their behalf. He started to feel dozy, his eyelids flickering in their attempt to stave off sleep, his thoughts becoming vague and intermittent, when suddenly he heard the high-pitched tone of his mother's voice calling.

'*Giuseppe, vieni giù?* Breakfast is going cold.'

The words startled him and rubbing his eyes, he exclaimed a muffled 'coming'. He rose gingerly from the bed, pushed back his hair, smoothed out his shirt with the palms of his hands and walked towards the bedroom door. He braced himself for a multitude of questions. 'Now for the Spanish Inquisition,' he muttered, raising his eyes to the heavens, his favourite Monty Python sketch passing fleetingly across his mind, but with as broad a smile as he had ever worn before in his life.

11

Joe was not the only one thinking and dozing that Sunday morning. After seeing Joe off down the street, Sue had re-entered her house and gone into the kitchen where she made herself an instant coffee. Her stomach was aching she missed him so much. She really wanted him to return so that they could go back to bed and sleep in each other's arms for the rest of the day. It surprised her how much it had hurt when he said he had to leave and that pain continued to course its way around her body. It was a pleasant pain, though, as she was reassured by his asking her out again and believed his request to be truly genuine. But why did Friday have to be so far away? She was just so impatient. So desperate was she to see him again, the next few days would feel like a lifetime.

After finishing her coffee, she went back up to her bedroom and slid back under the duvet. She lay there dozing, hugging his pillow tightly, so wishing it was Joe himself. The distinctive whiff of his Brut aftershave was still very evident. She really hoped he had enjoyed her attempt to pleasure him and that he was not annoyed at her not going any further. Although there had been two other boyfriends before, her sexual experience was not wide and she lacked confidence in herself. She would provide him with whatever he wanted next time and she hoped she would live up to Joe's expectations, thinking that he must have had hundreds of girlfriends in the past.

How could someone so handsome and attractive not have? There was no way she was likely to be the best he had ever been with and the thought worried her. Perhaps he did not really want to see her again and just fobbed her off about the following week. Her mind was a tsunami of emotions, not knowing what to believe. She turned over to her right side, carrying the pillow over with her and then turned back again. Soon, however, her heart beat more slowly, pumping blood and transmitting calm and a few minutes later, with her mind less stressed, she fell asleep.

After what seemed only a few minutes later, she was wide awake. The bright sliver of daylight between the curtains startled her, indicating that the early morning had already passed. When she turned over to look at the bedside clock, the green numbers glowed less brightly and she was surprised and slightly taken aback to discover that it was nearly midday. She lay back down on her back, still hugging the pillow, her senses keen and alert. She felt thirsty and in need of the bathroom but the warmth of the duvet and smell of the pillow, allied to the thoughts of the previous evening created a lethargy and a desire never to leave the bed. She contemplated the day ahead. Nothing was planned. It would be a typical lazy Sunday afternoon. She was sure Helen would ring or call round at some time, so nosy would she be to know how the evening had gone. She smiled to herself when Helen's expectant, wide-eyed and open-mouthed gaze came to mind. In a flash, she remembered how Joe had agreed to ask Pete to make up a foursome the following Friday and she knew that Helen would be excited beyond words. She hoped Joe would succeed with Pete, but he hadn't seemed to think it would be a problem.

At that particular moment, lying in bed on that October Sunday morning, Sue was as happy as it was possible to be. One minute, she really liked Joe, now she was convinced she was falling in love. How she wished he would come back later that day, ask her to marry him and move into the house with her straight away. She knew it was a dream but the thought was delicious and she never wanted it to leave her. 'Get a grip,' she scolded herself. 'Don't let's get ahead of ourselves.' Sue had always had a sensible, practical side to her nature which had always kept her in good stead. How she now wished this was not a part of her character. She just wanted to let herself go and believe the totally fantastic.

It was when Sue pulled the duvet higher up and over her chin that the recollection of Joe's going downstairs in the early morning suddenly came to mind. It would not have appeared so unusual had Joe not said that he had only gone to the bathroom. She knew this not to be true and for a moment she was perplexed as to why he had said it. For what reason had he gone downstairs? It was probably nothing but why could he not admit to it? Maybe he just wanted to nose around, which was very unlikely, or fetch a glass of water, which he did not. Very strange. He had seemed a bit jumpy when he left but she hadn't thought it so noteworthy at the time. It couldn't be much, she concluded, but the thought still lodged at the back of her mind.

'Time to get up,' she said sternly to herself a few minutes later, with huge reluctance. She placed the pillow to the side of her and pulled back the duvet. A sudden coolness drew goose bumps from her bare skin. So late was she rising that the early morning central heating had already switched itself off two hours earlier.

She swung her legs round, slid her feet into her slippers, with their images of Mickey and Minnie Mouse looking up at her, and took the three paces to her wardrobe, inside of which was hanging her fluffy white cotton dressing gown with Goofy's toothy stare prominent on the breast pocket. She put it on and tied the belt tightly in an effort to warm herself up more quickly.

She left the room and, after a hasty stop in the bathroom, walked down the stairs and directly into the kitchen where, after switching the central heating back on, she filled a kettle with water and waited for it to boil while leaning against the stack of drawers where she kept the kitchen utensils. As the water came to boiling point, she took a mug from a cupboard, placed a Tetley's tea bag inside and poured the water on top. She replaced the kettle and added some milk from a bottle in the fridge and stirred in two white cubes of sugar. She left the tea bag and spoon in the sink and moved into the living room, cupping the mug with both hands. The heat it generated felt very comforting. She turned on the television in an attempt to catch up with some of the day's news and sat down on the sofa. Curling her legs underneath herself with the agility of a cat, she stared at the television, not really absorbing any of the words expressed by the BBC news anchorman. Her mind kept drifting back to Joe's early morning venture downstairs and she found her curiosity difficult to expunge. Instinctively, she got up from the sofa and walked back into the kitchen. Once inside and still cupping the mug of tea, she scanned the room, trying to observe whether anything was out of place. Everything appeared to be in order. She moved into the hallway and did the same. Her eyes stopped on the wartime pictures but once again, everything seemed normal. Sue felt more reassured as she re-entered the living room, once more surveying the whole area, for what, she did not know. Feeling more relaxed and with the slightest of shrugs of her shoulders, she sat back down on the sofa, took a sip from her hot tea and looked at the television. As she did so, her eyes were drawn momentarily towards the small table in the bay window. She stared at it for a few seconds and then, squinting slightly, she clearly saw some tiny, faint smudges of darkness standing out against the lighter surrounds of very fine dust. The faint smudges were beside the handle of the right-hand drawer and it dawned on her straight away that they were fingerprints. She placed the mug of tea on the small table next to the sofa and walked over to the bay window, her eyes never leaving the handle of the drawer. She looked more closely at the prints and it was evident that the drawer had been opened, the drawer that contained her father's Luger, the drawer she never opened. Despite her immense curiosity, she could not immediately bring herself to open it and for what seemed an age, she fixed her gaze intently on the drawer handle. Perhaps Joe, and she was convinced by now that the fingerprints were Joe's, had just wanted to have a quick peep at the gun. It was perfectly understandable. Why had he not asked her the evening before? Maybe he thought it would have upset her and with some relief, the puzzle of Joe's wanderings downstairs was solved. However, although she had not opened the drawer since the death of her parents, she could not at that moment prevent herself from doing so. The prints by the handle were too powerful an invitation to do so, like a Siren luring a sailor towards her. She flipped up the small brass ring, inserted her right index finger and pulled it towards her. The drawer did not budge, surprising her, as she was convinced it had not been locked beforehand. Perhaps Joe had locked it instinctively. With added curiosity, she placed her right index finger and thumb either side of the tasselled key and turned it to the left. Once unlocked, she inserted her finger in the brass ring for a second time. The drawer was heavier than she remembered and the ring pressed firmly into her flesh as it slid towards her. Looking into the drawer, she took a sharp intake of breath as she saw at once that the Luger was missing. She stood stock still, her mouth slightly agape, her finger still holding the ring as she contemplated the empty space. She brought her left hand up to cover her mouth in shock. Her stomach felt empty and her legs a little unsteady. The papers at the back of the drawer only accentuated the empty space at the front. Doubts began to cross her mind. Had the gun been there? It had been a very long time since she saw it last. Had her father hidden it somewhere else before he died? There was no obvious place elsewhere in the house and anyway, after her parents' death, she had cleared out many drawers and boxes and cubby holes and found nothing. Maybe her father had hidden it in the shed or up in the loft or even sold it without her knowing? It was all very unlikely.

Sue soon understood that she was clutching at straws, trying hard not to believe that Joe had taken it. The correct word was 'stolen' but she did not want to believe that of him. And yet it was the only explanation and it must have been around his person when he left the house. She thought he had been a little stand-offish and edgy and now it was starting to make sense. But if so, why? Was it just a boys' thing; cowboys and Indians, war and stuff like that and his curiosity had got the better of him? Maybe he just wanted to show it to his friends and return it to her later? None of this was plausible, however. Perhaps he wanted to fire it like her father, to experience that surge of adrenalin? He often talked of the excitement of playing rugby, the hard-edged experience of going into battle. Maybe this was something similar? But could he fire it? Were there any bullets? She pondered long and hard and remembered distinctly that there were. She clearly recalled the rectangular box that rested beside the gun in the drawer. That, too, was missing. She looked down more closely into the drawer and saw clearly the very faint line of dust about two thirds of the way towards the right-hand side that marked the separating point between two objects either side of it, namely the gun and the box of bullets, she established. There was no doubt about it. Joe had taken the Luger and the bullets. She slowly eased the drawer closed, her mind in deep confusion, and went back to sit in the corner of the sofa. The television was still on but she took nothing in. Why had he taken it? She could still not fathom an answer. She repeated her earlier opinions. Was it just to show it to his friends or to fire one or two shots somewhere for the kick of it? Did he want to shoot a rabbit or something in the woods? Sue could not work it out. Was there a more sinister motive? It quickly dawned on her how aggressive and angry Joe could become when discussing Welsh independence, how he hated the English and how he had failed to apologise for wanting Prince Charles dead. And she could never forget his face of rage, almost demonic, when he stood snarling over the prostrate figure of James

Harrison. What had he said? "I swear one day I'll kill you, you bastard." Sue felt the hairs on the back of her neck stand on end as she considered this and a fine film of perspiration formed on her upper lip. She so loved this boy that she could not believe what she was thinking and she scolded herself for her wild imagination. But what was she going to do? Sue hated confrontation and knew that she would find it nigh on impossible to accuse him of taking it right to his face. She also knew that this might drive him away from her and that would be devastating. But she could not just stand by and do nothing. She had an obligation to her father at the very least. She could not just brush aside the fact that a handgun and bullets for which she felt responsible were now outside of her control and in the hands of her boyfriend. There had to be some simple explanation. Quickly summoning up courage and feeling more emboldened, she decided that she would have to confront Joe. She was determined to do so but almost as quickly, her courage faded and she asked herself, 'Can I?'

12

That very same day in Windsor Castle, a setting more different to the homes of Joe and Sue it would be difficult to imagine, the Prince of Wales was reclining, cross-legged, in a green-leather, studded wing chair in his personal quarters, having just returned from attending the service in St. George's Chapel with his mother and father, the Queen and Duke of Edinburgh. His Private Secretary was sitting opposite him, a low, yew coffee table between them.

The previous evening, he had spent some private time with his mother in her favourite room in her favourite residence and they had discussed his position in life. It was clear to the Queen that her son was finding it difficult to establish a clear role for himself and that he was becoming increasingly frustrated at his inability to express his views on subjects important to him, such as architecture and the environment, in fear of entering the world of politics which the British constitution strictly forbade. On more than one occasion, Jim Callaghan, the Prime Minister, had had to mention Charles's interference to Her Majesty during their regular weekly meetings at Buckingham Palace.

During the conversation with his mother, Charles had become quite emotional when expressing his frustrations and admitted to feeling the pressure that was building in the media for him to find a bride who would one day become Queen. His mother also reminded him that it was his duty to find a suitable consort. Charles could not understand how finding an appropriate bride should be considered a duty. Surely love and feelings were the only necessary ingredients and he had plenty of these for his beloved Camilla. If only she was not already married, another issue that added to his frustrations. It irked and saddened him to know that he would never marry her.

The Queen believed Charles to be totally self-indulgent and she told him so directly to his face. What was important was carrying out one's duty and earning respect and she was concerned that Charles was in danger of failing in both these endeavours. She was certain her subjects and particularly those in Wales, thought poorly of him. He was the Prince of Wales for heaven's sake, but who would have thought it? He rarely spent any time in the country and barely took any interest in its affairs and indeed seemed to go out of his way to avoid visiting. The Queen understood how peculiar it would appear to Welsh people to see Charles on their television screens wearing a kilt, staff in hand, walking the hills of Scotland. Wales has beautiful mountains and hills, she thought. Couldn't he walk there and at least show some empathy with the country? She remembered back a few years to Charles's investiture at Carnarvon and how the Welsh people, with their unique warmth and friendliness, had taken him and the rest of the Royal Family to their hearts. But it was clear to her that since that day, such warmth had cooled and certainly towards her son.

'Charles, you have to understand that in this day and age it is not possible to hide away from the public's attention. We live in the era of the television and are more visible to the people than ever before. This leads to expectations and there is no doubt that the Welsh would certainly appreciate your taking a greater interest in their country.'

'I suppose you are right. It has not escaped me,' Charles replied in a resigned manner. 'I have to admit this was clearly brought home to me the other day in Carnarvon. My office has already briefed the media that I shall be undertaking more public engagements in Wales. I'm meeting with my Private Secretary tomorrow to put some meat on the bones and plan some initiatives to help restore my standing. The message is clear.'

The Queen smiled, trusting in Charles's sincerity.

* * *

Now ensconced with his Private Secretary, they discussed what Charles had titled his 'Welsh Agenda'.

'Attendance at the Welsh Institute of Directors' Annual Dinner is a possibility, sir. It would be a fine opportunity to understand business needs in the principality.'

'Oh, not another dinner; just ghastly,' Charles groaned, his shoulders slumping. For a moment, there was silence. 'Fine, go ahead and arrange it,' he replied without enthusiasm. 'What else?' he continued grumpily.

'There is the Royal Welsh Show in Builth Wells in the summer. You have not attended that for a number of years.'

'Mmm, that would be interesting. I rather enjoyed it the last time I went if I remember. It is a beautiful part of Wales with more country people than from industry. Yes, I should like to attend that.'

'Of course, there is the National Eisteddfod to consider,' the Private Secretary recommended though his pronunciation of the Welsh cultural festival left something to be desired and Charles at first did not understand what he meant.

'Oh, the "Ice steth fodd",' Charles replied, annunciating the three syllables very slowly and deliberately for his Private Secretary's benefit. 'I was hoping you would not remind me of that. It is just so dull and rather strange, what with grown men dressed up as druids and as almost everything is spoken in Welsh, it is impossible to understand what is going on.' After a moment's thought, Charles continued, 'I am being a little unfair, the music and singing are quite extraordinary, in fact quite wonderful. Fine, put it in the diary.'

'It may be an opportunity to address the audience in their native tongue, sir?'

'Yes. That would impress them. The language is so difficult but from a written script I can manage it like before.'

As his Private Secretary scribbled down some notes in a gold-embossed, leather-bound diary, Charles gazed up towards the ceiling and then out through a window where the gloom reflected a typical October day. Water streamed down the panes as the rain lashed at them. He became pensive while his Private Secretary remained waiting for the next instruction. Eventually, Charles commented, 'I am very happy with these arrangements but I do believe we should explore the possibility of a more popular event, one which would engage the whole nation.' He had pondered his mother's words of the previous evening, concluding once again how in tune she was to modern-day life, more so than she was given credit for in the media. 'I have to be more visible to all the Welsh people,' he added.

'May I make a suggestion?'

'By all means.'

'Sport is always an effective avenue to exploit to promote oneself,' the Private Secretary advised rather pompously, 'and Wales certainly has a fine team when it comes to rugger,' the last word spoken as only an Old Etonian could. 'I do recall your attending a match in Cardiff just prior to your investiture which gained substantial media attention at the time. Perhaps you may want to consider attending another this coming winter during the international championships. I do not believe any other event will capture the country's imagination more than these games.'

Charles looked directly at his Private Secretary, his eyes wide in delight, and the latter could see immediately in his expression that he had found the proposal an excellent one. 'Yes, marvellous, well done. A high-profile rugby match. Yes, excellent. I shall wear my burgundy Welsh tie with the three feathers, making obvious where my allegiances lie and I must brush up on the National Anthem which I shall sing lustily before the match starts.'

'I can arrange that the BBC directs their cameras towards you during the anthem. The symbolism will be very effective. I can also ensure that you are introduced to both of the teams on the field of play before the match begins. That will magnify the exposure.'

'Yes, excellent, excellent. You should find out who Wales will be playing so that we can choose the most suitable game and you must make an announcement to the media as soon as possible about my attendance.'

'I took the opportunity beforehand, sir, in anticipation of this meeting to enquire into the schedule of the international rugby tournament. We have had good fortune because one match stands out as overwhelmingly the most appropriate. Wales will be playing England, their outstanding sporting enemy, at Cardiff Arms Park. Your popularity will soar to new heights when the Welsh people observe where your allegiances lie on such an important and symbolic occasion.'

'Yes, that would seem a most appropriate occasion to show my allegiances. My only problem is deciding in which direction I should project them.' Prince Charles guffawed loudly, his Private Secretary following, sycophantically.

13

Joe had never felt so stupid that Monday afternoon as he gazed out of the classroom window at the swaying branches of the horse chestnut trees outside. He also felt immensely frustrated. He had had it all worked out but with his eyes raised upwards towards the darkening skies, he could not believe the misjudgement he had made, making him wonder how his teachers could have ever thought him bright enough to go to university.

'Killaaaani!' boomed the deep bass voice of Elwyn Roberts, Head of Mathematics at Coed-Y-Lan. 'I hope we are not disturbing you. Please feel free to request we keep our voices down if we are,' he continued sarcastically.

The other pupils in the class looked down at their desks, one or two of them smiling, hoping not to be detected by the exasperated Mr Roberts. Joe turned his head slowly towards the front of the class where the Head of Mathematics was standing, hand on hips, looking straight back at him, his face a mask of unhappiness, bordering on anger. With his black gown fanned out behind him, Joe's immediate thought was that he looked like Batman.

'I'm sorry, Mr Roberts, I was just trying to work out the sum of the square on the hypotenuse of the right-angled triangle you have on the board. I find it helps my concentration sometimes to gaze outside at the chestnut trees.' Joe had responded so calmly and plausibly that Mr Roberts was uncertain whether to accept his explanation or not. 'I was also wondering, sir, whether Pythagoras did the same himself as he worked on his theory. The gentle rustling of the branches in the warm air of ancient Greece would have helped his concentration as well, I'm sure, sir,' Joe added, his expression dour as if to give greater credence to his statement, 'so long as he was careful to avoid any conkers dropping on his 'ead, that is.' This was too much for Pete who could contain himself no more and spluttered into laughter, triggering off the majority of the other pupils in the class.

'Alright, that's enough,' Elwyn Roberts shouted in a futile attempt to silence the students. He had taught too many of them for far too long over the years to be taken in by any facetiousness. 'Well, Joe Chilani, you'll have plenty of time to gaze out of your window at home this evening to help your concentration, as will the rest of you,' turning his attention back to the other students, 'because if you turn to page sixty-three of your text book, I want you all to do the exercises from that page right up to page eighty-five, and I expect all your exercise books to be delivered to me in the staff room by nine-thirty tomorrow morning. And if you think that's excessive, then you only have Joe Chilani to thank for that.'

A loud groan filled the classroom as the students leafed through the pages and noted the amount of work they had been set. The smiles and sniggers quickly turned to open-mouthed exasperation. Joe said nothing, totally unconcerned. His mind was already considering the solution to his misjudgement. For the whole of the previous day, he had been excited at the prospect of taking the Luger up to the woods behind the school at the end of the day to fire off a shot or two. How he had not worked out that the early evening would be too dark angered him. He shook his head in disgust. 'Stupid, so fucking stupid, I am,' he whispered silently to himself with a slight shake of the head. As a result, he made up his mind to skive off school and go up to the woods the following day.

* * *

As Joe lay awake in bed early the next morning, his eyes followed the fast-slow progress of a tiny spider as it scurried from the angle of ceiling and wall to the poster of the electric-blue, satin-suited Agnetha from ABBA, Blu-Tacked to the back of the bedroom door and who seemingly only had eyes for Joe. The spider's movement was quite mesmerising and Joe wondered whether the spider world contained the same assortment of characters found in the human world. After all, this spider seemed to have an excellent taste in women unlike the pretentious daddy longlegs of the summer which had scrambled up the wall to his Marc Chagall reproduction print. The thought drew a half-smile to his lips. However, it was not long before his mind turned to the barely believable prospect of his firing a World War Two Luger later that morning. He tried to imagine what the gun would be like; how loud it would be, how accurate, how stiff the trigger, whether there would be any kick or recoil? His only experience of guns came from the films he had seen on television or at the White Palace and County cinemas in town. Clint Eastwood seemed to handle them pretty well and as Dirty Harry, he had a

Magnum 44 to handle, "the most powerful handgun in the world which can blow your head right off." His mind wandered to James Harrison and he pictured a scene, a delicious scene. "Do yuh feel lucky, well, do yuh, punk!" 'That's Hollywood, this is reality,' Joe analysed coldly. The thought shivered him and he pulled the duvet a little higher over his shoulders.

Downstairs, Joe could hear the various sounds reflecting the comings and goings of his family. As precise as a Swiss clock, the door slammed at five past eight as his father left for the restaurant. He regularly returned after ten o'clock in the evening and it was not unusual for Joe to go days without seeing him, though they slept under the same roof. The customary seductive aromas of sizzling bacon and strong coffee tempted him to uproot from his bed, but today, he had planned to feign illness and remain in his bedroom until the house was empty. Marco would soon be off to school with his friend Paul who would rap on the back door at eight-thirty sharp. Though Joe attended the same school as his brother, they rarely, if ever, went together. His mother would leave at around nine o'clock to do the daily shop and then to go on to the restaurant for the busy lunchtime period. She would be back home by two-thirty. She never worked in the evenings, the home being everything to her.

'*Giuseppe, dove sei?* It's late. Breakfast is on the table.' His mother's voice sounded up the stairs.

'I'm staying in bed today, Mum,' Joe shouted down, feigning a croak in his voice. 'I'm not feeling very well. I've got a terrible headache. Tell Marco to say I won't be coming in.'

A minute later, Joe's mother was at the door. '*Stai male? Un mal di testa, ma come?*'

'I dunno, Mum. I felt it coming on yesterday evening but it got a lot worse during the night. I've got a bit of a sore throat as well. P'rhaps I've got the flu starting?' Joe added a bout of coughing for effect.

'Shall I call Dr James?'

'No, don't bother him. I'm sure I'll be fine. I remember the last one I had went away quite quickly. I'll just stay in bed today and see how I feel later. I may even go into school for a bit this afternoon if I feel better.'

'*Sei sicuro?*'

'Yes, Mum, I'm sure. There's no need to fuss.'

'I'll bring you up a Dispirin. That should help.'

'Ta, that'll be good.'

Before leaving the bedroom, Joe's mother pulled his duvet up even further, tucking it tightly under his chin. She returned a few minutes later with a glass holding a half-inch of cloudy water, the final speck of white dissolving before Joe's eyes and a hot mug of coffee, both of which she left on the bedside table.

'Try and get some sleep.'

'I will, don't worry.'

When she left the room, Joe sat up, drank the water and picked up the mug of coffee from which he took a large slurp. He remained sitting up, his mind wandering to the woods. He would have to make sure that nobody was around. It was unlikely at that time in the morning that anybody would be traipsing through the dense woodland close to his home and behind the school which led up towards Mayfield, high up on the hill. He glanced at the other bedside table, bringing to mind its lethal contents. He had five bullets at his disposal and decided he would fire only two, though he knew he would find the temptation to fire more irresistible. He thought he might want to carry out one more practice run closer to the day. It was all becoming so real now and he felt a dull ache in his stomach at the thought. A picture of the big day came to mind and he shut his eyes at the image. His breathing became more pronounced and he took two deliberate deep breaths, his eyes still closed, in order to remain calm and composed.

He finished his coffee, placed the mug on the bedside table, lay back down and stared up at the ceiling, both of his hands on the pillow behind his head. No particular thoughts came to mind. He heard the rap on the back door and Marco's "bye" to his mother followed by the sound of the door closing and murmurings as Marco and Paul walked around the side of the house and underneath his bedroom window to the front gate below.

A few minutes later, his mother returned, this time dressed in a navy-blue skirt, white blouse and fastening the buttons on her red and blue check cardigan. 'You're sure you'll be alright now? Are you sure you don't want me to call Dr James?' Joe's mother fussed as she picked up the empty glass and mug.

'No, Mum, I'll be okay. Don't you worry, it's nothing, really.' Joe's voice was quite firm, reflecting a degree of irritation.

'*Ci sono cannelloni nel frigo*. They take twenty minutes to heat up and there's some Angel Delight as well.'

'Ta, Mum. That's great.'

'You're sure you'll be alright?'

'Yes, Mum,' Joe yelled in exasperation and this time his mother left the room without saying another word.

A few more minutes passed by before Joe heard the

front door slam and all of a sudden, there was quiet everywhere. The faint tapping of his mother's heels soon dissolved into silence as she followed the same path as Marco and his friend. The slam of the front door seemed louder than usual and he wondered whether he had upset his mother with his sharp tone of voice. He knew he ought not to be so abrupt, a characteristic he had shown his mother on far too many occasions in the past and he was determined to try and be less so in future. He had promised himself this a number of times before without success and deep down he knew he would probably fail again next time. It was just part of his character and he found it a struggle to change it. It bothered him when his mother was upset for she was a wonderful, kind and loving person who was totally devoted to her family. He knew he took her far too much for granted. He loved his mother dearly and would protect her to the ends of the earth. He chastised himself for not expressing that love directly to her more often.

Joe's mind wandered once more to the big day and his only regret was the pain his family would experience afterwards, especially his mother. He wondered and worried whether they would be strong enough to handle the aftermath. The thought made him feel sick. He desperately hoped they would understand what he had done but without question, their lives would change forever and they would probably be consumed with an overpowering guilt. Once again, Joe's stomach knotted at the thought and he felt a cold sweat coming on, but his resolve did not waver. After the dust had settled and the Welsh nation understood the enormity of what he had done, change and independence would come to Wales in time, he was sure of it, and his family would be proud of him. He was sure that Sue would be proud of him as well and he realised straight away that the fact she had entered his mind at that moment showed the depth of feeling he already had for her. This was not a good time to get involved with someone, he cursed himself, but he feared that with Sue it was unavoidable. He could not wait to see her again at the end of the week and he knew his heart was lost. He hoped that her heart was lost to him as well. These waves of emotion were starting to unsettle him so he abruptly pushed aside the duvet and swung his legs round to the side of the bed, sliding his feet into his slippers in one movement as he had done on hundreds of occasions before like a finely-honed machine. He sat still for a minute, his head tilted downwards and his mind emptied itself of all its negativity. He gazed at the bedside table and knew it was time to get a move on. Incongruously, the image of Elwyn Roberts came to mind as it was at around this time that he would be expecting the homework he had set yesterday afternoon. He wondered how many other of his classmates would bunk off school today. Roberts would probably chide him sarcastically in front of everybody tomorrow, making clear the doubts he had about Joe's sickness. Of course, he would be correct, but not for the right reason, he thought. 'What a twat,' Joe muttered under his breath. He knew he could handle Roberts and his image passed as quickly as it had arrived, without concern.

Joe finally stood up, fiddled with his balls a second, threw off his pyjamas and took a couple of paces to the armchair in the corner where he slipped on his grey sweatshirt and shorts. He picked up his wallet from the desk and took out the small key. He inserted it into the drawer and unlocked it. With his senses heightened, he pulled it towards him and looked down at the exercise book that was covering the Luger. He placed the book on the bed and gazed down at the yellow felt cloth for a brief second before picking up the snuggly wrapped handgun. He removed the cloth, laying it on the bed next to the exercise book and held the gun in the palm of his hand. He lifted it once or twice to accustom himself to its weight. It was truly beautiful, with its iconic shape and glistening metalwork. Sue's father had taken very good care of it. There was a tiny catch which he assumed would release the magazine from the handle and with some nervousness, he picked at it with his fingernail wondering whether any bullets were already loaded. The magazine released instantly with a reassuring click. It slid out easily and he saw that it was empty. Joe could not resist having a pull at the trigger but it did not budge and momentarily he became anxious. He saw another catch which he thought could be the safety and moved it slowly in the only direction possible. He tried the trigger again and this time it pulled easily with only a slight resistance. Joe was unsure whether this would be the case when the gun was loaded but then this was one of the reasons why he was going up to the woods with it later, he told himself. He placed the gun down on the bed and took the box of bullets from the drawer. He opened it and took one out. He picked up the magazine and examined how to place the bullet inside. Joe worked it out quickly enough, estimating it could hold approximately eight at any one time. He felt very relaxed as everything worked so well with no worrying squeaks or resistances to concern him. Joe removed another bullet from the box and thumbed it into magazine. He was tempted to take another but decided that two were enough for now. He closed the box of remaining bullets and put it back in the drawer. He placed the exercise book back on top, shut the drawer and locked it. He replaced the key in his wallet and walked over to his wardrobe where, next to his kit bag, was a smaller spruce-green duffel bag which he had used when in primary school. He had not picked it up for many years but he thought it the ideal size to carry the Luger to the woods. After dusting it down, he loosened the white strings around the top and placed the Luger inside, once more wrapped in its yellow felt cloth. It fitted perfectly. He drew the strings tight to secure the bag and placed it by the side of the bed. As Joe set off for the bathroom, his excitement grew at the knowledge that he would soon be firing the handgun.

Once returned, Joe slung off his sweatshirt and shorts, leaving them in a heap on the floor and put on some fresh underwear. He pulled on his Wranglers and burgundy Doc Marten boots. His mother hated the boots and chided him for looking like a football hooligan but they were comfortable and sturdy and absolutely the right footwear for walking in the woods. He slipped on a new charcoal-grey sweatshirt with the word 'Gola' showing large across the chest, put his wallet in his back pocket, picked up the duffel bag and made his way downstairs into the kitchen. After a quick couple of pieces of toast and a glass of milk, he took his green Parka with fake-fur hood trim from the peg on the back of the cupboard door under the stairs and put it on whilst staring at the duffel bag on the floor, which the family's elderly, ginger tabby, Sunshine, was sniffing curiously. Finally, he picked up the bag and slung it over his right shoulder. It felt very strange carrying the bag again after so many years. He left the house by the back door, locked it, placed the key under a flowerpot and followed the same path his brother and mother had followed earlier, round the side of the house, through the front gate and on to the street in front.

Joe strode purposefully along the street for a couple of minutes and then turned left up a gradual incline towards the woods. Fortunately, he did not need to pass in front of the school to get there. He could clearly see the tops of the trees above the two rows of houses above him and he followed a path upwards in their direction. The paved path that wound itself round the side of the houses soon gave way to a turf one, flattened by years of constant use, primarily by youngsters going in search of blackberries from the abundant bushes that ran alongside the track, as Joe himself had once done. As he continued his walk, the incline became steeper and the bushes and trees narrowed in on him as the track became passable only in single file. As a young boy during the summer months, he would be repeatedly stung by the nettles on his bare arms and legs along this path and this painful memory floated back into his head as he instinctively kept a watchful eye out for them. He knew that he would soon come across an opening of flat ground within the woods, free of trees, known affectionately by everybody as Wembley, where Joe and other boys used to congregate for a game of football and a chat. Joe and his group of friends had not been there for a couple of years but Marco often went. Joe thought it wise to check out this area for if he was to come across anybody in the woods that morning it was more than likely to be there, perhaps some truants on the skive.

Fortunately, the place was deserted when he arrived. He had timed his entering the woods that morning to coincide with school lessons and he had every intention of being back home before the mid-morning break. Occasionally, one or two boys would venture up to Wembley during those twenty minutes for a cigarette and he clearly wished to avoid them. A few tabs littered the area as well as some torn pages of buxom, naked women from a pornographic magazine. He wondered if this had anything to do with Marco and whether his brother was moving on at last from the *Beano* and *Tiger*.

Turning to his right, the woods became denser and darker. Joe thought this an appropriate way to go. As he walked deeper into them, he had to fend off branches with his hands and forearms as they crossed his path. His step became much slower and at times he had to stop dead in his tracks and twist back some branches in order to continue. He worried that by entering such a dense area, he would not find any small opening to fire the Luger. After walking for another five minutes, he noticed that the darkness around him was giving way to some brighter daylight. He soon ascertained that the area in front of him was opening up a little and finally, where a shaft of sunlight beamed down through a gap in the trees as if a spotlight in a theatre, he stopped. Was this a sign? Was the Almighty keeping an eye on him? Would He approve? They were senseless thoughts, he knew, but the gravity of his mission made his mind think in such an irrational way that these small signs took on an importance which he would have normally believed ridiculous. The piece of ground on which he found himself was flat and grassless from the lack of natural sunlight rather than from constant use by passers-by. It was a very quiet area and as there was not a breath of wind, he heard neither leaves nor branches rustling away. He thought he might hear some small animal or bird noises but again, nothing. Everything was still and he cupped his ears to try and decipher any human sounds at all. He concentrated hard, but once again, nothing. So heightened were his senses that he had the illusion that many prying eyes were staring at him, but he soon snapped out of this illogicality and reassured himself that this was as good a spot as any to fire the handgun. Joe scanned around him for a target. Although surrounded by trees, he knew there had to be some distance between him and a target to avoid any ricochets. After a moment, he noticed a narrow opening between the trees immediately to his right, through which, at a distance of some fifteen feet he estimated, he fixed his eyes on the thick trunk of a horse chestnut tree. The trunk was wide enough for him to think he could not miss and whilst the distance would be much further than that on the big day itself, it was appropriate. After all, the purpose of the day was solely to accustom himself to the Luger. On the fatal day, he knew he could not miss.

He took the duffel bag off his shoulder and placed it on the ground in front of him. He squatted down on his haunches, loosened the ties and pulled out the gun. He removed the cloth, placing it back in the bag. He stood upright and held the gun by the handle, his right index finger resting lightly on the trigger. He went to unfasten the safety catch but cursed himself when he noticed he had forgotten to secure it in the first place. He realised he had been carrying a loaded, unsecured weapon and his mind wandered off to all the cowboy films he had seen when guns, accidentally dropped to the ground, discharged of their own accord. He did not know how likely such a thing could happen but he reminded himself to be much more vigilant in future. If he was to accomplish his mission, no small detail could be ignored.

Joe could hear his heart beating just a little faster in anticipation for this was an important moment. Adrenalin flowed freely around his body like electricity through copper wiring. He steadied himself, licked his lips which were suddenly dry with nerves and raised the Luger to shoulder height, his arm ramrod straight, and pointed it in the direction of the tree trunk. His left eye closed as he lined up the rear and front sights of the Luger, focusing hard on the green-brown bark. He had no specific target in mind other than around five feet up from the tree's base, dead centre. He would not be too perturbed if the first shot went astray as he only wanted to get used to the lethal weapon in his hand, the pressure needed on the trigger, the kick, the sound. His hand trembled a little but he was comfortable in his position. Finally, after a quick lick of his lips, he pulled the trigger. The sound was deafening, on a totally different dimension to what he had been expecting. A faint line of smoke snaked from the barrel and a brief burning smell hit his nostrils. He had not anticipated any of this. He immediately surveyed the whole area, sure that such a noise could be heard for miles around. His nerves were becoming shredded and it took him a full minute to believe how extremely unlikely it was for anybody to hear it. As he regained his composure, he was pleased to learn that the trigger was no stiffer than when he had tried it in his bedroom and that the kick was small to negligible.

With the gun hanging loosely by his side, he walked over to the tree truck and saw a clear bullet hole in the thick bark, quite central and approximately seven to eight feet from the base, certainly above his own height. The slight kick had still been enough to jerk his arm upwards a fraction but as distance would not be an issue on the day, Joe was unconcerned. The bullet hole was a perfect circle. To be truthful, he was not sure whether the bullet was embedded or not within the trunk or whether it had bounced off somewhere on contact. It was irrelevant. Slowly, he walked back to his original position. Once again he steadied himself, took aim, paused and with the experience of the first shot behind him, he soon found the threshold for the trigger to release the bullet. The noise was again unnerving but the whole experience was more reassuring. In examining the tree trunk once more, he found that the bullet hole was a foot lower than before and very central. Joe was very happy. In fact, he was ecstatic. He already felt well in command of the weapon. Only the sound was a real surprise. He believed he could carry out his mission right away if he needed to, but with the pleasant knowledge that he still had enough bullets left over to afford another practice session if he felt it necessary. He was highly confident that such a critical part of his plan was now in order.

After packing away the Luger in his duffel bag, Joe retraced the route he had taken through the woods and within thirty minutes he was sitting comfortably at his kitchen table waiting for the kettle to boil. A mug depicting the Apollo 11 moon landing sat in front of him with instant coffee granules inside. He had detected no sounds of note on his journey back and was certain that nobody had seen him in the woods firing the handgun. On his immediate return, he had bounded up the stairs to his bedroom, unlocked the bedside table drawer, replaced the Luger under the exercise book, relocked the drawer and returned downstairs.

With the water in the kettle bubbling away, he wiped away the small amount of mud that had clung on to his boots and left them in the utility room. After pouring the water into the mug, he followed up by pouring milk into a bowl of Rice Crispies. The famous snap, crackle and pop bore no relation to the sound of the bullet blasting from the barrel of the Luger, he thought, grinning. He was very pleased with the way the morning had gone and that the mode of operation and target of operation were clear and under control. He knew the way he had obtained the weapon was fortunate and it niggled him whether Sue would ever discover it missing but he concluded that for such a mission he would be more than happy to take as much luck as was going. After rinsing out the mug and bowl, he knew he had one final, important task to carry out that morning. He walked over to the telephone in the hallway. The number he rang was embedded in his brain.

'Owain here,' Joe said. There was a palpable hesitation on the other end of the line before the listener acknowledged him. 'I've got what I need. You know what I mean. There's no need for you to do anything.'

The listener could not prevent the strong sense of surprise sounding from his voice. 'That's great, Owain. How did you get it?'

'That's no concern of yours.'

'We were on the point of getting one as well.'

Owain smiled and shook his head at the insincerity. 'Well, it's not necessary now.'

'That's...'

'There's nothing else you need to know. It's done.' And with that, Owain cut the call without even a goodbye. Joe stood momentarily by the telephone looking at himself in the hallway mirror, his mouth stretched from ear to ear in delight. It felt very strange calling himself by another name, the one they had agreed they would all use should anybody need to contact another member of their anarchist group.

'Owain Glyndwr,' Joe whispered. 'I wonder what he was like,' as Joe pondered the revered last Welshman to hold the title of Prince of Wales back in the late fourteenth and early fifteenth centuries and who had led the revolts against English rule in Wales. 'I hope I can do him proud.'

Reality soon hit home, though. Everything had been relatively easy so far when compared to the essential necessity of representing Wales against England at Cardiff Arms Park. He had a chance, a small one if he was honest with himself, like a punter backing an outsider against the outstanding Red Rum at the Grand National. But to make the team, he would have to play each game over the coming weeks to the very utmost of his ability if he was to catch the eye of the selectors, because if he was not chosen to represent Wales in that particular match, his whole mission would go straight down the plughole.

14

'Hi, gorgeous. You know Pete, don't you?' Joe introduced his friend as they both stood outside Sue's front door.

'Of course. Come on in. Hi, Pete,' Sue responded as she received a kiss on the cheek from Joe before offering her hand to Pete. He shook it weakly with a shy smile and shifted nervously on his feet, his cheeks warming slightly.

'Bang on time, half-seven on the dot. I hope you're ready 'cos the table's booked for eight-thirty. Helen's with you, I hope?' Joe enquired. Pete looked up, wide-eyed, in anticipation of the answer.

'She's just trying on a new lipstick and jacket of mine upstairs.' Sue indicated the living room and Joe and Pete both entered, where Joe cast a quick glance at the walnut table from which he had taken the Luger. 'Make yourselves comfortable while I get myself ready. Would you like something to drink?'

'No thanks,' Joe replied, 'we don't have enough time.' The firmness of his tone conveyed to Sue the need to get a move on.

'Would you let me wear one of your jackets?' Pete asked Joe mischievously, under his breath, when Sue left the room.

'No fucking chance. And if you mention lipstick, I'll smack you one.' Both of them smirked and kept the sound of their laughter low.

'Where are they?' Joe mumbled to Pete impatiently as he saw another five minutes pass on his wristwatch. He was about to stand up and call upstairs when the door opened and the two girls walked in. An overpowering smell of perfume hit their nostrils as they both jumped smartly to their feet.

'This is Helen,' Sue announced grandly as she glanced sideways at her nervous friend, whose cheeks instantly blushed crimson.

'Hi, Helen,' Joe and Pete replied at the same time.

Pete's cheeks warmed up once more and a few butterflies began fluttering in his stomach. He stretched out his hand and shook Helen's rather formally but he could not pluck up the courage to peck her on the cheek. Joe and Sue cast a sly look at each other and smiled. Helen was considerably taller than Sue with straight black shoulder-length hair, so black that Pete wondered whether it was dyed or not and for some unfathomable reason, the picture of Morticia Addams came suddenly into his head. She was rather lanky and quite skinny, almost too thin for her height, and despite wearing a tight-fitting cheesecloth shirt, the top three buttons of which were undone, there was no obvious cleavage formed by her small breasts. She did have beautiful Elizabeth Taylor-like violet eyes, however, which complemented the dark-red lipstick she had selected from Sue's collection. Her face lit up like a lantern when she smiled and there was no doubt that Pete had already taken a fancy to her, more so than when he had seen her at a distance in town, in the rugby clubhouse or in the Maltsters.

'Right, let's go. It's already ten to eight and you never know how long it'll take us to park in Cardiff.' Joe was taking control, his characteristic impatience coming to the surface.

On leaving the house, they all walked over to Pete's father's Austin Maxi which was parked a few yards down the road. Pete had agreed to drive for the evening as he had worked it out with Joe beforehand that after the meal, he would drop him and Sue off first before carrying on to Helen's house. Joe had advised Sue of the arrangements during the week and she was happy for her friend to spend some time alone with Pete afterwards. She knew she would be bursting with excitement the following morning to discover how the two of them had got on. The mustard-coloured Maxi was not the sexiest car in the world and Joe felt a little embarrassed to be seen in it, particularly when he was trying to impress his girlfriend. He dreamed of owning a red Dino Ferrari one day, just like the one Tony Curtis drove in *The Persuaders,* but for the moment beggars could not be choosers. It was not lost on him that this dream would soon be shattered.

'My God, you should've seen Robbo on Tuesday.' Pete broke the ice as they wound their way to the A470 trunk road to Cardiff. 'He was absolutely champing.'

'Who's Robbo?'

'Oh, he's our maths teacher, Elwyn Roberts,' Pete replied. 'Joe wound him up so much on Monday, he gave the whole class a ton of homework to do which he wanted handed in first thing in the morning. The only thing is, about a third of the class rang in sick and a good few of those who did come in 'adn't finished it all. He was well pissed off, I can tell you. I was one of the goody-goodies, though I did get half the exercises wrong.'

'Why Joe, what did you do?'

'Oh, nothing much, I just wasn't paying too much attention in class an' he had a go at me, that's all.'

'Nothing much! You only tried to tell him you hoped Pythagoras kept an eye out for conkers falling on his head when working on his famous theory in Ancient Greece. The sarkie way you said it cracked everybody up, so Robbo dished out the homework.'

'You said what?' Sue exclaimed utterly bewildered and looking nonplussed at Helen, who returned her look, nonplussed herself. Despite this, they still laughed out loud, though neither of them wished to admit they did not find the story all that funny.

'Robbo was particularly annoyed 'cos Joe was one of those who cried off sick.'

Joe sighed deeply, annoyed that Pete had mentioned this and the expression on his face hardened.

'You made up you were sick?' Sue enquired in a surprised tone from the seat directly behind Joe.

'I didn't make it up, I was sick.'

Pete ribbed his friend. 'Come off it, you're never ill. I can't believe it a coincidence that the day we get a ton of homework, you suddenly go down with summing.'

'I keep telling you, I was sick. I had a bad cold and a sore throat.'

'Yeah, yeah.'

'You didn't tell me you'd been ill,' Sue piped up, digging further.

'It wasn't much and next day I was fine anyway. There was no reason to mention it. It's no big deal. You're worse than Robbo, you are.' Joe directed this last remark at Pete. 'Next day he was alright with me anyhow. At least someone believed me.'

'Well, I suppose he can't accuse you of summing he can't prove but I tell you, on Tuesday, it was pretty obvious from his expression that he didn't believe you.'

'Well, that's his problem. He's such a tosser, he is. He gesson my wick.'

'Language, language.'

Sue leaned back in her seat and gazed out of the window to her side, not saying a word. Joe appeared the picture of health and he was certainly in great condition the previous Saturday as memories of their night together sprang back to mind. Also, she recalled, when he rang on Wednesday, he sounded fine. There was no hint of a sore throat or cold in his voice. She couldn't accuse him of anything but she wondered whether there was any connection between his absence from school and the missing Luger. It seemed far-fetched but the stolen handgun bothered her tremendously and she was determined to mention it to him at some stage.

'What did you do on Tuesday then?' Sue's tone was more accusatory than she wanted to convey and she bit her lip in annoyance. Even Helen turned her gaze towards her, her face a picture of curiosity.

For a few seconds, there was quiet in the car as they awaited Joe's response. His pulse rate jumped a little higher before he replied. 'I just stayed in bed most of the time and I didn't get up until my mother came home in the afternoon. I was feeling a lot better by then. It was really boring but that's life, I suppose.'

'You didn't go out at all 'en?' Sue said this in such a way that Pete and Helen were wondering whether she was accusing him of seeing someone behind her back.

'No, not at all. It's like I said, I stayed in all day. Anyway, what is this? You sound like Kojak interrogating some suspect or other.'

'Just interested, that's all.' Silence returned and the atmosphere became a little oppressive.

'Soon be there,' Pete eventually pronounced as he eased the car through Cardiff city centre. Sue stayed quiet. She had noted the delay in Joe's response and his very defensive answer. The demons of doubt all began to dance around restlessly in her mind.

* * *

'We've a booking for four at eight-thirty. Sorry we're a bit late. The name's Chilani.' The manager of the Positano restaurant in Church Street looked down briefly at the open page of an A4-size diary on his desk, ran a pencil through a name and asked the two young couples to accompany him to a corner table which was positioned directly beneath a fishing net with fake starfish attached and which hung rather precariously across the angles of walls and ceiling.

'*Italiano?*' enquired the manager.

'*D'origine italiana, ma sono nato qui. Non è la mia prima lingua e non la parlo molto bene.*' The manager, who had lived for many years in Italy, smiled and complimented Joe on his response and accent. Helen smiled, too. Not only was he tall, good looking and athletic, he was clever as well. She envied her friend hugely. Pete thought he was just showing off. They made themselves comfortable at the table and Pete twisted himself round to take in the décor of the restaurant. He felt immediately ill at ease for he had never been to such a smart establishment before in his life and he cursed Joe for not warning him.

'This is fabulous. What a lovely place,' Sue marvelled and Helen, her eyes wide open with wonder, concurred.

'Yeah, I like it 'ere a lot. I've been a few times with my parents and brother. It's very cosy and the food's great, I promise you.' The eyes of Joe's three companions continued to scan the restaurant, taking in the rows of empty Chianti bottles on the walls tucked snugly into their wicker baskets. In fact, there was one on their table but this time with a short stubby red candle protruding from it, which a waiter promptly lit. Red wax was encrusted around the wicker and Pete could not resist picking at it with his fingernail.

'Look Sue, David Essex!' So loud was Helen's excited shriek, the whole restaurant turned their eyes towards her.

'Where?'

'There, over there; the photo on the wall. Can you believe it? David Essex has been here.' All their eyes followed her gaze towards a series of framed photographs that lined the wall above the small bar in the opposite corner. Helen's face beamed with delight as her eyes fixed on the pop star, his shoulder-length, wavy hair framing his smiley face and his left arm hugging the shoulders of a much shorter, balding and portly, middle-aged man.

'David Essex? You don't like 'im, do you?' Pete asked rather grumpily.

'You must be joking. He's fantastic, just gorgeous, he is. I can't stop myself shaking just thinking about him. Just look his eyes, his hair, that smile of his. Oh my God, I'm so excited. I wonder if he sat in this very seat I'm sitting in now. I can't believe it.'

'He's orrite, I suppose. Anybody else we know in the photos,' Pete replied nonchalantly, trying to change the subject. They all scanned the wall above the bar. It was clear some photos were older than others, borne out by the fact that the same portly gentleman appeared in all of them, his hair ranging from thick to thinning to thin and its colouring from black to peppery to grey.

'There's Kevin Keegan in that one, look, with the poodle perm, and Tom Jones, I think, in the one next to it.' Sue pointed in the general direction of the wall, her eyes squinting to gain a better focus. 'The man in all the pictures must be the owner or something.'

'Hey, Pete, go and ask whether he wants his picture taken with you,' Joe asked cheekily, his face breaking out into a broad smile. The two girls both laughed.

'Ha ha,' Pete replied. 'I could say the same about you.'

'Yeah, but when I play for Wales, I'll be up there, you watch. Tom Jones'll 'ave another Ponty boy next to him to keep him company.' Joe's response was so confident his attraction instantly grew for the two girls. A waiter approached their table and handed each of them a menu. He asked in broken English whether they would like an aperitif.

'Half a lager for me,' Pete responded abruptly.

'Sue, Helen, what would you like?' Joe asked, remembering his manners. Pete took note and shrunk a little.

'I'll have a vodka and orange, thanks.'

'Me, too.'

Joe hesitated for a moment then asked for a Campari Soda.

'Oooh, Campari Soda. Who's come over all posh 'en?' chided Pete when the waiter had left the table.

'You're such a pleb,' Joe returned rather snobbishly.

The drinks ordered, they all buried their heads in the menus. With the exception of Joe, their eyes went straight to the prices and though very reasonable by the standards of such restaurants, Pete and the two girls gulped somewhat. Sue and Helen were uncertain whether the boys would be picking up the bill and their stolen glances at each other, with concern etched across their faces, revealed all that was necessary as they read each other's minds. Their worry dissipated, however, when Joe commented out loud, 'Go ahead, girls, choose what you want. This evening's on me an' Pete.'

'Are you sure?' Helen replied. 'That's very kind of you both. Thanks very much.'

'Yes, thank you. That's lovely of you,' Sue agreed.

Pete's face remained hidden behind his menu and he barely acknowledged the two girls. Joe and Pete had agreed beforehand that they would share the cost of the meal, though Pete had initially been reluctant and tried to argue that in these times of women's libbers, the girls should pay their own way. Joe chastised him for his lack of generosity and promised him that the restaurant was not too expensive. In fact, the expression "not much dearer than the Wimpy" had played a large part in Pete eventually conceding. Not much dearer than the Wimpy! I'm gonna kill him later, Pete decided. He had enough money on him to cover a figure he had calculated in his head but it would hurt and he knew things would be tight for a good few weeks to come. The waiter returned, order pad and pencil to the ready. This time, Pete did not jump in.

'Sue, what d'you fancy then?' Joe asked.

'We're all having starters, I assume?' Sue looked at everybody expectantly.

'Absolutely,' Joe replied. The corners of Pete's mouth turned downwards as he registered the greater expense.

'I'll have egg mayonnaise to start and then the lasagne to follow.'

'Sounds good. Helen?' Joe continued as the waiter scribbled away.

'Egg mayonnaise for me as well then fett.., fettu.., fettuci.., how d'you pronounce that?'

'Fett..ou..chee..neh. The 'c' is like a chee sound in this instance, like in church, as it's followed by an 'i',' Joe butted in before the waiter could open his mouth.

'Okay, I'll have fett..ou..chee..neh al..la car..bon..ara,' Helen carried on hesitantly, looking up at Joe and hoping that her pronunciation was adequate.

'It can be a bit confusing can Italian. For example, virtually everybody pronounces my name Chill...ani when in fact it's pronounced Kill...ani. The 'c' before the 'h' gives it a hard sound. My mum goes mad when she hears Chill...ani. She was almost shouting at the telly the other day when Ponty were on and the commentator kept getting my name wrong.'

Oh, gerron with it, big 'ead. We 'aven't got all day. Pete caught the eye of the waiter who was probably having the same thoughts as him and he addressed Pete with a slightly impatient tone. The restaurant was busy and he did not have time to listen to an Italian language lesson.

'And for you, sir?'

'Prawn cocktail and the sirloin steak, please,' Pete replied unadventurously.

'And how would you like your steak, sir?' The waiter wrote 'medium' on his pad before Pete had even opened his mouth.

'Medium, please.'

'For you, sir?'

'I'll have a small spaghetti bolognese to start followed by the cotoletta alla milanese.' Joe's voice was commanding and his accent convincing. 'You can bring some chipped potatoes and a selection of vegetables for the two of us as well,' he went on before Pete had any opportunity to place his own order.

'Any wine with your meals?'

'A bottle of Barolo and a bottle of San Pellegrino, please. I hope that's okay with you?' Joe asked, addressing the girls. Both of them nodded their heads, not knowing what to expect.

'Two bottles of wine?' Pete enquired of Joe, worriedly calculating a new number in his head as the waiter collected all the menus and set off in the direction of the swing doors to the kitchen. 'That's quite a lot.'

'San Pellegrino's mineral water, you twp.' Both Sue and Helen sniggered while Pete went quiet and his cheeks suffused with blood.

'What! Water in a bottle? You're joking? That's really weird. I get mine out the tap at home,' Helen chuckled, throwing her thoughts into the conversation slightly bemused. She addressed her next remarks to Joe. 'So I hear you've had one or two dramas with your rugby lately?'

'You must be referring to my suspension. Yeah, I suppose so. You can't imagine what a bunch of pillocks those committee men can be. It was totally out of order and put me back quite a bit. I reckon I've got a chance of making the Welsh team this year.'

'Really, that would be brilliant,' Helen replied as she took a bread roll from the wicker basket the waiter had left behind.

'I reckon you'll make it,' Sue butted in. 'All the boys at school think you're playing better than any other centre in Wales and the newspapers are talking you up a lot.'

Pete remained quiet as he considered suspiciously the packets of grissini sticks resting alongside the bread rolls in the basket. He finally decided to try a packet but struggled to open it. He was on the point of using his teeth but thought it might look a bit common.

'What's the next step?' Sue carried on. 'How d'you gerrin the side?'

'For the moment, I've just gotta keep playing well every week. A key time is the New Year. On the eighth of January, there's the annual trial match, the Probables versus the Possibles. I think the match is in Swansea this year. I've gotta try and get selected for that game. If I do, anything is possible.'

'Probables? Possibles?' Helen enquired, buttering her roll. 'What's all that about?'

Pete broke in, not wishing to be left out of the conversation. He had given up on the grissini and furtively placed the packet back into the wicker basket. 'Well, it's basically a match between those players likely to make the Welsh team, the Probables, against those players who are doing well and have a chance of breaking into the team. They're called the Possibles for obvious reasons. Usually the established stars like Gareth Evans and Jim Morgan are picked for the Probables. Unfortunately for Joe, Geraint Lewis, who plays in one of the centre positions Joe's after, is a definite for the Welsh team as he's bound to be captain. What's interesting about this game is that as the match goes on, the selectors on the sidelines can make changes whenever they like so some reserves get a chance, too, and if someone is playing really well or they wanna look at different combinations, some Possibles move up to the Probables and vice versa.'

'Gerraway! During the same game? That's odd.'

'Yeah, I suppose so but that's the whole point of it. It's a real trial game. The big stars are very clever, though. They'll cry off with some imaginary injury on the eve of the game so there's no chance of them being shown up. They'll rely on their reputations. In fact, I don't think Gareth Evans has ever played in one.'

'Yeah, but he's absolutely brilliant. He can do what he likes,' Joe added admiringly.

'So you might make the Possibles?'

'I might even make the Probables if I play really well in the coming weeks. There's no reason why not but realistically, I've got a better chance of making the Possibles. I'd be happy just to make the reserves if I'm honest as I'd definitely get on at some stage.'

'What then? What happens if you play well?'

'Easy. Then I'll get picked to play for Wales, I suppose. The first international is right after the trial, at home to Ireland. After that, it's Scotland away. To be honest, I'm not too fussed about those two games.' They all looked at Joe in amazement. Sue, in particular, stared directly at him for this was not the first time she had heard him say this and it puzzled her then as it puzzled her now.

'Not too fussed!' Pete exclaimed just as the waiter started to place their first courses on to the red and white check tablecloth in front of them. 'Not too fussed, are you mad?' he went on. 'I'd give my right arm to play for Wales and here you are with a really good chance and you're not too fussed.' The last three words came out slowly and with great emphasis.

'How come?' Helen interrupted as she cut into a piece of egg and applied some mayonnaise.

'Well, the big match is against England at the Arms Park which comes straight after these two. That's the one I really wanna play in. You know, they're the old enemy and all that. I'd give anything to be picked for that game.'

'Only because they're not much good,' Pete interjected, grinning.

'Oh, I dunno about that. They're getting better and that James Harrison is pretty good you've got to admit,' cautioned Helen, 'and very good looking, too, by the way.' She smiled and cast a sideways glance at Sue who smiled back.

'Good looking!' Pete exclaimed. 'He's not all that,' he carried on, a hint of jealousy in his voice. Joe remained quiet, his expression as indecipherable as a high-roller poker player so as not to reveal his inner feelings. His stomach churned, though, at the mention of Harrison. His pulse rate quickened and he needed to take a deep breath to calm himself down. He hoped the others had not noticed.

'He's a piece of English shit.' Joe made this statement in a very forceful manner, unsmiling, and with his eyes looking directly at his pasta dish. He twirled some spaghetti around his fork and it was obvious to his companions how much he disliked, even hated Harrison.

'Sue told me how you smashed him into the advertising hoardings the other day.'

'Yeah, that's how I got suspended but I'll tell you something, that's nothing compared to what I've got planned if I get picked for the international.' Joe's statement was expressed with such feeling that momentarily everybody went quiet around the table. Pete knew how competitive Joe could be but his tone was much sterner than he had ever heard before. Helen thought that Joe was showing the passion and commitment necessary to become an international rugby player and she admired him for it. Deep down, she fancied him rotten, though she could never reveal that to Sue. Sue was becoming increasingly puzzled. She accepted that Joe was a passionate and committed rugby player but his words and manner seemed to go beyond that normally expressed by other players when discussing sporting competition. She had the nagging feeling he was up to something but could not think what. She could still not believe the missing gun had anything to do with it. That was crazy, surely?

'Why is there all this animosity between us an' the English?' Helen asked.

'Because they fuck us about all the time and have treated us like third-rate citizens throughout our history. Even today, those cunts look down on us, belittle us and make us out to be a bunch of servile idiots.'

'Hey, Joe, don't hold back now, just tell us what you really think,' Pete interrupted a little cheekily, bringing forced smiles to the faces of the two girls who were embarrassed by the foul language. Sue's smile quickly melted away as she stared at Joe disapprovingly.

'I'm sorry, excuse my language, I just feel very strongly about it, that's all.' Joe's tone had moderated.

'Is it true, though? Things seem okay to me. I've got a friend in Cheltenham and she's lovely. I don't see any English people lording it over us today. Everything's cool.'

'That's not the point. We could be so much greater if we controlled our own destiny, ran our own industry, our own lives. I tell you, it won't be long before the government closes down all the pits. There'll be mass unemployment, you watch. Steelmaking will be the same. We'd never allow that to happen. Also, there's a strong possibility of finding oil off the coast of Pembroke, it's been in all the papers. That's our oil and all the money that generates should be spent by Welsh people in Wales. Look what's 'appening in Scotland. The English are taking all their oil and gas and that's why there's such a fuss up there. Also, look at all the water being piped into Birmingham and the Midlands from the Welsh mountains. That's our water and if we had our own government, we'd charge them for it and make a fortune. With coal, oil and water, we can be rich and live independently but much more than that, we can be a proud nation again, not at the beck and call of the English.'

'But we are a proud nation.'

'You know what I mean, proud in the sense that we can control our own lives and look the English in the eyes as equals and not as servants. We should do it for all our ancestors as well who were shafted, exploited and brutalised for centuries.'

'All our ancestors! You can talk,' Pete butted in incredulously.

'You know what I mean. I feel as Welsh as much as you do.'

'You should become a politician,' Helen interjected admiringly.

'Politics is a waste of time. It can only get you so far. Plaid will just keep faffing around, doing sweet FA. It needs summing much stronger than that, something that will really ignite this nation of ours and make the English sit up and take notice.'

'What d'you mean? Some sort of armed struggle like in Northern Ireland?'

'P'rhaps,' Joe responded enigmatically. He was about to continue when the waiter arrived and poured some wine into each of their glasses before taking their starter plates away. As he was about to restart, Helen interrupted.

'You sound like a lot of the boys at school, doesn't he, Sue?'

'Yeah, I think we had this conversation in the Caesars Arms the other day.'

'That's right, I remember. I'm quite intrigued by this. You both reckon there are others around who think the same as me?'

Pete began to eye the restaurant as he became disinterested in the table's conversation, having heard it all before. His eyes settled on a pretty, blonde-haired girl sitting at a table near the bar and who was smiling broadly. Unfortunately for Pete, she was smiling at her partner who was sitting opposite her. Their hands were touching and Pete concluded he was a lucky bugger. As Joe became more animated, an elderly couple at another table peered over in their direction. Pete smiled back at them, arching his eyebrows to convey his exasperation.

'Oh, yeah, loads. But it's all just chat, you know. They go on about it all the time but it's nothing really.'

'Why's that d'you think?'

'What d'you mean?'

'Why do they just talk about it? Why don't they go out and do something about it, you know, protest, agitate a bit, kick up a stink and fight for what they believe in?'

Sue joined Pete in staying quiet as Helen led the conversation with Joe. 'Well, I'm not really sure. As

I said, it's just chat. I suppose they don't really know what to do or how to organise themselves. Deep down, they're probably just resigned to the fact that this is how things are and that nothing'll ever change. It's true some of the boys get quite angry but I can't see them doing anything nasty or violent, like. That's far too extreme for them.'

'D'you think so? Don't you think they just need a lead, someone or something to encourage 'em to take some action, to stir 'em up a bit? It's interesting what's 'appening in Northern Ireland. I know there's always been an IRA, well at least going back to the turn of the century as far as I know, but it's only really in these last few years that they've come to the fore and had any real success. Are the Irish so different to us here?'

'You're not suggesting a WRA, are you?' Pete scoffed.

'What d'you mean by WRA?' Helen enquired somewhat befuddled, looking at Pete.

'WRA; Welsh Republican Army, duurrrr.'

'Oh, I gerrit now,' Helen responded a little embarrassed, lifting her head back.

'Why not?' Joe butted in.

'You're mad! What's up with you? Have you gone all soft in the 'ead or summing?' Pete blurted out, a family of four next to them turning their heads in his direction. This was the first time he had heard Joe make reference to a possible terrorist organisation.

'Well, something like that.' Joe toned down his views. 'You can't ignore the fact, though, that a...' Joe hesitated to find the correct words, '...a violent struggle, for want of a better expression, has far greater impact than political bullshit. What's needed is something awe-inspiring, something tremendous, with real impact, to really get things going, not just 'ere but all around the world.'

'You really 'ave gone soft in the 'ead,' Pete responded, raising his eyes to the ceiling before casting glances towards Sue and Helen who both smiled back.

'I'll give you an example. Remember Bloody Sunday a few years back when the Paras shot all those innocent Catholics, in Derry, I think it was. I know it was terrible an' all that but this event strengthened the IRA and resulted in much greater support for them and since then, they've been incredibly active. Look what they did in Guildford.'

'Yes, look what they did in Guildford,' Sue interjected, her voice loud and angry. 'All those innocent people out for a quiet drink in the pub blown to pieces. Disgusting it was. Whoever did that are just murderers, scum who should be strung up.'

'I know it was awful but the government is getting worried about their strength and support and take my word for it, the North will join up with the South one day.'

'You're dreaming,' Pete interrupted, shaking his head. 'Anyway, Ireland's different to us. They've got this Catholic-Protestant problem an' it's hardly rocket science to work out why the IRA got stronger after what the Paras did. It's different 'ere, though.'

'No it's not and we shouldn't just talk about Ireland. What about the PLO and their fight with Israel or ETA with the Spanish? Remember at the Olympics when the PLO shot those Israeli athletes? You know, it was terrible, like, don't gemme wrong, but it brought their situation to world attention and now they're getting plenty of support for their cause. Their situations are basically the same as ours. People whose lands have been occupied by another power, just fighting to get back what's truly theirs. Why's that so different to us 'ere in Wales?'

'You've really gone off your rocker now. How anybody can support the PLO after what they did in Munich is mad. And this someone or something that's gonna stir up the Welsh people, what d'you 'ave in mind? Are you gonna be that someone riding out on a white charger with sword in one hand and flag in the other?' Pete asked sarcastically with a little laughter and slight shake of the head, though the two girls were all ears in waiting for Joe's response.

Joe's lips parted and he seemed to be on the point of uttering some words when he abruptly closed them again and remained silent. The seconds ticked by as his three companions stared expectantly at him. But Joe did not say anything and eventually just picked up his wine glass and took a slow drink. Pete and the two girls passed the most fleeting of glances between each other but when another few wordless seconds lapsed, they soon concluded that Joe had no intention of answering the question. Each of them took a sip from their drinks, the atmosphere around the table somewhat suffocating. It was Pete who finally addressed Joe and with some force. 'You've been talking absolute bollocks if you pardon my French. What are you on? Have you been eating magic mushrooms with Kev Davies or summing?' Turning to the two girls, Pete explained how their classmate Kevin Davies was well known for indulging in a number of strange and illegal substances.

'We'll see,' were the only words Joe said, his voice barely a whisper, and he turned his head away and looked down at his cotoletta, which had just been served by the waiter. He did so in such a manner that it was obvious to all that he did not wish to continue the conversation. The others, too, looked down at their meals, breathing in the enticing aromas. Helen took another careful sip from her glass of San Pellegrino, trying to decide whether the addition of some bubbles made the water taste any differently to that which came out of her taps at home. She was more concerned whether they would give her hiccups than anything else. Pete was pleased that such a heavy and absurd conversation had come to an end and made another mental calculation of the cost of the meal. Sue's emotions, however, were in turmoil, spinning around wildly inside her head. She cut into her lasagne and took a first mouthful. Despite it nearly burning the tip of her tongue, she remained stern-faced as she gazed down at the sizzling pasta in front of her. Butterflies were fluttering around alarmingly inside her stomach. The missing gun was bad enough but it was Joe's refusal to answer Pete's question that was the real cause of her anxiety. She had the clear impression he was up to something. Or was she just becoming paranoid? It was ridiculous to think that Joe might become involved in some terrorist atrocity. Or was it?

15

'Thanks for dropping us off. I'll speak to you tomorrow, Helen. Thanks for a lovely evening, Pete, and drive carefully.' Sue tapped Helen on her shoulder from the rear of the car as she stepped out through the already open door.

When they had left the restaurant, Pete had escorted Helen to the front passenger door. Helen picked up on this first real attempt of his that evening to take a closer interest in her. It felt a little disconcerting to suddenly feel like one of a couple. She liked Pete but did not fancy him as much as she thought she might, though she would accept any further invitation to go out with him as she thought there was a chance that the relationship might develop. She had known he would drive her home later in the evening and that the two of them would be alone together for the first time but she hoped he would just drop her by the door without exerting any pressure for a kiss or more. She had plenty of experience of handling such situations and felt confident she could handle Pete. Now, if it was Joe, then that would be something completely different.

Joe had already got out of the car and was standing by Pete's open window as Sue said a final word or two to Helen. He looked down at his friend and smiled at him, knowingly. Pete's expression, however, remained glum. For the whole journey back to Pontypridd, he had been quiet and had left it to the others to engage in conversation. It did not help that he had been the only one not drinking as the girls laughed and even shrieked at some of Joe's more risqué jokes. He had heard them all before anyway. Pete's moodiness was more down to the number of notes he had had to remove from his wallet when the bill had arrived. He had come well prepared and still expected to have a couple of nice crisp fivers available to him at the end of the evening. The fact that he had had to use them all upset him, particularly when he noticed that the drinks' bill had accounted for much more than half the total and he had hardly drunk anything himself. It had not helped his mood when Joe had requested three grappas for him and the girls at the end of the meal and then a final one for himself for the road. The girls had not even enjoyed them as the burning sensation made them splutter and their eyes water. Wimpy prices my arse, he thought, and he was determined to ask Joe for a larger contribution when they were alone together next. He had thought about asking him for more at the table but did not want to appear tight-fisted.

'Now you 'ave a nice evening, you two,' Joe slurred, 'and watch his 'ands, Helen.'

'Shurrup, will you?' Pete responded, his cheeks flushing with embarrassment.

Eventually, the car pulled away and Sue and Joe remained standing, looking momentarily in its direction before moving away and towards Sue's front door.

'Well, I thought that went well,' Joe started, breaking the brief silence that ensued between them.

'Yeah, it was a lovely evening, really good fun. Pete can be a bit quiet at times, though. D'you think he enjoyed it?' Sue enquired as she inserted the key into the lock.

'I'm sure he did. It's not easy when you're the only one not drinking. Anyway, I think he likes Helen. Wha' d'you reckon?'

'What do you mean, what do I reckon?'

'Well, you know, does Helen like him now she's got to know him better?' Joe wiped his feet on the doormat as he followed Sue into the hallway.

'I'll tell you tomorrow after we've chatted but I'm not that convinced. She took more of a shine to you.'

'Well, that's to be expected, innit? You can 'ardly blame her.'

'Watch your head when you go in the kitchen. The door's only three feet wide.' Joe grinned as he took off his bomber jacket and placed it over a kitchen stool before sitting on another. 'Tea, coffee?'

'Mmm, I fancy something a bit stronger. D'you 'ave a can or summing?'

'No beer, sorry, but I've got some white wine open in the fridge. Is that okay?'

'Yeah, that'll be fine, ta.'

'Actually, I think I'll join you.' Sue pulled open the top door of the fridge and removed the bottle of Blue Nun, her fingers tingling from the chilled glass. She placed it on the table next to Joe before opening the cupboard door above the sink to remove two tumblers. 'You don't mind these glasses, do you?'

'Why, what's wrong with them? They're fine. Who d'you think I am, the Prince of Wales or summing?'

'Well, the way he's been going on, it wouldn't surprise me if he popped in the house some time.'

Joe frowned, not understanding this last comment. 'What d'you mean?'

'Don't you ever read anything in the papers other than the sport?' Sue poured the drinks and then continued. 'Apparently, he's gonna embark on a tour of Wales or something like that, you know, going to the Eisteddfod, a few town visits, stuff like that. I think they mentioned he's gonna go to the match against England next year as well. You never know, you might meet him if you get picked. If you do, could you ask him for a couple of tickets for the girls?'

'Say that again, Prince Charles is going to the England match next year?' Joe's face was expressionless and he did not react to Sue's amusing quip.

'Yeah, well that's what they say in the papers. Anyway, what's the problem?'

'Oh, no problem, it's just interesting to know,' Joe replied enigmatically. He stared into space for a few seconds as if trying to evaluate what this would mean for his plan on the day. Instinctively, he felt a great opportunity had opened up in front of him.

'Hello, hello, are you still here?' Sue tried to grab Joe's attention, waving her hand in front of his face.

'Are you sure he's going to the game?'

'I told you I read it in the paper,' Sue bellowed in frustration. 'I dunno if they're right or wrong, it's just what I read. I'm not his secretary or something. I don't run his diary. What's the big deal?' Sue took a large gulp from her glass, stood up from her stool and went over to the sink to rinse it out. She felt some annoyance as Joe seemed to blank her out, more intent on knowing the movements of the Prince of Wales.

'It's no big deal.' Joe's mood lightened and he rose from his stool and placed his left arm around Sue's waist. 'You 'aven't got the 'ump with me now, 'ave you? Come and sit on my lap.'

Joe, however, was astonished when Sue grabbed his wrist and flung his arm away from her while spinning away from his clutches and walking straight out of the kitchen. Joe stood motionless for a second, totally nonplussed, trying to understand what had brought this on. It was the first time he had experienced any resistance from Sue to his advances, well, outside of bed anyway, or any unhappiness. He was taking a gulp from his tumbler when he heard Sue yell for him to come into the living room where she had seated herself on the left-hand side of the sofa. Joe placed the glass in the sink, burped quietly, left the kitchen and went into the living room, sitting down beside her. He could see straight away that her expression was serious and that she was somewhat agitated. She could not look him in the eye.

'Are you okay?' Joe asked softly.

'I'm fine.' Sue's harsh tone contradicted her reply. She hesitated, clearly struggling to say what she had on her mind.

'Are you sure? You look a bit, you know, a bit,' Joe, too, was struggling to find the correct word, 'a bit, well, flustered if you know what I mean.' He wasn't sure if such a word truly reflected what he saw in Sue but it elicited a response.

'I want to ask you something that's been bothering me.' Sue's stomach felt hollow and the words came out slowly, increasing the impact of the question to follow. Joe picked up on the mood and tone and sat quietly, his face a blank, totally in the dark as to what Sue wanted to know. He waited patiently as Sue tried to find the courage to go on.

'I don't want you to take this the wrong way.'

Joe's heart started to beat a little faster and he felt a knot form in his stomach. Outwardly, his face did not change. It felt as if she was going to impart some bad news like not wanting to see him anymore. As Sue failed to follow up on her statement, Joe's patience broke. 'What is it you don't want me to take the wrong way? Come on, spit it out.'

Sue raised her head and looked him straight in the eye. 'It's not what you think. It's just something that's been on my mind for a while.'

'You're talking riddles now. What is it you want to say?' Joe hesitated before saying the words he hoped never to say. 'Do you want to finish with me? Is that it?' He said the words softly and lowered his eyes sheepishly and for the first time in their relationship, Sue saw a vulnerable Joe. Instantaneously, Sue took Joe's right hand and placed it on her lap, caressing the back of it nervously with her thumb.

'No way! Why would I want to do that? I'm totally in love with you, you must know that. I have been from the moment you turned up at the door for dinner.' Sue's emotions came out in torrents and she moved towards him and hugged him tightly, Joe's bristle lightly scraping against her soft cheek. She could not see Joe's face which was suddenly wide-eyed. What the fuck is going on here? he asked himself. He couldn't figure it out at all. It felt wonderful to hear Sue say such things for it reflected his feelings towards her, too. He was about to reciprocate when Sue leaned back and resumed her distant position. 'It's because I love you so much that I'm finding it so hard to ask you what's on my mind. It's probably nothing and I don't want you to think I'm accusing you of anything but you know the other day, when you came round and we were chatting about lots of stuff.'

'Yeeaahh, go on.'

'Well, I dunno if you remember but one of the things we talked about was my dad and how he loved anything to do with the war and how he collected memorabilia and stuff.' Joe sighed inwardly at Sue's inability to get to the point but said nothing. 'Well, you might remember that one of the things we spoke about was a gun he owned, a German Luger, which he kept in the drawer over there.'

Now that she had said it, Sue looked down at the carpet, not wishing to witness Joe's undoubtedly angry face. Instinctively, Joe looked over to the small table under the window and tensed up instantly. He had been found out. He could not believe it. He thought she said she never opened that drawer and here they were just a few days after he had taken it and she already knew. He was determined to brazen it out and remain calm and collected so that she could not pick up on any incriminatory body language or change in facial expression.

'Yeah, I remember. Go on.'

Sue looked up and observed no visible change in him. In fact, his disarming response, said in the manner of someone keen to resolve a mystery himself, threw her somewhat. He seemed to genuinely know nothing about what she was talking about and he certainly did not appear on the point of turning angry.

'Well, when I opened it the other day, it wasn't there.' Once again, Sue tried to pick up on any change in body language. Joe remained relaxed, his facial expression one of mystification.

'You don't think I took it, do you?' Joe's voice was calm, not in the least threatening.

'No, absolutely no way,' a stressed Sue replied quickly and loudly, clutching his hand. Joe did not believe her but he felt he had gained some initiative. She was clearly finding it difficult to accuse him outright.

'What would I want with a gun? That's just ridiculous. I know I've done some pretty stupid things in my time but I promise you and I really want you to know this, I would never steal a gun to shoot someone or something. I could never do that, never. I really want you to know that. It's important to me that you do.'

'No, I know you didn't take it and I believe you.' Sue stroked Joe's hand and then held it firmly. Her emotions were such that her eyes darted to the left and right and then directly at Joe once again before she looked away altogether. She nervously adjusted her position on the sofa and looked down suspiciously, as if the cushion was full of creepy-crawlies. She cursed herself for not being able to accuse Joe directly.

'Hey, calm down, calm down, you're all over the place.' Joe placed his left hand over Sue's, his tone commanding. 'I can see you think I might have taken it, but please believe me, I did nothing of the sort.' Despite the lie which unsettled him and knotted his stomach, Joe remained calm and Sue did not detect anything to make her disbelieve him. He was so assured that she began to doubt whether he had in fact taken the Luger, but her doubts were momentary. She was certain he had. 'Are you sure it was in there? Could it be somewhere else, in another drawer, in the loft, in the shed out the back, anywhere?'

Sue did not reply and a deathly hush fell over the room which made them both feel very uncomfortable. It was Sue who finally restarted the conversation. 'I thought it was in there but I'm not so sure now. I don't know where else it could be, though.' Sue's voice was less stressed and agitated. 'P'rhaps I'll take a harder look around later and see what crops up.' Sue knew she had lost her momentum. Joe had given his answer to her question, though she knew he was lying. But what could she do about it? If she accused him of lying, he would undoubtedly react angrily and such an accusation would mean the end of their relationship. She could not countenance that. Nevertheless, the gun was missing. He had taken it. She did not know why but she could not bring herself to believe he would use it. But what could she do now? She did not know. At least she knew what his position was. 'You're probably right. It may be in the loft with some of my dad's other stuff. If I'm honest, I haven't looked in that drawer for yonks. Maybe I'm just mistaken and my dad moved it before he died. It's no big deal anyway.'

Once again, the room went quiet. Joe did not reply though his heart rate remained high. Sue seemed genuinely uncertain as to what had happened to the Luger and Joe started to feel confident that he had got away with it. Deep down, he felt rotten lying to Sue and this feeling only reinforced his love and desire for her. When he thought Sue was leading up to finishing their relationship, the numbness that came over him was a sensation he never wished to experience again. The relief at her outpouring of love was overwhelming. As his love for Sue grew, he knew the thought of losing her afterwards was the one thing that would test his resolve more than anything. He did not want to think too much about it for the moment as there were many months yet before the big day and so much could happen in the meantime, principally his not being selected for the Welsh team.

'Come 'ere.' Sue slid sideways towards Joe and he held her lovingly in his arms. He kissed her lightly on the top of her head. 'Don't worry, it'll turn up. These things usually do,' he whispered reassuringly in her ear. His tone of voice was so confident that Sue wondered whether he was considering returning it.

'I suppose it will.'

'You really 'ad me worried there. I thought you were gonna finish with me. My stomach went all hollow. I love you so much that even thinking about it kills me.'

Sue grasped his arm and squeezed it firmly, turning her face so that their lips met. Joe's words had electrified her and she longed to return his love, physically and immediately. 'Let's go upstairs.' They both rose from the sofa together, hand in hand, Sue leading the way, her thoughts only that of making love. 'Did you manage to get to the chemist's?' she asked a little shyly.

'Sorry, but I couldn't face up to it.'

'What d'you mean?' Sue's tone could not hide her disappointment.

'Well, Mrs Parry works the till in Boots and my mum knows her really well. I'd die if I put a packet of johnnies in front of her.'

'Oh, okay.'

A few moments of silence ensued as they walked up the stairs and entered Sue's bedroom. She was deflated at this unexpected turn of events and could not hide her disappointment in the expression on her face.

'Are you okay, Sue? You look a bit down in the dumps,' Joe enquired, peering into her eyes. 'There's nothing wrong, I hope?'

'Yeah, I'm fine, don't worry.' Sue's attempt at a jolly tone and smile were half-hearted.

'You sure? Sorry I bottled out in Boots. I hope you understand.'

'Sure, there's no problem,' Sue replied nonchalantly.

'That's good. I don't want you to 'ave the 'ump with me again.' Joe smiled inwardly at Sue's obvious disappointment as they both started to undress separately. He deliberately took his time taking off his clothes to prolong her discomfort. 'No, I couldn't face Mrs Parry, I'm sorry, but that's not to say I couldn't face the johnny machine in the Maltsters.' And chuckling in the same manner as Muttley when he's annoying Dick Dastardly, he held up a small packet and showed it to Sue.

'You sod!'

16

'Giuseppe, there's someone called Owen on the phone,' and with that, Marco left the receiver on the table and returned to the living room. Joe's heart beat a little faster as he got up from the armchair and walked slowly into the hallway. He pushed the door three quarters closed behind him but noticed his mother washing up in the kitchen.

'Hello.' After just a few seconds of speech from the other end of the line, Joe interrupted him. 'I'll call you in ten minutes,' he whispered, 'stay by your phone.' Not waiting for a reply, Joe placed the receiver back on its cradle.

'Who's Owen?' Marco seemed to appear from nowhere by his side.

'Never you mind.' Joe's stern expression, stare and tone of voice told Marco in no uncertain terms not to ask him again and to stay out of his business. Marco wandered off into the kitchen. Joe followed him and grabbed his brown duffel coat from the cupboard under the stairs. He then strode through the kitchen and put on his boots by the back door.

'*Dove vai?*' Joe's mother asked him where he was going as she wiped away at the dishes stacked in the rack on the draining board. Joe did not reply directly and only advised that he would be back in half an hour. Mrs Chilani was used to the comings and goings of her elder son and thought nothing of it, though Marco never took his eyes off him, knowing he was up to something. Ten minutes later, Joe was waiting for Dafydd to pick up the phone as he shivered in the phone box at the bottom of Graigwen Hill.

'Hello.'

'Owain here.'

'Owain. Only rang earlier to find out if you…'

'I know what you're on about.'

'It's…'

'No, forget it.'

'But this…'

'No! You heard what I said.'

'The…' But Dafydd had no time to finish the sentence for Joe had slammed the phone down, left the booth and marched purposefully back up the hill.

1977

17

"And the Wales team to play Ireland at Cardiff Arms Park next Saturday is as follows: Full-Back...John Evans; Right-Wing...Gareth Evans; Left-Wing...Jim Morgan; Centre and Captain...Geraint Lewis; Centre...Steve James..."

'Noooooo!' Joe screamed as he sprang up from his chair and pushed the desk over in front of him. Pete, Dave and three other school friends all jumped up smartly to avoid it as Joe tore himself away and slammed the door behind him as he hurtled out of the classroom. The gathering of schoolboys all looked at each other without saying a word. There was nothing to say. Joe had not been selected for the first rugby international of the season against Ireland the following Saturday. They had all been huddling around the battered transistor radio Pete had brought in to listen to the announcement of the team during their lunch break at one o'clock. A few minutes later, two of their teachers and several more pupils entered the room.

'Well?' asked Gerald Jenkins, the senior PE teacher, though the lack of excitement in the room and upturned desk gave obvious clues as to the decision of the selectors.

'He didn't make it, sir. They picked Steve James.' Everybody in the room was deflated and disappointed for their star player. They all felt Joe had a chance of selection, particularly after his performance in the Probables versus Possibles trial match played on the Saturday just gone.

'Pity that. What a disappointing way to start the year. He really thought he'd make it, particularly after Dewi Griffiths's write-up in the paper this morning. He reckons he's the best centre in Wales, better even than Geraint Lewis.'

'Steve James, he's fucking crap,' Pete snorted. 'Sorry 'bout the language,' he added quickly and apologetically, remembering that two teachers were in their midst. They both glared at him, Jenkins sternly, but said nothing. They both felt the same way.

'He plays for Aberavon, doesn't he?' Dave carried on, lifting the desk back up on to its legs and picking up the pens, books and ruler that had flown off it.

'Yeah and that's where Bill Johnson comes from. I could swear his voice perked up when he read out his name a few minutes ago. He's chairman of the Big Five, the national selectors. It's no wonder James got in. Who the fu... heck do they think they are, these Big Five? None of 'em are from Ponty and that's why we never get anybody picked. A bunch of pillocks the lot of them if you ask me.'

'Look, there was always a chance Joe wouldn't make it,' the reasoned voice of Gerald Jenkins broke in. 'I agree with you he's better than James but it's all about opinions at the end of the day. I know Dewi Griffiths and Bob Parry-Jones on the telly talk Joe up a lot but even they 'ad their doubts 'cos of his age and whether he could handle the pressure. It may have come a bit early for him but I'm sure he'll get there one day.'

'Let's 'ope so. I was hoping to cadge a ticket from him. Now I've got no chance.' They all broke out into wide smiles.

'Where's he gone?'

'Dunno. He just stormed out. He screamed out something, pushed the desk over and shot away. He's steaming. I don't think we'll see him again this afternoon. I'll try him later 'cos a few of us are supposed to be meeting up in the Maltsters tonight for a celebration drink. Sue and Helen are coming down as well. I suppose we'll still get pissed out of our heads anyway and 'ave a good ol' moan. I'm sure he'll turn up.'

'We didn't hear that, orrite, boys!' The two masters did not want to be seen to condone underage drinking, though they knew it was rife.

'Absolutely!' Pete glanced at the rest of the boys and they all nodded their heads vigorously in agreement. They respected the two masters and would not want to get them into any trouble. He continued optimistically, 'He's still got a good chance for the Scotland game, though. Ireland are not bad this year and who knows, they might even beat us on Saturday. That Mulligan in the centre's shit hot and p'rhaps it's not such a bad thing Joe's missed out. He'll show James up and then Joe will get in, you watch.'

'Let's hope so. It would be brilliant for the town and for the school. Can you imagine that, the first schoolboy to play for Wales since God knows when? Mind you, if he does get in, he'll come up against Harrison when we play England and he's seriously good. Did you see that try he scored on *Rugby Special* against Wasps on Boxing Day? Unbelievable it was. He's so fast and really strong. I can't stand the bugger but you've got to give it to him, he's really good. And let's not forget he gave Joe a bit of a runaround when 'arlequins played Ponty last year. I dunno, perhaps it might be better for Joe to leave it for this season. He'll be bigger and stronger next year, I'm sure.'

'No way!' Pete's loyalty shone through. 'He's ready now and he'll take Harrison, Mulligan, James, Geraint Lewis, anybody you want to name, anytime.'

Before the conversation got out of hand, Gerald Jenkins broke in. 'Let's not get ahead of ourselves here. It's a shame he didn't make it for Saturday but let's see what happens. There's another three internationals to come this season and you know, with injuries, bad form and the like, he could still make it but there's no point trying to predict the future. What will be, will be. Anyway, lunch will be over soon so let's get back to your lessons. If Joe doesn't turn up, I think everybody'll understand, even Hoppo, so he won't get into any trouble, I'm certain. If he's not back and you see him tonight, tell him from me to keep his chin up. Knowing Joe, I'm sure he'll get over it quickly.'

* * *

But Joe wasn't getting over it quickly. After storming out of the classroom, he hurried past all the boys and girls milling around outside in the corridors and bolted down the front steps outside the main entrance to the school and marched purposefully towards his home. Some boys and girls were making their way back after lunch and moved smartly out of Joe's way for it was apparent he was in a furious mood and unlikely to shift his position. He knew he would not return that afternoon and did not give any consideration to the consequences. He left his satchel and coat hanging on the back of his chair, but these were the furthest things from his mind.

As he turned into his street, he broke into a trot, swung open the front gate and shot up the steps towards the garden. He flung the gate violently behind him and it clanged loudly as it bounced back and forth. After following the path round to the back door, he lifted up the flowerpot and picked up the key. He unlocked the door and, after closing it firmly behind him, kicked off his shoes and ran upstairs to his bedroom. Once inside, he closed the door, locked it and threw his blazer on to the armchair in the corner. He tore off his tie and threw that at the armchair as well, though it fell short and lay eel-like beneath it. Joe undid the top two buttons of his shirt whilst at the same time flinging himself on to his bed where for the first time in the ten minutes that had passed by since the announcement of the team, a semblance of calm returned to his being. He lay back, put his hands under his head and stared directly upwards at the ceiling. He noticed a black speck close to the lamp shade in the middle and tried to work out what it was, how it got there and how it seemed to defy the laws of gravity. Just another of life's great mysteries, he concluded, just like how he had failed to make the Welsh team. For a moment, he thought of his mother, whom he knew would be home within an hour or two depending on whether she had any shopping to do or how busy it had been in the restaurant at lunchtime. He'd make an excuse for his being there, a headache perhaps or just the truth. He'd say the teachers had given him permission to skip the afternoon due to his disappointment. She'd understand that, because although she cared nothing for rugby and in fact wished Joe never played the game, she knew how important the sport was in Wales and was well aware that Joe had a chance of being selected for the forthcoming international matches. Her friends and customers all reminded her of this and she felt immensely proud, as did Joe's father and brother.

'Yeah, she'll understand,' Joe said to himself, 'when I tell her the truth.' Then, after a short delay, he bellowed at the top of his voice, 'IT'S BECAUSE I'M FUCKING USELESS AND MY PLAN IS A LOAD OF SHIT. WHO THE FUCK DO I THINK I AM, BELIEVING I COULD PLAY FOR WALES?' Letting off this steam made him feel better. He took two deep breaths and began to compose himself. After a few moments, his thoughts became more rational and he reassessed his situation. On the positive side, the match against Ireland was not important in itself and had no bearing on his plan. What was important was selection for the England game which came after Ireland and Scotland. He had been desperate to play in the Irish game for he reckoned that once he was in the team, there was a good possibility he would stay in it. Thinking logically, he reasoned that the opposite might also be true in that if he played badly, he would be dropped and unlikely to return that season. This thought comforted him. Maybe this is what will happen to James and Lewis and he would get picked in their places later. It was all ifs and buts, but the logic of his thinking brought him some peace of mind. He was still not in the team, though, and a cold sweat came over him at the realisation that time was running out. He felt impotent, not knowing what he could do. He would just have to carry on playing well for Pontypridd and hope for the best. There was no point getting into a panic at this stage but he knew that that time was not too far away.

Joe was realistic enough to know that his selection for Wales would be difficult and he had given thought to alternative plans. But no others attracted him. Nothing would remotely compare or carry the impact, real and symbolic, of the Wales versus England rugby international and so important and crucial, indeed vital, was his mission that only maximum impact would suffice. The pictures of the day were clear in his head; the huge crowd, the massive television audience, the dignitaries, the drama. He dreamed of the consequences afterwards; the gathering of young Welsh people, the plots, the violence, the worry of the establishment, their eventual capitulation, the joyous scenes in all the towns and cities as a Welsh Parliament in an independent state is established. Vainly, Joe even dreamed of his place in history, of the admiration of the Welsh people. He would be a hero for being the catalyst for such tumultuous events. There might even be a statue of him somewhere, one day.

No, it had to be Wales versus England. He had received a serious setback but there was still time to put it right. He turned his head to the left and set eyes on the bedside table. Without hesitating, he jumped smartly off the bed and took a single stride to the armchair where he grabbed his blazer. He took his wallet from the inside pocket and, after opening the small pouch, pushed aside some of the coins to reveal the tiny key, which he removed. After placing the wallet on the bedside table, he inserted the key in the drawer, unlocked it and pulled it towards him. He lifted up the old exercise book and removed the felt wrapper from the Luger. He cast a worried glance towards the bedroom door and reassured himself that he had locked it when he had first entered the room. He picked up the gun and held it in his right hand. It felt heavier than he remembered. Was he losing his strength? Just a nonsense thought, he concluded. He gazed down at the weapon and marvelled once more at its shape and glistening steel. But when it came to it, when there was no turning back, did he really have the balls to use it? He closed his eyes and pictured the scenes of the day. His heartbeat quickened and his stomach heaved at the images in his head. It would take unimaginable courage to carry it through, of that there was no doubt. Nonetheless, at that particular moment, he felt strong and committed and determined and his resolve, if anything, was greater than ever. But he knew it was easy to believe such things sitting on his bed in the comfort of his own home. How would he feel in front of forty five thousand excited and animated spectators when the moment of truth was right upon him? He knew he would only have a tiny window of opportunity. He closed his eyes and took a deep breath, visualising that specific moment. He raised the gun. Yes, he could do it. He was certain. There was no doubt about it. He hoped.

The slam of the front door broke his dream-like state. 'Shit, she's home early.' He quickly wrapped the Luger in the yellow felt cloth, placed it back in its original position, put the exercise book on top and closed the drawer. After locking it, he put the key back into the pouch of his wallet. He ran his hands through his hair and smoothed the wrinkles out of the front of his shirt as best possible before silently unlocking his bedroom door and walking down the stairs, towards the kitchen.

'Oh, you gave me a fright. *Perchè sei qui?*' A startled Mrs Chilani enquired why her son was home as she stretched up to place cans of baked beans into a cupboard high above her eye line.

'It's nothing. I'm just disappointed I didn't get picked for the match, that's all, and wanted to be by myself. I couldn't face being in school. I wouldn't have been able to concentrate anyway. The teachers said it would be okay,' he lied.

'I heard the news, I'm sorry. Most of our customers said not to be too despondent. They told me to tell you to keep your spirits up and that you'll get there eventually. *Un po' di pazienza, Caro.*' Joe's mother gave him a hug and they held each other briefly as she told him to be patient.

'Yeah, sure,' Joe responded rather unconvincingly, breaking away from her. 'Anyway, I'll be fine. There's no point worrying about things you can't control.' It was one of his most commonly used expressions and he perked up instantly.

'*Una buona tazza di tè?*'

'Yeah, tea'd be nice. Ta, Mum,' Joe replied and he pulled back a kitchen chair, scrunching up his face when he scraped one of its legs inadvertently across the floor. 'You watch me. When I do get picked, I'll show everybody, everywhere what it takes to be a proud and committed Welshman.' Joe's eyes were distant and unblinking and his face a blank. He failed to register any of his mother's activity around him as she poured water into the kettle and fetched some milk from the fridge. His words sounded messianic in tone but she barely gave a moment's thought to what he was saying as she had no interest at all, whatsoever, in any of the international matches. She thought it was such a rough, tough, brutal game and wanted nothing to do with it. Mistakenly, she was wrong to believe he was talking about rugby.

18

'Bye, Mum.' Joe bolted from the kitchen table having eaten his tea in five minutes flat. He grabbed his duffel coat and shot out the back door. His mother barely had time to acknowledge his goodbye whilst Marco remained immersed in *Tiger* and didn't bat an eyelid as Joe flurried around.

In the same time it had taken Joe to eat his tea, he had run down the hill and into the Maltsters in eager anticipation of meeting Sue, Pete, Dave and Helen and whoever else had made the effort to turn up for the supposed celebration drink. Despite the earlier disappointing news, he still expected a good crowd to turn up. The quiet afternoon hours had had the desired effect of calming Joe down and placing things into their proper perspective and in fact, over several cups of tea, he'd had a long conversation with his mother about a number of different subjects, the first time he had spent so much time chatting with any member of his family for as long as he could remember. When Mrs Chilani had finally determined that the ironing could wait no longer, Joe returned to his room and thought how difficult the aftermath of his plan would be for her, his father and brother. Such thoughts upset him and as the moment drew closer, he knew the impact on his family and Sue would be his toughest test of all. Once again, he took two deep breaths, which he always found helpful to clear his mind when these negative thoughts took hold.

On entering the pub, Joe saw a gang of familiar faces sitting around three small rectangular tables, which had all been pushed together. The dark-brown table tops were so heavily marked and stained that even Jackson Pollock might have considered the intricate shapes, patterns and squiggles a work of art. He knew he was late, having dozed off in his room and only waking when his mother yelled up the stairs that his tea was going cold. Five minutes in the bathroom, five minutes to change clothes, five minutes for tea and five minutes to reach the pub only five minutes late. Not bad, he thought, considering. He immediately approached Sue and they held each other briefly and kissed delicately on the lips. Her sad expression and words of regret were mirrored by everybody around the table. In addition, Joe received consoling pats on the back from those seated closest to him. He acknowledged everybody, noticing that Pete and Helen were sitting at opposite ends of the tables. Not another bust-up, he thought. He wondered what the matter was this time. Their relationship would not have been out of place on *Crossroads*.

'Thanks everybody for coming. I know the news was disappointing but I suppose that's the way it goes sometimes. There was always a chance I wouldn't make it. In fact, if I was 'onest, it was a bit of a long shot.'

'Oh, I dunno 'bout that. Everybody reckons you're the best centre in Wales, well, equal to Geraint Lewis, at least, but certainly better than Steve James. I can't believe he's been picked. He's such a lump and so slow. The Paddies will run rings round him on Saturday, you watch. I reckon you'll be in for Murrayfield, no problem.'

'Well, thanks for that, Dave, let's just wait and see. Right, let's 'ave a whip. A pound each for starters, I reckon.'

All the boys delved into their pockets for the cash whilst the girls rummaged around in their handbags before producing the crisp green notes. Pete gathered them up and folded them over in his hand. 'Right, I've got the kitty. Who's 'aving what?' he asked. Everybody placed their orders and Helen volunteered to help him carry the drinks from the bar. Pete ignored her and asked Gethin Harris to accompany him instead. As they left for the bar, Joe glanced sideways at Sue who raised her eyes to the heavens in despair. She peered over at Helen, who looked glum, her eyes fixed on the floor and chin seemingly stapled to her chest.

'Hey, Phil, thanks for coming on Saturday by the way. It was good to see your ugly mug there and I could hear your support from the pitch. I'm sorry I didn't get the chance to see you after but I was being pulled from pillar to post by the selectors. I really appreciate it, though.'

'No sweat,' he acknowledged, dropping his eyes and flushing with pride. Phil Jones was a mad-keen rugby supporter, a year below Joe in school. His knowledge of the game, teams and players was extraordinary, particularly for someone who was so lacking in athleticism and co-ordination himself. He could barely run and catch a ball, but his enthusiasm when playing the game was total and he was never afraid to get up and try again after being smashed to the ground. Phil was usually a quiet type though very well-natured and popular in school. When talk turned to rugby, however, his eyes shone brightly and he became very animated. Joe liked him immensely. He was the one person able to be present at the Probables versus Possibles trial match in Swansea the previous Saturday and Joe valued his support hugely. Sue had wanted to attend but her Saturday job at the Co-op prevented it, particularly as the cover she had arranged had gone down with a cold a couple of days earlier. Whilst Joe would have liked her to be there, he had been afraid his concentration would lapse in some foolhardy attempt to impress her. So when Sue told him she could not go, Joe was not too disappointed. His kind words of understanding had been comforting to her.

'How can they pick Steve James? It's ridiculous,' Phil sighed, shaking his head and eyeing everybody in the group around him. 'How he even started in the Probables is beyond me, to begin with. It's only because he plays for Aberavon and we all know where the chairman of the Big Five, Bill Johnson, comes from. It's scandalous, really.' All the boys nodded their heads in agreement just as Pete and Gethin returned with two trays of drinks. The girls nodded their heads as well, though more out of loyalty and camaraderie than out of any understanding as to what was being said. 'All he did was stick to his position and pass it on to Lewis. He didn't make one break or put in any nice long kicks to the corners though he had plenty of time and ball. The one time he tried a grubber, he completely fluffed it and it bounced back off the defender right past him and the Possibles nearly scored a try. His defence was alright, I suppose, but an international centre needs to have more than that. And d'you remember his one cap last year against France? What an embarrassment, that was. The Froggies just flew past him all the time. No wonder he got dropped. I can't see 'ow he's any better this year.'

'So, Phil, you're not his biggest fan then,' Pete interjected matter-of-factly, a twinkle in his eye. The group all burst into laughter, Dave embarrassingly so, as he spluttered his beer down his multi-coloured tank-top.

The crowd in the Maltsters was building up gradually, one or two of the clientele passing by Joe to express their disappointment. Mr Collins, who owned the travel agency in Mill Street and who was a good friend of his father, even bought a round of drinks for the whole group, which was greatly appreciated. Gethin Harris rose from his chair. 'I'll go and put some music on.'

'I'll come with you,' Helen jumped in, leaving her seat at the same time. Selecting records could be quite hazardous in the Maltsters as darts often pinged off the wire of the dartboard which was positioned right next to the jukebox. Pete was taken by surprise at the keenness in Helen's voice and he kept his eyes trained on the pair of them as they walked away.

'I thought they messed you about a bit on Saturday,' Phil carried on, looking directly at Joe. 'You start off as a sub and then with ten minutes to go in the first-half, they take off Emyr Thomas and give you a go in the Possibles. You only had the one chance, but you got half past Steve James and slipped the ball through to Martin Harvey who made good ground. He's a tremendous flanker, by the way. God knows 'ow he didn't get picked. I remember that chip ahead as well which put their defence under pressure. You did more in those ten minutes than James did all game.'

That's neat, that's neat, that's neat, that's neat, I really like your tiger feet, rang out from the speaker above them as Gethin and Helen pondered their next selections.

'God, they've got crap taste in music,' Richard Morgan intervened haughtily. He was affectionately known as Dinner due to his emaciated frame.

'Oh, I dunno. I think Mud are really good,' Ann commented.

Dinner blushed a little as he quite fancied Ann and so pathetically contradicted his own comment. 'Yeah, actually, you're right. Mud are pretty good.' Joe and Sue once more caught each other's eye and smiles crept across their faces.

'And then, at the start of the second-half, they take you off and leave James on. In fact, he played the whole game.'

'I did play the last twenty minutes for the Probables, remember, Phil. I took Geraint Lewis's place and played alongside Steve James.'

'That's true and you played well, but the ball never really came your way because James never passed it to you. He passes it to Lewis all day and then when you change sides, he either went into contact himself to set up a ruck or passed inside. He never wanted you to 'ave the ball 'cos he knew you'd do something with it and put pressure on his place 'cos they were always going to pick Lewis. It was just a case of who was gonna play alongside 'im and there was no way James was going to try and make you look good.'

'It's funny you should say that 'cos I had the same impression myself. I never got the ball when I was next to him. Afterwards, because I finished the match in the Probables, I kind of felt I had a really good chance of being selected and some of the stuff I read in the papers raised my hopes as well. But it's true, they'll never drop Lewis and James did nothing to help me. The selectors always had James in mind to play. He's such a cunt, that Bill Johnson. James must be shagging him.'

'Joe! Don't use that word. It's horrible.' Sue looked sternly at him whilst all the boys began to laugh. Dinner leaned back and slowly dragged at his cigarette, imagining he was Al Pacino in *The Godfather*, not taking in what Joe had said. He thought he looked cool and was sure that Ann could not fail to notice. What Ann could not fail to notice, more like, were Dinner's clothes stinking of smoke and the yellow nicotine stains already appearing on his fingers. She turned towards him and grinned. Dinner took this as a sign that he was making the right impression and that Ann was no doubt gagging for it. However, the only impression Ann had was how unattractive he looked and how she could possibly get round to the other side of the table.

'Wharrelse did you put on?' Sue enquired of Helen as she and Gethin returned to their seats. Pete took a large gulp from his glass, his eyes fixed on the two of them as they sat down. Was that a deliberate brushing of arms? He'd better watch it if he gets too close.

'After *Tiger Feet*, we put on *Blockbuster*, *Metal Guru*, *Dancing Queen*, *Bohemian Rhapsody*, *Puppy Love* and just for you, *Starman*.'

'Oh, that's lovely.' Sue smiled at her friend. 'I love *Starman*, it's one of Bowie's best.'

'*Puppy Love*!' Pete blurted out exasperated. 'Are you mad or what? Donny fucking Osmond. Are you joking?'

'It's a lovely song.' Helen defended her choice firmly.

Pete looked down at his empty glass and laughed, shaking his head. Without acknowledging Helen, he suddenly got up, the glass in one hand, the wedge of notes in the other. 'Right, what are we all 'aving? Same all round?' The boys all nodded their heads, one or two of them downing what remained of their pints at the same time.

'I'll miss this one,' Sue interjected. 'You're going a bit too fast for me.' Her glass of white wine and soda remained nearly full to the brim.

'Me, too,' both Ann and Helen concurred in unison. 'I'll be legless by nine o'clock at this rate,' Ann added.

'Oh, go on, you'll be orrite,' Dinner commented, picking up on the remark.

'No. I'll definitely give this one a miss,' Ann replied firmly, turning her face away from him to avoid the smell of smoke.

As Pete set off for the bar, beckoning Dave to come and give him a hand, Phil tried to continue his interrupted assessment of the Welsh team selection. Ann thought the rugby conversation had gone on for far too long and although she liked Phil, he could be a bit of a bore in her mind so she took the opportunity to move away from Dinner and take Dave's place next to Helen so that she could chat with her on another subject. Dinner was disappointed but there was no change in his facial expression and pose, head upright, cigarette held high, rather effeminately, the smoke floating away slightly behind him over his right shoulder. His thoughts turned excitedly to a Roxy Music album cover where Bryan Ferry, the epitome of cool in his mind and the only rival to Al Pacino, was wearing a khaki army shirt. He wondered where he could get hold of one. Ann would die for him if she saw him wearing it, he convinced himself. None the wiser as to which retailer might stock the shirt, his thoughts quickly returned to Michael Corleone.

'What you day-dreaming about this time, Din?' Joe had noticed Dinner's vacant stare, his mind miles away.

'I was just wondering whether I should slick my hair down like Al Pacino in *The Godfather*,' he replied in all seriousness. The table burst out into loud guffaws though Dinner's face took on a perplexed expression, wondering what was so funny. Even Phil stopped talking rugby.

'Hey, girls, wha' you reckon?' Joe enquired. 'D'you think Dinner should grease his hair down and do you think it'll make him look like Al Pacino?'

'More like Al Capone,' Dave replied as he set down a tray of beers, smirking.

'That's the trouble with you, Dave, you've got no style. How can you wear those bovver boots of yours? They're just for yobs, football hooligans and those Bay City Rollers trousers look ridiculous. When you came in with your dirty old man's mac on I couldn't work out if you were Les McKeown or Columbo.'

'Hey, nice one, Din. That's quite funny for you.' Joe was taken aback at the unexpected witticism.

'They're orrite by me. I couldn't give a toss what I wear. Hey, my dad's got some Brylcreem at home. Tell you what, I'll bring some into school tomorrow and we'll see what you look like. I could do with a laugh. I bought a few bags of pork scratchings as well. Hey, Din, you'd better take a couple as you could do with a bit of fattening up.' The laughter continued cruelly and even Ann started to feel a little sorry for Dinner.

'Don't bother asking me for a tab again. You can forget it next time.'

This worried Dave as he always asked for a final drag of Dinner's cigarette to get his fix of nicotine. 'Oh, don't do that to me, please! I'll do anything for you, even call you Al,' he replied sarcastically, kneeling down in front of him and attempting to kiss his hand as if Dinner was the new Don.

'Fuck off,' was Dinner's very un-Godfather-like response.

'Hey, Joe…' Phil was champing at the leash to restart the rugby conversation.

'Good name for a song,' Pete interrupted as he folded the wad of notes into his back pocket before retaking his seat.

Everybody looked up at him bemused until it clicked with Joe. 'Oh, I get it now. *Hey Joe*, you know, the Hendrix song.'

'Oh, very funny.' Everybody started to snigger around the table. Phil tried to start again. 'Hey, Joe…' Everybody burst into more silliness and giggles and Dave stood up to play air guitar and to sing the first few bars of the song. The alcohol was starting to take its effect. Even Phil smiled to himself. 'Hey, Mr Chilani..,' he resumed to even louder guffaws. 'Come on, it's not that funny. Hey, Mr Chilani…' The laughter finally subsided. '…Steve James could be a real problem if he's that in with Bill Johnson. You know, even if he has a crap match against Ireland, they may still pick him for Scotland. He'll be 'ard to shift.'

Joe had not thought too deeply about this situation. He had convinced himself that by being selected for the Probables last Saturday, he had had as good a chance of being picked for the international as Steve James. But now, Phil's assessment started to worry him. Four Aberavon players had been selected for the match against Ireland and three of those were very contentious. Aberavon were even having a poor season. His own club, Pontypridd, had lost just three games and yet only he and Rocky Evans had been selected for the trial. Rocky had been outstanding for the Possibles and the Probables front row had buckled on a number of occasions under his pressure. And yet, he had not been moved up to the Probables and it was no great surprise when he had not been selected for the international.

'Rugby politics! They do my 'ead in. It's just not fair. It doesn't matter 'ow good you are, it's whether you're in with the selectors or not. That's all that counts these days. It's a fucking disgrace.' Joe gulped down half his pint as if that would somehow reinforce his point.

'It doesn't help when your own club is against you either.'

'What d'you mean by that, Phil?' Sue interjected.

'Well, it seems pretty obvious to me that the rugby committee is not very keen on Joe. After the Boxing Day match against Cardiff, I was in the bar in the Athletic Club with my dad and some of his friends and apparently one of them was talking to Stan Williams about the Five Nations and who he reckoned had a chance of being selected for the team. He thought Rocky deserved to be picked and even Leap, though he must be nearly fifty! But he didn't even mention Joe. When my dad's mate asked him, Stan the Man was dismissive and reckoned Joe was too young and lacked discipline,' he gave a gentle nod towards Joe, 'and that you were likely to give away penalties or, even worse, get sent off. I saw Williams talking to Bill Johnson and another one of the Big Five, Howell Rees, I think it was, for ages afterwards and I'm sure they must have been talking about the Welsh team and what Williams thought about it.'

Joe started to bristle and he recalled the demeaning way Williams had spoken to him after the Harlequins game. The beer was also flowing freely through him and his voice was starting to sound louder and louder. 'It's funny you should say that. I reckon you're right. That slob Williams has definitely got it in for me. He's such a wanker and I'll be really pissed off if it's true he's been talking me down. You'd think he'd be pleased that someone from Ponty might play for Wales but at the end of the day, he's just an old-fashioned, bigoted twat. You know, he's one of those dinosaur types who think a woman's place is in the kitchen, the tosser.'

'He sounds like a good bloke to me,' Dave interrupted mischievously, a twinkle in his increasingly slitty and pissed eyes. The girls all looked daggers at him. 'Sorry 'bout that, girls. Actually, he's wrong, I agree with you. Everybody knows a woman's place is in the bedroom first, then the kitchen.' Ann thumped him on the arm playfully, biting her bottom lip.

'I dunno what I'm supposed to do anymore,' Joe carried on, ignoring Dave. 'The papers talk me up, the telly talks me up but I'm still miles away from the team.'

'I think you're a bit closer than that,' Phil commented, 'but I know where you're coming from. I still think you've got a great chance of being picked this year. Look, it's very likely Mulligan will piss all over James on Saturday and he'll come under pressure...'

'You say that,' Joe butted in, 'but the Paddies are rubbish and Wales should win easily and even if James is crap, they won't change a winning team.'

'I think Ireland are a lot better than you give 'em credit for. But even if you're right, he'll still be under pressure when Wales go to Murrayfield 'cos Scotland are good and we might even lose this year 'cos we never do well up there. There might be a few changes after that.'

'I'm not bothered about Scotland, it's England I want.' Joe looked straight ahead and through Phil, who was sitting opposite him, as if he was not there. His expression became distant and serious as he gulped down the remaining half-pint of his beer in one go. All the boys, Sue and Helen turned towards him. Ann was considering going over to the jukebox. She was more interested in music.

'You must be bothered about Scotland, it's your next opportunity,' Phil replied incredulously.

'Yeah, I am, don't gemme wrong, but England is the one I really wanna play in. It's crucial, essential I play in that one.'

Sue stared at Joe who continued to look straight through Phil. He had that same serious and determined expression that worried her at times due to the sheer scale of its intensity. She also noted that this was not the first time Joe had placed all importance on the England game. Instinctively, she knew Joe was planning something and she shivered slightly at the thought. The stolen Luger still played on her mind. Are the England game and the gun connected or was she just reading too much into things? It's too far-fetched, surely, but it did worry her. She remained silent with her thoughts.

'Yeah, well, England is the big one in that they're the old enemy and all that but they're so rubbish that down 'ere at the Arms Park, we'll put thirty on 'em. Scotland is the big threat in the championship this year, p'rhaps with France. England's only got a couple of decent players like Harrison and Meadows. Harrison's pretty shit hot, though. You've got to give it to him.'

'In more ways than one,' Helen blurted out saucily, smiling at Sue who smiled back.

'James Harrison?' Ann appeared to wake up. 'Isn't he the one who's married to Vikki Adams? He's absolutely gorgeous, not quite David Cassidy, but not far off.'

'Harrison, he's gonna get the shock of his life. Like all those English bastards, he won't know what hit 'im.' So matter-of-factly and chillingly had Joe expressed these words that the table chatter descended into silence.

'Well, you're gonna have to play a lot better against 'im than when you did last year.' It was Pete who finally spoke. Sue was not convinced that Joe was talking in a rugby context and she stared hard at him trying to delve into his brain. Joe remained quiet, his mind elsewhere.

'What's interesting is that on the Saturday after the Scottish game, the week before the England game, Ponty are playing Aberavon here in Ponty, and they'll probably pick the team for England the following Monday.'

'God, Phil, you're like a computer,' Pete butted in, looking startled. 'Is there anything you don't know about rugby? You even know the fixture list weeks ahead.' Everybody smiled around the table, though Phil's cheeks reddened a little and he looked down at the floor sheepishly.

'You're like a machine.' Dave concurred with Pete.

'A lurve machine,' Dinner added incongruously. They all looked at him in bemusement.

'Wharra you on about?'

'Wharra you on, more like?'

Dinner failed to reply and took a swig from his drink, very self-conscious, but trying to remain and look cool. Even he did not know why he said it. It was just a phrase he liked which came to mind. He wasn't even a fan of Barry White and always avoided anything written about him when he read *Melody Maker*. Just keep calm, look cool, he said to himself as he exhaled a large ring of smoke, followed by a succession of smaller ones from his mouth.

'Anyway, getting back to the real world,' Phil broke in, raising an eyebrow, his expression somewhat perplexed, mirroring those of his friends, 'the Aberavon match would pitch you directly in opposition to Steve James. It's an opportunity to get one over him, a final trial if you like. If you ran rings round him, it would be impossible for the selectors to ignore you for the next match against England. The press would have a field day if you didn't get picked.' Joe's ears pricked up and he stared at Phil, absorbing the implication of his every word.

'Aren't we getting a bit ahead of ourselves 'ere,' Gethin commented, digging down deep with his index finger to retrieve the last tiny morsels of smoky bacon crisps from their bag. 'If James is crap against Ireland, Joe'll probably be in for Scotland. Conversely, if James plays well in the internationals or even if Wales win and he plays average, they'll still pick him for the England game even if Joe gets the better of 'im against Aberavon. It's all ifs and buts and you never really know what's going on in the heads of the selectors.'

'Talk about stating the bleeding obvious,' Pete interrupted sarcastically and forcibly, glancing at Helen. 'Hey, Geth, why don't you just shurrup until you've got something interesting to say,' he continued aggressively. Gethin looked at Pete, stunned at the sharpness of his tone.

'Hey, there was no need for that,' Dave retorted.

Pete took a large swig from his pint glass and, after wiping his mouth with the back of his sleeve, went quiet. His face was crimson and his brow sweaty and he appeared to be on the point of blowing his top. Everybody around the table was puzzled and they all looked at each other in wide-eyed amazement.

'Let's just calm it down.'

Sue caught Helen's eye and wondered if Pete's mood had anything to do with his on/off relationship with her friend. Though he was one of Joe's best friends, Sue was not all that keen on Pete. He could be charming at times and initially Helen had liked his attention and company. But it soon became apparent that he was only after one thing, which Helen refused to provide, and a very obsessive nature came to the fore. He would frequently show anger towards Helen and on two occasions he had stormed out of pubs, leaving Helen behind all alone. After evenings of frustration and fury, Pete would always apologise subsequently and they would rekindle their relationship. However, at a New Year's party only a few days before, Pete, plied with alcohol, had manhandled her at the top of the stairs of the house where the party was taking place and tried to force her into a nearby bedroom. Helen had to physically grab his wrists before slipping under his grasp and fleeing down the flight of stairs into the living room. Sue had been there with Joe. Helen explained what had happened and being upset, she had decided to walk home. Sue had accompanied her and only returned well after midnight so missing the celebration with Joe. She was furious with Pete, as was Joe, who scolded his friend, calling him every name under the sun and threatening to smash his face in if he did anything similar again. Pete knew he had done wrong and asked Sue to apologise to Helen on his behalf before grabbing his coat and leaving for home.

But now, Sue could not understand why Pete had been so aggressive towards Gethin. Had he tried it on with Helen? Had they been getting close? Helen had never mentioned Gethin before in any amorous sense. She looked at Helen who just shrugged her shoulders. Joe was aware of what was going on around the table but he took no interest. His mind was racing in a number of different directions, fortified by drink.

'Pete, pass me the kitty, will you? I'll get another round in,' Dave requested.

'I'll come with you.' Pete got up from the table and walked over to the bar. He knew he had stepped over the line and needed to regain his composure away from the table.

Dave got up behind him. 'The same again?' he enquired. Everybody nodded their heads approvingly.

'Gessome more crisps in and pork scratchings, will you? I'm starving and I need something to absorb these beers.'

'Good idea.'

'Some dry roasted peanuts as well if you don't mind,' Sue added. 'Not the salted ones. They're really bad for you apparently and much more fattening.'

'P'rhaps we should get those for Dinner then?' Gethin replied, smiling, and Dave laughed out loud as he picked up the girls' empty glasses, the rims of which were smeared with pink lipstick. Dinner just stared into oblivion, his head held high, not responding. He's a bit odd, Ann thought.

'I didn't realise we were playing Aberavon before the England game. You're right, Phil, if I come up against James and do him over, I've got a good chance of being picked for the international,' Joe mused. Always the emphasis on the England game, Sue thought.

'That's right but hopefully you'll be in the team before then against Scotland.'

'D'you reckon James will play in the Aberavon game, though?' Joe asked, showing no interest in Phil's comment about the Scotland game. Once again, Sue picked up on this. 'You know what I mean, players always feign some injury if they want to miss a game against a rival who would have more to gain. What's the point of playing if there's a chance you'll get shown up? Knowing Steve James, he'll just crap out.'

'Could be, but who knows, he might be under a load of pressure himself. If Wales are playing poorly and his position is under threat, he'll feel the need to play and put one over on you, his main rival. He might have no choice. If he craps out under these circumstances, they'll probably pick you.'

'I'm sure Bill Johnson and Stan the Man Williams will have something to say about that. They'll find any old excuse to talk me down. I reckon Johnson's shagging Williams as well as James.'

'A ménage-à-trois,' Dinner threw in casually.

'Yeah, something like that, Din,' Gethin replied, not really sure what a ménage-à-trois was. Everybody laughed around the table, except for the girls who thought Joe's comment too crude.

'Pardon my French, girls, or should I say, pardon Dinner's French, literally. Ah, more beer!' Joe looked up to see Pete and Dave returning from the bar, flinging bags of crisps, nuts and pork scratchings in every direction.

'Put him in the slips,' Dave bellowed as Phil plucked a misdirected bag of cheese and onion from above his head. 'So 'ave we decided if Joe's in the team yet?'

'Don't worry,' Helen replied with a twinkle in her eye, 'Phil's got it all worked out.'

'So there'll be a repeat of Joe against Harrison then,' Dave continued in light fashion before downing a third of his new pint in one go. He looked at his Albright suspiciously. 'D'you reckon they water the beer down 'ere,' he whispered.

'Nah! Albright always tastes like that. Gnat's piss, it is. I dunno how you can drink the stuff,' Gethin commented before taking a good swig of his Guinness, which left a line of white foam on his top lip.'

'I hope that's Guinness around your mouth, Geth,' Joe remarked enigmatically. 'You haven't been servicing Bill Johnson like Steve James has, I hope?'

'That's disgusting!' Sue screamed, understanding the comment immediately and punching Joe firmly on the shoulder.

'Ow, that hurt.'

'I hope so. That's disgusting what you said,' though everybody around the table was laughing. Gethin wiped the Guinness away quickly from his mouth. Ann dropped her eyes a little shyly and with his leg shaking slightly, Dinner wondered if she picked up on the joke and whether, in fact, she did the deed.

Pete changed the subject. 'So are you gonna stiff-arm Harrison over the hoardings again, assuming you play against England, which Phil assures us you most certainly will? Phil, you should be the chairman of the Big Five, not that wanker, Johnson. That was superb when you did that. All hell broke loose. Can you imagine that on national telly? It'd be brill.'

'All I can say is that if I play in that match, I'll certainly leave my mark.' Joe wondered if he was revealing too much of his intentions and knew there was a danger of the drink loosening his tongue. He left the statement in the air as he grabbed his beer and took another swig.

'Not just on telly but in front of Prince Charles as well 'cos I read he's gonna be at the match, too. Part of his, "look how much time I spend with my loyal subjects campaign". He's such a toss-pot.'

'Well said,' Joe concurred, wiping his mouth and making a grab for a bag of nuts on the table. 'He's a total twat. What's jug ears got in common with us 'en? Why doesn't he just stay put in England or Scotland or wherever it is he lives, the wanker?' Joe's voice was becoming raised and his tone was turning more aggressive.

'Who saw Morecombe & Wise on Christmas Day?' Sue tried to change the subject as Joe placed a handful of nuts into his mouth. She recognised the tell-tale signs, as did most of the others, that Joe was about to go off on another one of his anti-English tirades.

'Who didn't? They were brilliant, just so funny. My dad was splitting his sides laughing. Just hilarious, they are. Did you see Angela Rippon dancing? She was amazing. I'd die for legs like that.' Ann smiled as she recalled the newsreader's dance routine on the show.

'Why, are Eric and Ernie coming to the match as well 'en? If they do, the last thing they'll see is a comedy show, I promise. I tell you, Harrison an' all the English are gonna get it well and truly if they pick me. He's no different to Prince Charles. They're both arrogant twats who take great pleasure in looking down on us from their high horses. What is it about us Welsh? We seem to be more than happy to let the English run their rule over us. They couldn't give a stuff about us. We should be governing ourselves. We don't need 'em. We just need to stand up to them and show a bit of courage and tell 'em to fuck off. And when I say courage, I mean courage. Not fancy words or anything like that but a bit of aggression, something to make 'em take us seriously.'

Pete, Dave and Sue's eyes connected and they all felt a sense of unease. Ann and Gethin had not heard such vehemence from Joe before and were surprised and yet enthralled. Ann welcomed the move away from rugby conversation. Helen looked longingly at him. She loved it when he became serious and aggressive.

'Well, Joe, one day, who knows? Maybe Wales will have its independence but I don't think things are too bad as they are now.' Dinner's comment was uttered with such an air of calmness and complacency that Sue knew that Joe would explode with all the fire of the true believer. She was not mistaken.

'It's just that fucking attitude that pisses me off about people today.'

'Keep it down, Joe,' Sue intervened, noticing how the heads of the pub's customers sitting closest to their table had turned towards them.

'Why should I? The whole of Wales should wake up and listen. We're a fucking disgrace. All small nations with a grievance are fighting hard for independence and we just sit on our fat arses doing fuck all. Look at the Basques, the Irish, the Palestinians. They're taking huge risks, fighting and dying for their cause.'

'And killing lots of innocent people along the way.' Ann was not afraid to raise her head above the parapet and argue back in disgust.

'Not always so innocent,' Joe retorted weakly and unconvincingly.

'Let's not go there, Joe,' Pete remarked, like Sue, trying to change the subject.

'No, let us go there!' Joe yelled, his eyes staring directly and aggressively towards him. 'We've been downtrodden for years. The English have always looked down on us and made us feel inferior, trying to rule our lives. Where are all the jobs? Not 'ere they're not. That government in London looks after itself. We should be in control of our own destiny.' Joe's tone had moderated and he was almost pleading with his friends around the table to take what he was saying seriously. 'Surely it makes sense for us to govern ourselves. We are a nation, after all, for God's sake, with its own language, its own culture, its own way of doing things, its own personality and I tell you, the way things are going right now, that's all gonna change and we might as well all lie down and die if we allow it to happen.'

'I think you're exaggerating a bit.' Ann tried to intervene reasonably but she was shot down by a tirade from Joe.

'Exaggerating! Are you stupid or summing?' Joe's tone was rasping and ugly.

'Joe, that's enough,' Sue retorted angrily. 'Apologise to Ann for that. That's totally uncalled for.'

'It's alright, Sue,' Ann replied to her friend whilst everybody else around the table sipped their drinks, their eyes avoiding contact with Joe's. 'I don't think it's unreasonable to hold the views you have and I'm sure there are many who would agree with you, but these matters should be resolved through politics and democracy. If the majority of Welsh people believe what you believe in, then fine, let's become independent. There are ways of bringing this about but only if there's a majority. But if you look at Plaid's support in the recent elections, they're miles behind Labour and even the Tories so there's no desire at all for Welsh independence.'

'Ann, you're talking bollocks.' Everybody looked at each other, smiled and shook their heads in the knowledge that Ann was totally in the right. Sue was inwardly furious at Joe's behaviour towards her friend but said nothing as she knew that Ann was more than capable of arguing for herself and did not seem put out by the rudeness coming her way. 'And I'll tell you why,' Joe went on, only stopping for a moment to take another large swig of his pint. 'People in this country know that Plaid will never succeed so they can't be bothered to vote for 'em. But deep down, they believe in what Plaid stands for. It's no different to those other countries or regions fighting for independence. The politics in those lands will never represent what people truly believe in 'cos the main parties are all basically loyal to their states just like they are in this country. People know the only chance they'll have of getting their own way is through an armed struggle and when they see this succeeding, more people will follow. There's no doubt about it; history tells us this. Think back to the United States. It was a war that succeeded in getting the English kicked out of there, or Mexico when they fought the Spanish. I tell you, the English are gonna be booted out of Northern Ireland one day, and sooner rather than later, believe me, and when that 'appens, we'll all be sitting here in the Maltsters thinking why the fuck couldn't we have done the same ourselves? Have any of you ever read anything about Michael Collins?' Before anybody could open their mouths, Joe carried on. 'Michael Collins was a famous IRA leader back in the early part of the century and just through sheer personality, determination and courage, he galvanised hordes of young Irish people down in the west of Ireland to take up arms and fight the English. And he succeeded when the Irish Free State was created. The IRA is doing the same up in the north today and you watch, they'll get their way eventually. The point I'm making is that we can achieve this as well. The only thing the Welsh people need is for someone to lead them in the struggle.' Joe suddenly stopped talking, allowing his words to sink deep into the minds of his friends. He looked up to await a response, gazing at Ann, in particular, but nobody replied. He finished off the beer in front of him and asked Pete for the kitty.

'Here it is. It's getting a bit low. P'haps we'll 'ave another whip after this round.'

Joe just grabbed the cash and made no acknowledgement towards him. He shot off to the bar without asking anybody what they were having. Nobody made an initial move to help him. They all just stared at each other, a mixture of bemusement, bewilderment, incredulity and admiration etched across their faces. Sue, in particular, looked annoyed. She hated Joe when he was in this mood. Everything was perfect in their relationship except for when he was like this. She tried to put it down to the drink but she knew Joe was like this even when sober. Okay, perhaps the drink had made him somewhat ruder than usual and she felt mortified for Ann, but in essence, she had to accept that he felt very strongly about Welsh independence and that he truly had a deep-rooted resentment, even hatred, for England and all things English. That's just the way he is, she concluded.

'Is he serious?' Phil whispered, keeping a close eye on Joe at the bar. 'Am I missing something but is he advocating some form of violent action against the English?'

'No, you 'eard him right. It's not the first time he's gone on like this,' Dave replied in a resigned manner. 'I'm sure the beer's not helping but he's pretty consistent in his views.'

'He's a nutter,' Gethin said in a low voice before noticing he still had half his pint in front of him and that he was falling behind the others. He tried to take a large gulp but he struggled.

'Wha' did you say?' Pete stared menacingly at Gethin. Everybody's ears pricked up at the threatening tone, particularly Sue and Helen.

'I said he's a nutter, having views like that, just crazy.'

'You'd better watch yourself.' Pete was now pointing his finger directly at Gethin, who looked back, startled.

'Oi, calm down, Pete.' Dave put a hand on his shoulder. 'What's up with you tonight, you're a bit feisty?' Helen looked down at the table trying to ignore them.

'I just don't like anybody talking about Joe behind his back like that, that's all.' Pete grabbed his pint glass and peered inside at the dregs. His face was red with fury and his shoulders were tense. He tipped his head right back and tilted the glass to a vertical position, his tongue licking at the tiny drops of beer that ran slowly down inside. When it was totally drained he calmly placed it on the table. For a few seconds, it was all peace and quiet but then, without warning, he flung himself across the table faster than a Michael Holding toe-crushing yorker to where Gethin was taking another sip from his glass and the two of them ended up on the floor, with Pete on top, raining punches down on him. Half the glasses on the table crashed to the floor and Helen moved sharply to her right to avoid the flailing arms. Gethin had a good hold of Pete's wrists and so prevented any heavy blows landing on him. His shirt was torn, however, and drenched in beer.

'You keep your hands off her, orrite! She's got nothing to do with you,' Pete yelled as he tried to free his arms. Dave and Phil immediately rushed over and tried to pull Pete away. In a flash, Bob, the barman, hurtled towards them, manoeuvred himself in between Dave and Phil, grabbed Pete with all his considerable might and threw him to the side of Gethin.

'You, gerrout now!' Bob shouted, pointing at Pete, 'an' you can gerrout, too,' looking directly at Gethin.

'I 'aven't done nothing,' Gethin protested, still lying on his back.

'Gerrout, both of you, now!' Bob had no sympathy. Their friends were standing around them with the exception of Dinner who had calmly moved his chair back away from the commotion and lit another cigarette. Three couples who had been sitting close by were also standing but they soon regained their seats as the fighting died down. Helen and Sue were standing next to each other, Sue's arm around Helen who was visibly shaken.

Pete jumped up and with his face full of rage, he grabbed his green Parka from the floor on to which it had fallen. He strode quickly and purposefully towards the front door, putting his coat on at the same time. As he left, he slammed the door behind him. He did not once look back. Gethin got up more slowly, still bewildered at the turn of events. He made a futile attempt to close his torn shirt and wipe away the beer before raising his eyes to the heavens and shaking his head. Now that Pete had stormed out, he hoped that under cool reflection, he might be allowed to stay but Bob had not left the scene and repeated forcibly for him to get out.

'It had nothing ...'

'Just gerrout!' Bob was in no mood to listen to any mitigation.

'It's best you leave, Geth,' Phil reasoned and he passed him his black trench coat. Gethin took it slowly, looked apologetically at his friends who shook their heads in sympathy and walked towards the door. He could feel the eyes of all the pub's customers digging deeply into his back before finally exiting.

Bob left the scene and everybody returned to their places. Dinner slyly moved his chair round towards where Ann was sitting, now that more space had been created and before Ann had any chance to move herself. She groaned inwardly.

'What was that all about?' Phil began, shaking his head and looking up towards the bar to see whether Joe would be returning soon with a new round of drinks.

'I dunno. He's been in a mood for ages, has Pete. He must have thought that Gethin was getting a bit too close to you, Hel. What d'you reckon?'

'It's nothing, let's just leave it,' Helen replied softly, Sue squeezing her shoulder more firmly, concerned for her friend.

'I 'ope Pete's not waiting for him outside,' Dave suddenly blurted out. They all looked at each other with worried expressions on their faces. Nobody said anything. Eventually, Dave volunteered to take a look. He left his seat and walked out of the pub. Everybody stared intently at the front door for what seemed like an age before Dave re-entered. He immediately shrugged his shoulders. 'I couldn't see either of them so I assume everything's okay. If it's not, well, there's nothing we can do about it now.' They all looked at each other once more before relaxing.

'Now where were we? Yeah, that's right. We were talking about what Joe had been saying.' It was Phil who picked up the conversation. The mention of Joe's name made them all turn their heads towards the bar to see where their friend was. All they could see was his back as he waited to be served. Bob had temporarily gone to the toilets to clean himself up so leaving the bar short-staffed and the service slow.

'I'll go up and help him with the drinks in a minute,' Sue offered.

'He might be able to handle 'em himself, being as there are two less this time,' Dave responded with a smile, his friends grinning.

'I can respect Joe's views and even understand 'em to a certain extent but I got the impression he wants to be some great leader who everybody will follow to kick the English out of Wales.'

'Yeah, summing like that, I think.'

'Dew, I think he's gone a bit soft in the 'ead. Sue, you are looking after 'im now, aren't you?' Dave added jokingly.

'Oh, don't worry, she's looking after him alright, aren't you?' Helen replied with a wink, earning herself a playful elbow in the ribs from Sue.

'Don't worry, he's fine,' Sue responded unconvincingly. 'He holds the views he does. So what, it's not as if anything'll come of it.' She looked down at the table to see if any crisps remained, though, in reality, it was more a ruse to avoid eye contact with her friends. The missing Luger returned to her thoughts. She could not get it out of her head and the stress of trying to evaluate whether Joe had any intention of using it or not was starting to unsettle her. She wished she could share her concerns with someone like Helen or Ann, or even Dave, or anybody, but if Joe got to know, he'd be furious particularly after he had assured her he had not stolen it in the first place. If he thought she didn't believe him, she feared he would finish with her this time for certain. If there was no trust, there was no relationship. And she could not expunge the thought that any worries she had were downright crazy. Joe, shooting someone? That was ridiculous. This wasn't some melodramatic television drama, this was real life. These things didn't happen.

'Yeah, I wouldn't worry about it,' Dave intervened. 'It's just the drink talking. It's all a load of rubbish. Ann, you had it in one.' Ann smiled back at him which annoyed Dinner but whose expression remained unmoved all the same.

* * *

When Joe left his seat to go up to the bar, his mind was spinning furiously like a top. The more often he expressed his views, the more just he believed the cause and the more resolute he became. He loved to listen to the great orators in history like Kennedy or Martin Luther King or even Michael Foot amongst today's Parliamentarians. He found them truly inspiring and he wondered if his little oration at the table had inspired his friends or only himself. A bit of drink always helped and didn't he once read that Nye Bevan had always liked a tipple before taking to the platform. Ann, the stupid old cow, just represented the apathy that existed today, the very reason why Wales would always be subservient to the English. His other friends were no better. They were not serious people with strong views about anything and they did not possess the will to change things. Drink, girls, rugby, other sports, pop music; that's all the boys were interested in and as for the girls it was boys, relationships, clothes, marriage, kids, that's all, perhaps with a few pretty-boy pop stars thrown in as well. They were happy the way things were. Well, I'm not, he thought, and I'm going to do something about it.

'Joe, Joe, I'm not disturbing you, am I?' The lilting tone of Bronwyn, the bar girl's voice, broke into his reverie. Rumours abounded that she was Bob's love interest, though at twenty years of age she was not even half his age. They never discussed their relationship publicly although all his male friends privately envied his being able to fondle her size 38 DD bosom.

'Sorry, Bron, miles away. Same all round, you know, the same as Pete ordered last time,' Joe replied, his eyes automatically homing in on her chest.

It was when Bronwyn turned to fetch the pint glasses that everybody in the pub heard the almighty crash of tables and glass and raised voices emanating from Joe's group of friends. Those at the bar, including Joe, spun around and observed the commotion. From the corner of his eye, Joe saw Bob hurtle through the swing door of the bar counter and menacingly approach his table at such speed that, for a moment, he thought Bob was going to launch a Kung Fu kick, Bruce Lee-like, at Pete and Gethin wrestling on the floor. Joe just stood there bemused, wondering what was going on. It probably had something to do with Pete breaking up with Helen because he had been in such a bad mood for days and, in particular, this evening. Perhaps Gethin had got a bit too close to her, he thought. As Bob broke them up and ordered them from the pub, Joe shook his head despondently and turned his back on the scene. Bronwyn was still transfixed and staring open-mouthed at the commotion, two empty pint glasses in her hands. Though Joe was now facing her, he did not hurry her to complete the round. He looked down at the coins he was passing from hand to hand, deeply pensive. Am I kidding myself? The scene only served to confirm his thoughts of a moment ago and once again he shook his head slowly. Do I really believe that stupid fuckers like Pete and Gethin are going to get involved and commit themselves to driving the English out of Wales? Aren't most boys of their age the same? The alcohol had certainly stirred his emotions, firstly in a positive way by reinforcing his resolve and commitment but now negatively by bringing to mind the doubts he had about youngsters today.

And yet, he recalled the words of Sue and Helen who had both independently stated that they knew boys who expressed the same views as him. Dafydd, Ieuan and Robert were also adamant that an undercurrent of militant nationalists were in place just ready to be given a lead. Admittedly, he did not know any of them but surely they would not have said what they said if there was no truth to it. No, he was convinced like-minded people did exist, maybe not his immediate friends, but then he couldn't expect everybody. After all, the IRA was only a tiny minority when compared to the whole Irish Catholic population. He only needed a hardcore to follow his lead and then, over time, as momentum built, the rest would follow, if not in body then certainly in mind and by then, that would be enough to convince the English to grant Wales its independence just like they had done pretty much everywhere else in the old Empire. When it came down to it, history told him that the English would surrender to concerted and just direct action.

'Hello, Joe, hello, can you hear me? That'll be one pound sixty-five. My God, you really do 'ave a lot on your mind tonight.'

'Sorry, Bron.' He apologised once again as he pulled out a note and counted the relevant change from all the coins in his hand. Just as he handed over the money, there was a tap on his shoulder and Sue appeared behind him. 'Thanks, can you manage these? I can take the rest. What 'appened over there?'

'Pete got a bit uptight with Gethin about Helen, that's all. He can be such a dick sometimes. He's been awful to her lately. It's his entire fault and he knows it. Can you ask for a tray? I'm gonna spill these, I'm sure.' Bronwyn had read Sue's mind and she passed over a tray before Joe had even had time to turn around.

'You didn't half miss something a minute ago, Joe. Pete just went psycho with Gethin,' Dave remarked as he grabbed his pint of Albright from the tray. He thought he'd give it one more try. 'Shit,' he added as he spilled some of the beer on to his fingers, 'I always do that,' and he flicked some drops behind his back before sucking at the rest.

'I saw it from the bar. Idiots, both of them.'

As they made themselves comfortable, they noticed there were two extra pints on the table. Joe had failed to advise Bronwyn that with Pete and Gethin thrown out, they would not be needed. 'Looks like we've got a couple spare,' Dave observed. 'I've no doubt we'll take great pleasure in helping Pete and Gethin finish their drinks.'

'Fantasticamundo,' Dinner chirped, aping the Fonz, another one of his idols.

'P'rhaps we should give 'em back some of the whip?' Helen pondered.

'No chance!' Joe was adamant. 'If they want to behave like a couple of twats, that's their problem. Lerrem pay for embarrassing us as their friends.' Everybody nodded their heads in agreement.

Phil took up the conversation. 'If Steve James doesn't...'

He barely got out a few words before Ann shouted him down. 'Enough rugby, please!' she bellowed, waving her hands furiously in front of her.

'Well said, Ann,' Sue agreed, supporting her friend. 'No more rugby, politics, Pete or Gethin for the rest of the evening, orrite!' Helen nodded her head in an exaggerated manner, pursing her lips at the same time. The sisterhood was taking over. All the boys remained silent, taking the opportunity to sink a good quarter each of their pints. 'It must have been half an hour ago when I asked but who saw Morecombe and Wise on Christmas Day?'

The rest of the evening passed off without further drama. There was much laughter, drinking, flirting and light-hearted conversation. Even Dinner smiled once or twice and contributed a funny line or two in his laconic way. There were many groans from the boys when Helen and Sue returned from the jukebox and the syrupy singing of the Osmonds sounded from the speaker above them and there were many whoops and much encouragement as the same two began dancing to David Bowie and ABBA. Their corner of the pub was like a private party in all but name, though none of the other customers seemed to mind. In fact, as Bob called time, the whole pub was singing along to *American Pie*. Bob had a broad smile on his face. Yes, there had been a fracas but he was used to that. He was smiling because he estimated his takings for the evening to be similar to those of Christmas Eve, very healthy indeed. It also helped his mood to know Bronwyn was staying over that night.

Joe, too, was smiling and laughing and singing though not dancing despite Sue's best efforts, tugging hard at his arms to bring him to his feet. Beneath it all, however, his mind was racing. At the end of the evening, his thoughts took him back to the original purpose for their being there in the first place. It was meant to be a celebration of his being selected to play for Wales. Reality hit him when he reminded himself that he had failed in this objective and he became more sullen when he understood better the implication of this failure. All his friends and everybody else in the pub had been sympathetic, but sympathy was not going to get him anywhere. As much as he tried to believe it, selection for the Welsh team was not totally in his hands. He could play well but if the incumbents were doing okay and Wales were winning, his chances were diminished. Underpinning all this was the belief that some prejudice existed against him among the selectors and even within his own club. If it was not for the drink or the convivial atmosphere, he would have felt quite depressed. But thanks to Phil, God bless him, the human computer and rugby oracle, a pinprick of light did appear at the end of the tunnel in that there was the possibility of his playing against Steve James in a club match just one week before the England international. It would be a final opportunity, a chance to outplay him and to force the hands of the selectors. It was a straw to clutch on, only a straw and not a very strong one at that, but at least it was something.

19

The *Tiger* comic flopped on to the doormat the second Mr Chilani had finished with that morning's *Western Mail*. Sunshine ran towards the front door, sniffed the comic, looked around in a befuddled fashion and returned to the armchair in the living room. The clatter of the letterbox always had this effect on her. Once there, she was never interested in any of the findings. None of the Chilani family could understand why after thirteen years she continued with this fruitless routine. A very strange cat, they all concluded. Usually, Marco would jump from his chair to retrieve the comic but this was no usual morning. Instead, he grabbed the newspaper and went immediately to the back page.

Prior to this, Marco had been impatiently eating his *Frosties* as his father read the paper at breakfast, a hot cup of tea steaming in front of him and two pieces of toast on the plate beside it. Hidden behind the newspaper, Marco could not see his father's face but only the fine line of cigarette smoke which floated away to the ceiling.

'What's it say, Dad?'

There was no reply and slightly fearfully, Marco did not repeat the question. It seemed to him that his father was forbidden to say a word until he had left the house for without fail, each morning, he would take his seat, light a cigarette and grab the newspaper. Instantaneously, his wife would place the cup of tea and toast in front of him and a few digestive biscuits on a plate in the middle of the table. After fifteen wordless minutes, he would stand up, grab his coat and cap from under the stairs and stride towards and then out of the front door. The only difference this late February, Saturday morning was that he was taking much longer than normal to read the paper.

'Here you are.'

Marco was quietly surprised to learn that his father did indeed possess a tongue as he saw him leave the table. The lead story on the back page revolved around that afternoon's rugby match between Pontypridd and Aberavon. However, the main interest in the match was not so much who would come out on top between the two sides but more, who would come out on top in the showdown between Joe Chilani and Steve James. Many commentators believed the winner of this showdown would almost certainly be selected to play for Wales the following Saturday against England.

Although Marco was somewhat indifferent to what went on in his brother's life, even he had been consumed by the debate raging in the principality as to who should play alongside Geraint Lewis in the centre for the forthcoming international. Whilst Joe's name had frequently appeared in print, the coverage during the past week was of a much greater magnitude than usual with a number of photographs and short biographical details accompanying every article. What's more, Joe was being discussed on national Welsh television during sports' bulletins, with film of him in action. On one occasion, he even gave a lengthy interview about his ambitions, his family, his prospects and what it would mean to be selected for Wales.

Joe's family had felt quite nervous when he appeared on screen for this interview, hoping he would come across well. They were proud of what Joe was achieving on the rugby field but they were not used to the accompanying media spotlight. His mother hoped he would speak correctly and fluently, which he did, but she kept to herself her annoyance that he had not brushed back his hair and that his tie was slightly askew. She was more shocked at the broadness of his Welsh accent which seemed accentuated on screen. Marco was relieved he had not said anything which might embarrass him, fearing some mild ridicule from his friends, though it annoyed him when Joe said he was the only good rugby player in his family. His father as ever kept his thoughts to himself but those who knew him best felt that afterwards, he walked just that little bit more purposefully, that he held his head that little bit higher and that his chest protruded that little bit more proudly.

Marco devoured the coverage in the newspaper and not the *Frosties* which soon turned into a brown sludge in his dish. His tea, too, became cold and his mother gently chided him to drink it up quickly. It was as if Marco had become deaf for he gave no reaction as he continued to read the rugby coverage. It was quite clear that the stakes were high for both Joe and Steve James. As the prophet of all things rugby, Phil Jones, had forecast during that boozy, punchy night just after New Year in the Maltsters Arms, the upcoming match between Pontypridd and Aberavon would indeed have a major say in deciding whether Joe would be selected for the Welsh team.

During the past couple of months, Wales had made an indifferent start to their Five Nations campaign. As expected, they had convincingly beaten a typically erratic Irish side whose form as ever veered between hot and cold like a defrosting vindaloo. Whilst Tony Mulligan had twice easily skipped past Steve James during the game, the latter did have the satisfaction of scoring a try and making a final pass for another. Unsurprisingly, after such a comprehensive victory, the selectors made no changes for the next game against Scotland. Joe was disappointed that James had kept his place though, reluctantly, he had understood why. He was encouraged, however, at comment in the media about James's indifferent tackling and how such a weakness would be targeted by future opponents.

The match in Edinburgh had proved to be a much more challenging affair for the Welsh and although Wales had lost by only a handful of points, there was no denying that Scotland had been dominant and had deserved their victory. The scoreline, it was accepted, had flattered Wales. As ever, whenever Wales lost an international match, criticism throughout the principality was fierce and often irrational, but not unexpected. The position of many players in the team came up for discussion, none more so than at prop forward where the advocates of Rocky Evans were granted full licence to support their player as the Welsh scrum had buckled embarrassingly on a number of occasions against the committed Scottish forwards.

Rocky Evans was not the only Pontypridd player to have his supporters. The clamour for Joe's inclusion in the national side was now deafening. Whilst it would have been unfair to single out Steve James as the person mainly responsible for the Welsh defeat, it was clear that his lack of strength in the tackle was putting his team under pressure and the Welsh back row was often in retreat to bolster up his defence. As usual, James's passing was precise and on one occasion, a clearing kick under severe pressure near his own tryline earned him generous applause as the ball flew into touch close to the halfway line. However, on another occasion, an interception and feed to James by the mercurial Welsh fly-half, Bleddyn Howells, had shown up Steve James's lack of speed as he was easily caught and tackled within ten yards by his opposite centre despite the latter having to stop and turn before tracking back to catch his opponent. The thirty thousand Welshmen in Murrayfield, the one hundred thousand in the pubs of Edinburgh and the three million watching on television back in Wales all gave out a collective groan which could probably have been heard at Twickenham where England were playing France at the same time. If James had taken that chance, Wales might well have sneaked a victory. The only person who did not groan was Joe as he watched the match in the Pontypridd RFC clubhouse. He knew straight away that this one incident would help his cause no end. Phil Jones was watching the match in the clubhouse as well and he turned instinctively towards Joe. They caught each other's eye and smiled.

'*Che cosa dice, Marco?*' Even Mrs Chilani was keen to know what the papers were saying about the match in the afternoon and, in particular, about her elder son. After a momentary pause, Marco précised the comment with his mother all ears as she washed up the dishes.

'Basically, it says that a strong performance by Giuseppe this afternoon should be enough for him to get picked next week. They're really having a go at Steve James, saying he would have to have the game of his life to save his place. There's some comment, though, about whether Giuseppe is ready, you know, how young he is and all that. There's one guy who thinks that James should play next week whatever happens because experience will be everything against England. But saying that, there's no doubt most people are on Giuseppe's side. There's some stuff about how good James Harrison is and that Giuseppe's tackling is much stronger than Steve James's and how that'll be important next week.'

His mother had switched off at the mention of tackling, Steve James and James Harrison. She had no interest in rugby or the various players. It was enough to know that most of the opinion was on Joe's side. She knew it was important for him to play for Wales and she knew that her family would be the centre of attention in the town if, indeed, he was selected. But despite all of this, she was so caring of her son and so fearful of the physical and violent nature of the sport that if Joe walked into the kitchen at that very moment and said he would give it all up, she would embrace him with delight.

Marco placed the newspaper on the table and scampered to the front door. Now that he knew what was being written about his brother, his attention turned to *Tiger* and the latest adventures in the lives of Roy Race, Skid Solo and Johnny Cougar. As he picked up the comic, he saw a dishevelled Joe walking slowly down the stairs out of the corner of his eye.

'*Dov'è tuo fratello?*' Mrs Chilani asked Marco, wondering when Joe would make an appearance. Before he could answer and on cue, Joe ambled into the kitchen, rubbing his eyes, barefoot, and wearing a sweatshirt which did not co-ordinate with his striped pyjama bottoms. His hair was unkempt and he stifled a yawn. Mrs Chilani wondered whether this was the fine specimen of a man they were writing about in the newspaper. It was barely credible.

'Just some coffee, Mum, and some juice, thanks. I won't have anything cooked today. I'm not really hungry. I'll have a piece of toast, that's all.' Joe gave his order before his mother had the chance to voice any alternatives.

Marco returned to the table and immersed himself in his comic, oblivious to his brother's presence. As his mother poured the coffee, Joe took the newspaper and scanned the back page quickly. He knew what was at stake this afternoon and knew the general commentary around the match in the media. There was no reason to get absorbed in yet another article. He turned to the front page where the beaming smile of the fresh-faced Prince of Wales stared back at him. Joe looked into his eyes and for a moment there was a real connection between the two of them as if Prince Charles was physically there in front of him. Joe's demeanour became more severe and he felt his chest heave slightly at the thought that if everything went to plan, one week from today, he would indeed be staring into the Prince of Wales's eyes and not just at a photograph of him. He might be smiling at opening a new shopping centre in Swansea yesterday, Joe thought, but I wonder what his face will be like when we meet next week. He threw the paper down and even Marco drew his eyes away from his comic as it slapped hard against the wooden table. Joe took two deep breaths to regain his composure before drinking the glass of grapefruit juice in front of him. His mother re-poured the juice the second he placed the empty glass back on to the table. She could see that Joe's mind was distant and so chose not to enter into any conversation with him, thinking that he must be concentrating on the match in the afternoon. How wrong she was.

'Ta, Mum.' Joe rose from his chair, walked past his brother and set off for the bathroom. Marco had been expecting a flick of the ear or some sarcastic comment on his way but neither of them came. Joe ran the bath before returning to his bedroom to undress. He walked back to the bathroom and stepped into the hot, steamy water. After sitting down, he scattered a few flakes from the Radox box, turned off the taps and slid himself forwards so that only his head protruded above the surface. He closed his eyes and felt beads of perspiration forming on his forehead. Everything was still and quiet and the thought flashed across his mind that this might well be the last Saturday he ever spent at home. Despite the hot water, the thought chilled and unsettled him. He had hoped that the bath would help him to relax and clear his mind of the tumultuous events of the following Saturday, which he struggled to shake from his mind, but it was difficult.

The previous night had been terrible. He had slept in fits and starts and the darkness only exacerbated his worries. His resolve had been severely tested. Why was he doing this? Does it really matter? What would be the effect on his family and Sue? She had already lost her parents in tragic circumstances. Was it fair to put her through another horrific event? Was he strong enough, really strong enough to carry it through? He had had such serious doubts and misgivings that he tore himself away from his bed and switched on, not just the bedside lamp, but the main light in the room. He had sat on the edge of his bed for what seemed like hours. The light had helped but now the silence tormented him. He looked at the clock next to the bedside lamp. Still only two-thirty. He begged for the next hours to pass quickly, to hear the comforting sounds of his family traipsing around the house or the purring engines of motor vehicles on Graigwen Hill to the side of the house. He eventually decided to listen to Radio Luxembourg through the crackle of his small transistor radio. He switched off the two lights and lay in bed with the radio next to his head on the pillow. The sound was wonderful to his ears and it helped him get through the night.

Thankfully, the steaming bubbly water gradually took effect and his mind and body began to relax. He reached out for the yellow flannel which was resting beside the Radox box on the rim of the avocado-green bath tub, dipped it in the water, wrung it out and placed it flat over his face. He shut his eyes immediately. He could no longer feel the beads of perspiration running down his temples as the absorbent flannel did its job. He felt so warm and comfortable that he wondered whether he would be able to rid himself of these feelings in time to harden up for the match in the afternoon. The match in the afternoon; the biggest match of his life. So unsettling had the night been and so vivid the images of the scenes next Saturday, he had barely given a moment's thought to the game against Aberavon and his confrontation with Steve James. Under the flannel, his mind suddenly turned to it. His relaxed state bred confidence. He believed he was superior to Steve James. He was stronger, a better tackler and faster. He also knew that his forwards would be too strong for the opposition and that this would make it easier for him to perform in the game as he was likely to be on the front foot more often than not. James, in contrast, would be on his heels. It would be difficult for him to have any impact when on the back foot. Not only that, the attendance was likely to be large due to the publicity the match had generated and Pontypridd supporters were renowned for their vociferous support. This always spurred him and the rest of the team on and the noise would undoubtedly be several decibels higher than normal. He also knew that Rocky would be fired up as there was every chance he, too, would be under consideration for selection the following week. His thunderous drives would raise the noise levels even higher and Joe made a point of recognising when Rocky was on the charge so as to be on his shoulder in support as quickly as possible.

Joe's mood changed, though, as he thought about Stan Williams and the rest of the committee members sitting next to each other in their customary prime seats in the grandstand like members of the Politburo. Dressed in their black pullovers, blazers and coats, their faces severe, perhaps the Gestapo was a better analogy, he thought with a slight chuckle. 'Wankers', he muttered under his breath. No doubt they would find something negative to say to any member of the Big Five in attendance. He would just have to take their opinions out of the equation by playing so well that selection was guaranteed.

* * *

The contrast between the Pontypridd dressing room and Joe's bathroom at home could not have been greater. Instead of warmth, there was cold; the freezing, skin-numbing wind whistling through the entrance of the grandstand and making its way into the two dressing rooms. Instead of quiet, there was noise; the incessant chat, the clattering of studs on concrete, the thuds of players striking themselves and their teammates to become accustomed to the collisions they would shortly be experiencing. Instead of the sweet aroma of soap and water, there were the less appealing ones of farts, belches, Deep Heat and wintergreen. Instead of calmness of mind, there was anxiety and tension.

Before entering the dressing room, Joe had stopped off in the clubhouse. He had requested his usual small bottle of Lucozade and as ever, offered to pay. The money was never accepted. He was unsure whether the energy drink made any real difference to the way he felt but so accustomed was he to drinking it that psychologically he would have felt weaker without it. A bit like Samson without the hair, he often reminded himself. At the far end of the bar, Eamon Murphy was sitting in his customary position on a high stool, Guinness in hand. He always complained that it never tasted like the Guinness in Ireland but he never switched to anything else. He was smiling and laughing and joking with two members of the club who were undoubtedly already on their third or fourth pints. Joe never understood how Eamon could remain so relaxed before a match and particularly how he could drink alcohol. He always claimed it was just the one, though Joe swore blind he frequently saw him partake of a Jameson whiskey chaser or two as well.

'There's our new Welsh international over there,' Eamon bellowed over the tops of the heads of his company as he looked in Joe's direction. 'Have a couple of bottles today, Joe, for extra strength. Actually, forget that, we don't want you running off the pitch for a piss when Aberavon are on the attack.' Everybody laughed and Joe smiled back. He had often tried to respond wittily to Eamon's jibes but so often had the words fallen flat in comparison to the Irish master's, he just grinned back, cheesily.

'Good luck, Joe. We're all behind you, butt.'

'Thanks, Dai,' Joe replied as he took the Lucozade from the barman. As he unscrewed the top, Joe registered surprise as he saw Dave, Phil, Dinner, Pete, Sue and Helen enter through the main doors. 'Nollike you lot to be here so early before a match?' Joe enquired whilst hugging Sue at the same time. She squeezed him tightly and kissed him full on the lips, her mind filled with memories of the passion they had enjoyed at her home the previous evening. She had so wanted him to stay the whole night but he had made his excuses about wanting to be properly rested for the game and left early. So stressful had the night turned out to be, he wished he had stayed.

'We just wanted to catch you before you changed, you know, this being such a big match an' all that. We met up in the Llan for a quick one then came on over.'

'That's really good of you all. Appreciate it,' Joe responded, placing his hand on each and every one of their shoulders to register the fact. Helen blushed and lowered her eyes coyly when he gently squeezed hers.

'I dunno how you can drink that stuff,' Pete snorted, screwing up his nose as his eyes arrowed in on the Lucozade bottle. 'I'm gonna get myself a proper drink. What's everybody 'aving?'

'That's why Joe's gonna play for Wales and you're rubbish,' Dave shot back and everybody chuckled.

'Ha ha. Now what's everybody 'aving, that is, everybody except Dave?'

'So how you feeling?' a smiling Dave enquired of Joe as Pete turned his back to try and gain Dai's attention behind the bar.

'Not bad, a bit nervous if I'm 'onest. A bit tired as well. I slept really badly last night.'

Everybody looked simultaneously at Sue as Dave saucily enquired, 'Aye aye, and why's that 'en?'

'Don't look at me,' Sue responded in a voice loud enough to turn the heads of those close by. Her cheeks flushed red and she lowered her voice. 'It's got nothing to do with me.'

'We believe you,' Helen replied, in a way that made clear that none of them did. Joe smiled at Sue but remained non-committal.

'You'll be orrite. The pressure's mainly on Steve James. I'm sure he didn't wanna play today but he's been forced to, to try and save his place.'

'You're wrong about that. There's as much pressure on me as there is on 'im. I can feel it, don't you worry,' Joe corrected Dave as Sue squeezed his hand.

'We saw Bill Johnson get out of his car with someone when we came in, probably another one of the Big Five. He was parked just by the BBC van. Look, Dewi Griffiths has just arrived, over there.' They all turned their heads in the direction of the main doors.

'The chairman of the Big Five, the BBC and the chief rugby correspondent of *The Times* newspaper. You can certainly tell it's a big match.' Phil uttered his first words and as ever, he was right on the money.

'Oh, thanks, Phil,' Joe mocked sarcastically, 'as if I need any more reminding.' He grabbed him in a playful headlock and ruffled his hair.

'Here we are.' Pete passed round the drinks. 'Here's your Guinness, Phil, gnat's piss for Dave, lager for me and Din and two Bacardi and Cokes.'

'Ta, Pete.'

'So where did Bill Johnson go?' Joe asked. 'I can't see 'im anywhere.'

'He went into the committee room. Stan Williams met him and they went in there.'

'Well, that's me fucked. He's probably telling Johnson at this very moment not to pick me. "He's too young, it's a big risk, no discipline, his time will come."' Joe put on an effeminate voice, mimicking that of Stan Williams. 'I may as well go home.'

'Don't be silly,' Sue admonished him. 'If you play well, they'll have to pick you.'

'I wish it was as easy as that.'

'Look, Dewi Griffiths is coming over, I can't believe it.' Dave's eyes were open wide in wonderment as the legendary Welsh international approached them.

'Well, Joe, I hope you have a good game today.' Griffiths offered him his hand whilst all his friends remained silent, slowly sipping at their drinks and hoping that Griffiths would not speak to them. They were so much in awe of him they would not know how to reply.

'Thank you, Mr Griffiths,' Joe replied, shaking his hand.

'Just a word of advice. Play your natural game out there and be patient. I'm sure there'll be plenty of opportunities in the game for you. Don't worry, you'll be orrite.'

'Thanks, I'll try.'

Dave's cheekiness got the better of him. 'Mr Griffiths, I hope you'll write something positive about Joe in

Monday's paper. He'll be a real grump if he doesn't get picked and it'll be us who'll 'ave to put up with 'im.'

'Well, I'm only a reporter, not a selector,' Griffiths replied with a smile, 'so don't blame me if Joe's not picked.'

'But everybody listens to you. What do people say? "What Dewi Griffiths says, goes."'

'Now if only that were true. Don't worry, if Joe plays well, I'll make sure to say so.'

Dave was on a roll, and being unable to stop himself, said to Griffiths, 'Joe told me you could have a night with his girlfriend 'ere if you support him on Monday and you've gotta admit she's pretty tidy.'

There was an explosion of laughter, though Sue found the comment less than amusing. 'Stop it, Dave!' she screamed. A bemused Dewi Griffiths looked at Sue and smiled. He did not know what to say. Even Mr Cool, Richard Morgan, aka Dinner, spluttered into his glass at that one.

'Well, Joe, have a great game and good luck.' Griffiths shook his hand once more, turned on his heels and walked away.

'I can't believe you said that.' Sue thumped Dave as hard as she could on the arm, biting her bottom lip.

'That's a classic,' Pete opined. 'I'll never forget that one.' They all dissolved in fits of laughter, even Helen, though Sue's face remained puce with anger.

'Come on, it's only a joke,' Joe said with concern, putting his arm around her shoulder before scolding Dave in her defence as he turned towards him, 'and a very bad one at that!' His tone was firm though not threatening.

'Sorry, Sue. I just couldn't resist it.'

'Don't worry about it,' she replied sharply, not meaning it.

'Right, I'd better be going then.' Joe picked up his kit bag and kissed Sue on the cheek. She grabbed his free hand and squeezed it firmly.

'See you here after the game. Good luck.'

On this final expression of encouragement, Joe turned away and marched towards the main grandstand and the dressing room below. He lengthened his stride and called out to Martyn Prosser, the team's hooker, who was ten yards ahead of him. He caught up with him and they entered the grandstand together.

* * *

They were nearly ready to go out. The referee had already popped his head into the dressing room to advise he would be back in five minutes to call them on to the field. The various stinks and sounds now included pungent body odour and bull-like snorts as each player prepared himself mentally as well as physically for the game ahead. Steam was already rising from the jerseys of those players who had warmed up on the pitch as the dampness of the shirts mixed with the heat of their bodies. Martyn Prosser and the loose-head prop, Bill Hopkins, had locked their arms and shoulders together, both of them grimacing and sweating profusely with the effort as they drove hard against each other, rocking from side to side. Nobody disturbed them even though space was at a premium. Outside the dressing room, the distant sound of studs clattering on concrete, in time to shouts from one to ten, indicated that Aberavon were coming to the end of their preparations.

Out of the corner of his eye, Rocky Evans saw Leap Thomas wind some white bandaging around his head, his final ritual before calling the team together for the customary rallying call. Immediately, Rocky got up from his place and went to sit next to Joe. Joe had prepared in his normal way and, after so many games for the senior team, was less intimidated by the frenzy of activity around him than when he had first appeared. At that time, he was genuinely terrified and wondered how he had managed to get himself into such a position. Now he was being spoken of as a potential Welsh international, someone whom others looked up to, and he thrived on this power and responsibility.

As usual, Joe had changed quickly and been the first to run out on to the field to warm up, ball in hand, waiting to be joined by some of his teammates. As ever, he passed Eamon Murphy who, having yet to enter the dressing room, was enjoying a final cigarette by the entrance to the stand, his kit bag at his feet. For ten minutes, Joe performed a multitude of stretching exercises which kept Murphy entertained. 'It'll be your fault if I play like an eejit today, Joe. I'm already knackered just looking at you.'

After his stretches, Joe did some sprints up and down the field, often passing the ball side to side with a teammate. Once he felt warm, he left the field and returned to the dressing room to begin his mental preparations. Rocky found him sitting down, hunched over, his head almost between his legs. A line of perspiration was running down a temple and occasionally, Joe drew some deep breaths. This was an important time for him. He was visualising the action ahead, seeing himself run hard through any gap that might appear in the opposition's defence. He also visualised an opponent running hard and aggressively at him and how, by steeling himself, he would throw himself into an equally aggressive tackle in return. He visualised being cool under pressure, ensuring that any relieving defensive kicks would find the safety of the touchline. In his own world, he did not initially hear Rocky's words and it took a sharp rap on the shoulder from the tight-head prop to gain his attention.

'How you feeling, boy?'

'Good, Rock.'

'Listen, there's a lot of chat and stuff about us playing for Wales next week.'

'You're as good as there, Rock. The Welsh scrum is rubbish.'

'Maybe, but I can't take anything for granted.' Rocky was virtually whispering and the two of them looked like co-conspirators plotting some coup as they sat in a corner, their heads touching and their faces hidden as they gazed downwards on to the harsh, grey, concrete floor now covered in muck and tape and globules of gob and snot when all around them, the loud and frenetic activity of their teammates gathered momentum. 'It's my life's ambition to play for Wales...'

'Same 'ere.'

'...and this is my chance. I won't get another one. I'm not young like you an' I won't let my family down. They're really proud of me and I'm gonna do it for them. Nothing's gonna stop me today.' Joe turned his head slightly and looked into Rocky's eyes. They were so intense, Joe knew he was as good as selected. 'Not only is pulling on the red shirt incentive enough but I've not forgotten that punch Meadows smacked me with 'ere last year. Remember that? Well, he's got one coming his way next week.' Joe smiled but said nothing. They could both see Leap Thomas rising from his place and about to beckon everybody to gather around him. 'But there's one thing I want you to know. I'm not going there next week by myself. I want another Ponty boy with me. You're fucking twice the player Steve James is. Jesus, I'm faster than 'im. Just get stuck in and show 'im who's boss. Wharrever 'appens, we're both going there together next Saturday, orrite!'

'Right, gather round, boys.'

As Joe and Rocky rose from their places in response to their captain's call, Joe's smile broadened further and they continued to look into each other's eyes. Rocky's words of support and encouragement had electrified him. Instinctively, they grabbed and hugged each other tightly, squeezing hard, warriors about to enter battle together. As the others gathered in a circle around Thomas, he saw the two of them still in the corner of the dressing room. 'Hey, lover boys, are you gonna come and join us or are you gonna go off and shag each other?' Joe and Rocky walked over to the gathering, prising the circle of teammates apart and adding their two links to this chain of ferocious, sweating manhood.

'Right, boys, we're gonna be going out in a minute. I can't be sure but I think Aberavon 'ave finished their final warm-up. You know why I can't be sure? Well, I'll tell you why. It's because I could hardly fucking hear them. They're a bunch of fucking pussy cats, the lot of them, shitting themselves, they are. No way are we gonna lose to these West Walian bastards, are we?'

'Right!'

'Well, ARE WE? I can't 'ear you,' Thomas bellowed at the top of his voice.

'RIGHT!' his teammates shouted in response, squeezing each other even more tightly. Taff Morgan, the diminutive scrum-half, thought his shoulders were going to dislocate, so tight was the squeeze of the huddle.

'I STILL CAN'T HEAR YOU!'

'RIGHT!' The response was so deafening that even those spectators on the opposite side of the field could hear it.

'WHAT ARE WE GONNA DO?'

'WIN!'

'WHAT ARE WE GONNA DO?'

'WIN!'

'LOUDER!'

'WIN!!'

'LOUDER!!!'

'WIN!!!'

Taff Morgan extricated himself from the group as he feared being crushed to death, so powerful the forces around him.

'Right, boys, find some space. On the spot, after me.' Thomas was satisfied with his team's response so now he beckoned them for one final warm-up. Just as the players were arranging themselves, Stan Williams popped his head into the dressing room to wish the team luck. Leap Thomas was in no mood to receive any uninvited guests. 'Gerrout!' he thundered at Williams, showing no deference to the club's president. 'Team only, gerrout!'

As Williams sheepishly turned away, Joe snarled at him, his face, twisted in anger, turning purple. 'Yeah, fuck off, you fat cunt!' Williams momentarily turned back but then retreated knowing full well he could not break into the camaraderie of a rugby team about to enter battle.

'Right, five slow then five fast.' In time, the team performed five slow jogs on the spot followed by five fast ones. 'Again!' The team responded to Thomas's command. 'AGAIN!!' Once more the team responded. The referee entered during this final flourish and caught Thomas's eye. It was time to go out.

The whole team was now glowing through perspiration as they made their line to leave the dressing room. Time for final farts and belches. As ever, Thomas's second-row partner, Ceri Evans, ran quickly off to the toilets to vomit. Joe grabbed a ball from the floor and pounded it hard into his shoulder and chest. He checked that his gumshield was in his shorts pocket. Beads of sweat glistened on his forehead and he felt a reassuring warm dampness down the middle of his back.

Aberavon had already run out on to the field and the players were gently loosening their limbs awaiting their hosts. A few seconds later, Pontypridd emerged from the dark tunnel under the stand and sprinted on to the field to the accompaniment of the roars and applause of their loyal supporters. Such support invigorated Joe and as he made his way to his position to await the kick-off, he looked around him and into the crowd to identify his close friends. He immediately saw Sue and Helen standing next to each other on the shallow terracing opposite the main grandstand and near the halfway line. Behind the two girls, he saw the heads of Dave, Pete, Phil and Dinner, all of whom were wearing black and white bobble hats, with the exception of Dinner who, to Joe's eyes, appeared to be wearing a lime-green, velvet fedora. What a dick, Joe smiled to himself. Pete seemed to be drinking from a small bottle. No doubt, Joe thought, that it was a half-bottle of whisky that they would pass around themselves during the game. The bobble hats and whisky were necessary as were the heavy coats, scarves and gloves for the day was truly freezing and plumes of white, condensed breath exhaled from the players' mouths. The sharp breeze brought with it a chill that penetrated the bones of the spectators and Helen was already complaining of frozen toes which Pete volunteered to warm up. The offer was sharply rejected. Though the match was taking place in mid-afternoon, the floodlights were already on as a heavy gloom hung over the ground and these lights only accentuated the diagonal lines of sleet that cascaded from the skies.

Joe was impervious to the conditions as he sought out Steve James just prior to kick-off. His opponent stared back whilst blowing on to his hands and jumping up and down to stay warm. On seeing this, Joe stood full-square in his line of vision, his hands on his hips, totally stationary as he tried to reflect the confidence he felt about their encounter. He looks lost to me, Joe thought. He's away from home, freezing, under pressure and with hardly any support. Joe could not wait to get started.

But Joe's confidence was misplaced. From the first lineout of the match, Ceri Evans soared high into the sky and gave quick ball to Taff Morgan who whipped the ball away quickly down the three-quarters line. Joe took the ball at speed and every instinct in his body told him to pass the ball further on down the line. But the second he received the pass, he saw Steve James fifteen yards in front of him shadowing his movement. Instead of passing, Joe ran hard directly at him. As they were about to collide, Joe tucked the ball under his right armpit and mustered every ounce of force he could generate. To his shock, however, when they collided, Joe was stopped in his tracks and the ball was dislodged from his grasp, bouncing forward. Joe felt he had run into the proverbial brick wall. James had been expecting such a play from Joe and steeled himself for the collision, anchoring his feet solidly into the turf. He turned his shoulder into Joe and though both of them ended up on the floor, it was clear to all the players and spectators who had come out on top in that first encounter. James was the first to rise and deliberately pushed down on Joe's head to help his movement upwards. 'Is that all you've got, wop boy? You'll 'ave to do better than that,' he whispered at the same time. Joe lashed out with his right arm as he began to rise but James had already moved away and he was left striking fresh air.

As the two sets of forwards gathered for the resulting scrum, Leap Thomas grabbed Joe's attention. 'Hey, Joe, that was perfect ball from the lineout, right off the top,' he stated, his expression severe. 'Look to move it out wide next time and don't get involved in any personal battles with James, orrite!' Joe nodded his head and retreated to his position, somewhat crest-fallen. On the sidelines, Phil and Dave looked at each other and acknowledged that round one was definitely in James's favour.

From the scrum, the Pontypridd forwards demolished the Aberavon pack, with Rocky Evans to the fore, driving his opposite number upwards and virtually over the backs of his second-rows. It was the first time he had ever had an aerial view of Pontypridd and feared it would not be the last. As the ball squirted out of the back of the retreating Aberavon scrum, their scrum-half managed to flick the ball away to Steve James who, back on his heels, was under severe pressure from the marauding Pontypridd back row. He managed to firmly hand off one opponent before spinning to his left to wrong foot another. After running five yards into space, he spiralled a left-footed kick forty yards downfield, the ball bouncing once before skidding into touch just ten yards from the Pontypridd tryline. It was a strong and classy piece of play and even the Pontypridd spectators applauded warmly.

'He looks up for it today.' Sue turned round glumly and stared at Phil hoping that her analysis of the game was incorrect and that the font of all rugby knowledge would put her right. Unfortunately, she was not mistaken.

'He certainly does.' Phil was in full agreement and frowned in worry.

'Give me another nip, will you?' Pete gestured to Dave and the latter passed him the whisky bottle. 'We're gonna need this. It's gonna be a long day.'

Joe's confidence waned in the knowledge that just five minutes into the match of his life, Steve James appeared to be on the top of his game whilst he had started poorly. For the next twenty minutes, both of them played steadily, with Joe lacking his usual commitment when taking on his opponent directly. He passed out some well-timed balls to the outside backs and his defence was tidy but he struggled to get truly involved in the match. This was his last chance, he knew, to make the Welsh side, to carry out his tumultuous and historic plan and in the murk and cold and sleet of this grim afternoon, he was blowing it. He felt as miserable as the day itself. He had underestimated James and the whole experience was turning into a nightmare. It couldn't get any worse, he assured himself. He was wrong.

Just before half-time, Steve James ran on to an inviting pass, which he took at speed, his eyes flicking left and right as he sized up his options. Joe ran up to close down the danger when James suddenly slowed and turned his body round slightly away from him. His fellow centre had taken a line behind James and was preparing to receive the ball in a classic scissors movement. James's slowing down and half-turn momentarily checked Joe's and his centre teammate, Pat's, forward advance. They both braced themselves for the scissors move when James unexpectedly turned back and burst through the gap between his flat-footed opponents at lightning speed. Joe and Pat had been fooled. It was a dummy scissors, with James feigning to pass but then retaining the ball as he attacked the space between them. Having breached this first line of defence, James continued at speed towards the Pontypridd tryline where he was confronted by Eamon Murphy at full-back. Before Murphy could make the tackle, however, James passed the ball on to his right-wing who tore over the line, running under the posts to make the conversion easier.

Initially, the spectators groaned at the poor defence, but when the try was scored, once again generous applause broke out. James's teammates all approached him after the try was scored, smiling and patting him on the back for a piece of brilliant play. As he ran back to the halfway line, he passed by a disconsolate Joe and grinned at him.

'What 'appened there, Pat?'

'Dummy scissors, Joe, and a fucking good one at that. Hard to know which guy to cover. He did it well; we'll just have to give 'im that one.' Joe knew Pat was correct but he found it hard to accept. Leap Thomas didn't say a word to either Joe or Pat but he didn't need to; the look of thunder on his face said it all.

The half-time whistle sounded immediately after the re-start kick and with his head hung low, Joe trudged slowly to the other half of the field, the picture of dejection. As he did so, Steve James fairly skipped by him, upright on his toes like a new-born foal. He had deliberately veered towards Joe and faintly brushed his shoulder as he ran past him. Joe turned round but James had already gone. What Joe did not miss, though, was the broad grin on his opponent's face. They both knew one thing. Steve James was running rings round him.

'Right, boys, grab your oranges and then gather round.' Leap Thomas's tone of voice left nobody unaware of the mood he was in. It was as filthy as the mud beneath his feet. 'What the fuck's going on? Nine points down to these fuckers, we should be ashamed of ourselves. We're stuffing 'em up front but you've got to use the ball better in the backs. There's too many wrong options, too many of you wanting to be glory boys. Remember, it's a team game. You've gotta work for the openings, you can't just blast through 'em at will.' These initial words were addressed to everybody in the team but there was no doubt whose eye Thomas caught when he said them. Joe nodded his head in agreement but in his guts he felt belittled. 'But I tell you what,' Thomas's tone was now one of exasperation and resignation, 'it doesn't matter 'ow much ball we get if we defend like we've done so far.' Once more Thomas glanced at Joe, but this time he sought out Pat as well. 'We've gotta keep our shape better and be sharper round the field. We're all fucking half-asleep. Come on! We're gonna lose this if we defend like we did in the first-half.'

Leap Thomas bought into the fact that rugby was a team game and that there should be collective responsibility either in victory or defeat so whilst he knew who were responsible for the poor first-half performance, he would never criticise anybody by name and would always make reference to the whole team. His confidence had been shaken, nevertheless, and he believed the team's tactics would have to change if they were to overcome their deficit.

'Right, come in closer and listen.' Crouched low at the centre of a circle of steaming, stinking manhood and beating his fist up and down on an imaginary drum to the rhythm of his voice, Thomas addressed his teammates slowly and calmly, this time looking intently into the eyes of each and every one of them. 'We're stuffing 'em up front. Their scrum is rubbish and we're nicking a lot of their lineout ball as well. What we're gonna do this half is keep the ball nice 'n' tight, really tight.' He sought out his key forwards, Rocky, Ceri Evans, Martyn Prosser and Bill Hopkins. They all nodded their heads in agreement. 'When we get our hands on the ball, we're just gonna drive it on and on. Taff, when you get it from us, I want you sniping round looking for support back inside, the same at the scrums. I want us to drive those fuckers right over their tryline, orrite!' Taff Morgan and the forwards all nodded their heads vigorously and one or two of them began to punch their own arms and chests in anticipation of the battle ahead. 'I only want the ball to go out to the backs as and when we've built up a good lead, orrite, Taff!'

'Right, Leap.'

'That doesn't mean you backs are just gonna be standing around.' Thomas swivelled his head and caught the eye of Joe, Pat and Eamon. 'When they've got the ball, I want you to go up as a line together, no gaps, and go up aggressively. Get in their faces. That Steve James 'asn't got a speck of mud on 'im.'

The backs nodded their heads though somewhat less enthusiastically than the forwards. Eamon Murphy puffed out his cheeks and turned towards Pat. 'Bejesus, we're going to freeze our bollocks off this half if they're not going to pass us the ruddy ball,' he whispered and Pat nodded his head in agreement, the disappointment obvious on both of their faces.

Joe was horrified. He knew his chances of playing for Wales were hanging by a thread and his emotions were in turmoil. All his plans were going down the drain because of one terrible half of rugby. He knew he had to play the next half like a man possessed and totally upstage Steve James if he was to have any chance of being selected. But now, his captain was barking out orders that the forwards would keep hold of the ball and not throw it out to the backs at all. He couldn't just be a spectator in the centre. He had to get hold of the ball and show James and the selectors what he could do. Leap Thomas was held in huge respect by his team and nobody ever questioned his tactics during a match and certainly not a seventeen-year-old schoolboy.

'We'll never beat 'em if we just 'ang on to the ball in the forwards. We know we can take 'em in the backs.' Joe's voice quivered as he spoke and he sounded desperate, which he was. His teammates had been about to break away from their huddle and resume their positions for the second-half but they all stopped in their tracks on hearing Joe's words. 'We nearly got through a couple of times and they're definitely gonna tire second-half. If we get the ball, we'll definitely score a couple of tries, no problem.'

Joe and Thomas were standing five yards apart and they stared into each other's eyes. Calmly, Thomas called the team together once more. 'Right, this is what we're gonna do this half. It's like what I said earlier. We're gonna keep the ball nice 'n' tight, really tight.' Thomas repeated his initial commands in a quiet, measured tone, exuding confidence. But just as he was completing the sentence, he paused and turned to face Joe before following up with a loud, 'ORRITE!' Nobody moved and he stared hard-faced and unblinking, for what seemed an age, directly at Joe. Joe could not hold the stare and he lowered his eyes to the turf, one or two of his teammates following awkwardly. Thomas added a final sting. 'You just concentrate on your tackling.'

The team broke for their positions and Joe trudged towards his, totally belittled, his head hung low in shame. Surprisingly and unexpectedly, however, Rocky Evans came up behind him and tugged at his shirt for attention. 'Joe, don't worry about it. I'm sure you'll get your chance this half. And like I said in the dressing room, I'm not gonna Cardiff next week by myself.' Joe smiled at Rocky, his spirits momentarily raised.

On the sidelines, though, the spirits of Joe's friends were at rock bottom. It did not take Phil to tell the others how Steve James had outclassed Joe during the first-half and from a distance, it was apparent to them that there had been some sort of disagreement involving Joe during the team huddle. As Joe trudged back to his position, his slow gait and hunched shoulders reflected his mood and Sue, in particular, was concerned. 'Come on, Joe!' she yelled with all her might from the touchline trying to raise his spirits. The shout was so loud and so unexpected that her friends and those spectators immediately around her were momentarily startled and turned towards her. 'Come on, Joe! Come on, Ponty!' she yelled once more.

Phil picked up on her encouragement and followed her lead. 'Come on, Joe! You can do it, keep it going,' he bellowed. As he and Sue started another round of encouragement, their friends all joined in and Joe did not fail to hear them. He looked towards the touchline and smiled. He could barely make them out through the sleet and murk, and Helen, with the hood of the sweatshirt she was wearing under her beige Afghan coat with white frills pulled tightly over her head and scarf covering half her face, was almost indistinguishable. On seeing Joe's smile, Dave clenched his fist, raised it to his chest and gritted his teeth to convey strength and determination. Joe nodded his head slowly on seeing this and his demeanour became serious as his mind turned to what he needed to do during the second-half.

As he feared, the opening minutes turned into a slugfest between the two sets of forwards. The pitch was cutting up badly and the inadequate floodlights barely made up for the increasingly gloomy day. The handling amongst the forwards was poor as the ball, now permanently smeared with a muddy slime, proved difficult to hold. Scrum after scrum followed and Joe could feel his body temperature drop noticeably as he and the other backs became virtually redundant. At each scrum, Taff and his opposing scrum-half would try to dry the ball on the front of their jerseys but so dank were they, they only seemed to make the ball even slipperier. To make matters worse for Joe, Aberavon, too, had given up on playing an expansive game and they resolved to keep the ball in the forwards. Though they had been bettered during the first-half, they knew that throwing the ball out to their backs on such a dreadful day would only lead to mistakes from which their opponents could profit. They also had a lead to protect so the longer the match became literally bogged down in the mud, the more time was on their side. This was something Joe did not have and as the match headed towards the midpoint of the half, his thoughts were turning to desperation. He constantly kept his eye on Steve James but his opposite number and rival for the Welsh jersey seemed content to hold his position and cover any threatened attacks. He was ahead on points and being cautious, waiting for the final bell to ring when he knew he would have his arm raised and be declared the winner. Could Joe land the knockout punch to change everything? It did not seem so and he was lost as to what he could do.

From the sidelines, the level of noise from the Pontypridd supporters had dropped as the freezing sleet and wind and poor spectacle in front of them sapped their energy. Dave picked up on this and turned to Phil. 'This match is going nowhere,' he stated worriedly. 'It's a stalemate and we're gonna lose if we're not careful. Joe's 'ardly had a touch of the ball. Let's try and get the crowd going a bit.' He led the chants of *"Pont..ee, Pont..ee..."* and Phil, Pete, Sue, Helen and even Dinner joined in. They kept the chants going and the rest of the supporters followed suit, roaring *"Pont..ee, Pont..ee, Pont..ee, Pont..ee..."* at the top of their voices. On hearing this, the Pontypridd players took inspiration, puffed out their chests and gritted their teeth for a final effort.

A series of strong forward drives led to an excellent touch-finder by Taff Morgan deep into Aberavon territory. From the resultant lineout, and leading by example, a highly-motivated Leap Thomas caught the ball directly from in front of his opponent's outstretched hands despite it being Aberavon's throw-in. His fellow forwards surrounded him in support and they mauled their way towards the tryline. Five yards short, Rocky Evans took the ball from Thomas, broke out from the back of the maul and drove for the line which he made by blasting over the tackles of the opposition scrum-half and blind-side wing.

The crowd roared and applauded loudly and the chants of *"Pont..ee, Pont..ee, Pont..ee…"* were now joined by chants of *"Rock..ee, Rock..ee, Rock..ee…"*. Further applause followed as the conversion was successfully kicked. Leap Thomas felt a great deal of relief as, with just ten minutes to go, his half-time change of tactics had finally paid off and Pontypridd were back in the game, now only three points behind. The whole team was re-energised and even the redundant backs were screaming encouragement at their marauding pack of forwards. It was barely possible to make out who was who as each one of them was caked in mud and enough steam was rising from their bodies to drive a turbine. Joe was pleased at the score but in his guts, he was despondent. He had not been able to contribute at all during the second-half and with so little time to go, he believed his chance had gone. He just wanted the match to end, to go away by himself and reassess the situation. He had blown it. How could they drop Steve James now? Even if Pontypridd ended up winning, it would count for nothing.

A long raking kick from Eamon Murphy, his first touch of the ball during the second-half, caught the wind from directly behind him and slid into touch twenty yards from the Aberavon tryline. The crowd's roars were frantic, deafening and imploring. Time was running out, but Pontypridd had a good position. The Aberavon linesman signalled that the touch was a further ten yards away and the crowd roared in anger at his obvious gamesmanship. Pete was incensed and waving his fist furiously at him, bellowed in his direction, 'Hey, linesman, you got a turd in your eye or summing. The touch is never there, you cheating bastard.' Everybody around him roared their agreement. Helen and Sue just cringed.

'Come on, Leap! Come on, Ceri! Let's get up there and nick another one and show those cheating fuckers,' Dave bellowed, knowing that another steal from the Aberavon lineout would put Pontypridd on the attack. However, the throw-in was safely gathered by Aberavon and a maul formed with them in control of the ball. They held on, running down the clock, before finally releasing it to their scrum-half. He threw a fine pass to the outside-half who was standing just fifteen yards from his tryline and he prepared a relieving kick to touch. Just as he took back his kicking leg, however, his standing leg slipped on the sodden turf and he fell to his knees. With the Pontypridd wing-forward, Barry Phillips, now virtually upon him, the outside-half panicked and shovelled the ball on to Steve James. James was back on his heels and Joe saw his chance. He raced up to him like an Olympic sprinter and held him in an all-encompassing tackle before James had any opportunity to clear the ball. They wrestled briefly and then fell to the ground together. The laws of the game required Joe to release James, who promptly freed his hands, turned on to his side with his back to the opposition players and stretched out his arms to present the ball on the floor to his supporting teammates. It was exemplary technique and drew nods of approval from the spectators closest to the action as not only had he resisted the tackle but he had also put his team back in control of the ball.

Finally, finally, he had his opportunity. He had been waiting all game for it and despaired it would never come. This was the moment. This was it. The 'he' in question, however, was not Joe Chilani. It was Rocky Evans. He had made a promise to Joe. They were going to go to Cardiff together. He had kept his side of the bargain, he was sure. He had played well. No, not just well, but outstandingly well. He had demolished the Aberavon scrum. He had mauled like a terrier. He had driven strongly upfield, knocking off tackles and he had smashed his way over the line for a try. He could see that Joe had struggled during the first-half and that Steve James had responded well to the pressure he was under. In fact, he was shocked at how good he actually was. He knew the second-half had been dominated by the forward exchanges and that Joe had had no opportunity to shine. James had continued to not put a foot wrong. But now, finally, finally, he had his opportunity.

Rocky saw Steve James's outstretched arms, protecting the ball and saw that his support player was his fellow centre. Rocky calculated that he could ruck over James and arrive at the ball at the same time as the opposition player. Being four stones heavier in weight, he was confident he could drive him off the ball, releasing it potentially for a Pontypridd teammate to come in behind him, take the ball and score. This, however, was not his main concern. As he arrowed in on the ball, he rucked over Joe who was still lying on the floor next to Steve James. With tremendous forward momentum, he strode over James and with all his seventeen-stone might, slammed the mud-caked, slimy, size eleven rugby boot that adorned his right foot straight into the back of Steve James's right hand. James shrieked in agony as he felt the aluminium studs break three of the hand's bones and he grasped it immediately with his other hand. Rocky continued on his forward drive, blasting James's teammate off the ball with ease. Rocky had been careful to ensure his forward drive was with no break in stride, so that the contact he made with James's hand could be construed as an accident. He avoided the more obvious stamping movement which could lead to a sending off by the referee and instant exclusion from selection for the Welsh international team. James's cries could be heard around the ground but the focus of the spectators' attention remained on the loose ball as Barry Phillips gathered it up and drove for the tryline. He was held up one yard short by the scrambling Aberavon defence and Phillips's forward teammates piled in behind him to try and force him over. Aberavon dug in deep, however, desperately protecting their three-point lead. They knew a try here and the match was lost. The ball remained held up and the referee jockeyed from one side of the maul to the other to see if Pontypridd had any forward momentum. If not, he would have to blow his whistle and award a scrum.

Joe remained on the ground, transfixed by Steve James's initial cry and subsequent loud moaning as his rival knelt beside him clutching his wrist. He was in great pain, his face screwed up, and he resembled an ugly gargoyle. His cheeks were crimson and despite his eyes being tightly shut, tears had found their way from under the lids and dripped on to the ground. 'Fuck, fuck, fuck,' he cursed as if this would somehow help ease the pain. Joe looked at him and then at the hand he was holding.

It seemed as if it had been inflated by a tyre pump so swollen did it appear and despite the muck that acted as camouflage, there was no missing the bright redness of the skin that glowed like a traffic light through a fog. Across the redness were four perfectly formed circular craters. They were a deep purple in shade and all were seeping tiny droplets of blood. The studs had penetrated deeply into the flesh. Joe could not take his eyes off them.

'Joe! Joe!' Taff Morgan screamed. Joe remained rooted to the ground not responding to his scrum-half's call. 'JOE!' Morgan's cry even drowned out the curses of Steve James. Joe reacted and looked at his teammate. 'Gerrout there, left, now! There's nobody there.' Morgan eyed the opposition tryline in the left-hand corner which Joe saw was undefended. He understood Morgan's command, jumped to his feet and took a few paces to his left. Just as the referee was about to blow his whistle for a scrum, Morgan dug out the ball from the entanglement of limbs and boots, the maul having collapsed to the ground, and passed it to Joe. With the Aberavon tryline only three yards in front of him, Joe cantered over under no pressure and touched the ball down. The referee was upon him in a flash, arm raised, and with a loud blow of the whistle, awarded a try.

The crowd erupted. Everybody in the grandstand was on their feet peering into the gloom of the left-hand corner, applauding loudly, shaking the hands of their neighbouring spectators and grabbing the shoulders of those in front of them. So, too, in the terracing opposite where Joe's friends all hugged each other. The chant of *"Pont..ee, Pont..ee, Pont..ee..."* rang out.

On the field, Joe's teammates patted him on the back, their smiles as wide as the Severn Estuary. They all

sought out Rocky Evans whose initial drive over the ball
had set up the score. He was more concerned with Steve
James, however, and he jogged over to the stricken
player who was still kneeling on the ground, but this
time in the company of the Aberavon trainer who was
applying a filthy wet sponge to the back of his hand,
which unfortunately for James, did not transmit any of
the fabled magic to ease his pain. Rocky's concern was
not so much for the player, though he would make a
point of searching him out after the game to apologise,
but more to evaluate what damage he had caused. He
could not see the covered hand but he felt sure that a
bone had been broken for he was convinced he had
heard the sound of a twig breaking when he had made
contact and amidst all the muck and dirt and water on
the field, he could not see any twigs. As he made his way
back to the halfway line, he kept his eye on James who
was now being accompanied off the field by the trainer.
His face remained twisted in agony and despite the bitter
cold, he was sweating profusely. His arm was extended
and held by the trainer and as he applied more pressure
with the sponge, his head shot upwards at the sharpness
of the pain. Not only had he played well, Rocky
reflected, but he had carried out this final task just as
well, also, and a broad smile crept across his face. He
continued to receive the compliments of his teammates
who were largely unaware of what had happened to
James. More importantly, the referee ignored him. He
had got away with it.

Joe, too, was jogging back to the halfway line,
receiving more pats on his back from fellow teammates
but like Rocky, he did so looking over his shoulder at
Steve James walking off the field in obvious agony. In

fact, he so wanted to know how badly hurt James was, he stopped before reaching the line and looked intently at James's departure from the field. It was a serious injury. He had seen it close up and the pain etched across James's face confirmed it. What did this mean? He tried to make sense of what had just happened. He's got to be doubtful for next week, he thought. He felt sure the hand was broken but he could not at that moment bring himself to admit that James would not be available for the international. He was not certain, how could he be? Perhaps it was not as bad as it looked. Everything would become clearer later when the extent of the injury was known. But just for a split second, it flashed across his mind that he would be selected next week. James has got to be out, surely? He was lost in a trance, still following James's progress off the field, until he finally lost sight of him as he made his way down the tunnel under the grandstand and towards the dressing room. Indeed, Joe did not even register the huge roar when the conversion wide out by Taff Morgan was successful. As Taff ran back to his position, he passed by Joe who was still rooted to the spot, mouth open wide, staring at the tunnel entrance. 'Come on, Joe, the match isn't over yet,' Taff reminded him.

Joe heard the comment and turned slowly towards his position. Instinctively, he looked towards the forwards to seek out Rocky. Despite the driving sleet, Joe picked him out at once amidst the muddy bodies and plumes of steam. It was not difficult as Rocky was the only one with a wide smile on his face looking directly back at him, his gumshield an oblong of sparkling whiteness contrasting vividly against his black and rain-streaked face. For the first time, Joe understood that this had been no accident as he had originally thought. It took him just a split second to comprehend what Rocky had done and to remember the words he had spoken before the match and at half-time. Rocky had kept his promise. It was at this moment, as the two of them fixed eyes on each other, that Joe finally knew he would play for Wales next Saturday. His face broke out into the widest of smiles and it lit up the grey surrounds like the sun breaking through the clouds of a gloomy morning. He could not stop himself screaming in euphoria, which drew looks from the players around him, wondering what had got into him. He was not embarrassed and he floated back to his position as if on air.

There was hardly any time for the kick-off and once Pontypridd had gathered the ball and fired it into touch, the referee blew his whistle to end the match. Loud applause and a sustained chant of *"Pont..ee, Pont..ee..."* burst out from the crowd and all Joe's friends gave each other big hugs. Sue had been trying to gain Joe's attention after he had scored his try and was a little disappointed he had not looked her way. Now that the final whistle had gone, she tried once again but Joe ignored his friends and ran straight over to Rocky Evans and embraced him in ecstatic delight. 'I'll never forget what you just did for me,' Joe whispered into Rocky's ear, still hugging him like a young boy might his father.

'Told you we'd be going together. I won't be so lonely now.' As they broke apart, Joe turned towards his friends who were walking across the pitch in his direction.

'Gerraway! Don't hug me,' Sue shrieked, 'you're stinking!' She agreed to a kiss on the cheek after which Joe, in jest, rubbed his face all over hers. 'You sod!' Sue scolded him as she spluttered and spat out a couple of muddy blades of grass. Joe shook his friends' hands, while smiling at Sue, patting them on the back.

'What 'appened to Steve James?' Phil enquired. 'We could see him go off and he looked in a lot of pain to me.'

But before Joe could reply, a frozen Helen broke in and forcibly requested that they resume the conversation in the clubhouse once Joe had showered and changed. 'I'm gonna die of cold if I stand out here any longer,' she added. Her statement was accompanied by a grimace as her eyes turned downwards towards the bottom of her jeans and boots which were covered in mud right up to her knees. And before anybody else could say a word, she was off, squelching her way towards the clubhouse. Her friends all agreed and followed after her, leaving Joe to sprint over to the far side of the field to clap off the opposition before disappearing into the dressing room.

* * *

It was fully an hour before Joe walked into the clubhouse, slinging his kit bag to the side of the lobby where a number of coats were hanging on rails. His hair was slicked back and still damp from the hot shower, glistening under the strip lights. His black club tie with the Old Bridge emblem was neatly knotted around the white collar of his shirt and he wore the club blazer with pride. He glanced over and around the hordes of dried-out spectators, now warming up nicely and enjoying their pints, and saw his friends in the exact same spot where he had left them before the game, occupying a corner at the far end of the bar. He threaded his way towards them through the crowd, cheeks glowing, and accepting many pats and words of congratulations on the way. After giving Sue a gentle squeeze, his first words concerned the only thing on his mind and were addressed to his friends with a desperate inquisitiveness not dissimilar to that of a small boy wishing to know what he had received for Christmas. 'What's the word on Steve James? How bad's his hand? I couldn't find out anything in the dressing room. Have you seen him around anywhere?'

Pete pushed a pint of bitter towards him along the bar as Phil responded. 'I think it's pretty bad. Those Aberavon guys over there told me they'd heard it was broken. When I went for a piss, I saw someone getting into the back of a car still in Aberavon kit an' I'm pretty sure it was 'im. They were probably taking him off to hospital.'

'That means you'll play for Wales next week,' Helen added excitedly, giving Joe a hug that led to his spilling some of his beer.

'Could be, but you never know.'

'Oh, come off it,' Dave interjected forcibly. 'It was either you or 'im and he'll be out for ages.'

'I suppose so.' Joe was inwardly excited but there was caution in his reply. 'I was really lucky today. He was playing well and I couldn't get my 'ands on the ball an' when he went past me in the first-half for their try, I could've died out there.'

'He played really well, the best I've ever seen him considering the conditions,' Phil agreed. 'He was unlucky to break his hand. What 'appened? Did you see the incident?'

'As clear as anything. Rocky drove over 'im going for the ball and accidentally trod on it,' Joe replied insincerely.

'Somehow the words 'accidentally trod' and 'Rocky Evans' don't seem to go together in the same sentence,' Dave responded mischievously, a knowing smile breaking out across his face. They all smiled in turn and nodded their heads.

'Only Rocky knows the truth.' Once again, Joe lied. He changed the subject. 'Anybody seen Bill Johnson?' he enquired. Now that Joe believed himself to be in pole position for selection next week, he was keen to learn the whereabouts of the chairman of the Big Five. He was hoping he would come over and tip him the wink before the side was officially announced on Monday. He surveyed the room but could not see him anywhere.

'I've not seen him in 'ere. He's probably 'aving a drink with the committee. He was sitting next to Stan Williams all through the game.' Joe cursed at Pete's reply. Stan Williams would not support him and he wondered whether he was bad-mouthing him at this very moment. 'Don't worry, Joe, Fat Stan doesn't pick the side and Steve James is out. You're bound to be picked.' Joe appreciated Pete's follow-up but would have felt more at ease if it had come from Phil whose rugby antennae were much sharper.

'Hey, I think Dewi Griffiths is coming over,' Dinner advised, looking over Joe's shoulder. The Welsh rugby great was side-stepping his way past the mass of thirsty drinkers who stood in his way, much like when doing the same on the rugby field in his heyday, and approached where Joe was standing. Joe turned his head and looked over his shoulder instinctively.

'Watch what you say this time.' Sue's tone towards Dave was sharp and her look threatening.

'P'rhaps he's coming over to take up the offer.'

Sue elbowed Dave hard and fully a third of his beer spilled on to his belted black and white patterned Starsky cardigan.

'Hey, watch it.'

'You deserved that,' Sue replied unapologetically.

Dave was still wiping the beer off his cardigan with the back of his fingers when Dewi Griffiths reached them. He touched Joe on the shoulder and he turned round, feigning surprise at his presence. 'Well played, Joe. That was a hard match in really tough conditions.'

'Thank you, sir.' Dewi Griffiths commanded such respect that it did not seem out of place for Joe to address him as if one of his school teachers.

'A real day for the forwards. It's never easy when you're a back on days like these. I should know; I've been there many times.'

'That's true. It was really frustrating out there. They defended well and we were lucky in the end.'

'What happened with their try? Steve James just seemed to glide between the two of you in the centre. I've never seen him move so quickly.'

Joe's face remained unmoved but inside, his guts were churning at the question and comment and recognition that James had outplayed and outthought him during that moment. 'Just a misunderstanding between us, that's all. I thought Pat was going to take anybody running in his space so I let him go. It was his man. James is not all that quick, it just seemed that way 'cos neither of us went for him and we were rooted to the ground.'

Joe's reply placed too much blame on Pat and was ungracious towards James but Dewi Griffiths had seen too much rugby in his time not to know the truth. 'Mmm, perhaps,' he answered, clearly unconvinced. After an awkward second or two during which they both took sips from their drinks, Griffiths resumed. 'James showed a lot of composure out there today considering the pressure he was under. He was very solid but so were you by the way,' Griffiths added quickly, not wanting to give the impression he was a fully paid-up member of the Steve James appreciation society. 'Considering the conditions, you're handling was good and the pressure you put on James helped lead to your try.'

'Thanks. I'll be the first to admit it wasn't one of my better games but that's the way it goes sometimes.' Joe could sense that Griffiths had not been too impressed.

'Looks like a bad one he's picked up, though. It's definitely a broken hand so his season is pretty much over.'

'Yeah, it looks like. I was sorry to see him get hurt.' Joe's reply was mature and straight-faced and Griffiths took a quick gulp from his glass to finish his drink. As he placed it back on the bar, he looked directly at Joe and smiled. Joe smiled back but then couldn't resist saying, 'Well, actually I'm not if you really wanna know.' Griffiths laughed out loud and Joe and his friends followed suit.

'No, I bet you're not,' Griffiths replied, a broad smile stretching across his face. 'I think your guardian angel was smiling down on you today, or should I say, Rocky Evans, more like.'

'You could say that,' Joe returned with a smile.

'Anyway, I must go. One or two others I need to speak to before I leave. Anybody seen Bill Johnson?'

'I think he's in the committee room, Mr Griffiths,' Phil replied.

In hope rather than expectation, Sue plucked up the courage to ask Griffiths to put a good word in for Joe with the chairman of selectors. The audacity of her request brought a smile to Griffiths's face but he said nothing. All Joe's friends looked intently at him, hoping to hear some positive words. Griffiths bent down to retrieve a small briefcase from near his feet and avoided any eye contact. He paused momentarily to survey the room, to seek out some other person he might want to speak to. He turned his head left and right until he finally caught sight of someone. He folded his coat over one arm and made to leave. His silence during these few key seconds and refusal to rise to Sue's request discouraged Joe and his friends and they all stood around nervously as Griffiths prepared to leave. Politely, he wished them all an enjoyable evening as he turned on his heels. But then, all of a sudden, he turned back to Joe and offered some words of wisdom. 'Enjoy the game next Saturday and keep your wits about you because Harrison is twice as slippery as James.' And with these words and a final smile, he left.

Before Joe could reply, Griffiths was gone. Sue hugged him tightly and Dave yelled out his delight, excitedly. Phil, Dinner, Helen and Pete all smiled and grabbed Joe by the shoulder and arm. Griffiths's message was clear. Joe had his endorsement and Griffiths's opinion was highly valued. Even Joe felt more relaxed, knowing what an important ally he had.

'I think this calls for a celebration,' Pete blurted out as he tried to grab the bar girl's attention.

'I think it's really gonna happen.' Sue took up the conversation, holding Joe's hand firmly and looking him directly and lovingly in the eye. 'You're really gonna play for Wales next week. Can you believe it? It's incredible.'

'Let's all calm down now. Griffiths is a reporter, he's not a selector. He doesn't always get his way.'

'Yeah, but he's really important and he wants to speak to Bill Johnson tonight. After what he's just said, he's bound to put in a good word for you. And let's not forget, Steve James is out, injured.'

'He's not the only other centre in Wales, you know.'

'Yeah, but all the others are crap and everybody knows it's between you and 'im. All the telly and newspapers have been going on about it for weeks.'

'Suppose so.'

'Right, grab your drinks, everybody,' Pete intervened as he passed them round to his friends.

'Ta, Pete.'

'Right, let's all be upstanding.'

'We are upstanding, you pillock.'

'Oh, right. Well, let's just raise our glasses and toast Joe. To Joe Chilani, Welsh international rugby player.'

'Joe Chilani, Welsh international rugby player,' they all replied, raising their glasses in Joe's direction before taking large swigs from them.

The people close by all turned to face Joe's group of friends and smiled and one or two of them raised their glasses in salute as well. Even Joe's worries faded away in this show of high confidence. He really did believe he was going to play for Wales against England the following Saturday.

20

'Wow, you all look fantastic, just stunning.' Joe's eyes lit up when just a couple of hours after their celebratory toast, Sue, Helen and Ann approached his table in the far corner of the clubhouse from the main entrance. In those couple of hours, Joe, Pete, Dave, Phil and Dinner had continued talking and drinking whilst the two girls had gone home to change for the evening's disco. On their return, they had met up with Ann, who, having taken Sue's previous Saturday job in the Co-op, had been unable to attend the game during the afternoon. With her indifference to rugby and the weather as it was, this had not caused her any great hardship. As people drifted away, some tables had become available and the boys selected their usual one in the corner.

Not only Joe's eyes had lit up. 'Blimey, you all look storming.' Dave concurred with Joe's view as he eyed the girls up and down in a lecherous manner.

'Well, don't make it sound as if it's so unusual, will you?' Helen replied haughtily. 'We always look gorgeous,' she added, putting her hand behind her head and arching her eyes to the skies, posing as if she were Farrah Fawcett in *Charlie's Angels*.

Sue, who was dressed in her favourite black trousers, black stiletto boots and cream blouse, went to sit next to Joe, with Dinner having to shuffle sideways to free up a space for her. Helen went to sit next to Dave, purely because he was the furthest away from Pete while Ann reluctantly sat in the only other space possible, between Pete and Dinner. Dinner, in his fantasy world, took this as a sign of interest in him.

'Phew, you've certainly splashed on the smellies,' Dave commented as he screwed up his nose. 'Wharrisit, Charlie?' he asked ungraciously.

'Gerroff!' Helen was indignant. 'I don't wear Charlie. It's Chanel N° 5 if you wanna know,' she continued a little pompously.

'Chanel N° 5! You're kidding. That must've cost a bomb.'

'It's my mum's, actually, but don't tell her I took some if you see her in town,' she whispered conspiratorially.

'You look very nice, Ann. I like your necklace.' Dinner broke his silence with some charm which Ann replied to with genuine gratitude though she thought his eyes were wandering much lower down than the bottom of her necklace.

Rockin' Robin Williams was setting up his decks and lighting system in the background and was as ever the butt of Eamon Murphy's jokes. 'Hey, Robin, this young lady here wants to know if you're going to play any T-Rex records tonight and she doesn't mean the ones from prehistoric times you usually play.' Rockin' Robin just smiled, knowing there would only be one winner if he took on Murphy in some banter.

'So you obviously haven't moved very far since we left you at the bar; just the ten yards from there to here.' Sue was speaking softly with Joe as she watched Helen accompany Dave to the bar.

'Can't really see the point of going 'ome only to come straight back out again. It's nice just to relax here. Rugby really takes it out of you, you know. Anyway, so many people came up to wish me well for Monday, you know, keeping their fingers crossed, like, I could never have got away.'

'You must be really excited.'

Joe did not reply straight away and the expression on his face remained earnest. He struggled to find the right word. 'Scared, if you really wanna know,' he finally managed to say. Once again, he paused before carrying on. 'Next Saturday is gonna be incredible and I just wanna be sure I'm up to the challenge.' As he spoke these words quietly and without emotion, he held Sue's hand and squeezed it lightly.

'You'll be brilliant. You deserve it so much. I'll be so proud of you.' Sue leaned her shoulder into Joe's and rested her head against his.

'I hope you will be.' Joe turned his face to make eye contact with her. After a short pause, he repeated the phrase. 'I hope you will be.' Sue kept her head on Joe's shoulder and neither of them spoke a word. She assumed he was talking about running out for Wales next Saturday. This unusual need of his for reassurance placed some doubt in her mind.

The proximity of the date and the knowledge that he would almost certainly be selected made Joe feel morose and vulnerable, and he considered whether he should share his plan with someone, though he knew he could not. As he watched the clubhouse filling up with young people, excited at the prospect of dancing, drinking and flirting, he scanned the faces of the boys and men and tried to evaluate who would follow his lead, who would take up the fight, who would endure so that Wales would be rid of the English forever and be a proud nation once again. It dawned on him that by this time next week, it would be all over and his place in history assured.

'You're quiet?'

'Just thinking, reflecting on things.'

'Anything in particular?'

'Nothing really, just thinking about what it'll be like next Saturday. It'll be a hell of a day, that's for sure.' Sue could sense Joe's tension and picked up the tremor in his voice as he spoke and she squeezed his hand in recognition. 'You will be proud of me, I really hope you will.'

The comfort of Sue sitting next to him, the warmth of the clubhouse and the relaxing effect of the alcohol all conspired to lower his guard and he was tempted to reveal all to her. She would understand, surely? he said to himself. She would help him even, particularly during the coming week when he knew he would need the very utmost in support. Sue would provide that, she would understand. The past months had been difficult enough keeping his plans to himself but with next Saturday so close, he was in desperate need for reassurance. He turned his face towards Sue and looked directly into the almond-shaped eyes he loved so much and took some shallow breaths. He hesitated as he tried to find the right words and glanced quickly around to fathom whether anybody else would hear him. Dave and Helen were still at the bar, Pete and Phil were ensconced in conversation and Ann was slyly looking around the room while feigning interest in Dinner's opinion as to why Bryan Ferry was cooler than Marc Bolan. Joe was about to open his mouth when the whole clubhouse was shaken by Keith Richards's unmistakable opening guitar riff to *Brown Sugar* as it blasted from Rockin' Robin's stark black speakers. At the same time, the clubhouse lights dimmed and the whole place was transformed from drinking den to dancing club. All of a sudden, Joe's mood was shaken from its torpor and the loudness of the music put an immediate stop to what he was going to reveal to Sue.

'Fuck me, is Robin deaf or summing?' Joe blurted out, wondering if anybody around the table could hear him.

Everybody's head rose up as it was now impossible to converse, much to Ann's relief in particular. The words that were spoken were intermittent and more easily understood through reading lips than receiving sound. Sue noted that Pete and Phil's eyes were beginning to wander around the room, clearly evaluating which girls had arrived and whether they were alone or with partners. Dinner started to roll yet more tobacco into a Rizla paper and Ann took the opportunity to move away from him and sit next to Sue.

Joe sat back, his head rocking back and forth to the beat, his mouth miming Mick Jagger's vocals. The following Saturday suddenly seemed very far away and he was relieved that he had not opened up to Sue. What was he thinking of? He must be mad. The blasted drink had nearly got to him again, lulling him into a false sense of security. It could have all ended there and then if it hadn't been for Rockin' Robin.

Dave and Helen returned from the bar, both of them carrying small, round and battered metal trays advertising Welsh Bitter, the distinctive green and red colours virtually scratched away. They placed them on the table and everybody sought out their own drink, nodding in appreciation. When Mick Jagger stopped singing and Noddy Holder took over, the volume lowered somewhat. Someone had clearly had a word with Robin. Joe had seen Stan Williams waddling in the general direction of the DJ and he wondered if it had been him. If so, for the first and only time he could remember, Joe was in agreement with the club's president.

'That's better. I can hear myself think now. Thanks for the drinks, Hel, Dave,' Sue remarked.

'Here comes Gethin.' Dave motioned towards the door as their friend approached them. Helen's ears pricked up and she looked over towards him in an eager manner. She shuffled sideways in the bench seat she was sharing with Dave, leaving no doubt in Gethin's mind where he was expected to sit. Joe looked at Pete to check whether there were any obvious signs of a red mist descending but he seemed calm enough. It did not stop Sue from whispering to Joe to keep an eye on him, nonetheless.

'Bad luck, Geth, just missed the round. A pound in the kitty and here's some shrapnel to get yourself a pint.' So before Gethin could even unbuckle the belt of his long black trench coat, he was off to the bar where, with a deflating feeling, he observed it was three layers deep with thirsty customers.

Joe was half-listening to the conversation around the table when, by chance, he caught the eye of Stan Williams who was sitting amongst a large group of people on a long table by the side of the bar, situated the furthest point away from Rockin' Robin's speakers as was possible in the clubhouse. Williams hated the Saturday night discos and wished no more than to sit with his friends and discuss the day's rugby in peace like he did every other night of the week. He reluctantly had to accept, however, that without the regular Saturday night's takings, the club's already difficult financial position would become quite perilous.

The two of them stared at each other for what seemed an age but which was, in reality, only a few seconds. Williams's expression was dead-pan and it was he who broke off the eye contact first. This unsettled Joe for although they were of different generations and attitudes, they had never failed to at least acknowledge each other, often pleasantly, whenever their paths crossed. Nevertheless, Joe was certain that Williams had deliberately locked eyes with him and even more certain that when he looked away, there was a hint of embarrassment, as if he knew something he could not share with him and that if this was the case, the news was more likely to be bad than good. Maybe he was reading too much into it. After all, he had been very sharp and rude to him in the dressing room prior to the match. Perhaps it was no wonder he appeared none best pleased. It played on Joe's mind, nonetheless, as a packet of pork scratchings struck him in the face, flung gently in his direction by Dave. It startled Joe and his hands flew up in reflex, disturbing his private thoughts.

'What you day-dreaming about?' Dave asked as he tore open a bag of salt and vinegar crisps.

'Norralot,' he replied unconvincingly, leaning over Sue to pick up the packet from the floor. After sitting back up and crunching a mouthful of scratchings, he decided to share his concerns with his friends. 'Are you sure you saw Stan the Man with Bill Johnson after the match?' Nobody could mistake the sense of worry in Joe's voice, however much he tried to disguise it.

'They were in the committee room together, definitely. I saw 'em go in.' Phil reaffirmed his earlier comment.

'Mmm.' Joe's facial expression now reflected the worry in his voice. He glanced down briefly at the table top, picked up his pint glass, swilled the beer round but enigmatically did not continue the conversation. It took Pete to pick up on his mood.

'Oh, come on now, you're not worried about Williams shafting you with Bill Johnson, are you? Don't worry about it? You're in the side, definitely. Williams is just a fat slob. He doesn't have any influence over who plays for Wales.'

'Yeah, Pete's right,' Dave concurred, 'and remember, Dewi Griffiths was gonna have a word with him and come on, who's Johnson gonna listen to, him or Stan? And aren't you forgetting something, James has bust his hand so unless he breaks all the rules of medical science, there's no way he can play next week.'

'Yeah, I suppose you're right,' Joe agreed, reluctantly, and logically he knew they were, though it would have made him feel better if Phil had said the same rather than remaining quiet. 'I'm just a bit jumpy, you know. I can't really believe I'm gonna be in the team, like.' Sue slipped her arm in his and gripped it tightly, smiling proudly, just as Gethin finally returned from the bar and sat in the seat next to Helen.

'Right, next round,' Dave burst out. 'You're turn at the bar, Geth.'

'Piss off,' and everybody laughed.

The spirits around the table and everywhere in the clubhouse were high as the drink took effect, mixing potently with the steady stream of rock, pop and dance music. Soon, the dance floor was filled with girls, including Helen, Sue and Ann, whilst everywhere else around the clubhouse, groups of boys and men continued with their chatter though never taking their eyes off the girls gyrating away, hoping to catch the eye of one or another for later attention. Though still quite early in the evening, one or two of the dancing queens were a little bit worse for wear from the alcohol, most of it consumed at home as they tried on various outfits before venturing out. The combination of drink and high heels accounted for a young girl out celebrating her sixteenth birthday and as she completed an elaborate spin whilst singing along with the exquisite vocals of Diana Ross imploring *Ain't No Mountain High Enough*, her foot caught the strap of one of the many handbags littering the floor and she crashed to the ground just avoiding Sue and Helen. As her friends came to assist her, cruel laughter rang out from a group of boys leaning against the bar. The young girl, embarrassed and red in the face, galloped off to the toilets, two concerned friends tottering directly behind her like chicks following their mother hen.

Joe smiled as he witnessed the scene and he stared lovingly at Sue as she helped the fallen girl back to her feet. He could not take his eyes off her. He was so lucky to have such a gorgeous girlfriend and he noticed how Dave, Pete and Phil were all looking at her as well, though no man alive could surely prevent himself from staring at and admiring her small tight behind as she bent over.

The concern Sue had for the girl spoke volumes of the kindness and generosity that was part of her nature. Though a stranger to her, she was genuinely worried. Joe continued to stare at her and he knew he was in love, that this was the girl he wanted to marry, to have children with. The death of her parents had made her vulnerable and he wanted to hold her and protect her and make her know that she was not alone. Why had she come into his life at this moment? He reflected on this in real anguish and his stomach heaved slightly. He was going to hurt her, he knew. No, it would be worse, he would destroy her. How could he do this to her? Once again, the demons of doubt awoke from their slumber and flew around his mind, teasing him. He could feel himself weakening and if he had been told there and then that he had not been selected for the Welsh team, the sense of relief and delight would have been overwhelming. But he had encountered these demons on numerous occasions before and he knew how to fight them off and in an instant, his resolve returned. He would not fail. He would be strong enough. There were no doubts. But still, there was sadness and a deep-rooted concern at the effect his actions would have on Sue, his family and his friends. After the initial devastating shock, he hoped they would come round and be proud and even admire him. Yes, they would, he was sure of it. They would understand the cause. How could they not? It was unquestionably right. No unreasonable person could dispute it.

Still deep in contemplation, Joe took a sip from his beer and began scanning the room. He felt comfortable in the clubhouse; it was like a second home to him and being one of the stars of the team, he was made to feel like a king. Everybody had a word for him, a pat on the back, a drink. They loved him. But he knew he would never play for Pontypridd again and the thought saddened him. He saw Leap Thomas in a far corner towering, Gulliver-like, over a throng of admirers. He had presence and respect. Thomas had apologised to Joe in the dressing room after the game for the harsh words spoken at half-time which had so belittled him in front of his teammates. Joe knew he would do the same again in similar circumstances but his concern for him showed strength not weakness and sublime man-management skills. He was a true leader. Would he take up the cause? Joe hoped so. With Leap on board, the English would be finished.

As the evening progressed, Joe joined in the conversation with his friends but his mind was elsewhere and he did not absorb much that was being said and contributed little himself. He wished more than ever for Sue to be beside him, to provide the comfort only she could when the demons returned as they fleetingly did, no doubt sated on the bitter ale he was drinking. But Sue was on the dance floor, invariably trying out some new movements with her friends, smiling, laughing, the picture of happiness and enjoyment. The girls had been away from the table for what seemed like hours, the remnants of their fingerprint and lipstick-smeared glasses looking flat and uninviting. The conversation among the boys was becoming increasingly more difficult to hear as Robin cranked up the volume and longer periods of silence ensued. As they were unable to converse easily, their attention turned to the dance floor, their necks and eyes straining to consider which girls might be worth tapping. At this moment, their courage weakened and frequent, nervous sips of drink were taken.

Pete was determined to dance with Karen Dixon, not only because she was a very pretty girl but also because he knew Helen thought the same and he hoped she would be upset at his giving her attention. Gethin's eyes were very much on Helen and on a number of occasions she had smiled back at him from the dance floor. Or, he hoped her smiles were directed at him for he couldn't be sure and his courage faltered. There was also the added complication of Pete. They had made up of sorts after their fracas at the beginning of the year but if he made his intentions obvious towards Helen tonight, who knows how Pete would react. Maybe it was just better to sit there and listen to the music. Phil had left the table some time ago and was chatting animatedly to Taff Morgan. Joe noticed the Pontypridd scrum-half looking over Phil's shoulder every now and then and on a couple of occasions he caught Joe's eye, raising both of his to the skies. Joe smiled back. He loved Phil, but by God he could bore you to death about rugby sometimes. Dinner continued to roll his cigarettes and sip his drinks and always appeared to be looking down at the table and never directly into anybody's eyes. His fixed facial expression never changed as if the supply lines of emotional thoughts from his brain never arrived. He was too cool to contemplate the girls on the dance floor and he would never dream of actually going up to tap one. He was content in his misguided belief that Ann truly fancied him and he would wait for her to come to him. Dave was as ever on the point of drunken paralysis, stumbling badly when he stood up from his seat, bumping into people as he staggered to the bar or toilets and shouting deafeningly when Robin played one of his favourite tracks. Girls were always of great interest to him until the drink took hold. Once it did, there was no way he would attempt a move on anybody. Like clockwork, he only ever took to the dance floor right at the end of the evening for some head-banging as Robin rounded off his set with Black Sabbath's *Paranoid*. The girls always left the floor at this stage and Dave would round up all the boys, somewhat aggressively at times, to join him, even if they did not want to. He would invariably end up falling over and lying down flat on his back, out to the world. He was eternally grateful that his friends always managed to get him home.

As the throbbing beat of Status Quo's *Caroline* came to an end, Robin changed the mood and as if by telepathy, someone dimmed the lights further. The wonderful *My Cherie Amour* sounded from the speakers and the dance floor emptied save for two couples who held each other and moved gently in time to Stevie Wonder's loving vocals. The girls returned to their seats, their cheeks rouged through exertion, their shirts slightly damp down their backs and the faint whiff of perspiration mixing with their perfumes.

'Phew, that was great,' Sue began as she looked disapprovingly at her drink before taking a sip. She crinkled her nose as the taste of warm, concentrated orange juice slipped down her throat. Ann volunteered to get some more vodkas and orange and took the remainder of the kitty from Gethin. There was barely enough for one.

'God, boys, how much have you lot been drinking?' she exclaimed as she separated the few coins in the palm of one hand with the index finger of the other.

'Another quid in the kitty,' Dave blurted out as he rummaged in his jeans pocket for his wallet.

'Boys only,' Joe intervened, 'as we're doing most of the drinking.' Dave turned up his eyes towards him, a little disgruntled, but said nothing.

'Anybody seen Karen Dixon?' Pete asked nonchalantly but loudly. 'I think I'll ask her for a dance.' He tried to avoid Helen's face but couldn't resist a quick look sideways to gauge her reaction. She barely acknowledged the words. 'Now where is she?' Pete went on, eyeing the room in an exaggerated manner. 'I saw her earlier and she was looking absolutely stonking. She gave me a massive smile so I reckon I've gotta chance there.' Sue and Helen exchanged quick glances and gave the slightest of shrugs.

'She's over there with Eamon Murphy,' Dave responded, flicking his head in their general direction, 'an' if I'm not mistaken he's got his hand on her arse so I think you're out of luck.'

'Don't blame her,' Sue broke in, ''cos not only is he really good looking, he's really funny, unlike someone round this table I can think of.' Everybody exploded into laughter, with the exception of Pete, whose face turned as black as coal.

'Have I missed something?' Ann enquired as she returned from the bar.

'Only Pete making a tit of himself,' Sue replied.

'Beers, boys?' Pete asked grumpily, finding an excuse to leave the table. As he left for the bar, everybody just smiled at each other.

'You're okay, aren't you?' Sue asked her friend, touching her forearm lightly.

'Oh, God yes, don't worry,' Helen replied, casting a quick glance at Gethin who smiled back a little shyly. He took a big swig from his pint for courage and to gather his thoughts. If he was going to ask her to dance, he had to do it now for the slow records would not last forever. He remained silent before eventually but clumsily dipping his toe in the water.

'He's superb is Stevie Wonder. Such a brilliant song, this.' His words were spoken hesitantly and directed at nobody in particular.

'A lovely song to dance to as well,' Sue replied more loudly than usual. 'You like it, too, don't you, Hel?'

'Oh, yeah, it's lovely.'

Even Gethin could pick up the hint and in a voice which he hoped came over commandingly but which, in fact, only highlighted all the nerves he had in his body, he asked Helen for a dance.

'Thanks, that'd be nice,' and Helen got up sharply from her seat to accompany him to the dance floor before he had time to change his mind.

'You'd better hurry,' Dave shouted out, 'the song's about to finish.'

And indeed, as Gethin slipped his arm around Helen on the dance floor, the song came to an end and they released each other quickly and stood there avoiding each other's gaze. They shifted on their feet, both of them unsure what to do next. A tongue-tied Gethin had never felt so uncomfortable. The time before Robin spun his next disk seemed like an eternity to him. He was about to suggest returning to the table when the opening piano notes to Elton John's *Your Song* tinkled from the speakers. Once again, he opened his arms and held Helen and they began to move in time to the music. Helen's hold was quite firm and Gethin's nervousness evaporated.

Sue couldn't take her eyes off them and she smiled when at last they began their dance. Instinctively, she looked for Pete at the bar but could only see the back of his head. She leaned forward in her seat and was about to reach out for her drink when Joe stood up and took hold of her hand. 'Let's dance,' he whispered. Sue was a little taken aback because Joe only ever danced or, more likely, stumbled to one or two slow records right at the end of the evening, but without hesitation, she allowed herself to be led towards the smooching couples on the dance floor. Just as she was about to embrace Joe, she caught Helen's eye, who grinned back, contentedly.

Sue settled her head on Joe's shoulder, closed her eyes and immediately felt the warmth and comfort that his body and the beautiful music provided. Joe's hold was firm and delicate at the same time and Sue sensed straight away that she was providing a wonderful comfort to him as well. His next words stunned her, though. 'I love you, Sue, more than you can ever imagine. You're everything to me.'

Such compliments from Joe were rare and hardly ever delivered outside of the bedroom. Often, they were said as if Joe had to force the words out of him, as if it was a sign of weakness to admit such things. It had never bothered Sue because she knew deep down what he felt for her and she knew that her father had been the same with her mother. In fact, it seemed a very common trait amongst the male population of Pontypridd to suppress their feelings and it was a culture she was accustomed to. She raised her head from his shoulder, leaned back a fraction and looked him straight in the eye. 'That's lovely. I love you so much, too.'

Her head returned to his shoulder and their hold became even firmer. Joe ran his fingers slowly and lightly up Sue's back and she sensed a need in the way he held her that she had never experienced before. It was unusual but delightful at the same time because she wanted him to know that she was there for him whenever he wanted and his words and embrace suggested that this was such a time. Joe moved his face slightly away from her and then brought his mouth towards hers. After some delicate brushing together of lips, which sent delicious shivers of electricity down their spines, Joe opened his mouth and Sue needed no second invitation. They kissed with feeling, oblivious and uncaring as to what anybody else might think around them. *Your Song* ended and John Lennon's *Imagine* replaced it but the two of them barely noticed as their bodies remained in close embrace. Sue wondered about Joe's mood for he appeared more vulnerable than she had ever known him before, vulnerable and nervous. She believed it was finally dawning on him that he was on the point of playing for Wales. The high expectations and worry that invaded his body whether he could perform at the highest level of the game were clearly unsettling him. She held him even more tightly as she thought about this. She would provide him with the comfort and strength he would need. Joe reciprocated her tighter embrace with one of his own and those shivers of electricity down Sue's spine began to turn into greater waves of arousal. Then, all of a sudden, Sue felt a tiny droplet of water high on her right cheekbone and she realised that Joe was crying. So shocked was she at this, she leaned back slightly to view his face but Joe followed her movement, keeping his face close to hers for he was embarrassed to let her or his friends see him. But he could not hide his moist eyes and droplets of tears from her.

'Hey, Joe, what's wrong?' Sue's tone was soft, understanding and puzzling all in one.

'Nothing, it's just, oh, I dunno, it's just, you know, I love you so much and find it so hard not to be with you that, well, it just gets to me every now and then, like now.'

'That's okay. Don't worry, I'll never leave you, you know that. I love you with everything I've got.'

'I know and it's wonderful. I really need you, Sue... desperately. I'm just so, so, what's the right word, you know, edgy, nervous, worried, all these things.'

Sue pushed her body against his and although the two of them were still on the dance floor, they were hardly moving, their bodies only going through the motions of dancing as the importance of the conversation took hold.

'Hey, I'm here for you. You know that. Don't be afraid.'

'I know.' After a short hesitation, he added, 'I'd really like to stay tonight.'

It was usually pre-arranged when Joe would stay over at Sue's and this was one evening that had not been. He still found it impossible to tell his mother he would be staying at her house so he continued to tell occasional, little white lies about how he would be sleeping at Pete's or Dave's. He liked to forewarn his mother and it was for this reason that he always pre-arranged his stays with Sue. He knew his mother knew what he was up to and that there was always the danger of her bumping into Pete's or Dave's mother in town, but he continued in this way. He was not at the stage where he could discuss sleeping with girls with anybody in his family and his mother was not at the stage where she could easily confront him about it.

'Of course you can stay. I'd love that.' Her right hand gripped Joe's forearm. Joe said nothing in return but his loving caress of her body told Sue everything she needed to know about his gratitude. She became intrigued at Joe's mood and need and wished to delve more deeply into it. 'Don't worry about the game next week or all the publicity and stuff. You'll be fine. Is that what's bothering you or something else, p'rhaps?'

'Let's go and sit down.'

Though John Lennon had not yet come to the end of his song, they left the dance floor, hand in hand, snaking their way around the smooching couples and returned to their places at the table. A fresh pint sat invitingly in front of Joe but he ignored it. He was deep in thought, on the point of admitting all to Sue, but still holding back, unsure how she would react. He was truly in turmoil and he did not engage Sue in any conversation. He had not even thanked Pete for the beer though he was sitting opposite him, alone. Sue did not fail to miss the angry expression on Pete's face and the fact that he was staring hard towards the dancing couples and towards one couple in particular. She hoped he would not make a scene over Helen and Gethin, but at that moment, she was more intrigued as to how Joe would respond to her question, if at all.

Joe roused himself from his stupor and also noticed the look of fury on Pete's face but he said nothing. As if by reflex, he wiped both of his eyes with the back of his hand in an attempt to cover up any evidence of tears in front of Pete. He was sure that with the darkened room and Pete's attention elsewhere, he would not be found out. He sighed loudly but then said in a whisper, 'No, nothing else, really.'

His reply was clumsy and enigmatic, indicating clearly to Sue that there was something else on his mind. She paused for a brief moment before exploring more herself. 'You can tell me if there is. I won't tell anybody, I promise.'

'No, there's nothing.'

The tangible hesitation before Joe replied only hardened her belief that there was something on his mind that he was not sharing with her but he'd responded in the negative twice and she did not wish to pursue it any further. If he wanted to open up to her, then let it come out naturally. Joe slid along his seat closer to Sue and put his arm around her back and placed his other hand on her arm. He leaned his head against hers. His signs of affection pleased Sue and she placed her hand on his thigh. The security of his presence was comforting and she smiled to herself. He was certainly an enigma. She knew that from the very first time they had gone out together. It was not one of his better traits. In fact, by far, it was his worst, and occasionally when she was feeling vulnerable herself, her mind would wonder what little secrets he was keeping from her. Don't be so paranoid, she would scold herself. Doesn't everybody have their own little secrets? In truth, she did not feel insecure with him at all. She knew he was very attractive. It did not need her friends to tell her that but she knew how he felt for her even if he could hardly bring himself to admit it, unlike this evening. It was always pleasing to know from Dave and Pete how Joe spoke lovingly about her in front of them and she could understand how, somewhat irrationally, it was often easier to speak about one's feelings with a friend rather than directly with one's own partner. As these reflections permeated her mind, his beautiful words spoken earlier returned and she experienced a wonderful reassuring warmth inside her. She was still not certain what had led him to say them but hey, so what! This was a positive enigma, not one that she would try endlessly to evaluate.

But all these thoughts of Joe suddenly drew from one of the darker compartments rooted in her brain the puzzle of the missing handgun. Periodically, this mystery would rear its head but as time went by, less so. If Joe had taken it all those months ago, he had not done anything with it and so her worry as to why he had taken it diminished and in fact, she was increasingly more of the opinion that perhaps he had not taken it at all. But it still bugged her and she was determined to get to the bottom of it one day.

Joe remained quiet and immersed in deep thought beside her. Resting her head on his shoulder, she remained silent herself. She looked sideways, out of the corner of her eye at the dance floor and saw Helen and Gethin continuing their slow dancing to 10cc's *I'm Not In Love*. She loved this song and mimed the words to herself. The way Helen was holding Gethin suggested the exact opposite of the song's title and Sue's eyes opened wide in surprise at the sight of her hand wandering down to Gethin's behind, triggering him to copy her action in response. Sue also noticed the two or three light kisses Gethin placed on Helen's cheek and how Helen had turned her head to receive a couple more on the lips. All thoughts of Joe vanished from her mind for the moment as she considered her friend. Would this be the start of the loving relationship Helen had always wanted? She certainly hoped so for Sue liked Gethin a lot and he would be good for her friend, she was certain. The dance floor was now heaving with couples, so much so that there was barely any room to move, resulting in many couples dancing out of time with the music as they bumped into each other. Frequently, some girls had to stop dancing altogether and bend down to retrieve their handbags which were being nudged around the floor by errant feet. Sue continued to study the couples, intrigued to see who was dancing with whom. Joe gazed in their general direction but did not really take anything in. Sue then saw at the back of the dance floor Ann's arms wrapped around Phil's neck. They were not dancing but just standing there kissing passionately. Ann's neck was bent right back, so forceful was Phil's kissing. Excitedly, Sue turned to Joe and exclaimed, 'Look, over there, look, at the back, Ann and Phil, snogging! Can you believe it? She's such a dark horse, she never mentioned Phil to me at all. Look, Joe, look!'

Joe did look but he was not bothered. His mind was still in another place and he did not reply. With a huge smile on her face, Sue shook Joe's arm vigorously to draw a comment but he remained silent and Sue gave up. She strained her neck around some couples to see if Ann and Phil were still kissing. They were and her smile grew even wider. Dinner was sitting at another table with another friend rolling another cigarette. He, too, had seen Phil and Ann kissing but noting how he was virtually breaking her neck, he reasoned that she was not enjoying it and would soon return to his charms. Just be cool, he reminded himself, that's what girls like.

Sue was so entranced with Ann and Phil that it took her a brief moment to comprehend the streaking blur across her eye line and subsequent raised voices and commotion. She had taken her eyes and attention off Helen and Gethin but Pete had not and the two light kisses on the lips were enough to bring out his rage and he flew from his chair faster than a Bjorn Borg forehand smash and he launched himself head first into Gethin. His aim was so accurate that Helen remained kissing fresh air, untouched, like a scene from a Tom and Jerry cartoon, as her dancing partner was blasted away in a blur, at warp speed, as if on the Starship Enterprise. Pete, however, was unable to avoid other dancers and the force of his tackle on Gethin led to two other couples crashing to the ground at the same time as them.

'You fucking cunt, doing that to me, fuck you.' Pete began throwing punches at Gethin as he straddled him on the floor. Gethin lifted his arms in front of his face and he tried to catch Pete's hands as the blows rained down on him. His expression was like that of a startled wildebeest trapped by a hungry lion but he succeeded in deflecting the majority of Pete's punches away from him. 'Fucking bastard, muscling in on my girl like that.'

'Your girl! Do me a favour,' Gethin yelled back, finally gripping Pete's wrists to stem the blows. Before Gethin managed to say another word, the dead weight of Pete was suddenly lifted as Taff Morgan and Eamon Murphy physically threw him off him, grabbed Pete by the scruff of the neck and marched him smartly out of the main entrance before pushing him violently in the back and on to the rain-sodden tarmac outside.

'You're barred, you wanker. If we see you in 'ere again soon, you'll be getting one of these, orrite!' Both Taff and Eamon stared down at him, the former brandishing his right fist to accompany his words.

Back in the clubhouse, the commotion had settled down, with Helen and Phil helping Gethin back to his feet. They were soon joined by Sue who put her hand on Helen's shoulder to signal her concern. Rockin' Robin changed the mood and the pounding beat of the Osmonds' *Crazy Horses* blared out from the speakers.

'He's stark raving mad is Pete.' Gethin brushed himself down in some annoyance. 'What's his problem? He shouldn't drink so much if he can't hold it, the twat.'

'It's just he's still got the hots for Helen,' Sue replied and as if to reassure him and help her friend out added, 'but they stopped seeing each other ages ago and you were never too bothered anyway, were you, Hel?'

'Yeah, that's right,' Helen responded sheepishly. 'We went out for a bit but it was nothing in the end.'

Gethin had recovered his composure and put his arm around Helen. 'You okay?' he asked.

'Yeah, fine.' Helen smiled back and they kissed quickly on the lips.

'Let's go to the bar. I'll gerrem in.'

As Gethin, Helen, Ann and Phil moved off, Sue stopped momentarily and looked back at Joe who remained sitting in his place, his face expressionless. He had witnessed the commotion but instead of running over to help diffuse it as he would usually have done, he just stared blankly at the scene. He shook his head in sadness as he had done when Pete and Gethin had had their first dust-up in the Maltsters. It was a scene he had witnessed virtually every weekend, involving various different protagonists and he wondered deep down whether there was any real discipline amongst the Welsh youth of today to engage the English in a committed conflict. They all certainly liked to fight but it was kids' stuff, fuelled by alcohol. When it really came down to it, were they really up to the challenge? At that particular moment, he had only doubts.

'Be with you in a sec,' Sue said to her friends before breaking off to join Joe. 'Are you okay? You look a bit down.'

'I'm fine, just pissed off with Pete, that's all. He's such an arsehole, sometimes.'

'I thought you might've tried to stop them fighting. Are you going to check if Pete's alright?'

'I'm fed up of busting up fights. It's so pathetic. They should all grow up.'

Sue was surprised at his use of the general and the plural rather than focusing just on Pete. Once more, Joe went quiet and Sue sat down beside him, a little self-conscious. She looked up towards the bar where her friends were all mingling, awaiting service. She was about to break the ice and invite Joe to join them when he addressed her first. 'Come on, let's go. I've 'ad enough for tonight.' His tone of voice was soft and welcoming and Sue did not hesitate to agree to his wish. They both stood up, gathered their belongings and walked over to the bar. 'We're gonna be on our way.'

'So early?' Phil asked surprised.

'Yeah. It's been a long day and the match took a lot more out of me than I thought.'

'Aye, aye, are you sure that's the only reason the two of you are leaving?' Gethin added mischievously, winking at Joe.

Helen and Ann both looked at Sue who smiled, her cheeks reddening a little. They both smiled back knowingly. Sue moved her head closer to her two girlfriends. 'Call me tomorrow. I wanna know everything and I mean everything you two get up to tonight. You haven't escaped my attention, you know,' she whispered. The two girls grinned but said nothing.

'Come on 'en, Sue, let's go. See you all.'

'See yuh.'

Joe and Sue strode out of the clubhouse and pulled up the collars of their coats. Fortunately, it had stopped raining, but a stiff, cold, northerly wind was blowing and Sue, taking Joe's arm, hugged him tightly as they set off for her home. Briefly, Joe looked back at the clubhouse and the one set of rugby posts visible to him at that time of night. It saddened him to walk away from the club that meant so much to him for possibly the last time, and tears formed once again in his eyes.

21

Joe was lying on his back, staring up at the lampshade in the middle of the ceiling he had got to know so well. Though it was only seven o'clock in the morning, he had been fully awake for an hour. Across his chest, Sue's head lay lightly. His right arm tingled as it bent round Sue's naked back, hugging her to him. The pins and needles were mild, though, and he did not try to adjust it. His thoughts turned to the coming afternoon and the tasks he needed to carry out. All the time he had planned just the one but now, he knew, it had to be two. The quiet of the morning and softness of the bed helped relax Joe against the harsh reality of the following Saturday, the proximity of which was unnerving. A sliver of light shone faintly through the tiny gap between the curtains and across the bed and in his anxious state, he wondered whether it was being cast by God Himself, as if He knew what Joe was planning and providing him with the necessary determination.

Sue groaned softly and shifted her head a little as the first stirrings of life coursed through her body. The right arm across Joe's body tightened further as she sought even greater comfort from the heat it provided. She lightly traced her finger along two parallel jagged grazes on the side of Joe's chest, courtesy of Aberavon studs received the previous day. Her lips kissed the yellow and purple bruises so lightly that Joe hardly felt them.

'Mmm, this is so nice.' Sue's sleepy voice was only just audible and the hint of hoarseness reflected its dehydrated state and the passive smoke she had inhaled the evening before.

'The best feeling in the world.' Joe's reply was full of love and charm and though Sue's face was hidden from him, he sensed the tiny widening of her mouth on his skin as she smiled in accord with his sentiments.

To Sue's eyes, Joe certainly appeared more relaxed than he had been at the club and his love-making that night had been the most tender she had ever experienced. She could see the scars, the contours of hard muscle, the slow rise and fall of his chest. She could even hear the slow, regular heartbeat. But she was not conscious of the sickening knot in Joe's stomach which formed on and off dependent on when the anxiety of the following Saturday broke the barriers and filtered into his brain. Unbeknown to Sue, this was such a moment. Joe wondered about the shock of this moment next week and the despair of Sue and his family. The Sunday papers would carry headlines they could never imagine. The silence of this waking hour tormented him. Why could it not be Saturday already? Another six days of this would be torture and did he really have the strength to resist all the negativity and doubts? Life in Wales was not so bad, he tried to reason. But it was: servile, down-trodden, patronised, gutless, weak, pathetic even. His belief in these sentiments remained strong and to be the catalyst to rid Welsh people of the words he associated with them was not only right but heroic, a great service to the Welsh nation that would never be forgotten.

'I'm gonna have to make a move.'

'Why so early? Can't you stay another hour or two?' The sleepiness in Sue's voice had gone and her tone was sharper and tinged with disappointment.

'Sorry, but I can't, not today.'

'Why? Are you doing something special then?'

Joe hesitated palpably before responding. 'I need to get back and have a quick bath and scrub-up 'cos I don't wanna miss church this morning.'

'Church!' For the first time that morning, Sue raised her head and looked directly into Joe's eyes.

'What's wrong with that?' Joe replied less than convincingly.

'I never took you for a church-goer. You never mentioned it to me before. In fact, you said you always tried to avoid your mother on Sundays 'cos she kept badgering you about it.'

'Yeah, that's true, but that's not to say I don't mind going every now and then,' Joe lied. Sue stared hard into his eyes and said nothing which discomfited Joe immensely. 'What's the matter? What's wrong with going to church?' Sue remained silent and moved her elbow off him and lay down by his side. She clearly had a sulk on and refused to touch him. 'It's important to me, Sue. Please believe me.'

'Sounds more like an excuse to me,' Sue retorted grumpily. 'You never mentioned church before. You just want to get away.'

'If you don't believe me, just be outside St. Dyfrig's at ten-thirty and you'll see me there.'

Joe knew she wouldn't be there and Sue knew that she wouldn't go but the sincerity in his voice mollified her and she snuggled up closer to him in a calmer frame of mind. In fact, Joe was not making excuses. He did plan to go to church with his mother and brother that morning. When attending St. Michael's Catholic primary school, he was obliged to go to church every Friday in addition to the usual Sundays and the importance of Jesus, Mary, Joseph and all the disciples was drummed into him at the earliest of ages. Indeed, Joe had loved all the biblical stories and had frequently said private prayers to himself. As he got older, he lost religion, unable to reason out the great miracles that he had once taken for granted. But such an upbringing meant that religion would always play a tiny part in his life, a prayer here and there for peace of mind and if he ever needed the strength and comfort that God could bring, it was at this particular moment. For this was the last Sunday before the tumultuous events of the following weekend and the last chance to say his prayers in the house of God. Not only would he pray for strength but he would pray for his family and friends and for Sue, all of whom would need fortitude beyond imagination this time next week. He would ask God to take care of them and to give them the necessary understanding to help them through the forthcoming traumas.

The tornado of emotions spinning through his brain was overwhelming him and in an attempt to escape them, he pushed Sue's arm off him and flung back the duvet in an overly aggressive manner. He swung his legs round in a flash and sat by the side of the bed for a moment, his head in his hands, looking down between his legs at the carpet. The abruptness of his movements had the desired effect and emptied his mind somewhat of these unnerving feelings and a greater calmness swept over him. He turned to face Sue. 'Sorry 'bout that but if I don't force myself, I'll never leave.' Sue edged herself towards him with a smile on her face and attempted to place her hand on Joe's half-erect penis. Joe stood up sharply with a firm, but unconvincing 'no' and took one stride to the armchair to gather his clothes.

'Just a little longer, pleeeaaassse.' Sue's tone was at its most suggestive but Joe quickly put on his underpants and trousers, following up with the rest of his clothing.

'Sorry.'

'I'll come down with you.'

Sue was resigned to the fact that Joe would not change his mind and leapt out of bed, gathering up her dressing gown. She followed him out of the room, along the landing and down the stairs to the front door where Joe put on his shoes which he had left on the doormat the previous evening. He turned to face Sue before opening the door. 'Thanks for a lovely evening and for yesterday at the club. You were really there for me when I needed someone.'

Sue held both his hands and pulled him towards her. 'I'll always be here for you,' she whispered in his ear. They held each other for a full minute without saying a word, Sue on tip-toe, resting her head on Joe's left shoulder. 'The big day tomorrow…it's so exciting. I'll call you straight after school. I can't believe I'm going out with an international rugby player.'

'Well, let's just wait for the announcement first and not count our chickens.'

'You're so cautious; you're definitely in.'

'We'll see, hopefully, but I don't wanna tempt fate.' But Joe's voice exuded confidence.

'What you doing after church, O Lord Jesus Christ?' Sue spat out the words sarcastically, bowing in reverence in front of him.

'The usual, you know, lunch and then a couple of things I need to do.'

'Like what?'

'I'll probably touch base with Pete as well and see 'ow the pillock's doing.' Joe had deliberately not answered Sue's question and changed the subject.

Fortunately, the mention of Pete's name reminded Sue of Helen and the relationships that appeared to be forming the night before. 'Oh, I remember now, last night, Helen and Gethin, Ann and Phil. I must speak to the girls today and find out what went on. Can you believe it? Did you see Ann snogging Phil, the little hussy?' Sue was so excited that she hopped around on the spot and her face shone like a full moon on the darkest of nights. Joe smiled in response, let go of Sue and opened the front door.

'We'll speak tomorrow,' and with a final quick kiss on the lips, he was gone.

* * *

'Hello. It's only me.'

Joe's mother looked away from the bacon she was frying and towards the slam of the front door and the greeting shouted from the hallway. Joe was bounding along and entered the kitchen where his father had his head immersed in the *Sunday Mirror* and his brother waited patiently, head in hands, for his breakfast. Neither of them acknowledged him. '*Dove sei stato?*' Mrs Chilani enquired of her son's whereabouts. 'And Marco, take your elbows off the table.'

'I stayed over at Pete's last night. He was in a right old state so I had to take him home. He was steaming drunk, just all over the place he was and he got into a fight with

Gethin as well so I had to cool things down a bit. Sorry I didn't call from the club but there was a massive queue for the phone. We didn't get to his house till gone twelve and I didn't want to disturb you.' Mrs Chilani turned back to the frying pan while Marco cast him an unbelieving glance. 'Just summing quick, Mum, 'cos I wanna have a bath. I'd like to go to church with you today.' Marco's head turned sharply towards his brother and he frowned. He wondered what had come all over him and was annoyed that he no longer had an excuse himself to get out of church that morning.

'*Bene*,' Mrs Chilani replied nonchalantly while cracking open an egg.

Before Joe sat down, his father got up, placed the newspaper on the sideboard, gathered his coat and cap from under the stairs and left the house. Joe ate his breakfast quietly and replied monosyllabically to Marco's questions about the match against Aberavon. The newspaper's headline centred on Steve James's broken hand and only two paragraphs into the match report suggested strongly that Joe was now certain to be selected for the forthcoming international. Joe read the report with satisfaction, ignoring his brother. With a final slurp of his grapefruit juice, Joe rose from his chair and made to go upstairs. 'I'm gonna have a nice long soak in the bath so if you want a poo or piss, do it now 'cos I don't want you disturbing me when I'm in there, orrite!'

'I've already been,' Marco responded, not bothering to look up at his brother.

'Ta, Mum,' and with that he shot up the stairs, ran the bath, stripped off in his bedroom and immersed himself in the steaming water, foaming with Badedas. He looked at the bottle with uncertainty wondering what had happened to his favourite Radox.

An hour later, Joe was sitting in the living room waiting for Marco and his mother, reading a paper. He was devouring the sports pages, glancing only momentarily at the headlines on the front. He was wearing his graphite-grey flannel trousers and black tasselled slip-ons, which shone brightly in the sunlight that beamed through the window thanks to his mother's obsession with polishing shoes. He wore a crisp white shirt under his navy-blue lambswool pullover. Freshly shaven, black hair slicked back and still rosy in the cheek after his bath, even his mother commented how handsome he looked when she entered the room, fastening her wristwatch at the same time. She was proud that her friends and cousins would get to see such a good-looking boy today when they arrived in church, particularly after commenting that they had not seen him for a very long time.

'Marco, take off that sweatshirt and put a pullover on like your brother. You're not wearing that to Mass. And brush your hair.' Marco slowly left the room and returned sulkily to his bedroom to change.

The three of them entered St. Dyfrig's together, Joe and Marco a pace behind and either side of their proud mother. As they walked up the centre aisle, they cast glances left and right and smiled acknowledgements at those they knew and who were already seated. When they found some available places in a pew, they edged their way along and Joe and Marco sat down while their mother knelt on the burgundy cushion in front of her and said a prayer. As usual, the church was only half-full and Joe scanned the congregation for anybody else he knew. When the Mass began, an air of solemnity took hold and Joe's thoughts returned to the events of the forthcoming Saturday. He closed his eyes and shivered slightly, inducing Marco to turn and look up at him. When it was time to kneel, Joe closed his eyes once more and whispered a quiet prayer. 'Please, Lord, next Saturday will test my resolve and strength beyond anything I've ever experienced before in my life. Please give me the determination to succeed in my task so that this wonderful country of mine will rise to fight and find justice. I know how hard it will be for Mum, Dad, Marco and Sue, so please, Lord, look after them, give them strength, give them the ability to understand what I have done so that they can be proud of me as I am of them. I am ashamed I ask this of You, me who never goes to Mass or hardly ever prays. I do not deserve Your help but at this particular, critical time, I know that I cannot go ahead without You. So I ask for Your help with all the gratitude I can muster. Thank you, Lord.'

When Joe finished, he saw that the rest of the congregation was already standing up and he felt a tear running down one of his cheeks. Marco looked up at him baffled and wondered what was up with his brother. This did not last long, though, for he was already bored silly and wishing the priest would get on with it and finish. Joe and Marco sat down when many of the congregation, including their mother, went up to receive Holy Communion. Joe was tempted to receive the Host himself but not having confessed his sins for over two years, he did not feel that he should. He remained seated, deep in thought and pleasantly relaxed after saying his prayers. Marco was so disinterested in the whole proceedings he even began to see what was under the soles of his shoes to pass the time, picking at some tiny stones that had embedded themselves into the rubber. Joe shoved him hard enough for Marco to bump into the person seated on the other side of him and with his cheeks blushing, he quietly apologised before thumping his brother weakly on the thigh with his fist.

Two hours later, not only was Marco's purgatory a distant memory but like his brother, Joe was also in a very contented frame of mind. They had just finished their Sunday lunch, one of the highlights of the week for both of them. Their mother was a truly fantastic cook, though regrettably, neither brother complimented her enough on it. Joe could never understand the often repeated saying that a man subconsciously looked for elements of their mother in a girlfriend. It seemed weird and he was adamant it did not apply to him. But these moments after Sunday lunch did make him believe his already wonderful relationship with Sue could be even better if she could match his mother's talents for cooking. Perhaps there was some truth in the saying after all.

Today, Mrs Chilani had roasted a leg of lamb and her two sons had irritated her when she pulled the dish out of the oven. As it rested on the table awaiting carving, they both picked at it with their fingers, tearing off the succulent meat from the bone. The aroma was so tempting it was impossible to wait those extra few minutes before it arrived at the table. Sunshine quickly joined them in the kitchen looking up at them with her huge, desperate eyes, willing them to throw her a morsel. A few roasted potatoes went missing from that particular dish as well before it reached the table. It seemed to Mrs Chilani that her boys had already had enough to eat before taking their seats at the dining table and she shouted at them to stop picking as it would ruin their appetite. At the table, Joe plunged in first to take down more meat, selecting the darkest pieces as he liked his lamb well cooked. If Marco beat him to a piece he liked, Joe was not averse to taking it straight back from Marco's plate, to his great annoyance. The biggest fights, however, would take place over crackling whenever their mother cooked pork. On those days, Marco would quickly take the biggest bits and run away from the table to eat them before his brother could get hold of him. Only when their father intervened and admonished them sharply did the boys calm down.

The lamb and potatoes were trimmed with peas and carrots, both smothered in butter and Joe drowned his plate in gravy before finally adding some mint sauce, the smell of which he adored. The green mint floating in the ocean of brown gravy looked mildly disgusting to those of a weaker disposition but to Joe it provided the most fantastic taste. When Marco turned up his nose, Joe reminded him that this was the reason why he was so big and strong and why he was such a little runt.

The lamb was followed by another one of the boys' favourites and in Joe's eyes, a work of art that should be admired rather than eaten. Their mother's sherry trifle was what all the angels in heaven must be eating for it was truly historic. Even Sunshine's patience could not hold when this appeared on the table as she jumped up and ignoring everybody and everything, slinked towards the dish. She never made it as she was unceremoniously thrown back on to the floor where Joe tormented her by putting some of the thick cream on the top of her nose and out of the reach of her tongue. Sunshine always found a way to get it in the end, though. The sherry trifle was large enough to last a week in most households but not in this one and it was eaten at one sitting.

The two boys moved from the table and to the armchairs, feeling their stomachs and decidedly sleepy at the same time. Their father remained at the table, his head immersed in *The Sunday Times*, one of the three papers he took on Sunday. He continued to sip from his wine glass and he lit the first of what would be a number of cigarettes that afternoon. The winter had been a boring time for Marco as he rarely went out on Sunday afternoons and he would constantly badger his father to go for a drive in the car. For some reason, which Joe could never fathom, Marco liked to go to the service station at the Severn Bridge where despite the heavy lunch, he loved to eat chips smothered in tomato sauce and mustard and drink Coca Cola. Joe could not understand how small Marco was for he ate a huge amount for his size. He must have worms, he would tell his friends, to Marco's great annoyance. Marco was impatiently waiting for the start of spring in a few weeks' time for then he would plonk himself in front of the television and watch the Sunday League cricket coverage for hour after hour. He loved cricket, much more than rugby or football and had ambitions to play for Glamorgan one day. If Barry Richards or Clive Lloyd were batting, he would aggressively tell everybody in the living room to keep quiet, even his father, so that he could concentrate and enjoy the thrilling stroke play of his two cricketing heroes.

As Joe sat in the armchair watching his mother clear the table, a task none of her family ever volunteered to help her with, his mind returned to the terrible traumas his family would be experiencing at this precise moment the following week, and the contrast with this peaceful, lazy Sunday afternoon could not have been greater. However, unlike other times when such thoughts entered his mind, at this particular moment he felt calm and in control of his nerves. He congratulated himself on going to Mass that morning for the prayers he said had unquestionably brought the peace of mind he hoped they would. It was clear that the Church would be there for his family to provide support in the days, weeks and years to come and this knowledge gave him great satisfaction. He also believed that he would not now be alone, that God Himself would look over him during the tumultuous week to come. Had not His own son made a huge sacrifice and mankind been saved as a consequence? Joe had never thought in these terms before and it eased his mind immensely. He could still not reason out the existence of God but at this moment, religion was playing a key role in providing him with the necessary determination and resolve and he vowed to return to prayer during the week when those two despicable enemies of his, weakness and doubt, wreaked havoc in his mind as they would most certainly do.

Joe could feel himself falling asleep so with a start, he jumped up from the armchair, causing his father to turn away from the paper momentarily. Sunshine had been curled up fast asleep on his lap so Joe's sudden movement threw her off and disorientated her briefly before she scampered out into the kitchen.

'I'm going up to my room. I've got a difficult essay to write for tomorrow.'

'Are you going to come for a ride in the car later? Dad, we are going for a ride in the car later, aren't we?'

Their father did not reply to Marco's question and his silence was taken by Marco as discouraging.

'No, not me. This essay'll take ages. I've got to concentrate quite hard so don't disturb me, orrite!'

'What's it about?'

'Stuff you won't understand.'

'Try me?'

'It's an analysis of how important the construction of canals was to the Industrial Revolution in the last century if you really wanna know.'

Marco said nothing, totally perplexed and stared hard at his brother before muttering 'stupid subject' under his breath and walked away. Joe retired to his bedroom, closing and locking the door behind him. He hoped his family had got the message not to disturb him. He prepared himself for the two tasks he had to undertake.

* * *

The evening light had started to dim as Joe walked sheepishly into the kitchen where his family was gathered around the table. Some cold slices of lamb and jars of mint sauce and Branston pickle were at its centre and on the sideboard, a large Madeira cake was awaiting cutting.

'*Finalmente! Vuoi prendere una buona tazza di tè?*'

'Ta, Mum, tea'd be nice.'

His mother poured him a cup as he sat down, those in front of Marco and his father already steaming. She put a plate in front of him and Joe took down some lamb and Branston. He suspected that the best pieces had already been taken. His eyes were bloodshot and Marco wondered if he had been crying. His mother also noticed and addressed him. 'Your eyes look red.'

Joe was discomfited at the comment and thought quickly on his feet before replying. 'It's nothing much. It's just I've been staring at this piece of paper for ages and writing non-stop and my eyes got tired. I've been rubbing 'em a bit, that's all.'

'It must be a long essay, you've been up there hours.' Joe thought Marco was fishing. His acute senses would make him a good lawyer when he grows up, Joe reflected.

'Yeah, mainly 'cos I couldn't get to grips with it and kept scrubbing stuff out. It was harder and took much longer than I thought it would. Did you go for a drive in the end?'

'No!' Marco's tone was sharp and he looked up at his father with an air of discontent.

'You missed *Rugby Special*.' Mr Chilani finally spoke.

'Yeah, I heard you call me but I was too immersed in the essay. Who was on?'

'Harlequins and Rosslyn Park was the main match. It was a good game. Harlequins won 21–18. Might be a good thing you didn't watch it,' his father added enigmatically.

Joe looked at his father, puzzled. 'Why d'you say that?'

'Because James Harrison was playing and he scored two great tries. You'll have to watch him like a hawk next week if they pick you.'

'Might be better you miss this match and play the next one,' Marco commented unhelpfully, with a smirk. Joe's face turned angry and biting his lip, he fixed unblinking eyes on his brother, discomfiting Marco to such an extent he was forced to look away and shift uneasily in his chair.

'Fucking Harrison.'

'Oi, watch your language!' Mr Chilani turned aggressively towards Joe with real fury in his face. 'Don't think you're being clever using language like that.'

'Giuseppe, I hope you don't use language like that outside of this house. *Sei cattivo*,' his mother chipped in, admonishing him.

'Sorry, I won't use it again.'

'Well, let's hope not.' His father's serious expression and look towards Joe emphasised who the boss was in this household.

'Harrison's no problem. You watch next week. He's gonna get the shock of his life.'

Joe's mother quickly cleared the table so that she would not be late for *The Onedin Line*. Her family had already moved into the living room after their supper to settle down in front of the television. The mention of James Harrison had unsettled Joe, however, and his mind began to fill with numerous conflicting thoughts. He stared hard at the television, finding it difficult to concentrate, and he commented briefly to his father how downhill it had gone since his all-time favourite programme, *The Golden Shot*, had ended a couple of years earlier. He used to be as thrilled as Bob Monkhouse, Anne Aston and the whole studio audience whenever a contestant managed to fire Bernie's bolt from the crossbow and cut the thread over the bullseye. Incongruously, this image came to mind and he hoped his aim would be as certain the following Saturday.

'I'm gonna bed.'

'This early? You like *The Onedin Line*, don't you? It's on in a minute.'

'Yeah, but not tonight. I might tinker a bit more with this essay,' he replied insincerely. 'Anyway, tomorrow's a very big day and I feel a bit on edge so I just wanna get some sleep.'

And tomorrow was indeed a very big day. Joe's mind had been on so many things this Sunday that it was only late on that he remembered that the Welsh side to play England was being announced at one o'clock. He was confident of selection, everything pointed towards it. Nothing could go wrong. This was it.

22

"And the Wales team to play England at Cardiff Arms Park next Saturday is as follows: Full-Back...John Evans; Right-Wing...Gareth Evans; Left-Wing...Jim Morgan; Centre and Captain...Geraint Lewis; Centre...Ray Douglas..."

'Noooooo!' Exasperated expressions of incredulity rang round the classroom. The schoolboys and teachers who were gathered round the single transistor radio all leaned back in disbelief and looked immediately towards Joe, their mouths agape. Nobody had been able to concentrate on their lessons that morning in anticipation of the announcement and when the bell and buzzer had sounded, everybody rushed off to scoff down their lunch quickly before meeting up in Joe's classroom.

The sense of excitement that morning was palpable and his fellow school friends were even more nervous than Joe was himself. He had devoured the morning papers and was convinced he would be selected. Dewi Griffiths had been as good as his word in *The Times* saying the time was right for Joe's elevation to the team, that the Welsh back division was in need of the attacking flair he would bring and that with James Harrison in mind, the Welsh defence required the robust tacking only Joe could provide. 'Game, set and match,' a relaxed Phil had said to him when they walked out of assembly together. And if Phil was confident, Joe was confident.

The mood was quite different now, however. A sense of unease pervaded the room and nobody knew what to say. Even Gerald Jenkins, the senior PE master, was stunned.

"*Outside-Half...; Scrum-Half...; Loose-Head Prop...;*"

The names of the rest of the team continued to crackle out from the radio but very little interest was being paid to them. Joe was in shock. Unlike his omission from the first match of the international season when he stormed out of the classroom, he remained seated, tiny beads of perspiration forming on his brow and upper lip, his heart doubling its rate of beat. He stared at Pete, Dave and Phil open-mouthed, his face a ghostly white, without registering their presence.

"*Hooker...; Tight-Head Prop... Richard Evans;*"

'Rocky's in,' Phil uttered, breaking the silence, 'brilliant.' But even this did not filter into Joe's brain. He was trying to understand what it all meant. He had blown it. It was all over. His plans were in ruins. The tiny beads of sweat on his brow linked together and a fine trickle ran down one of his temples. He was yet to utter a word.

'I'm sorry, Joe. That's real bad luck.' Gerald Jenkins placed his hand on Joe's shoulder. 'I know it's disappointing but you'll get there, don't worry.'

"*Second-Row...; Second-Row...;*"

'Ray Douglas! What the fuck's going on?' Pete snorted, his voice trembling with anger.

'Williams! Watch your language,' Jenkins bellowed at Pete, his face mirroring Pete's tone of voice. He leaned over and cuffed him around the head. 'This isn't the first time I've warned you. Come and see me at the end of the day and feel lucky I won't report this to the headmaster.'

'Sorry, sir, I just lost it a second.'

'No matter, see me at the end of the day,' Jenkins repeated sternly.

"Wing-Forward...; Wing-Forward...; No. 8...."

The boys shifted uneasily in their chairs, one or two of them rising and looking to leave. Joe remained statuesque in his, not moving a muscle, his head buzzing with hundreds of incoherent thoughts; What now? What happened? How come? Unbelievable, the Luger, Mum, Dad, Sue, Marco, James Harrison, Prince Charles, Cardiff Arms Park, Stan Williams, Dewi Griffiths, Phil; stupid, useless, fucking failure. He had not heard a word Gerald Jenkins had said nor had he felt the consoling pat on the shoulder.

'It's unreal. How can they pick Ray Douglas over you? It's just beyond. You ran rings round him the other day. It's a disgrace. The selectors should be ashamed of themselves.' An angry Phil made an effort to start up some conversation, shaking his head, unable to believe what he had just heard.

"The six reserves are...John Phillips; ...Harry Watkins; ... Ceri Hickman;"

'Yeah, it's just ridiculous, it is, unbelievable, a total disgrace,' Dave agreed, also shaking his head and pursing his lips, his face turning crimson. All the other boys shook their heads as one and uttered the same sentiments. Nothing, however, grabbed Joe's attention and he began to feel quite nauseous. He could vaguely make out the comforting words in the background: 'Don't worry, next time, bad luck, ridiculous, unreal, unbelievable, disgrace,' but they meant nothing.

"...Steve Lewis; ...Glyn Burnell; ...Joe Chilani."

What was that? Did he just hear his name on the radio? He swore he did. For the first time in a couple of minutes,

Joe gave some reaction to the events around him. He raised his eyes bemused, bewildered even, but this time his eyes were wide open, looking around him like a new-born lamb. It was Phil who confirmed aloud what Joe believed he had heard. 'You're in as a reserve! Did you hear that!' All the boys smiled and looked at Joe who in turn looked directly into Phil's eyes and held his stare. For a few seconds, there was silence as they tried to understand what being a reserve meant. It was the last thing they or anybody else had considered.

'Reserve; that means you'll get on if someone gets injured,' Gerald Jenkins offered. Having witnessed Joe's despondency, he talked up the selection, encouraging the other boys. 'That's superb. Well done, Joe, you're in the Welsh squad. Fantastic, innit, boys?'

'Yeah, just brilliant.' And although the congratulatory words were well meant and accompanied by wide smiles, the sense of disappointment that he had missed out on making the actual team remained and the congratulations were a touch muted and certainly did not bear any resemblance to the ecstatic reaction that would have emanated had he made the starting XV.

Joe's face became brighter, full of curiosity, the new-born lamb in a world it did not yet understand. He struggled to evaluate what being a reserve meant for his plan. 'Thanks, boys, appreciate it,' he responded hesitantly. 'Being a reserve means I'll be at the game, wonnit?'

'Course you will. Like Mr Jenkins said, if someone gets injured you'll be on and even if it's only for ten seconds, you'll win your cap.'

'Yeah, but only if they're in Joe's position. There are five other reserves as well. There's Joe and Glyn Burnell who can cover for the centres, wings and full-back, fly-half even, so you know, if one of them does go off, he's got a great chance of getting on.'

'What about beforehand?' Joe interrupted, looking at Phil and Mr Jenkins, his mind working overtime and totally disinterested in the analysis of how he might win his cap.

'What d'you mean?'

'Well, you know, beforehand, before the match starts, like. I'll be able to line up with the teams for the anthems, won't I?'

'Definitely, and I'll tell you why.' Joe was all ears as Phil answered him. 'Because Prince Charles is coming, both of the teams will line up to meet him, including the reserves. Usually, only the fifteen actually playing get on the field for the anthems but when some bigwig is in attendance and they don't come any bigger than Prince Charles, then everybody lines up so you'll definitely be there. God, I'd give my right arm to stand there and listen to the anthem wearing the red shirt. It's gonna be incredible.'

'You're sure now, aren't you? This means everything to me.' Joe was so anxious he demanded confirmation from his friend, his tone desperate.

'Believe me! In fact, it was in *The Echo* on Saturday. You musta missed it. There was a piece in there about the match next week and how Charles was coming and how not only him but half the Welsh Rugby Union Committee were gonna be presented to the teams. Yeah, there's gonna be a bit more pomp than usual, like. You know, the band's gonna play a bit longer, a red carpet, stuff like that. Just fantastic, it'll be. The hairs on the back of your neck are gonna be standing up like mad. I know they will be on mine an' I'm not even going. Apparently, the security's gonna be mega, too. You know, loads of cops to keep an eye on the crowd and plain clothes detectives dotted round as well.'

'Best job in the world. Can you imagine being a copper at an international? Getting in free with sweet FA to do,' Pete butted in, casting a worried glance at Mr Jenkins who this time did not admonish him as he had held back on saying the 'f' word outright. The PE master's facial expression, however, made plain to Pete that he was walking a very fine line.

'You're sure now, aren't you?'

'Yes, Joe. Trust me. You'll be on the pitch for the anthems.' Phil sounded a little exasperated at Joe's unnecessary doubts.

'You'd better make sure you wash your hand before you shake Charles's now, won't you, you know, him being royalty an' all that,' Dave interrupted, grinning.

'I've gotta better idea. Why don't you wipe your arse first then shake his hand. I'll crease up if I see him sniff it afterwards on the telly.'

'You're disgusting, Williams,' Mr Jenkins retorted but he had a smile on his face this time and everybody began to laugh.

'Shame you won't be up against Harrison, though. I'd have liked to have seen a rematch of you against 'im. The selectors have really fu... sorry, messed up picking Douglas.'

'But I'll still meet him on the pitch, though, won't I?'

'What d'you mean?' Phil asked slightly perplexed.

'Well, as I'll be on the pitch beforehand lining up for the anthems and warming up, like, I'll be bound to come across him, won't I?' Joe said these words as if staring into thin air and everybody went quiet, not understanding what Joe was talking about. He seemed to be in another world, his mind clearly focusing and picturing the scenes on Saturday. He failed to register the air of puzzlement in the faces of his friends. All that mattered to Joe was that he would be on the field on Saturday in close proximity to Charles and Harrison and in front of a huge television audience. He remained quite trance-like for a few moments but then it dawned on him as clear as anything that he had not failed. In fact, he had succeeded, not quite how he had imagined it, but nevertheless, he would be on the field of play.

All the hard work and commitment and excruciating pain had paid off. The work in the gym that strained his muscles until he thought they would explode; the weights that made his hands and arms and legs sore for days on end; the brutally long runs in rain and sleet and wind; the multiple sprints that made his lungs burst and left him gasping for breath and retching in agony. It had all been worthwhile. He had succeeded. He would be on the field for this momentous match. The realisation overwhelmed him. 'I've done it, I've done it, I've fucking done it!' he yelled, finally escaping from his reverie and looking at each person around him individually in the eye. 'I'm gonna be on the field on Saturday, I've done it!' He grabbed Pete's arm, clasping it tightly. 'I've fucking done it!' He did not care that Mr Jenkins was still in the classroom and the PE master, understanding the enormity of what Joe had achieved and the prestige he had brought to the school, ignored the expletives. Pete looked at him but Mr Jenkins's look back confirmed that he still expected to see him after school. 'Yeeaahh!' Joe screamed out at the top of his voice in euphoria, standing up from his chair, both of his hands clenched in fists in front of him. His face radiated happiness.

All the boys and masters were a little taken aback by Joe's reaction but they still smiled at his joy and sense of pride and achievement. Okay, he had not made the actual team but being a reserve was still an accomplishment in itself and there was every chance he would get on the field to win his first cap. Dave began to clap and everybody joined in, their faces wreathed in smiles. Soon afterwards, the boys began to filter away, the majority of them heading for the tuck shop to buy some goodies for the afternoon. Gerald Jenkins tapped Joe on the shoulder as he made to leave and asked him to pop in and see the headmaster whom he knew would want to congratulate him.

'So what 'appens now, Phil? Shall I expect a phone call from someone?'

'Maybe, I'm not sure, but I think you'll get a letter, probably tomorrow, giving you all the details about when and where to turn up. Usually, the squad meets up on the Thursday before the game at the Angel Hotel in Cardiff for a bit of a run through in the afternoon and on Friday and then there's the match on Saturday.'

'So I'll be staying over two nights?'

'Three, I think, 'cos there'll be a fancy dinner on Saturday night after the game and a big piss-up, I'm sure. And all for free, you jammy sod.'

'Make sure you don't forget your tux,' Dave blurted out.

'Tuxedo? Hadn't thought of that.' Joe had not given a second's thought to the dinner after the game and to the dress code. And he wasn't going to start now.

'So you'll be getting hordes of tickets to hand out to your friends 'en, no doubt?' Pete's question got to the heart of a very important matter and he, Dave and Phil all looked up at him expectantly.

'Ah, now this is something I did look into. Anybody selected is entitled to two complimentary tickets apparently and the option to buy two more.'

'Wha' d'you mean by complimentary?'

'Free, you twp.'

'Ah, that's what I thought,' Pete lied.

After a pause, Joe continued sternly. 'I'll come straight to the point. My father really wanted me to offer two tickets to Mr Collins who's a very good friend of his and I couldn't say no. I've also promised Sue one and she asked whether Helen could go with her. I'm sorry, boys.'

'What! Sue must be looking after you alright!' Dave's expression of horror was partly in jest as deep down inside, Joe's friends knew that she or his family would have first call on any tickets available. As it transpired, Joe had asked his mum and dad but they both declined. They both preferred to watch the match on television. When Marco had asked whether he could have one, Joe's reply was customarily withering.

'I promise I'll keep my ears to the ground when I meet up with the squad and if there's anything going, I'll let you know.'

The bell and buzzer sounded outside in the corridor and the boys all rose to go to their next lessons.

'We're still 'aving a drink tonight to celebrate, though, aren't we?' Pete asked.

'Ah, not tonight. Sorry, boys, but I'm out with Sue. She's cooking me a meal round her place.'

'So that's the secret. She's cooking for her ticket.'

'And something else, no doubt,' Dave chipped in mischievously and everybody started to laugh, Joe included.

'Tell you what, let's 'ave a piss-up on Wednesday as I'll be meeting up with the squad next day.'

'Sounds good to me.'

'Yep, I'm in.'

'Me, too.'

'Spread the word round. P'rhaps we can go on a crawl.'

'I know what, let's 'ave a real mega one 'cos it ain't often we can celebrate summing like this,' Pete carried on. 'You in, Joe?'

'You bet I am!'

23

'It stinks in 'ere.' Marco had entered Joe's bedroom that Thursday morning on the instructions of his mother to wake him up. It had already gone eight o'clock and his mother was about to shovel the sizzling bacon and eggs on to his plate downstairs.

'Piss off,' came a croaky reply from an invisible hump under the duvet.

'Come on. Mum says you've got to get up. Breakfast's going cold. You were so drunk last night, you woke me up when you got in, banging about making a racket.'

'Oh, diddums,' came the muffled reply.

'It stinks like a brewery in 'ere and you must've been farting all night as well. It's disgusting,' and with his fingers clasping his nose, Marco turned to leave the room. But before doing so he stopped, turned back to his brother and said, 'Oh, and I just wanna wish you well for the match on Saturday and I hope you get on.' And with that statement he was gone for, unlike Joe today, Marco still had school to attend.

As Joe lay in his bed, a pillow clasped firmly around his head, Marco's words resonated around his brain. It was the kindest thing he had ever heard his brother say to him and with a maturity that Joe did not believe he had at his age. It heartened Joe to know that in the difficult weeks, months and years to come, Marco was likely to be strong and a tremendous support to his parents.

He finally stirred and slowly shuffled his legs out of the bed. Marco was right. It did stink in his bedroom and this was only exacerbated when the trapped cocktail of smells floated free from under the duvet. He tried to find his slippers with his toes but failed abjectly. He sat on the edge of the bed, his eyes screwed up tightly and his head bent over almost resting on his lap. He had no energy and craved returning to bed. The taste in his mouth was like, as Pete loved to say, a Turkish wrestler's jock strap, and it seemed as if someone was pounding away on a big bass drum inside his head. He had to drink some water and for the first time that morning, he cautiously and slowly opened his eyes. The effect was like having hot needles stuck into them and he immediately closed his lids as he groaned in pain. He moved his right hand towards the glass of water he knew to be on the bedside table but in his blindness, he knocked it over and the telltale splash of cool droplets on his foot told him the consequence. 'Oh, fuck me, why do I do it?' He re-opened his eyes, this time gritting his teeth to tolerate the initial pain, and bent over to replace the toppled glass back on to the table, wiping it against the pillow first so that it would not wet the surface. The water on the floor seemed to absorb quickly into the carpet so he dabbed at it with the corner of his duvet to remove the surface moisture, hoping that his mother would not notice. He craved returning to his bed and for the first time in a long time, the aroma from the kitchen was a turn-off rather than a turn-on. Bacon and eggs in the current state of his stomach spelt trouble.

'*Giuseppe, vieni giù?*'

His mother's question whether he was coming down for breakfast was met by an initial silence but then Joe walked gingerly over to the door. He shouted back, 'Mum, I'm really tired so I'm gonna go back to bed. Marco can have my breakfast if he's still there.' Fortunately for Marco, he still was and he swiftly demolished the sizzling bacon and fried eggs on Joe's plate, ramming bits of his toast violently into the yolks before stuffing them into his mouth. A yellow gunge ran down his chin.

'Remember you have to be in Cardiff by one,' his mother yelled back.

Joe did not need reminding. This was the day he was meeting up with the rest of the Welsh rugby squad at the Angel Hotel and he had arranged to meet Rocky Evans at Pontypridd train station at midday. After a quick visit to the bathroom, to take in water rather than divest of it, he returned to his bed and lay down flat on his back. He felt more sober and the throbbing in his head was at least tolerable. He reflected briefly on the morning ahead and the things he needed to do and allowed himself only a short time longer in bed. Luckily for him, he did not have to go to school as he had been given a special two days dispensation in light of the fact that he had to meet up with the Welsh squad in preparation for the match. He did not envy Dave, Pete, Dinner or Phil who had all been sloshed out of their heads the night before and who were now, no doubt, dragging their shattered bodies out of their beds. Pete had kept lining up Vodka Martinis the whole evening to complement the never-ending supply of beer that was seemingly delivered by conveyor belt, so quickly did the pints appear. Pete always fancied himself as a bit of a James Bond and without question, the boys would all be feeling both shaken and stirred this morning. He remembered Sue and Helen walking him to his front door or at least he remembered being at his front door in their company. He did not remember leaving the Maltsters, or was it the Llanover they had been to last? He felt guilty at leaving Sue to go home by herself but then remembered that Helen was staying over with her so the guilt dissipated.

Ah, Helen, that reminded him. She had been so effusive and excited at the fact she would be attending her first rugby international that she had hugged Joe and tried to snog him just as he was coming out of the toilets, hidden away from everybody else. What would Sue think if she knew that? He had no guilt as he had resisted her and told Helen that for Sue's and Gethin's sake, it would be better to forget all about it. Joe smiled and then giggled to himself at the efforts being made by his friends to get their hands on her rugby ticket. Dave said his father would pay her treble time if she worked in his corner shop on Saturday whilst Phil promised to buy her the latest Stevie Wonder double album, *Songs in the Key of Life*. Dinner invited her to the Cardiff night club, *Flagstones,* where the great, the good and the cool of Cardiff society went, apparently, and he made it quite obvious that she should feel honoured to be asked to accompany him. Everybody creased up at this one and Helen's guffaws of laughter and sarcastic reverential curtsies meant that Dinner did not need to receive any formal reply.

'Hey, Din, I've just had a thought. Keep on coming up with those daft ideas and Helen here will give you the ticket just to shut you up. Hey, Hel, stop laughing, you'll do yourself a mischief.' Dave's words were mocking but as ever, Dinner remained calm, pulled slowly on his roll-up and gave off his air of superiority, once again convinced deep down that Helen in truth would have liked to have accepted.

Pete remained po-faced around the table whenever Helen was the centre of attention and he said nothing. Joe was thankful that Gethin had not been able to make the evening for he was sure Pete would have gone for him again. That reminded Joe. 'It was definitely the Llan we went to last as Pete is still barred from the Maltsters,' he muttered to himself.

He reflected on the week just gone as he pulled the duvet snugly over his shoulders. As ever, Phil was right on the money and the important-looking letter, embossed with the red initials WRU, landed on the doormat on Tuesday morning. Sunshine gave it a quick sniff but quickly ignored it, unlike Joe who tore from his kitchen chair to retrieve it. The problem with Phil being such a font of all knowledge was that when Joe read the letter, it said pretty much exactly what Phil said it would and so it was rather anti-climactic. It was congratulatory in tone and advised that he should be present at the Angel Hotel in Cardiff by one o'clock the coming Thursday. There would be training during the afternoon and on Friday, and a formal dinner after the match on Saturday. He was expected to bring a dinner suit with him. He would be free to leave on Sunday morning. He would be sharing a room and his roommate would be determined on Thursday. All reasonable expense claims would be met. This line was set out in bold and underlined at the bottom of the letter and left nobody in any doubt about the importance of keeping costs down to a minimum.

On that same Tuesday morning, Meirion Hopkins singled him out during assembly and he was invited on to the stage to receive the applause of the whole school. The headmaster spoke proudly of his achievement and the prestige it had brought on the school. His words were generous and inspiring, and Joe blushed at the compliments.

In contrast to the delight of his headmaster, the opposite was true in the media. There was universal surprise that he had not been selected for the team, the majority putting it down to his rather indifferent display against Aberavon, whilst others delved more deeply into the murky world of rugby politics. Dewi Griffiths was critical of his non-selection and forcibly scolded the selectors for their caution and concluded that James Harrison would be sleeping more easily in his bed knowing that Joe would not be up against him. Nobody doubted, however, that Joe's time would come and very, very soon, and that the experience of being in the squad, training and rubbing shoulders with the elite of Welsh rugby, would only do him good. He would be a big star in the future and one on whom Welsh rugby should hang its coat tails.

The second Joe arrived home on Monday evening, the phone rang and a nervous-sounding Sue was on the line. She was unsure how Joe would feel at being selected only as a reserve. She herself was bitterly disappointed as she had dreamed incessantly of the moment Joe would run out on to the field in front of her and Helen. They would still be at the match but all they were likely to see of Joe was the back of his head, sitting in front of them in the stand. Her spirits improved, however, when she heard his voice and his obvious delight. It surprised her as she thought he had been desperate to play. Perhaps he was just putting on a brave face for her, she concluded. Joe went round to Sue's home later that evening and she was greeted with a beaming smile when she opened the door. The dinner had been sumptuous, not quite up to his mother's standard but certainly not far off. Joe spoke about his excitement at being selected for the squad but most of the conversation revolved around the budding romances or not of their friends. Joe could read Sue like a book and he knew that her seemingly disinterested throwaway comments about Phil and Gethin were aimed at eliciting information as to what they thought about Ann and Helen respectively. Joe did not have the heart to tell her that they were only interested in knowing what chances they had of sex rather than the wedding bells Sue was hoping for her friends, both of whom had admitted a great deal of keenness towards the boys.

'Yeah, I think they're both pretty keen and I'm sure they'd like to see the girls again.'

'Really!'

'Yeah.'

'Oh, I do hope so. They're so lovely, Ann and Helen. They deserve to be with someone nice. Ann had such a big love bite on her neck this morning you'd think she'd been bitten by that shark in *Jaws*. She was so shown up in school when one of the teachers told her to take off the scarf she was wearing. She went so red the whites of her eyes were shining. He's a bit of an animal then, is he, Phil?'

Joe smiled in a non-committal way, knowing the real truth and silently exasperated at how seriously girls took their relationships so quickly. 'Phil, oh, he's an animal

alright... or by the sounds of it, a big fish, more like.'
They both burst out laughing.

After dinner, they made love in Sue's bedroom but
soon afterwards Joe had to leave. His embrace and kiss
on the doorstep were particularly tender and Sue could
not fail to notice the tear that ran down Joe's cheek or
the lump in his throat before he finally set off down the
road. A few hundred yards further on, Joe stopped and
sat hunched over on a low wall on a stretch of road
that was absent of any pedestrians. He put his head in
his hands and burst into tears.

* * *

'Giuseppe, I'll be leaving in a minute. Do you have
everything you need?'

'Yes, Mum.' Joe turned his head towards the
bedroom door where his mother was standing, one foot
in, one foot out, adjusting the zip on the side of her skirt.

'Oh, it smells in here. I hope you have a bath before
you leave.'

'Yes, Mum.'

'You're sure you have everything?' his mother
repeated.

'Yes, Mum,' Joe's tone becoming slightly exasperated.

She left the room and returned to her bedroom where
she put on her pink cardigan and continued her dialogue
with her son from a distance. 'Make sure you pop in and
say goodbye to your father before you catch the train,'
she shouted, sliding her gold-plated bangles high up her
wrist. Fortunately for Joe, the restaurant was situated
right next to the station.

'Don't worry, Mum, I will. I'll be with you about
quarter to twelve.'

A moment later, Mrs Chilani rushed into his bedroom and gave her son a kiss. 'Make sure you do now. Don't forget to lock the back door when you leave and please have a bath.' These were his mother's final words from the landing before she made her way downstairs.

'Yes, Mum,' Joe sighed but in such a low voice his mother did not hear him.

At last, he heard the thump of the front door and the distant tapping of heels on the paving slabs outside, signalling that his mother had left and that he was alone in the house. He had been waiting specifically for this moment before getting out of bed, his head still pounding from the alcohol of the night before. He took a sip from his glass which he had refilled when in the bathroom and grabbed his wallet from the desk. Sitting back down on the edge of the bed, he opened the part of the wallet that held coins and removed the tiny key. He unlocked the drawer and took out the Luger. The sight of it unnerved him and he immediately locked his bedroom door even though he knew nobody else was in the house.

Since that time in the autumn when he had gone up to the woods behind the school, he had removed the Luger from its drawer on only one other occasion but had never taken it out of the bedroom. He had wanted to feel it nestling comfortably in his hand once more. He had toyed with the idea of returning to the woods a number of times but had decided against it because of the risk of being seen. Joe felt confident that when the gun was in his hand on Saturday, he would be able to fire it with no surprises. For a full five minutes, he pulled repeatedly at the trigger. Click, click, click, click. Everything was in fine working order. He would not have the opportunity to try it again.

He placed the gun beside him on the bed and removed the box of bullets from the drawer. Quickly and easily, he loaded the magazine with the remaining three and clicked the safety catch into place. He ripped the cardboard box holding the bullets into many, tiny pieces, making it impossible to know what the box had once held and put them on his desk, ready to discard in the dustbin downstairs later. Joe then walked over to the wardrobe and removed his kit bag. He took out his boots, which were already sparkling after his mother's thorough cleaning and polishing, and even the usually mud-encrusted aluminium studs glistened when the sunlight pouring through the window caught hold of them. At the same time, he took a small hand towel, which he had placed in the wardrobe previously, and put it next to the gun on the bed. Once he had done that, he returned to the drawer of the bedside table. From the back, he removed a small transparent plastic folder. He wrapped the Luger in its felt covering and placed it in the towel together with the folder, tucking them snugly inside as he folded over the loose fabric. He then placed it in the bag, pushing it over to one end. Beside it and in order to create a level base, he placed the grubby polythene bag that contained his match paraphernalia. Once he had done this, he placed a much larger towel on top. Only then did he replace his boots, followed by an assortment of kit to train in.

The next hour flew by. He took up his mother's recommendation to take a bath, after which he felt very much better. He even managed a leisurely cup of tea and two pieces of toast smothered in butter and strawberry jam without any adverse effect on his stomach. Eventually, he was ready to leave and for the first time that morning, he experienced a welling up of emotion as he left the house through the back door. He locked it behind him, put the key under a flower pot and strode round the house towards the garden gate. He could not help himself stopping briefly to turn round and view his home. He stared up at the imposing edifice that had provided so much security and comfort over the years and cast a quick glance across the lawn and flower borders where the first daffodils of the season were starting to bloom. This was where he had lived all his life, where he had spent most of the time with his family. As his emotions built further, he turned sharply on his heel and with kit bag in one hand and a holdall in the other, he passed through the garden gate, refusing to look back, and descended the hill towards his father's restaurant, where he knew it would be almost impossible to keep his emotions in check. He took countless deep breaths during the ten minutes' walk and he kept hammering the message into his brain to stay strong. Finally, he arrived and entered the restaurant.

Unexpectedly, a whole host of smiling faces appeared in front of him accompanied by a marked increase in the level of noise. His parents had made their regular customers aware that he would be popping in before catching the train to Cardiff and before he could take two paces inside, he was engulfed by the excited well-wishers, shaking his hand, grabbing his shoulder and patting him on the back. Joe was overwhelmed by all the good wishes and fervent hopes that he would get the opportunity to play and this helped him gain a semblance of control over his feelings. One comment about Rocky Evans accidentally landing on Ray Douglas's knee in training drew loud laughter in which he joined.

As the commotion died down, it was time to face his parents who stood next to each other, smiling proudly. He hugged his mother and to her surprise, he lingered, holding her tightly. She was more concerned that he behaved well during the next couple of days, that he was good and that he did whatever he was told to do rather than anything actually to do with the rugby. He let go of his mother and still holding her arms, looked her straight in the eye, his own awash with tears. 'I love you so much, Mum,' were Joe's only words. He turned to face his father and held him in a tight embrace as well. His father did not say anything but Joe repeated the words he had said to his mother. His father clasped him firmly on the shoulder and at that particular moment, he was the proudest man on earth. Tears were streaming down Joe's cheeks which he was unable to stem, leaving warm trails before finding grooves that led them to the corners of his mouth. His tongue licked at the salty taste and so as not to extend his agony any further, he abruptly picked up his two bags, acknowledged the smiling faces around him and without looking back, left the restaurant and marched towards the station. He had arranged to meet Rocky by the ticket office but before entering, he stood outside for a minute to regain his composure. He wiped at his eyes with the sleeve of his jacket and took in three deep breaths. More relaxed but still on edge, he entered the station and saw Rocky sitting on one of the wooden benches waiting for him. A passer-by shook Joe's hand and wished the two of them well before rushing to catch his train.

'Hi, Rock.'

'Orrite, Joe?' Rocky rose from the bench and shook his hand. 'You been crying or summing? Your eyes are as red as a baboon's arse.'

'Just been saying goodbye to my parents and you know, there were a few well-wishers in there, like, and it just got to me a bit.'

'How're your mum and dad?'

'Good, Rock, good.' After a moment's pause, he added, 'The best.' Rocky smiled at him and touched his elbow.

'Got your tux, 'ave you?' Rocky's enquiry was made with his eyes squinting at Joe's two relatively small bags. He himself was carrying a bulging suit bag with shoulder strap as well as his kit bag. Joe had been prepared for the question.

'My mum's gonna bring it round the hotel tomorrow night. I had to buy one in town as I've never worn one before and she's been fussing about the length of the trousers all week. She 'asn't finished shortening 'em yet.' Joe had been careful not to show the official Welsh Rugby Union invitation to his mother or father. If his mother had known he had needed a dinner suit, she would have had him traipsing around Cardiff a whole day to find one.

'She's an angel, your mum is. If I'd 'ad more time, I'd 'ave left my suit with her to do mine as well. Borrowed it from my uncle, I did, and he's four inches taller than me but fortunately, he's just as fat.'

'She'd have loved that. She already spends half her time cleaning Eamon's kit.' Joe smiled.

'Right, shall we get first class 'en? We're on expenses, remember.'

'Can we? Bit extravagant, innit?' They both looked at each other a bit unsurely.

'Oh, fuck it. It's not often you play for Wales and it's not as if we're coming from Llanelli or somewhere far like that. It's only twelve miles after all so it can't cost that much. Let's get first class and we'll argue the toss with 'em afterwards if they kick up a stink. Orrite, Joe?'

'Yeah, let's go for it.'

* * *

As Joe and Rocky settled into the first class carriage, Sue was gazing out of the classroom window, her mind a million miles away from her history teacher at the front of the class pontificating about the Romans. She looked endlessly at the wristwatch Joe had bought her for Christmas, waiting for the bell to ring for the lunch break. She was desperate to speak to Helen again who was sitting two rows behind her. Helen's mind, too, was in a spin as she tried once more to make sense of Joe's drunken ranting from the night before.

The previous evening's pub crawl had been lots of fun but the two girls, knowing that they had to attend school the next day and clearly more conscientious than the boys, drank only moderately. Early on in the evening, it became obvious that the boys were embarking on a major drinking session and Sue had warned Helen that her stay-over would most probably involve a diversion to guide Joe home first before they could return to her own house. This had not bothered Helen and she even welcomed the opportunity to get her hands around him if he needed support. The two girls soon realised that this was highly likely to be the case when Joe downed a fresh pint of Guinness in four seconds flat just five minutes after arriving in the first pub of the evening. What she had not expected, however, were the menacing, threatening and puzzling words Joe had ranted later on during the short walk to his home.

'You watch me girls, Saturday's gonna be the biggest fucking day you'll ever know, fucking amazing it'll be, you watch. Fucking Harrison, fucking Charles the tosser, wankers, cunts won't know what'll hit 'em, fucking English twats, Prince of fucking Wales, my arse. Who the fucks he thinks he is? I tell you, you watch me, everybody watch me, fucking amazing it'll be, I tell you.'

Sue had got very angry with him as they staggered along, telling him to keep his voice down and that his language was appalling and that he was no better than all the football hooligans who were causing havoc the length and breadth of the country. Joe was not listening. Helen was also appalled at the language and the vehemence of his words but she knew from experience what drink could do to someone and what Joe thought about Wales and its relationship with England. She knew it was just a load of rubbish that would be forgotten the following day. The next words Joe blurted out chilled her but again she thought it was just the alcohol talking.

'You watch, I tell you, you won't see nothing like it ever. Ever I tell you, ever! It'll shake up the wooorrrllllddd,' Joe screamed Muhammad Ali style, arms raised aloft in triumph. 'When I pull that gun, fucking dead, dead I tell you, dead. Shake up the wooorrrllllddd, shake up the wooorrrllllddd.'

At the mention of the word 'gun', Sue stopped dead in her tracks and took a pace backwards. She stared intently at him, like a cat focusing hard on a bird in a garden, leaving Helen to prop him up as best she could. She did not say anything and ignored his protestations as to where she had got to. For a full minute, they stood on the spot, with Helen taking his weight as his knees threatened to give way. Eventually, Sue made the first move and supported him under his right arm and they thankfully arrived outside Joe's front door without further incident.

The walk to Sue's house passed in a flash. Helen tried to make light conversation but Sue ignored her, her mind clearly elsewhere, her face absolutely thunderous. Even when they arrived and warmed themselves up in the living room, Sue remained silent as she sat as still as a statue on the sofa. Helen went into the kitchen to make some tea but when she returned, Sue had her head in her hands and was crying floods of tears. It was only then that Sue had revealed everything to Helen about the missing Luger and how she was sure Joe had stolen it. They spent hours working out how he could have taken it, whether it had been possible, whether Sue had made a mistake, whether it was still in the house somewhere, whether her father had an unknown storage area. Sue wanted to believe all these other possibilities and Helen's voice of reason did at times make her believe that perhaps she had been mistaken but she knew she was kidding herself. And now, it was becoming clear. Joe in his drunken state had, in effect, admitted everything. Helen's doubts, owing to the fact that alcohol made people say the most ridiculous things at times, checked Sue's conviction but only momentarily. He had the gun, he hated James Harrison, he hated the Prince of Wales and he had been desperate to play in this match. She knew he planned to kill them.

When will that bell ring? Sue thought impatiently as she looked yet again at her wristwatch. It's already three minutes late. Finally, it sounded and she closed her book and pad of foolscap faster than a David Nixon sleight of hand. She turned towards Helen and while everybody else was still rising from their desks, the two girls had already exited the classroom. A few minutes later, they were sitting opposite each other in a café in Hawthorn village, close to the school, a mug of tea steaming in front of Sue and a can of Tango in front of Helen.

'I still can't get my head around it, Sue. It's mad. I can't believe Joe would do anything like that. I haven't stopped thinking about it all day. I know what you say but it's just unbelievable.'

'It makes sense to me. It's doing my nut in.'

'Why don't I come round tonight and we'll search the house inch by inch. I'm sure the gun's there somewhere. It'll turn up.'

'I've already done that,' Sue replied sharply, shaking her head, a slight tremor in her voice.

'Yeah, but two heads are better than one. Or, why don't you ask your nan or your dad's friends if they knew somewhere he might have kept it?'

'I saw it in the drawer, Hel. I know it was ages ago but I saw it there.'

'You're sure you're not mistaken?'

'Hel, believe me, I saw it there. How many times do I have to tell you?' Sue's voice was raised and her tone reflected the stress she was feeling. Helen went quiet.

The huge workman sitting nearby with cement dust in his hair and all over his sweatshirt, jeans and boots glanced away from Luscious Linda from Liverpool on page three of *The Sun* newspaper he was holding and towards Sue. She glanced back and smiled apologetically, though noticing at the same time that unbeknown to him his stomach was resting over the edge of his plate of sausages, eggs and beans.

'Sorry for shouting, Hel. I'm just really on edge. We're just repeating ourselves from last night and this morning,' Sue carried on, not knowing what to say next.

'Why don't you ask him? You can call the hotel or even better, go down and see him tonight or tomorrow. I'll come with you, you know that.'

'I told you, I've already asked him.'

'Yeah, but not after what he blurted out last night.' Sue went quiet, knowing Helen had a point.

'He'll just deny it like he did last time. And like you said, he'll just make out it was drunken talk, you know, stupid stuff, just rubbish.'

Helen looked down and took a bite from the sandwich that had just been served to her. Sue took a sip from her tea. 'So what d'we do now?' Helen asked, wiping her mouth with a paper serviette.

'I dunno. I just dunno,' Sue replied, shaking her head.

'You're not gonna go to the police, are you?' Helen asked expectantly, her eyes remaining fixed on Sue whilst she took another bite from her sandwich.

Sue hesitated before replying to her friend. 'No. I can't do that. They'll think it's stupid. And even if they don't and confront Joe about it, what'll happen if it just turns out to be a load of rubbish. He'll go mad with me an' we'll be finished. I'd lose him over some stupid misunderstanding. How can we go out with each other if I call the cops on him?' Once again, Sue shook her head. She took her first bite from a soggy sausage roll, her mind seemingly far away, but then she resumed in a low voice. 'There's still one thing at the back of my mind that makes me believe he won't use it. When he told me he hadn't taken it that night, he said that even if he had, he didn't have it in him to kill anybody. The way he said it was really convincing, you know. He really wanted me to know that and I believed him. But now, I dunno.

Perhaps he's just a good liar for all I know. I just dunno, Hel.'

Helen placed her hand on her arm, responding softly and in a tone as reassuring as she could possibly muster. 'Sue, I know it all sounds a bit fishy but let's be realistic. This is Ponty, after all, not Hollywood. Joe's wonderful. You know that, I know that, everybody knows that. He's not some nutter. I know he feels strongly about Welsh independence but then so do loads of other people. I could imagine Joe going into politics one day and good for 'im. But come on, he's not going to shoot James Harrison and Prince Charles, is he? That's just ridiculous. Look, I've no idea what happened to the gun and I don't doubt what you say but I'm sure there's some simple explanation. Don't let this get to you. Saturday's gonna be a fantastic day. We're gonna be at the Arms Park watching an international. It's gonna be brilliant and your boyfriend's gonna be there on the field with a chance of playing. It's unbelievable, just fantastic, it is. Everybody will be so jealous of you. Don't ruin that by letting this gun business get into your head.'

Sue raised her eyes towards Helen, cupping both of her hands around the mug of tea and a semblance of a smile appeared on her face. 'Perhaps you're right,' she replied. 'I like your idea about talking to my nan or my dad's friends. They might be able to tell me something. It was ages ago when I saw the gun last, maybe even when my dad was still alive. I just dunno.' Sue felt a lot calmer and both of them looked into each other's eyes, smiling, as they held hands.

'Oh, bollocks!'

The loud expletive turned their heads as the huge workman realised his stomach was partly flopped over his plate of food. He looked sideways in embarrassment whilst wiping away some brown sauce from the bottom of his sweatshirt. The two girls pretended not to notice when they got up and left the table. They went over to the counter to pay and then left the café to return to school. After shutting the door behind them, they took three paces and then burst out into gales of laughter. As they strode, arm in arm, back to the school gates, the smiles never left their faces though the tight knot in Sue's stomach only highlighted the worry and anxiety she still felt.

24

It was early morning on Saturday, the day of the Wales versus England rugby international, and Joe lay on his side in his bed, wide awake, staring into space. The edges of the door were outlined in a ghostly white from the lighting in the corridor. He felt relaxed and in control of his emotions. He had thought about this morning for months, believing it would be the most stressful time of all, but now that the day had finally arrived, no restraining demons clouded his mind. He had gone over the reasons why he was going to do what he was going to do so many times; it seemed his brain had given up worrying about it. He clearly foresaw the events of the next few hours and that clarity mirrored the compelling reasons for his plan of action. There was not one shred of doubt, just certainty and resolve. As the first faint sounds of motor vehicles outside filtered their way into his hotel room, he knew for truly the very first time that he would succeed.

Joe's bed was soft and the room warm and he felt privileged to be staying free of charge in such luxury. He had stayed in very few hotels before in his time and the ones he had stayed in were usually quite bare and draughty with bathrooms on the landing. He had never stayed in a room with an en suite bathroom and minibar, although it had been made plain to everybody in the squad that the latter could only be raided at their own expense. He looked across to the digital clock on the bedside table where the numbers five and ten glowed red. His roommate, Ceri Hickman, was snoring loudly, still very much fast asleep. He did not know Ceri and Joe had been hoping to room with Rocky but the team management had insisted that players from different clubs room together to foster team spirit. Ceri Hickman, the huge Maesteg second-row, was also a reserve for the match and he believed this gave him free rein to indulge in a few drinks the night before. Accordingly, the room stank of stale beer and was strewn with Hickman's clothes as, in his drunken state, he had stripped off as quickly as possible before crashing out on his bed after coming in at one-thirty in the morning.

Joe still had a few hours before he needed to get up. He began thinking about the day ahead once more and recited a prayer to himself. He recalled the telephone conversation he'd had with Sue late the night before which saddened him and left him fighting back the tears, much to the merriment of one or two of his teammates who noticed. He felt that she had wanted to raise something specifically with him but had held back. The whole squad had been to the pictures to see *Marathon Man* and as he recited to Sue the antics of Rocky Evans seated next to him, she began to laugh and her sunny smile appeared in his mind. She seemed to lose her train of thought and her attempt to question him about something fell by the wayside. Did she want to ask him about the gun again? Had she sussed out he would use it the next day? He did not know but perhaps, inadvertently, Rocky had come to his rescue once again. After all, how could anybody not laugh at the thought of a seventeen stone, supposedly ferocious rugby player, burying his face in Joe's neck and holding his hand tightly as if he was his lover, when Laurence Olivier drilled into Dustin Hoffman's front tooth? And if that was not enough, the image of Rocky desperately trying to cover the wet patch on the front of his trousers with his hands when walking back to the hotel, having spilled his Kiora orange drink, had Sue in stitches. It had been a fun conversation and Joe was pleased to hear Sue laugh and in such good spirits but when he put the receiver back in its cradle, he felt wretched, sad and emotional and he scampered off quickly to bed. Now, as he lay there this early morning, everything was under control and he felt no emotion at all as he contemplated the day's events. Only the effect on Sue and his family hurt and weakened him and he instantly banished their memories from his mind. The comfort of his bed soon took hold, thankfully, and he dozed off straight away.

After what seemed just a few seconds, he woke with a start, his surreal, incomprehensible dream dissolving into the subconscious the instant he opened his eyes. The room was bathed in sunlight. He could hear movement around him and observed shadows appearing and disappearing faintly against the cream-coloured wall next to him. He looked at the clock. The red numbers, not now glowing, told him the time was eight-fifty. The whole squad was to meet up for breakfast at nine-thirty.

'Orrite, butt?' Ceri boomed, noticing that Joe had finally stirred.

'Yeah,' Joe replied, wiping the sleep from his eyes. 'God, is that the time?'

Ceri did not reply as he continued to fuss around the room, in particular searching for the underwear he had thrown off unceremoniously the night before. Once he had retrieved one of his socks from the top of the television, he sat down on the edge of the bed and began fiddling with his rugby boots. 'Have you got a stud spanner somewhere I can borrow? Bloody can't shift these ones with my 'and.'

'Yeah, sure, in my kit bag,' Joe responded, stifling a yawn. Ceri went over to the side of Joe's bed where he found his kit bag on the floor. He bent over and unzipped it. Only then did Joe realise his mistake. 'STOP! Leave it,' he blurted out and whilst still lying in his bed, he grabbed the bag straight out of the hands of his startled roommate. 'I'll gerrit for you,' Joe continued in a calmer tone and sitting up in bed with his back to Ceri, he rummaged around inside to retrieve the spanner.

'Dew, you gave me a fright. What you got in there, the Crown Jewels or summing?'

Joe did not reply as he finally located the spanner and passed it over to Ceri, calmly re-arranging the contents of his bag afterwards to exactly the same positions as before. How could he be so stupid, so careless? He reflected on this with some annoyance as well as relief. That moment could have blown everything. As he got out of bed, he zipped up the bag and returned it to its original place, commenting rather weakly, 'Sorry 'bout that, Cer. Didn't wanna make you jump but there's just some personal stuff in there, you know, a bit private.' He was about to add some more but stopped himself. No point digging an even bigger hole for yourself unnecessarily.

'Don't worry, butt,' Ceri replied, his attention firmly on his rugby boots. He stifled a muffled groan as he tried to loosen a stud. Joe's spanner did not improve matters and when Joe entered the bathroom, he heard a number of expletives. In the privacy there, he thought back to the indecision that had plagued him for weeks. Originally, he had planned to hide the gun in his holdall but had worried about leaving it in the hotel room for long periods during those hours when he was out training with the rest of the squad. What if a cleaner found it, perhaps a light-fingered one? He knew it was unlikely but he felt uneasy about being away from it. He also worried whether he would find a moment to transfer the gun into his kit bag. Accordingly, he decided to pack it in the latter in the knowledge that he would not have to transfer it and that it would come with him to the training sessions. His main worry, in this instance, was whether it would be secure in the dressing room when he trained, particularly as a spate of dressing room robberies was currently sweeping the principality. After much umming and ahrring, he reasoned that security around the Welsh squad was likely to be high and so decided that this would be the better option. All that indecision, all that worry, and he ends up inviting someone to enter the bag itself. What a fucking idiot, he thought.

* * *

The lobby of the Angel Hotel was heaving, though it bore no comparison to the hordes of people who thronged the main bar. Two burly doormen were regulating who could and could not enter the hotel through its narrow entrance on the corner where Westgate Street meets Castle Street and only a hefty punt of a ball away from the famous Cardiff Arms Park rugby ground across the road. The chatter was incessant and becoming increasingly raucous as the huge quantities of alcohol consumed took effect.

An American middle-aged couple, in matching Burberry raincoats and carrying genuine Louis Vuitton luggage, were trying to make themselves heard at the checkout, ruing the day they had made the booking and admonishing the poor clerk behind the desk. The various female staff, dressed in their matching heather-grey jacket and skirt uniforms, flitted purposefully from room to room, trying to avoid the attempted grabs and leers of the inebriated menfolk, some more than twice their ages. Four such men, with bright-white England scarves with the red rose prominent on both ends hanging loosely around their necks, strode down the elegant staircase to loud but friendly jeers from the mass of humanity below them. They saw only a carpet of red from the multitude of scarves, pullovers and hats, which impressed on them truly for the first time that they had ventured into the lion's den. A number of youngsters, fresh-faced and bright-eyed and with the front of the Artful Dodger, mingled among the crowd asking for any spare tickets or any swaps, namely one in the grandstand for two on the terracing so that a friend of theirs would be able to watch the game as well. They were more often than not met with varying degrees of politeness and negative response but three persistent boys eventually succeeded and with huge delight in their eyes ran off to tell their friends and to drink as much as was physically possible to make up for lost time.

The clock on the wall behind the two checkout girls showed just after one and it seemed mildly irrelevant to know that the time in New York was just after eight in the morning whilst that in Tokyo just after ten in the evening. All of a sudden, a deafening cheer resounded around the lobby as above them, a number of red-tracksuited figures appeared on the landing with various bags in hand and began the slow walk down the staircase. Those who chatted and drank on the steps edged tightly up against the balustrades, squashing against others and invariably spilling beer and lager on to the already sodden and grimy carpet. As the Welsh team captain, Geraint Lewis, followed by his teammates of all different shapes and sizes, walked down between them like Moses parting the Red Sea with his flock of Israelites in tow, Joe appeared on the landing, one of the very last in the long line of players. He looked very tense and his face was almost deathly pale in contrast to his usual darker complexion. Not only did Joe look nervous, he felt it. He could physically feel himself shaking and he was struggling to retain control of his emotions. The time was now close, very close, a time which not so long ago had seemed a very distant point in the future. The calmness of the early morning had been a mirage. He was frightened, very frightened, wondering how everything could have come about so fast and in the manner he had wanted. He was convinced he was blessed, that it was God's will which had guided him. And in these final moments of anxiety and fear, it would be God, he believed, who would help him to succeed.

The players had appeared from a large conference room on the first floor where they had been handed the famous red jersey with the white Prince of Wales feathers on the left breast. Each player had been called up in turn by Cliff Morgan, a famous international of the 1950s and one of the most revered figures in Welsh rugby. Joe had received his with pride to the applause of the others and a comforting pat on the back from the immortal Morgan. He had fought to hold back the tears, unlike Rocky Evans, who wept openly on receipt. Joe considered the shirt in his hand, the most iconic symbol of Welsh nationality. He felt the texture of the cotton and ran his fingers over the embroidered feathers. This is ultimately what I'm fighting for, he reflected, why I am doing what I have to do. As they broke up from the gathering, a red-eyed Rocky came over to him.

'Just look arrit, Joe. This means everything to me. Not long now and we'll be out there.'

'Yeah, Rock, my very thoughts. This is what it's all about. The red shirt, Wales.'

Ceri Hickman joined them and slapped his hand down hard on Rocky's shoulder before addressing him in a jocular tone. 'You big tart! If the English could see our big fat ugly prop forward crying like a baby, they'd laugh their cocks off.' Rocky smiled and Ceri thumped him playfully on the arm as he walked away. Joe said nothing and remained grim-faced.

'You nervous, Joe? You look it.'

'Yeah, you bet I am. Only natural, I suppose, an' I'm not even playing.'

'Don't gerrinto that frame of mind. Who knows, you could be on in the first minute.'

Joe did not immediately reply but then as they were walking over to the corner of the room to collect their kit bags, Joe put his hand on Rocky's arm and stopped him. 'You like my mum, don't you?' he asked.

'What d'you mean?' Rocky replied, somewhat perplexed at the question.

'Well, not like that I mean, but you know, you like her, don't you?'

'Course I do. Everybody likes Mrs Chilani. She's lovely. Always gives me a big smile when I'm in your place.'

'Do me a favour, Rock, I'd appreciate it if you spent a bit more time there in my dad's place. My mum likes you and's always asking after you. She'd love it if you popped in more often in future.'

'Yeah, sure, course I will,' Rocky replied, wondering what had brought this on. 'Will I get a few more chips than usual 'en?'

'I'm sure you will, Rock, I'm sure you will,' and with those words a smiling Joe and Rocky resumed their step to the kit bags, Joe's hand on Rocky's shoulder, comforted by his teammate's words.

But it only took a few seconds for his anxiety to return and the colour drained from his face when he left the conference room. Thankfully, as Joe proceeded from landing to stairs, he heard a familiar voice calling his name amongst the many in the lobby and this helped ease his tension. He turned his head in its general direction, surveying the throng below him. He heard the voice again, this time much louder. 'Hey, Joe... Joe, over 'ere.' Joe focused more intensely and then saw an arm held high up in the air trying to attract his attention. It was Dave and next to him he saw Pete and Phil. At the bottom of the stairs, he broke away from the line of red tracksuits and nudged his way towards them.

'How d'you get in 'ere?'

'Sneaked in when the doormen were busy. They're both a bit pissed, I think. It's a miracle they didn't see us. Guess what?'

'What?'

'Go on, guess what?' Dave repeated his question, his face wreathed in the broadest of smiles.

'WHAT?'

'We've all got tickets. Can you believe it? And all face value. East Terrace Lower, fucking brilliant.' Dave could not conceal his delight and did a tiny jig on the spot waving his ticket in the air.

Phil scolded his friend. 'Don't flash it around; someone'll make a grab for it.' Dave quickly tucked it into the deep pocket of his green Parka where it rested alongside a half-bottle of whisky.

For a moment, Joe relaxed in the company of his friends. 'That's excellent, boys, tremendous. East Terrace Lower? You'd better watch out for all the piss 'en,' he cautioned.

'What d'you mean?' Dave asked in puzzlement, casting a sideways glance towards his equally puzzled friends.

'Well, I've heard it's virtually impossible to get to the bogs when everybody's crammed inside so people just piss on the floor. Ceri Hickman was telling me it's like the Niagara Falls in there sometimes, you know, piss just running down the steps.'

'Gerraway! He's 'aving you on.'

'Honest. I 'ope you 'aven't got your best shoes on.' Instinctively, everybody looked down at their footwear.

'We'll just 'ave to finish off the whisky quick 'en so we can piss in the bottle if need be,' Dave grinned. 'Wish we'd got a full-bottle now.' Everybody started to corpse in laughter.

'How'd you wangle the tickets anyway?'

'Couldn't believe it. We were in the Old Arcade and this guy came over and offered 'em to us.'

'A tout?' Joe asked baffled, not understanding how they could have bought them at face value.

'No. He said he was from some rugby club up in North Wales, Ruthin, I think he said, and that they hadn't managed to sell all their allocation. So he 'ad these spare.'

'Couldn't sell their allocation? I can't believe that. Sounds a bit fishy to me.'

'Did to us at first but then he showed 'em to us and there you 'ave it. Just incredible, it was. You'd better get on now, some'ow.'

'Lemme have a quick look at it again.' Dave pulled out the ticket and showed it to Joe who then took it from his hand. 'Mmm, I'm not trying to be funny but the paper feels a bit thin to me. Sue's ticket seemed to be on much thicker paper.'

'Wha' you on about?' Pete interrupted, but for the first time since entering the hotel, the smiles vanished from all their faces.

'Dunno, just seems a bit thin to me, that's all. They are genuine, aren't they? The word round here is that a few forgeries are going around.' With that, Pete and Phil took their tickets out of their pockets and studied them carefully.

'They look orrite to me,' Pete carried on, glancing between Phil and Dave, both of whom looked a little worried.

'Lemme 'ave another look.' Joe grabbed the three tickets and studied them both sides and rubbed them roughly between his forefinger and thumb. 'You tossers, they're forgeries.'

'Gerroff! You're 'aving us on,' Pete blurted out less than convincingly. 'How can you tell?'

'Easy if you look 'ard enough. The serial numbers on the backs are all the same.' Joe's friends each seized their ticket from Joe desperately and compared the serial numbers, open-mouthed.

'Oh, no!' It was Phil, throwing back his head, who conceded first that the tickets were duds.

'Fuck, fuck,' Dave muttered under his breath, shaking his head. Pete just continued to stare at the tickets, lost for words.

'I'm sorry, boys. Anyway, don't give up. If I were you, I'd just get in a crowd and hurry through the turnstiles as quickly as possible. The stewards'll never know. They're pretty good forgeries. Probably best if you don't all go in together.'

'Come on, Joe, are you ready?' Joe turned towards the entrance and caught Rocky's eye. He could see some of the players were leaving to take the short walk across the road to the ground.

'Just a sec, Rock. I've gotta go, boys. I'm sure you'll get in.'

'Hey, we've gotta see your shirt first. They given it to you yet?'

'Yeah, it's in my bag by 'ere. Cliff Morgan 'anded 'em out a few minutes ago.' Joe unzipped his bag and pulled out the Welsh jersey. He opened it up and turned it round so that his friends could see both front and back. They were in awe of it, staring hard. Several other supporters in the lobby also turned towards Joe, straining to glimpse the iconic symbol of Welsh rugby.

'Wow, just look at it, it's brilliant. Twenty-one. P'rhaps not quite number ten but who cares?' Dave announced, making reference to Joe's number and that of the mystical fly-half position, so revered in Wales, and worn by some of the greatest rugby players who ever played the game. Phil moved forward and took a handful of the shirt and lightly kissed the embroidered feathers. He was so enthralled and ecstatic that if he had dropped down dead at that particular moment, his life would have been all worthwhile.

'Hey, Phil, pity you didn't go quite so gentle on Ann's neck the other night,' Pete blurted out and his friends all guffawed with laughter.

Realising that he had to get a move on, Joe quickly folded up the shirt and stuffed it back into his kit bag. Once that was done, he stared at his friends briefly before grabbing hold of the three of them and pulling them all into a huddle, their arms around each other's shoulders. He held on to them tightly for a few seconds and then raised his head to look them all in the eye. His own eyes were misty and his friends could see that he was welling up. 'You're the best friends anybody could've ever asked for,' he finally said. 'The best moments I've ever had in my life have been with you boys. I love you all more than you can ever imagine.' Their eyes lowered on hearing this, a little embarrassed. 'The next hours are gonna be massive. I can't tell you exactly what's gonna happen but it'll all become clear pretty soon.' They raised their eyes, perplexed. 'I'm never gonna forget you boys,' Joe continued, tears streaming down his cheeks and before anybody could say a word, he released them, picked up his kit bag and rushed to the entrance where Rocky was waiting outside. He wiped his eyes vigorously before reaching him. Pete, Dave and Phil all watched him leave and only turned back to each other when his red tracksuit disappeared from view.

'What was all that about?' Pete ventured, the three of them looking at each other, none the wiser.

'Dunno. He's just a bit emotional, that's all. He's gonna play for Wales, after all, with a bit of luck. I suppose it's understandable,' Dave replied unsurely.

'What's he mean about something massive happening that he can't tell us about?'

'Dunno. Bit weird that.'

In the background, a rosy-cheeked, excited supporter in a fawn-coloured duffel coat, red and white bobble hat and red and white scarf, all of which had seen better days, and who was holding an enormous green and white cardboard leek, the same height as him, tried to start up a chorus of "*oggi, oggi, oggi*". A desultory "*oi, oi, oi*" was heard in response, to his disappointment, as chatter about the game took precedence over singing and chanting for the moment. Crest-fallen, he sipped nervously at his pint, his immediate friends all sniggering around him. Dave turned his face away from the chant, wondering how he had managed to sneak the leek into the hotel without anybody noticing, when his face lit up and he offered his opinion. 'I know. I bet he's gonna ask Sue to marry him.'

'Nooooooo!'

'Could be. They're pretty close, they are, and he's mad about her. An' you've got to admit she's pretty storming.' They all nodded their heads.

'Yeah, could be. All that "I love you" stuff, "never forget you" stuff could be his way of saying it's the end of an era, like.'

'Could be.'

'Married, though! He must be off his 'ead.' They laughed and shook their heads in incredulity.

'Anyway, first things first. Who wants a beer?' And without anybody answering, they all smartly pushed their way into the hotel bar.

* * *

From in front of the Angel Hotel, two short lines of policemen in their fluorescent-yellow jackets formed a passageway for the Welsh players to cross the road, unimpeded, to Cardiff Arms Park. Holding up the rear of the players were Joe and Rocky, twenty yards behind everybody else. A huge gathering of well-wishers pushed up against the backs of the policemen, shouting out their encouragement, and forcing the two lines to sway backwards and forwards like black and yellow snakes slithering along, side by side.

"Good luck, Rocky."

"Stick one on Meadows for me."

"Don't take any shit from England, boys."

"Good luck, Rocky, get stuck in, boy."

"Good luck, Joe. Hope you gerron."

"Don't lose this one, boys, not to England, pleeaase!"

Some of the supporters tried to pat them on the back, stretching their arms over the shoulders of the policemen who invariably but good-naturedly leaned backwards to ease them away.

'Fuck me, Joe. Look at all these people. Must be thousands of 'em. We're doing this for them. I knew it'd be manic but I didn't expect anything like this.'

Like Rocky, Joe, too, was scanning all the faces of the supporters left and right, each one of them smiling and excited, often with brandished fists and gritted teeth for encouragement. 'You're right, Rock, we're doing this for them. This is more than just a rugby match. This is about Wales's place in the world, what we stand for.'

Rocky turned towards Joe and grinned. 'Bit heavy that but you're right, I suppose.'

They marched through the outer gates of the ground and made a short descent into the depths of the stadium and towards the dressing rooms. They left the crowds behind at the gates but both of them were still taken aback by the huge presence of policemen inside.

'God, Rock, there are more policemen 'ere than spectators. Bet there's no coppers crying off sick today. Probably on double time or summing like that as well, and they get in free to watch the game. It's orrite for some.'

'Norra bad time to do a bit of burgling, you know, what with no cops around to stop you, like,' Rocky replied, thinking of two work colleagues who had troubled the magistrates in their time.

'It's because Charles is 'ere, that's why there's so many of them. It's ridiculous. So many coppers just to protect one bloke. Fucking stupid, it is. Look over there, Rock, at those couple of codgers trying to gerrinto the Athletic Club. Fuck me, they've had to pass through two lines of policemen already and they still got frisked for their trouble. An' I bet they've been going there for years. It's just stupid.'

'You're right, Joe. Trouble with the Royals is that they're so protected they never get to mingle with anybody normal like us. That's why they're all a bunch of wankers.'

Joe looked at Rocky, nodding his head. 'Well said, Rock, well said. Couldn't agree with you more,' he concurred.

Privately, Joe was congratulating himself and feeling a warm glow inside because all his planning had been undertaken with the sole aim of proceeding unchallenged through security to gain access to the stadium. Playing for Wales was the only feasible means to accomplish this. He knew that security would be very tight but even he had not anticipated such a massive presence of policemen. But as he strode nonchalantly past them, accepting their best wishes with a pleasant smile, he thought about the Luger tucked safely at the bottom of his kit bag. Who would stop a player, who would frisk one or check his bag? Nobody, of course. He had dreamed of this moment, walking unimpeded into the ground. The dream was now reality. He wanted to yell out his success with all his might but settled on the broadest of smiles instead. Everybody was treating him like a God. If only they knew.

The first thing that struck Joe when he entered the dressing room was its cavernous size. The vast majority of those he had been in so far during his rugby career were pokey and claustrophobic with little room to lay out kit and match paraphernalia with any ease. Half-broken rusty pegs above splintered wooden benches were the norm. It was whilst sitting in such a miserable, grey, cold dressing room a few weeks back that he pictured himself in a prison cell which he envisaged to be very similar. It had not been the first time he had thought about this but that particular dressing room brought out the harsh realities of what a prison cell was truly like. The idea of being inside for years on end was devastating, truly horrific and it chilled him to the bone.

By contrast, in the Cardiff Arms Park dressing room, there was enough space to lay and hang out his whole wardrobe, he thought. In the middle of the room was a padded treatment table, its tan hide scuffed severely and sagging somewhat in its centre, available for anybody who wanted a quick massage before hostilities commenced and where ripped skin would be sewn back together after the game. On it lay a pile of match programmes, one of which each player took before finding a spot to change. Before doing so, they all studied the programme's contents quietly and, in particular, searched out their own names, proudly printed on the inside with grainy black and white photographs and short career details accompanying them. Joe did the same. There he was, amongst the reserves: *21 Guiseppe Chilani.* He frowned and cursed when he saw his Christian name had been spelt incorrectly with the 'u' before the 'i'. It was a common mistake which always annoyed him.

The atmosphere in the dressing room helped ease his tension as the throng of players, trainers and general hangers-on made him feel less alone. He even volunteered a quip at the hunched figure of Rocky beside him. 'Hey, Rock, who's Richard Evans? He's taken your place, I see.'

'Very funny.'

'Oh, that's you, is it? Never knew you 'ad a proper name.'

Rocky did not react and Joe could sense that his friend's focus was narrowing on to the battle ahead and that soon, Rocky's mind would be in match mode. Joe and all those at Pontypridd RFC knew never to disturb him when Rocky was preparing himself mentally for the game as he visualised the collisions and confrontations that were imminent. Soon, he would be sweating profusely, crimson-faced and snorting, ready for action, like a bull waiting to hurtle into a ring to face the matador.

As the minutes ticked by, the atmosphere began to change. Initially, everything had been quiet and calm. But now, the tension was starting to build inside the players. Joe observed a number of them in the same focused state of mind as Rocky and the activity in the dressing room increased markedly as each player began to undress and put on his kit, bandages and tapes. They then carried out some stretching exercises followed by some furious swinging of the arms and vigorous jumping up and down on the spot. Amidst this activity were the customary snorting, belching, flobbing and farting. The chatter was minimal with only the odd word and expletive audible. There was no Eamon Murphy character among them who was always babbling away and laughing when changing back at Pontypridd.

Joe, too, began to change, slipping on his jockstrap before the pristine white shorts. The red socks with white tops followed. Before he pulled on the famous red jersey with white collar, he gazed at it momentarily and as he did back at the hotel, he ran his fingers across the embroidered Prince of Wales feathers with the motto, *Ich Dien*, written at their base. He contemplated it. *I Serve* and Joe told himself that today he would truly serve his country.

'Together, Joe?' Joe's trance was broken by Rocky's suggestion to pull on the jerseys at the same time.

Joe smiled. 'Yeah, together. Ponty boys, together.' And with that, they pulled on the shirts. They tucked them into their shorts and then stared at each other before giving themselves a hug. 'Not gonna cry again are you, Rock?'

'Fuck off. I'm ready.' But Rocky was not quite ready. Joe noticed him looking down at his kit bag with the air of someone about to make a raid on it. 'Got any Vas in there, Joe? Left mine at home,' Rocky asked as he bent down.

Joe intercepted his movement, grabbed his bag and put it on the bench. 'Yeah, somewhere. Hang on.' He rummaged around inside and pulled out a small half-empty jar of Vaseline, encrusted around the rim, which he passed over to Rocky. He smiled as he witnessed

Rocky take big slabs from it with his sausage of an index finger, smearing the Vaseline around his ears and over his eyebrows like a prizefighter and then some on the inside of his thighs. Some things will never change, Joe reflected with a smile, like Rocky always leaving his Vaseline at home. He was worse than Eamon Murphy for scrounging.

'Thanks, butt.'

Joe tossed the jar back in the bag and then put on his tracksuit before finally pulling on his boots. He was the only player wearing the full tracksuit, though two of the other reserves were wearing their tracksuit tops.

'Cold or summing?' Rocky enquired as he rolled his neck muscles.

'Well, I'm up in the stand, nollike you.'

Rocky rolled his neck more vigorously and ignored Joe's reply. Some of the players left the dressing room, ball in hand, ready to carry out some warm-ups on the pitch and as the door opened, the singing of the crowd reverberated around the dressing room. The supporters were flocking into the stadium and the excitement and anticipation of the game ahead was building, not quite at its crescendo yet, but close. *Calon Lan* was followed by *Cwm Rhodda* which was followed by *Hymns and Arias* and then some roars as the players warming up saluted back to the crowd.

'Listen to that singing, boys, just fantastic, innit? The English will be crapping 'emselves in their dressing room. We gotta win today, boys. We gotta do it for the fans.' The words of the captain, Geraint Lewis, rang round the room and the passion in his voice was truly inspiring. Rocky, with beads of perspiration building on his brow and his face grimacing, thumped his chest furiously with alternate hands like King Kong on top of the Empire State Building.

Everybody around Joe was now transfixed in their own world as they switched their minds to match mode. Consequently, nobody took any notice of him when he picked up his kit bag and set off for the toilets. Once inside, he found an empty cubicle and locked the door behind him. As he did so, he heard the clatter of metal studs on concrete enter the toilets behind him. The formidable sight of size eleven Adidas Flanker rugby boots, with their three diagonal, yellow, parallel stripes, appeared at the foot of the cubicle next door. It unnerved him a little and he remained silent, not moving a muscle. Almost immediately, he heard a loud retching noise and the sound of water splashing as the nerves took hold of a teammate. A pungent stink accompanied the second retch but after two heavy coughs, Joe heard the sound of toilet paper being pulled and torn and the cascade of flushing water. The lock opened loudly and the clatter of studs trod a path out of the toilets.

With a deep breath, Joe placed his kit bag on the toilet seat, unzipped it and reached down to the bottom. He felt the Luger, wrapped in its cloth and hand towel together with the plastic folder, and pulled it out. He placed the kit bag on the floor and put the Luger on the seat. Unwrapping the towel and cloth, he held the gun in his hand and stared at it for a moment whilst quietly putting the plastic folder back in the bag. He unclipped the magazine, which slipped into his hand. He checked to ensure the bullets were still in place. Everything was in order. More clatter of studs resonated around the tiled toilets and soon after, the sound of piss splashing on porcelain. This time, Joe did not hesitate and he clipped the magazine back inside the gun's butt. The comings and goings of studs on concrete were now incessant but Joe was calm as he sought out the best place on his person to hide it. As anticipated, the pockets of his tracksuit top and bottoms were too shallow. Accordingly, he unzipped the tracksuit top and pulling down the bottoms to his knees, he unbuttoned his shorts. He tucked the Luger inside, the bottom of the barrel resting inside his jockstrap for further support, the cold steel making him flinch a little. The handgun's butt rested against his stomach on the outside of his rugby shirt. The safety catch remained on and Joe allowed himself a smile followed by a grimace when thinking of the consequences of it going off at that particular moment. He re-buttoned the flies of the shorts and pulled the white cotton cord tightly before knotting it at the front. Finally, he re-fastened the top button. The Luger felt reasonably secure. He re-zipped his tracksuit top and Joe felt confident that nobody would know that he was hiding something. He patted the slight bump on his stomach lightly as if it were that of an expectant mother. He knew that by placing his hand under the tracksuit top, he would be able to access the gun quickly and easily.

'You fallen asleep or summing?'

The question shook Joe but he remained calm and collected. 'Piss off,' he shouted back. Joe put the redundant felt cloth and towel back in his bag, checked once more that the gun was secure and pushed down on the silver-grey, chrome button in the middle of the cistern. The water flushed with an angry hiss. On leaving the cubicle, he saw Ceri Hickman looking at himself in the mirror, greasing back his hair, a tub of Brylcreem on the wash basin in front of him.

'What's with the bag? You got your own bog paper in there or summing? Always thought you Ponty boys were a bit posh.'

'Never you mind, Cer. Dunno about posh but at least we don't ponce up before playing.'

Hickman burst out laughing and blew himself a kiss in the mirror. 'Well, gotta look good, 'aven't you? We're on the telly, remember.'

Joe smiled and made his way back to the dressing room. The singing from the terraces and grandstands filled the corridor and Joe began humming the words, so uplifting and catching was the sound.

"Mae gan Iesu goran fry yn nheyrnas nef..."

On returning to the dressing room, he sat down and placed his head in his hands, the hard, cold metal of the Luger pressing firmly into his skin as he bent over. He had been so immersed in the atmosphere and in his own preparations that he had not given too much thought as to what was soon to happen. But now, with preparations complete and kick-off barely twenty minutes away, the enormity of what he was about to do flooded every sinew of his body and he shut his eyes tightly to try and fight off his weakness. He felt compelled to say a little prayer to himself. 'Please, Lord, I beg You to give me the strength to succeed, just for these next few minutes. Please, Lord, please. I ask You no more.' He crossed himself, which was noticed by a few of his teammates around him, but they did not say anything. The mellifluous voice of the Welsh coach, Bleddyn Thomas, drew Joe from his prayer and he raised his head.

'Right, boys, can I have a bit of quiet for a minute,' Thomas began. 'Before I pass you over to Geraint, I just wanted to remind you that 'cos Charles is 'ere today, there'll be a full line-up along the red carpet, reserves an' all, where you'll all be introduced to 'im. Ger will lead him down the line. Let's remember we're representing Wales today so no clever-dick questions or smart-arse comments, orrite! What's more, we all wanna look tidy so it's compulsory you wear your tracksuit tops.' A few of the players groaned. 'But one last thing,' Thomas said, pausing theatrically and looking into each and every one of the faces around him. 'Today's a day none of you will ever forget so go out there and enjoy it, get stuck in and kick the fucking shit out of those English bastards, orrite!'

'RIGHT!!' boomed out the reply, Rocky to the fore, beating the top of his head violently with his fists at the same time.

Bleddyn Thomas knew it was time to leave the dressing room alone to the players and he ushered out the physio at the same time as himself. Geraint Lewis took a few paces to the centre of the room and beckoned his teammates to gather around him. The fourteen who would take the field with him formed a circle, arms tightly grasping neighbouring shoulders. Joe and the rest of the reserves stood a pace behind them.

A surprise to Joe was that instead of the usual fire and brimstone of a captain's talk, Lewis was quietly spoken, his tone measured. But his words were no less powerful and inspiring. Hunched over in the middle of his circle of warriors, Lewis spun slowly on his heel, looking up into the eyes of each and every one of them, gauging each individual's state of mind. He saw resolve, determination, fear, expectancy, calmness and in Rocky's eyes, manic devilment. He lingered on him longer than the rest and noted the need to keep an eye on him during the game.

'I'm feeling good about today, boys. I like what I'm seeing around me,' Lewis began. 'Yeah, I like it a lot.' Lewis nodded his head slowly and deliberately in approval. His voice was soft but assured and this only extenuated his air of command. 'We're ready. I can see that. I'm happy. I know now that we cannot lose. This is our day and we're gonna do our nation proud.' The circle around him squeezed itself more tightly. 'It doesn't get any bigger than this, boys. This is the ultimate test, the biggest fucking match of our lives and we've got to give every ounce of energy in our bodies. We refuse to leave that field beaten, orrite! Just think for a moment of all those people who've helped put you in this position; your mums and dads, brothers, sisters, school masters, wives, girlfriends, coaches, all those who've sacrificed something to make you what you are. Do it for them. When things get tough out there, and they will, just think of that special person, draw on that energy and give every drop of blood you've got left in your bodies until you can't fucking move anymore, until the match is won and the English are defeated. We're a great nation, a great nation, the greatest on earth and we're privileged to be representing her today. Never forget that.'

Lewis paused but did not allow his teammates surrounding him to break away. He looked each one of them in the eye again, saying nothing. The circle swayed back and forth and side to side as the pressure of the squeezing gained force. Everybody was sweating profusely and three players had tears running down their cheeks.

'Yeah, we're ready. No doubt about it.' Lewis smiled and nodded his head in slow deliberate movements once more, exuding confidence, which rubbed off on the others. They felt unbeatable. 'No doubt about it. We're gonna win today. But boys, let's not forget to play with control out there. We've got to do the basics properly. I will not accept a lost lineout or scrum on our ball or any missed tackles. I will not accept it, orrite! I will not accept silly penalties and I will not accept bad passes. I will not accept missed kicks to touch. Remember wha' we discussed back at the hotel. Nobody thinks we can take on the England pack and that we're gonna run the ball everywhere. Well, we're not and I don't care that it's a fucking beautiful day out there. Forwards, you're to get stuck into them and destroy 'em, orrite! The pack is all England 'ave got. We stuff 'em up front and the game's ours. I don't wanna see the ball, I just wanna see you boys pulverize 'em, I do, smash 'em. I want an armchair ride, a nice fucking easy day, orrite! When they're beaten, we'll move the ball, but only then. I want this game to be tight, so fucking tight that I want to hear those English forwards squeal like stuck pigs as if someone's crushing their balls in a vice, orrite!

'RIGHT!!'

Once more, Lewis paused for effect and then smiled. 'Yeah, we gonna win today, no doubt about it, we gonna win. We're ready. Bryn...'

On cue, Bryn John, the team's scrum-half, took over, his job to warm up the players. 'Right, on the spot everybody, five fast, five slow, five fast, five slow. On me.'

Joe took a step back to allow the circle of players further room for their warm-up. Tears were welling up in his eyes and he wiped them with the back of his sleeve. Lewis's commanding presence made him think of Leap Thomas. There truly were leaders out there to fight the battle. Lewis and Thomas and many, many others, he was sure, would have their troops in the palms of their hands. They would do anything for them. Joe desperately hoped it would be the likes of Lewis and Thomas who would pick up the gauntlet he was about to lay down and lead the fight against England. He was optimistic. After all, was what Lewis exhorted in a rugby context no different to the much greater fight against the English for independence? They were on the same wavelength, surely? He was tempted to pull him aside and tell him what he was about to do and the reasons why but so immersed in concentration was his captain, he thought the better of it. It would all become plain very soon anyway.

The door opened wide and the referee entered the dressing room. Amidst the clatter of studs and shouts of encouragement, he sought out Lewis who nodded his head back at him. The five-minute signal. Joe shook and felt physically sick when the referee left the room and closed the door behind him. It was almost time. He took in huge gulps of air to try and calm his nerves but it was a struggle. It was time for him to get his own match head on, to summon up strength and determination and courage for the events ahead. He continued to gulp down air and for the final time, with eyes shut, he visualised the next few minutes. The images were clear in his mind, he was in control and his resolve did not waver the slightest. He pictured James Harrison in the virgin all-white shirt of England, the red rose sitting mockingly on his left breast, the enemy who dared bring his troops to Welsh territory. Everything he represented, Joe despised. His fury built as he visualised Harrison prancing on to the field of play, his mouth grinning in arrogance, his air one of total superiority. He saw Prince Charles being led down the lines of players, his vacant expression bookended by two Dumbo-size ears; a fresh-faced, puny, chinless individual, the Englishman who dared carry the title of Prince of Wales. He pictured Charles being introduced to Harrison, spending more time with him than with Lewis, laughing and joking, relaxed, laying down courtly instructions to his loyal knight to put the Celts back in their place.

'You orrite, Joe?' Ceri Hickman tapped him on the shoulder for it appeared to him that Joe was hyperventilating, his face bathed in sweat and anxiety with the stress of it all.

'Never felt better, Cer, never felt better in my life. I'm at peace. Let's go.'

25

'Isn't this brilliant, Sue? I can't believe we're actually here. Look at all these people, it's just fantastic.' Helen was literally bouncing around in her seat in the great North Stand that dominated the stadium, her face beaming with excitement as she looked to all parts of the ground, breathing in the atmosphere. Their seats were only four rows up from the front of the stand and only just to the right of the halfway line.

'It's just amaz...'

But before Sue could finish her sentence, Helen shrieked and grabbed Sue's arm so tightly, she nearly dragged her to the floor. 'Look, look, over there, Sue, look, over there. It's Vicki Adams. Can you believe it? Vicki Adams!'

'Where?'

'There, over there in the white coat wearing an England scarf.'

Sue craned her neck and, after a short struggle, finally succeeded in picking out the pop star who had two girls with broad smiles leaning over her, awaiting the autographs she was writing for them.

'I can see her now. She's married to James Harrison, she is; that's why she's here. Hope she has a miserable day.'

'Oooh, you're such a bitch, Sue. She looks a lot older in real life, though, doesn't she? She was in *Jackie* the other day with her new baby and some'ow she looked a lot younger in that.'

'And you call me a bitch! You don't still read *Jackie*, do you? Aren't you a bit old for that?'

'It was my sister's. I was just browsing through it,' Helen replied unconvincingly. The two girls dissolved into fits of laugher, Helen still holding tightly on to Sue's arm. 'Look at all the police. There must be thousands of them.'

'Now Helen, I must've told you a million times not to exaggerate.' Both of the girls creased up in laughter. Sue loved that joke and was never afraid to repeat it. It was the favourite of all those Joe had told her. 'Well, you know, what with Prince Charles being here and all that, it's gotta be expected.'

'Can you believe your boyfriend is gonna meet Prince Charles? It's unbelievable.' Helen continued to bounce around in her seat.

'Have you got ants in your pants or something?'

'Oh, Sue, I'm just so excited. I can't get over I'm actually here. Just listen to the singing. I knew it would be good but this is beyond. I've got goose bumps, it's just fantastic.' Sue smiled and tapped her friend's thigh before both of them joined in with the crowd's lusty singing of *Sospan Fach*.

"*Mae bys Meri An wedi brifo a Dafydd y gwas ddim yn iach…*"

'Look, the red carpet's down and they'll be out in a minute. It's only ten minutes to kick-off. We must give Joe a big cheer when he runs on.'

Helen's enthusiasm was infectious and Sue could not help smiling and feeling happy for her friend. Sue, too, was mesmerised by the panorama of colour, the movement and cacophony of noise around the stadium and the sense of anticipation as kick-off drew nearer. But the nagging fear that Joe was going to commit an atrocity with her father's handgun continued to gnaw away at her despite Helen's warm words of reassurance over the past couple of days. With the moment of truth fast approaching, she noticed her breathing was coming in short, rapid pants.

As if from nowhere and without warning, a line of rugby players wearing purple tracksuit tops jogged on to the field from beneath the North Stand before breaking into individual sprints and jinks towards one set of posts, avoiding the band of the Royal Regiment of Wales and their ceremonial goat. England had entered the field. Their captain, James Harrison, having led the line out, turned round and shouted loudly at each teammate as they bolted past him, his right fist brandished and his face, unshaven and sweating, the picture of determination. A mixture of reluctant applause and friendly booing rang round the stadium but Vicki Adams jumped up from her seat waving her arms furiously, her face wreathed in the widest of smiles. The Englishmen gathered close to their posts and formed a huddle, their captain at their centre. None of the spectators could hear his words but nobody could fail to miss the vigour of his lecture to his teammates, his right index finger jabbing directly and angrily at each and every one of them as he spoke through gritted teeth.

The noise level of the Welsh supporters grew in anticipation of the arrival of the home team and they roared "*Wales, Wales, Wales, Wales, Wales, Wales...*" at the top of their voices. Each exhortation became louder and louder as the team's loyal supporters implored them to enter the field. Sue thought Helen was going to have a heart attack as she jumped around in her seat and yelled out for her side. The seconds ticked by and still there was no sign of the team, as if it was teasing the crowd and demanding even greater exhortation. The home fans responded by bellowing *"Wales, Wales, Wales, Wales, Wales, Wales, Wales, Wales..."* until their throats ached, rocking the stadium to its very foundations.

And then, an almighty roar resounded around Cardiff Arms Park as those spectators opposite the North Stand, unbeknown to Sue and Helen, caught the first glimpse of red in the tunnel beneath them. Both of the girls leaned forward and when the Welsh team ran on to the field, they rose in excited applause as did all those in the stand around them. The chants of *"Wales, Wales, Wales..."* were now deafening and Sue could barely hear her friend's words of support next to her, even though Helen was shouting at the top of her voice. They expectantly awaited Joe's arrival and then, finally, right at the back of the line of players, they caught sight of the top of his thick black hair.

'Joe! Joe!' screamed Helen, looking first at him and then at Sue, her arms waving wildly in his direction. Anybody would have thought that it was her boyfriend who had entered the field, her actions not dissimilar to those she had made when welcoming David Essex on to the stage at the Capitol Theatre. 'Look, Sue, look!' Sue, too, was excited at seeing Joe and her smiling face projected happiness. But if Helen looked more closely at her friend, she would not have failed to notice signs of anxiety as well. 'Typical Joe, the only one wearing tracksuit bottoms, wanting to stand out as per usual.'

'Yeah,' Sue responded enigmatically. She kept a close eye on him and noticed how he sometimes placed his hand across his stomach as he jogged around the field. It was almost as if he had a pain there that he was trying to ease. On one occasion, she believed he had actually adjusted something and she felt a slight shiver down her spine.

'Look, Sue, he's looking our way. Joe! Joe!' screeched Helen, waving madly in his direction. Joe craned back his neck and looked up to where he thought Sue would be sitting and caught sight of the flailing arms. He saw Sue who copied her friend's actions by waving her hand at him. But what Sue saw made her chest constrict as instead of excitement and expectation, she saw a pale, drawn and nervous looking Joe who seemed to have aged many years. He lacked any animation and even from the distance of the stand, she could see that he had been crying. She stopped shouting and her smile left her as she stared at her boyfriend. Something wasn't right and she experienced a strange trembling feeling. It wasn't just the occasion getting to him, it was more than that, she was sure. Even Helen picked up on it. 'He looks very nervous, doesn't he?' she yelled at Sue above the noise.

Sue did not reply but then she saw Joe mouth some words to her which she struggled to make out. Joe looked intently into the stand but was unsure whether Sue had been able to understand what he was saying. 'I love you, Sue. I'm so sorry,' he repeated three times. Joe then turned to find his target.

Sue and Helen both concentrated hard on his mouth's movements, straining to make out the words. They looked at each other with worried expressions, saying nothing. Helen put her arm around Sue. They both wanted and didn't want to ask what he meant. Helen eventually ventured some words to Sue who had paled visibly beside her. 'He loves you so much, Sue. You're the luckiest person in the world. I didn't quite catch the last bit, though. What d'you reckon he said?'

'I think he said "I'm sorry" but I don't understand that.'

'I thought he said that, too.'

Helen was on the point of giving her opinion as to what Joe meant but after opening her mouth, she closed it again without saying a word. To an outsider, it almost appeared as if Joe was finishing his relationship with Sue. But that made no sense at all and she was totally perplexed. Sue, however, began to snap together the pieces of the jigsaw and the picture became much clearer, particularly when she saw Joe jog over to James Harrison, his hand still across his stomach. The realisation was like a punch in the stomach.

'Helen, he's gonna do something bad, I can feel it.' Sue grabbed Helen's arm and held it in a vice-like grip and she remained standing though everybody else around her had begun to sit down. 'He's gonna use the gun, I know it, I just know it.' Her voice was becoming hysterical and the people next to her and behind her looked in her direction. Her face grimaced with anxiety.

'Calm down, Sue, calm down.'

'Look, he's running up to Harrison. Look, Helen, look!'

Though the Welsh and English teams were both making their way to the red carpet to line up for the formalities, Joe jogged in the opposite direction and towards James Harrison, who was startled when Joe confronted him, snarling. 'You cunt. This is the day when everything's gonna change, when you and you fucking English know you're gonna be at war.' Joe's hand remained on his stomach and so obviously so that Harrison gazed downwards to see what Joe was doing. He felt that Joe was holding on to something. Both of them stood stock still, facing each other ten yards behind their respective teams who had nearly completed their line-ups. Some spectators wondered what was going on, including Sue, who feared the worst. 'I despise you. Everything you stand for is gonna be in ruins, you watch, when this great nation takes up arms. You can't beat the Irish and you can't beat us, you fucking English bastard.'

'What are you on about? Just fuck off back to the reserves where you belong.' With that, Harrison, his eye still on Joe's right hand, tried to move on and push past him but Joe took a step sideways, stopped him and looked him straight in the eye.

'You're finished, Harrison, finished, just like the rest of your countrymen. Your time has come.' Harrison was taken aback and hesitated momentarily. He saw Joe raise his right hand from his stomach but it was only to brandish his fist under his nose. Harrison pushed Joe hard in the chest and he stumbled backwards, struggling to retain his balance.

'What's going on here?' Brian Meadows had left the English line-up to see what was taking place behind him.

'Just a twat acting a twat, Brian.'

'Fuck off, Wop.' Meadows's words went straight to the point and were accompanied by his most menacing expression and he pushed Joe even harder. Rocky Evans was the first to Joe's side, followed by half the Welsh and English teams. Meadows and Rocky each held the other by the throat as teammates and officials tried to prise them apart. Soon their holds were released.

'You've got one coming, Meadows. I 'ope you've got eyes in the back of your 'ead,' Rocky snorted.

'Fuck off, Taffy.'

The crowd finally established what was happening and roared *"Wales, Wales, Wales, Wales, Wales, Wales..."* in approval and none more so than in the East Terrace where Pete, Dave and Phil stared open-mouthed and utterly bewildered at what their friend had just started.

'What's he doing? Fuck me, I think this deserves a nip all round. Pass the bottle, Dave.'

The commotion on the field died down and the two teams took their places once again along the red carpet. Geraint Lewis looked daggers at Joe whose face was blood-red and bathed in sweat. He felt Joe had completely lost his head and his expression, a mixture of fear, tension and aggression, did not bode well for the rest of the game. Hopefully, he would not be needed, Lewis thought, but his actions had stirred up the English team, of that he had no doubt, and that was something he could have done without. Joe did not return his gaze as he wandered to his position at the end of the line of players, alongside the reserves. He was breathing heavily, sucking in and exhaling air in large gulps as he tried to control his nerves. The sweat poured down his face and droplets fell to the ground from the end of his chin. He did not seem to notice and he made no effort to wipe his face. He looked straight ahead, his eyes vacant, and he seemed lost in his own world. He knew Sue was sitting up in the stand directly above him but he could not bring himself to look at her. Ceri Hickman, standing next to him, nudged his shoulder but Joe did not make the slightest movement to acknowledge him. Unusually for Hickman, he did not try to broach any conversation. He had finally concluded that Joe was a bit of an oddball.

The red carpet ran parallel to the touchline, along which the two teams stood, including the reserves and match officials. At its centre, another length of carpet ran at ninety degrees away from the long line and towards the tunnel under the North Stand. After a few moments, a gaggle of elderly gentlemen appeared, dressed formally in blazers and ties, the buttons of their shirts invariably straining to hold in their waistlines which had seen leaner days. At the head of this group walked the youthful Prince of Wales, bright-eyed and so fresh-faced it seemed as if he had not yet begun to shave. He tugged at one of the cuffs of his shirt as he conversed with one of the older men. Polite, rather than enthusiastic applause broke out when the crowd caught sight of him.

In the stand, Sue had no eye for the Prince of Wales. She continued to stare at her boyfriend and was beside herself with worry at the state he was in. She had been convinced he was going to pull the gun on Harrison but the incident had passed so quickly, she had been unable to react to prevent it or to warn anybody about it. Now, her mind was a mass of doubts, uncertain whether the melee that followed had stopped Joe from pulling the gun, whether he even had the gun or whether he ever intended to use it on Harrison. The confrontation with the England captain, though, had shaken her to the core and tears welled in her eyes. Helen, too, had been concerned and her enthusiasm waned in the knowledge that Joe was perhaps planning some atrocity. She was mystified as well at Joe's occasional holding of his stomach and like Sue, she became more convinced that he was holding and adjusting something under his tracksuit. She wrapped both of her arms around Sue to comfort her but neither of them said a word. They did not know what to do or whether they should in fact do anything. Confusion reigned in their minds.

But now, gazing down on Joe, Sue's concerns deepened. He looked dreadful, racked with anxiety, and he did not once look up at her as if he was ashamed to look her in the eye. Once again, Joe moved his right hand to his stomach but this time Sue was watching more carefully and she noticed him place it under the tracksuit top. He was definitely gripping on to something. Her mind was made up. Ignoring Helen, who was startled at her sudden movement, Sue turned sharply to the right and edged her way past the spectators sitting alongside her until she reached the concrete steps which led upwards to the exit from her part of the stand. The spectators were irritated at the speed at which Sue moved, treading on toes and kicking bags without a word of apology. Sue bolted up the steps and then, once inside the stand, hurtled down the other side, barging through late-comers as she tried to find the inner entrance to the big central tunnel. She had to warn somebody, an official, a policeman, a steward, anybody who could stop Joe. She would run on to the pitch herself, if possible. She now knew. It was certain. He was going to shoot the Prince of Wales.

Joe glimpsed the party of blazers with Prince Charles from the corner of his eye. He did not move his head and continued to look straight ahead. His hand under the tracksuit gripped the butt of the Luger and he flicked off the safety catch, an action he had mastered back in his bedroom. This only served to increase his anxiety further and he gulped in more air in an attempt to reduce it and retain some semblance of control. He could feel himself trembling and could not stop himself from shifting his feet nervously. His heart pounded and his breaths came in ragged gasps. The Prince of Wales was met first by James Harrison who, with charm and presence, introduced him to each member of the English team. He shared a joke with Brian Meadows along the way, no doubt recalling the fracas that had just taken place. After each English player had been introduced, there was a quick, final conversation and handshake with Harrison before the blazer introduced him to the referee who in turn presented his linesmen. Geraint Lewis then took over with a smile and led the Prince along the line of his team. He was getting closer, only a few more seconds and he would be in front of Joe.

Sue easily found the tunnel entrance but at this point she could go no further. Two stewards in fluorescent-yellow jackets and four policemen barred entry to anybody not involved in the game. Breathlessly, she went straight up to one of the policemen and pleaded, 'You've gotta help me. Joe Chilani has got a gun and he's gonna shoot Prince Charles. Please believe me. He's my boyfriend.'

'Joe Chilani?'

'Yes, Joe Chilani. One of the players, reserves on the field now. He's gonna shoot him. You've got to hurry.'

'And who may you be?'

An exasperated Sue raised her voice. 'I told you. I'm his girlfriend, Susan Jenkins. You've got to stop him. There's no more time.' The three other policemen joined their colleague and pedantically asked the same questions. 'Look, there's no more time!' Sue screamed, looking over their shoulders down the tunnel. The two stewards looked on with a wry smile, one of them commenting to his colleague about 'stupid bloody women'.

One of the policemen, who appeared to be in charge, raised his hand towards Sue, palm forward, and addressed her in measured tones. 'Just calm down, Miss Jenkins, please calm down for a moment. What makes you think he's going to shoot Prince Charles?'

'I know he is!!' Sue yelled. 'Please believe me. There's no more time.'

Sue's instincts took over and she disengaged from the policemen and stewards around her. Fired up with fury and with her mind acutely alert to the situation, she burst away from them, desperately, just avoiding the flailing hand of one of the policemen which she brushed off with a violent swing of her fist. She ran as fast as she could down the tunnel, ignoring the shouts of authority behind her, until she arrived at the side of the pitch, the darkness of the tunnel giving way to the green of the grass, the brightness in the sky and the kaleidoscope of colour in the stands around her. Various officials were startled to see her beside them and hesitated, not knowing who she was or what she was doing there. She seemed harmless enough. Arriving on the touchline, her feet on the red carpet, she looked to her right and saw Joe. The Prince of Wales was only one player away from him.

'Joe!!' she bellowed with all her might, fixed to the spot, some officials and players turning their heads towards her.

Joe saw her straight away and their eyes met and held for what seemed an eternity but which in reality was for just one second. Sue would never forget the fear in his eyes, the sweat on his brow and look of bewilderment on his face as he stared at her open-mouthed. He looked as if he was attending his own execution, which indeed he was. As Charles approached him, hand extended, Joe looked him in the eye and took one large stride backwards. He pulled the Luger from the waistband of his shorts and raised it upwards. The smile on Charles's face disappeared as he saw what Joe was holding in his hand. The trigger felt lighter than before but he knew this to be the effect of adrenalin, gallons of which was pumping through every vein in his body. It all happened so quickly that nobody had time to move. Joe raised the gun even higher and placed it against his right temple. Squeezing his eyes tight and without a moment's hesitation, he pulled the trigger and the bullet exploded in his brain.

'Noooooooooooooo!' Sue screamed before collapsing to the ground.

26

Several sixth form boys at Coed-Y-Lan were gathered in their common room behind the stage of the assembly hall. The room doubled up as a storeroom for battered old musical instruments, which were dumped at one end, all on top of each other. Oboes, clarinets, bassoons, violins, violas, double basses seemingly discarded like relics in a junk shop. They reflected a different age and some of them dated back more than twenty years. The boys today craved electric guitars, drums and keyboards instead.

In the middle of the room, equally battered and aged sofas, armchairs and hard-backed wooden chairs were strewn around. The boys lounged on them, their arms and legs in various shapes and angles to their torsos. Plugged into an electric point in one of the corners was a white kettle, smudged in black and grey fingerprints, rattling gently as it came to boil, a plume of steam streaming powerfully from its nozzle. At the foot of each of the boys, stained and chipped coffee mugs with dirty brown granules awaited the boiling water. Phil sniffed at the quarter-full pint bottle with silver foil peeled back to consider the milk's freshness. He flinched at the smell but declared it acceptable.

The events of the previous Saturday, only four days before, had not yet sunk in with anybody at the school, teachers and pupils alike, and most of them struggled with the media attention that had arisen. Reporters accosted pupils arriving and leaving the premises, requesting a few words about Joe. Pete had to be physically restrained on one occasion as he attempted to attack one of them. The headmaster, Meirion Hopkins, had made a dignified statement outside the front gates of the school on the Monday morning in full view of the television cameras but continued to be harassed for more opinion on Joe, his actions and whether other pupils might be of the same mind.

John Alderson broke the deathly hush with an inane statement to break the tension and start up some conversation. 'Dunno 'bout you, boys, but it just hasn't sunk in with me yet. It's unbelievable,' he broached.

'Yeah, it's just unreal.'

'I can't get my 'ead around it. I know he used to bang on a bit about nationalism an' all that, but I never thought it would come to this. It's just beyond.'

'Dave, you knew Joe better than us. Could you sense anything like this was gonna happen?'

'No way. not in a million years. It's unreal.' Dave looked down into his coffee mug which had been topped up with water and cupped his hands around it in an attempt to gain some form of comfort from the heat it generated. His face was a mask of sadness and incredulity and his eyes misted over.

'Thinking back, Joe often made sarkie comments about Prince Charles but, you know, nothing none of us 'ere wouldn't have said ourselves.'

'He couldn't stand James Harrison either. He hated his guts, in fact, but in the end he didn't do 'em any harm like Sue thought he would. He just used 'em for the publicity, like. He knew there'd be a massive audience so he kill... so he did what he did to himself to project his beliefs, like.'

All the boys took a sip from their mugs, dropping their eyes, unable to look directly at each other, still bewildered at the course of events and struggling to make any sense of them. They would not have been surprised if Joe had walked into the common room at that very moment. Saturday was just a bad dream, surely?

'Yeah, but Pete, it was much more than that, wasn't it?' Simon House interjected incisively. 'What he did was meant to be a catalyst for boys like us and everybody else in Wales to engage the English in some form of armed struggle. His letter was quite clear about it.'

'You're right, Si.' After a moment's pause, Pete tried to carry on but did not know what to say. 'I just can't get my 'ead around it,' he said weakly. 'It's not really 'appened, has it?'

'How's Sue?' Paul Kelly enquired as the conversation faltered, his voice soft and full of feeling. 'Anybody spoken to 'er recently?'

'I had a quick word with her last night,' Phil responded, shaking his head. 'She's in bits as you can imagine. Just totally devastated, she is. She was only on the line a minute. She didn't wanna talk. Her nan was with her. Helen and Ann are round there a lot as well.'

'That's right. I was talking to Helen last night but she says Sue just wants to be alone most of the time. It's really tough on her,' Gethin commented.

'What about his mum and dad? And his brother? I've not seen him in school this week, understandably. Anybody talk to them?' Nobody responded immediately and a sense of unease filtered through the air.

'My mum did briefly. She spoke to his mum. They're devastated,' Pete replied. 'We must go and visit them and pay our respects.' Pete's words were greeted by a unanimous though hesitant nodding of heads. None of the boys had ever had to pay their respects to anybody before after the death of somebody close to them and this unfamiliar territory unsettled them.

'You know Sue lost her parents in a car accident as well,' Dave butted in. 'It's just terrible what's 'appened to her. Can you imagine it, losing so many loved ones at her age? It's just awful. I 'ope she can recover from this. We've all got to do our bit to help.' Everybody nodded their heads vigorously.

'Must be like when there's a pit accident and you lose a lot of family all at once.' More nodding of heads followed.

'She also got a letter, didn't she?' Murray Phillips enquired, though he knew the answer already. 'D'we know wharrit said? There were no details in the papers or on the telly, unlike the other one.'

'Helen read it. Sue gave it to her to 'ave a look,' Gethin replied. 'It's a love letter basically. It wasn't very long and, after the police had read it, they gave it back to her. They don't think it has any bearing on any enquiries they 'ave to make. They were really good about it and none of the contents have been made public. Basically, Joe told her he loved her, that the moments he spent with her were the best of his life and that if his calling, for wont of a better word, hadn't been so strong, she was the girl he would've wanted to marry and 'ave kids with. He talked about the turmoil inside 'im and ended by saying sorry for what had 'appened.'

'Always was a bit of a soppy git was Joe,' Dave responded, and for the first time that afternoon some smiles broke out around the room.

'Where'd they find the letters again?' Dennis Morris asked.

'In his kit bag; in a small transparent folder. One addressed to Sue and the other one to, what was the title again, that's right, 'The People of Wales'.'

'I still can't get my head round what's happened. It's just mad, innit? Unbelievable, it is.'

'Yeah, Den, mad.'

The light from the two bulbs encased in their grimy plastic casing grew more prominent as the natural light faded from the windows. The room became more yellow-brown and when Pete rose from his armchair to make himself another coffee, a fine mist of dust rose with him. Once more the conversation faded as each boy continued to struggle with what Joe had done. Dave felt a knot form in his stomach and his eyes misted over again, necessitating the need to wipe them with the cuff of his shirt. It came as a relief when Dennis Morris addressed the gathering once more. 'I've read Joe's letter a few times now and it's just incredible, it is.'

'Yeah, Den. You'd never think Joe would write something like that.'

'Anybody got it with 'em? You know, the newspaper, like?'

Dave leaned over the arm of the sofa and picked up the Monday edition of the *Daily Mirror* from the top of a pile of newspapers that dated back to the beginning of the school year, six months ago. 'Here it is.'

'Read it out again, will you?'

Dave sat up straight and turned to page two where Joe's letter was printed. He coughed twice to clear the lump in his throat before starting.

The People of Wales

Saturday's dramatic events will have come as a great shock, but only through this and the letter you now read could I convey to you all, and to the rest of the world at large, my most profound love for this wonderful nation of ours and for the need to fight for its very existence.

Under English governance, our very way of life is being diminished and as a consequence, all that is distinctive and great in our country will soon unquestionably expire. I was not prepared to stand aside and allow this to happen.

Everybody in Wales needs to wake up to the fact that we must do everything in our power to retain and retrieve the wonderful characteristics of our beloved nation. To bring this about, it is essential that we govern ourselves and form our own Parliament, independent of any influence from London. But to achieve this, politics will get us nowhere; only an armed struggle will prevail. History has taught us that the English will always look after their own interests first and foremost and exploit the nations they rule. History also tells us that only through an armed struggle will anything change. The colonial uprisings throughout the old Empire have proven this.

In more recent times, I admire the courage of the IRA in their fight for the reunification of Northern Ireland with the South and of other great freedom-fighters elsewhere around the world. I despair at our lack of fight. We accept the status quo, they do not. This shames me and it should shame every person in Wales.

I wish passionately that my actions on Saturday will act as a catalyst for all you great Welsh people to think long and hard about your own individual response to my calling. England will unquestionably succumb in the end, believe me. But any fight will not be without hardship and sacrifice and no doubt it will be long and drawn out. I have made the ultimate sacrifice to generate the greatest amount of publicity and to raise the highest possible awareness of the overriding need for Welsh independence and to show my commitment to a cause I cherish and believe in with all my heart. I urge you to follow my lead, to organise yourselves and to rid these English from our lives.

I wish you strength, courage, determination, resolve and good fortune.

Giuseppe Chilani

With a sigh, Dave finished reading the letter and placed the newspaper back on its pile, clearing his throat once more and wiping a tear away from his eye. The common room remained silent, nobody venturing to speak first. Phil stared down at the floor, misty-eyed, his face the personification of misery. Pete followed suit, dabbing at his nose with his sleeve. The expressions on all the boys' faces reflected their sadness and shock, not knowing how to react to Joe's words. They had tried to work out their own individual positions the moment the letter had become public but they had all struggled hugely. Their brains remained scrambled.

'Well?' Dave finally volunteered, softly and croakily. An audience of sad and confused faces gazed back at him.

'It's just mad.' Gethin was the first to respond tentatively. 'An armed struggle, like in Belfast? It's crazy.'

'Yeah, I can't see that 'appening 'ere.'

'Bombs in the streets? Don't want any of that.'

'Absolutely. Fucking awful, it'd be.'

'Yeah, I agree. Speaking for myself, I don't think things are so bad anyway. Do you?'

'No. Life's orrite. I suppose things could be a bit better, you know, but you could say that about anywhere.'

'Yeah, it's orrite here. I can't be bothered with all this politics bollocks anyway. Doesn't really bother me who's in charge; Welsh, English, Common Market. They're all the same. Bunch of twats.'

'*Meet the new boss. Same as the old boss.*' Dinner spoke or rather sang his first words of the afternoon and with perplexed faces, everybody looked at him. '*Meet the new boss. Same as the old boss.* The Who. *Won't Get Fooled Again.* You know, it's a line in the song. It doesn't matter who's in charge, nothing ever changes.'

'Nice one, Din, I think.'

Pete got up from his armchair once more, finished his coffee and stretched out for his green Parka which was hanging from a half-broken aluminium peg on the back of the door. He placed the coffee mug back down on a desk. 'I've gotta make a move.'

The rest of the boys shuffled their feet. Some of them rose from the various assortments of chairs and edges of furniture whilst others grabbed coats and bags.

'Anybody out tonight?'

'Nah, *Sportsnight*'s on. Man United are playing.'

'Oh, that's right.'

'They're playing Liverpool, aren't they?'

'Yeah, cup replay. Gotta watch that.'

'There's interviews with James Hunt an' Geoff Boycott as well, I heard.'

'Really! Can't miss that 'en.'

As Pete left the room with Dave beside him, they gave each other resigned looks but neither of them said a word. They had read each other's minds, however, and both of them had come to the same conclusion, only confirmed by this animated interest in iconic English football teams and sports stars. What their beloved friend had done would all be in vain.

27

Six Months Later

Helen and Ann were sitting opposite each other on the
tangerine plastic seats in *Chilani*'s by the train station.
Helen had a chocolate nut sundae in front of her, Ann a
strawberry milkshake. The restaurant was busy as usual
that Saturday afternoon, with a high turnover of people
entering and leaving the premises. Despite the hustle and
bustle, Mr Chilani was standing quietly by himself
staring out of the window. One or two regulars passed by
him and he acknowledged them with a sad smile. His face
was ashen and lined and his hair markedly greyer than
only a few weeks earlier. He had aged ten years. Nobody
now mentioned Joe but nobody failed to notice the
physical difference in him either.

Marco was helping his father. He was all movement
and action, serving here, clearing tables there and fetching
stock from the upstairs storerooms or basement cellar. He
seemed to have grown in stature and gained presence and
the word was that despite his youth, he was like a rock to
his family. Joe would have been proud of him, Helen
thought, as he cleared a table quickly, wiped it down, re-
laid it and directed some new customers to it in a flash.
However, it appeared that he would have to remain a rock
to his family in another country for the *For Sale* sign that
hung on the outside of the building advertised not only the

business premises but also the family's intentions to move to Italy.

The decision to move to the midst of their close relatives was driven primarily by Mrs Chilani. She had not been seen in the restaurant and only rarely in the shopping streets since that fateful Saturday in Cardiff. She spent all of her time at home, visited every so often by friends and cousins. Invariably, however, she lived out her life in her mind, thinking endlessly about Joe and crying each day. Her homeland was too strong a draw for her now and she wished to escape Wales and what the country had done to her son.

As Helen contemplated Mr Chilani with sadness in her eyes, she took a mouthful of ice cream and looked once more at the entrance when the door swung open. But once again, there was no sign of Sue. 'Where can she be? This is getting ridiculous now. She's never this late,' Helen wondered.

'She's never late, full stop,' Ann concurred. They looked at each other but said nothing. Ann took a slurp from her milkshake and Helen picked a nut from her sundae. After wiping her mouth with a napkin, Ann broke the silence. 'She seemed alright the other day when I spoke to her. Said she'd definitely be here at one.'

'P'raps she's round her nan's and got delayed for some reason.'

'Yeah, probably that's it.'

'I've gotta make a move in a min, Ann.'

'Yeah, same here.' Ann took another slurp before continuing. 'So I'll be round your place at seven-thirty, yeah?'

'Yeah, that's fine. Thanks for driving tonight, Ann. Gives me a chance to have a drink. We'll pick Sue up. She knows we're coming round about that time. I mentioned to her about going to the Caesars Arms last night and she was up for it.'

* * *

Helen rang the doorbell for a third time but there was still no answer. The house was also in total darkness which was unusual. Helen walked slowly back down the path to where Ann was waiting in the car. 'No answer. Strange that,' she informed her friend.

'Mmm, d'you think she could be round her nan's?'

'Maybe, but she did say she'd be here. It's a bit odd, especially after not turning up this afternoon.' The two girls stared at each other, their faces a mixture of worry and puzzlement.

'Let's go an' see her nan. She's only round the corner.'

Helen rang the doorbell and a deep, hesitant ding-dong sounded from the inside. The door opened and a tiny, frail old lady wearing a red and blue check, woollen shawl around her shoulders looked surprised to see Helen standing in front of her. In one of her hands she was holding a bundle of brown wool, looped around some knitting needles.

'Oh, hello, Helen. What a lovely surprise. For a moment I thought it was Susan. She was meant to come round earlier.'

'Hello, Mrs Jenkins. We've just been round Sue's and there was no answer. We thought she might be round here.'

'No. I haven't seen her all day.' There was a moment's pause before she carried on. 'I do hope she's alright.'

'Would you have a key to her house, Mrs Jenkins? It's not like her to go missing.' Helen started to look worried.

'Yes, darling, I do. Would you mind going to see if everything's alright for me.'

'Of course not.' A minute later, Mrs Jenkins returned with Sue's house key and gave it to Helen. 'Don't you worry; I'll be back in a minute.' And with that, Helen bolted down the path to Ann.

In no time at all, the two girls were standing in Sue's front porch. Helen unlocked the door, nervously pushed it open and crossed the threshold. In the darkness, she struggled to find the light switch, patting her hand several times against the walls to her left and right. Finally, she found it and flicked it on. The immediate flash of whiteness made her blink once or twice. Ann would never forget the deep-throated scream she heard from Helen who was rooted to the spot in front of her and blocking her view. It chilled her to the marrow. Helen's scream passed to hysterical sobs, her right hand covering her mouth as Ann moved to her side. When she witnessed the scene, she collapsed to the floor. Sue was hanging from a rope tied to an upstairs banister, a chair on its side beneath her bare feet and Joe's neatly folded letter on the phone table in the hallway below her.

Epilogue

Five Years Later

'God, did you see that go up? Brilliant it was.' Dafydd, Ieuan and Robert were down on their haunches behind a thick hedge, a hundred feet from a beautiful thatched cottage outside the village of Northop Hall in North Wales. The small explosion had created a fire inside the property, visible to them through the frosted glass panes of the front door. The flickering forks of orange and yellow were gaining in intensity and black smoke billowed from the edges of the door and from the letterbox. The three of them were ecstatic and broad smiles crept across their faces. This was the third time they had firebombed the holiday home of an English owner and their campaign, together with like-minded anarchists from the newly-formed organisation, Meibion Glyndwr, was gathering a real momentum that was greatly concerning the authorities.

'Fucking teach 'em, wonnit? Be a long time before they consider buying our homes again.'

'Yeah, fuck off, you English twats.'

'There was a hell of a bang to that one. I think we're finally getting the knack of this.'

'Yeah, you're right. Thinking back, it's what Joe Chilani should have used instead of that gun of his. He could have taken out that wanker, Prince Charles, at the same time as himself.'

'Plus half the Welsh rugby team.'

'Yeah, but they were rubbish that year anyway, so we wouldn't have missed much.' The three of them all chuckled quietly to themselves.

'He always wanted a gun, did Joe. I thought he was gonna throttle you once, Rob, when you tried to suggest one of those dodgy explosive contraptions of yours again.'

'Well, it was the only thing we had at the time. Where the hell were we gonna get a gun from, come on? Lucky he found one himself. He was probably right, though, 'cos those first prototypes we made were pretty useless. Half of them didn't even explode. Joe had no confidence in them at all. They're a lot better now, though, as you can see.'

'Strange guy was Joe. He was prepared to kill himself for a cause but he was always adamant he wouldn't kill anybody else.'

'Yeah, I remember that conversation vividly. Fucking chilling it was in the multi-storey that night when he told us what he was gonna do. I know he'd been talking about it but I never thought for a moment he'd actually go through with it. I didn't sleep for days after that; I couldn't get it out of my head. If you remember, the plan for ages was to try and get at Harrison somehow before the match started. Joe hated his guts so much he was all for it. But what did he say that time? Ultimately, he could never bring himself to kill someone else. It was a line he could never cross. But he wasn't prepared to be hypocritical either. So by killing himself, he thought it would make it easier for him to incite others to carry out attacks against the English. You know, a sign of his real commitment, like.'

'That's right. And do you remember the time he said that even if he was capable of killing someone else, he could never face a lifetime in jail? The idea was unthinkable to him. He'd rather just die himself.'

'Unbelievable guts it took to go through with it; a bit like that IRA bloke, Bobby Sands, last year.'

'And when we knew Charles was gonna be at the match, he still couldn't bring himself to kill him. That would've been incredible. We missed a real opportunity there. I remember the last time I ever spoke to him. I wanted to try and convince him to shoot Charles but I couldn't get a word in edgeways and he slammed the phone down on me. Pity that.'

'Yeah, and the IRA weren't too impressed either. They gave us a terrible time, they did. They kept taking the piss about how we had someone in front of Prince Charles with a gun in his hand and we failed to shoot him. They couldn't believe it. It took 'em another two years before they had a chance with royalty when they blew up Mountbatten. We were ahead of them and we fucked up.'

'That's just the way Joe wanted it. We couldn't have changed anything.'

'Shame though, 'specially as the IRA are pretty much not talking to us now. If we had killed Charles or even James Harrison, everything would've been different.'

'You bet. With their arms and money and know-how, we could've got more people on board, I'm sure.'

'Yeah, you're right. Once all the fuss died down, nobody really took up Joe's challenge, though that Pete Williams mate of his is a right nutter. He's up for anything. Ultimately, it's taken the English paying through the roof for our houses to get people's blood boiling. Nobody here can afford to buy anything anymore. It's the same old story; people only get some fire in their bellies when they're being hurt in the pocket.'

'Yeah, you're right. The organisation's building up nicely now.'

In the distance, the faint sound of sirens wailing grew louder.

'We'd better get a move on. Come on, let's go.'